At the Doors of the Comédie Française.

Drawn and etched by E. Van Muyden.

OLYMPE DE CLÈVES, I. *Frontispiece.*

OLYMPE DE CLÈVES ❧ ❧ ❧
A ROMANCE OF THE COURT OF LOUIS XV. ❧ ❧ BY ALEXANDRE DUMAS ❧ VOLUME ONE ❧

Fredonia Books
Amsterdam. The Netherlands

Olympe de Clèves:
A Romance of the Court of Luis XV (Volume One)

by
Alexandre Dumas

ISBN: 1-58963-315-6

Reprinted from the 1893 edition

Fredonia Books
Amsterdam, The Netherlands
http://www.fredoniabooks.com

In order to make original editions of historical works available to scholars at an economical price, this facsimile of the original edition of 1893 is reproduced from the best available copy and has been digitally enhanced to improve legibility, but the text remains unaltered to retain historical authenticity.

INTRODUCTORY NOTE.

ALTHOUGH Monsieur Dumas, in the explanatory note appended to these volumes, cites contemporary authority for the final catastrophe as having actually taken place, we are not, of course, to assume that any other portion of Bannière's career, as traced in this story, is founded upon fact. The novelist is himself responsible for the plot so far as it is concerned with the fortunes of Olympe and her ardent and headstrong lover.

But the scenes which deal with the conspiracy (for it was nothing less) to corrupt young Louis XV., and force him to adopt a career of unredeemed profligacy, are founded upon indisputable evidence, adapted, of course, to the exigencies of the narrative. Indeed, the authority of contemporaneous memoirs may be cited in support of some of the most improbable details; for example, the queen's coldness toward the king, and the various anecdotes concerning Mademoiselle de Charolais.

It should be remarked that the dates are somewhat mixed to meet the requirements of the plot: the Duc de Bourbon and Madame de Prie were disgraced and exiled a considerable time before Richelieu's return from Vienna; four or five years, at least, instead of four or five days, elapsed between his return and the final surrender of Louis XV. to the charms of Madame de Mailly; and the episode of Bachelier's unsuccessful mission to the queen is usually assigned to a date considerably later still.

It would be difficult, within the proper limits of a note like this, to set forth all the elements which combined to form this conspiracy against the morals of the young king. The queen herself unwittingly helped on the scheme by her want of tact, and her failure to humor the whims of her capricious lord and master, who seems to have been afflicted with the royal disease — ennui — as no mortal ever was afflicted before or since. The daughter of a king who had lost his kingdom and had infinitesimal prospects of ever procuring another, reared in the strictest seclusion, and of an intensely devout and religious temperament, Marie Leczinska, though an amiable, tender-hearted, charitable princess, and a loving wife and mother, was ill fitted to preside over a court which subsisted partly upon memories of the halcyon days of the Regency, and partly upon the hope of seeing those days return.

In their interesting and clever work, "La Duchesse de Chateauroux et ses Sœurs," the De Goncourts devote much space to an enumeration of the various classes of persons who "did their utmost to bring about the accession of a mistress who would cause a revolution at Versailles, change the course of the stream of favor, and rejuvenate the whole government."

Prominent among them were those who were disgusted with the commonplace, peace-at-any-price policy of the Cardinal-Minister Fleury, whose dominion over his former pupil was absolute.

"But a curious thing happened," say Messieurs de Goncourt: "these machinations, which had for their real object the overthrow of the ministry and the minister, met with the assent at least, if not the active support, of the minister himself, on condition that he be consulted as to the selection of a favorite, and be assured of the *political* neutrality of the person selected."

The undeniable agency of Fleury in the corruption of his youthful sovereign is the saddest and most deplorable single circumstance of this whole sad and deplorable reign. His unlimited ascendancy over the king's will gave him more power

than Richelieu or Mazarin had ever known ; and
yet for no conceivable reason, unless to guard that
power against the fancied danger of a possible
return of Louis' affection for his lawful spouse, and
a consequent revival of the influence of the Duc de
Bourbon, he, an octogenarian, already within sight of
the tomb, and clothed with the highest dignity in the
gift of the Holy See, deliberately assisted to force
illicit connections upon the youth upon whose
future character and conduct the destiny of France
depended, and whose will had been his from his
cradle.

Fleury and Richelieu fitly typify the epoch which
has been well named by Monsieur Henri Martin the
period of the " Decline of the French Monarchy."

Monsieur Dumas has drawn a somewhat more
flattering picture of the Comte de Mailly than the
contemporary memoirs warrant.   He seems to have
been a dissolute, extravagant young gentleman ; and
one writer goes so far as to assert that he made the
contract which resulted in his wife's *liaison* with
the king, and that he made it against her will.
This statement is unsupported, however, and the
weight of evidence is against its probable accuracy
The Duc de Luynes, in his Memoirs, records the fact
that Monsieur de Mailly was imprisoned and exiled in 1739, because he persisted in continuing his

membership in the order of Freemasons, — at that time a novelty in France, and frowned upon by the authorities.

With his usual matchless skill, Monsieur Dumas has so interwoven history and romance that each embellishes the other; and the result is a harmonious and intensely interesting whole, albeit the period was conspicuously lacking in those stirring, chivalric incidents which furnished the themes for the marvellous romances of the days of the Valois kings and the first Bourbons. If there is little to appeal to the imagination and stir the blood, as do the exploits of D'Artagnan and his comrades on their expedition to England to recover Anne of Austria's necklace from His Grace of Buckingham, or the combat in which Bussy d'Amboise sold his life so dearly when called upon to pay the price of the love of "La Dame de Monsoreau," there is, on the other hand, much more of purely intellectual interest, — more perhaps than in any other of the historical romances of Monsieur Dumas.

The chapters which introduce us to the interior of the Jesuit novitiate are by no means the least interesting: the character of Père Mordon is carefully drawn, and is provided with an excellent foil in the person of the timid and irresolute Père de la Sante; and a world of information as to the objects and mode of government of this most remarkable and entirely unique organization is imparted in attractive form, and relieved from all possibility of tedium by the constant presence on the stage of poor Bannière, as the "awful example," whether in the chapel, in Père Mordon's sanctum, or in the Chamber of Meditation, with its cheerful embellishments in the way of mottoes and emblems.

The extraordinary pathos of the concluding chapters, although they do not perhaps form what is sometimes called a "good ending," will not in the eyes of the judicious reader detract from the singular charm of a story which is considered by no less competent a judge than the poet and critic, William Ernest Henley, to be a masterpiece of fiction.

In the reign of Louis XV. little sanctity attached to the marriage contract, and unchastity was very far from being looked upon as a crime. Under no other circumstances, perhaps, would the author have found it possible to depict a woman who, notwithstanding that her life was lived in accordance with a moral standard far below that by which the conduct of the nineteenth-century woman is measured, should yet so win our interest and affection, yes, and our respect, as noble, warm-hearted, loving, and true Olympe de Clèves.

LIST OF CHARACTERS.

Period, 1727-1729.

———◆———

LOUIS XV., at the age of eighteen, King of France.

MARIE LECZINSKA, his queen.

CARDINAL FLEURY, formerly Bishop of Fréjus.

MONSIEUR LE DUC DE RICHELIEU.

MADEMOISELLE DE CHAROLAIS,
MADEMOISELLE DE CLERMONT, her sister, } Princesses of the Blood.

COMTE DE TOULOUSE, Grand Admiral of France, son of Louis XIV. and Madame de Montespan.

COMTESSE DE TOULOUSE.

MONSIEUR LE DUC DE BOURBON, First Minister.

MONSIEUR LE DUC DE PECQUIGNY, captain of the King's Guards.

BACHELIER, valet-de-chambre to the King.

PHILIPPE V., King of Spain.

MADAME LA MARQUISE DE PRIE.

MADEMOISELLE PAULMIER.

ABBÉ DE POLET, confessor to Cardinal Fleury.

BARJAC, Cardinal Fleury's valet-de-chambre.

THE ARCHBISHOP OF PARIS.

M. FORESTIER, commandant of Swiss.

MADAME DE NESLE.

RAFTÉ, valet to Duc de Richelieu.

ABBÉ DE SINZENDORF.

COMTE LOUIS ALEXANDRE DE MAILLY, captain-lieutenant of the company of Scottish Guards.

LOUISE-JULIE DE NESLE, Comtesse de Mailly, his wife.

MADAME DE LAURAGUAIS,
MADAME DE VINTIMILLE,   } sisters of Comtesse de Mailly.
MADAME DE LA TOURNELLE,

OLYMPE DE CLÈVES, an actress.

JACQUES BANNIÈRE, a novice of the Society of Jesus, in love
    with Olympe de Clèves.

PÈRE MORDON, Superior of the Jesuits of Avignon.

PÈRE DE LA SANTÉ, a Jesuit Father.

L'ABBÉ D'HOIRAC.

CHAMPMESLÉ, an actor, afterwards an abbé.

MADEMOISELLE CLAIRE, maid to Olympe de Clèves.

THE HAIR-DRESSER to Olympe de Clèves.

THE GOVERNOR OF THE CITY OF AVIGNON.

LA CATALANE, an actress at Lyons.

THE MANAGER OF THE THEATRE AT LYONS.

JACOB, a Lyons money-lender.

THE VICAR OF THE ARCHBISHOP AT LYONS.

THE MARQUIS DELLA TORRA, an adventurer.

MARION, his wife.

PÈRE PHILÉMON,
LAURENT,   } retainers of Comte de Mailly.

A MAJOR OF DRAGOONS.

A MAGISTRATE OF THE CHÂTELET.

MARTIN, a keeper at Charenton.

CONTENTS.

OLYMPE DE CLÈVES.

I.

AVIGNON.

"SEE Naples and die," says the Neapolitan. "He who has not seen Seville has seen nothing worth seeing," says the Andalusian. "To remain without the gates of Avignon is to remain without the gates of Paradise," says the Provençal.

In fact, if we give credit to the historian of the Papal city, Avignon is not the foremost city of the South alone, but of all France and of the world.

Listen to what he says: —

"Avignon is ennobled by its antiquity; its situation is delightful, its walls superb; its soil fairly revels in its own fertility, its people are charming in their gentle manners, its palaces are magnificent, and its broad streets fair to look upon; its bridge is a marvel of architectural and mechanical skill, its commerce is flourishing, and it is famous in every corner of the globe."

Enthusiastic praise that, I should say! And yet we who come a hundred years after him who wrote these words are disposed to add something to them rather than to take anything away.

Indeed, to the traveller who journeys down the river to which Tibullus applied the epithet of *celer*, Ausonius *præceps*, and Florus *impiger;* to him who begins at

Montélimar to realize that he is in the South, by the warmer coloring of the landscape, the greater clearness of the air, and the more distinct outlines of objects; to him who sails with a shudder under the deadly arches of the Pont Saint-Esprit, each one of which has its name, so that one may know at once to what spot to carry assistance when a vessel is wrecked against one of them; to him who leaves at the right Roquemaure, where Hannibal crossed the Rhone with his forty elephants, and at the left the Château de Mornas, from the summit of which Baron des Adrets made an entire Catholic garrison leap off to the ground, — to such an one, Avignon, at a sharp bend in the stream, suddenly appears with royal magnificence.

It is true that the only thing which one perceives of Avignon at the moment that the city itself appears, is its gigantic château, the palace of the Popes, — a four-teenth-century edifice, and the only perfect specimen of the military architecture of that period; it is built upon the site of an earlier temple of Diana, who gave her name to the city.

But how does it happen, pray, that a temple of Diana could give its name to the future abode of the Popes of Rome? We will proceed to enlighten our readers upon this point, bespeaking that measure of indulgence which we have always noticed that readers are glad to extend to etymologists.

Ave Diana! (Hail, Diana!) said the traveller at the most distant point from which he could discern the temple of the chaste divinity, in the halcyon days of classical Latin, the days of Cicero, Virgil, and Augustus; *Ave Niana!* the boatmen had it in the time of Constantine, — a time when provincial idioms had already corrupted the purity of the Latin tongue; *Ave Nio!*

said the troops of the Comtes de Toulouse, de Provence, and de Forcalquier; hence *Avignon!*

Understand that this is history; we should be much less positive than we are, if instead of history we were writing a novel.

Thus you see that Avignon has been of all time a privileged city; moreover, she was one of the first to have a magnificent bridge,—a bridge built in 1177, by a young shepherd named Bennezet, who exchanged his pastoral crook for a pastoral frock, and was lucky enough to be canonized. To be sure, only three or four arches to-day remain to attest the quality of this structure, which was destroyed under Louis XIV., in the year of grace 1669,— almost fifty-eight years, that is to say, before the date when our story opens.

But it was towards the end of the fourteenth century especially, that Avignon was a glorious sight to see. Philippe le Bel, who had intended to bestow upon Clement V. and his successors in the Papal chair guards, a prison, and a place of refuge, really furnished them with a court, a palace, and a kingdom.

In very truth, that queen of luxury, of effeminacy and debauchery, which men called Avignon, did possess a court, a palace, and a kingdom; she had a girdle of walls which had been clasped about her ample waist by Hernaudy of Herodia, Grand Master of the Order of Saint John of Jerusalem; she had dissolute priests, who touched the symbol of the body of Christ with hands hot with lust; she had beautiful courtesans, sisters, nieces, and concubines of the Popes, who despoiled the tiara of its diamonds to make necklaces and bracelets for them; lastly, she had the plashing echoes of the fountain of Vaucluse, which repeated in amorous tones the sweet name of Laura, and lulled her to rest to the soft and licentious strains of the chansons of Petrarch.

It is true that when Gregory XI., at the earnest solici-
tation of Saint Bridget of Sweden and Saint Catherine
of Sienna, left Avignon in 1376 for Rome, where he
arrived on the 17th of January, 1377,— it is true that
Avignon was then shorn of her splendor, although retaining her arms, which are gules with three golden keys
facing one another, and supported by an eagle with
this device, *Unguibus et rostris ;* and was thenceforth
naught but a mourning widow, an uninhabited palace,
an empty tomb. The Popes indeed kept Avignon, which
was very productive property, but they kept it as one
keeps a château which one no longer uses as a residence;
they sent a legate there to take their place, but he only
did it in the same sense that an intendant takes the place
of the proprietor, or the night of the day.

However, Avignon continued to be the religious city *par
excellence,* for at the opening of our story she still contained one hundred and nine canons, fourteen beneficed
priests, three hundred and fifty monks, and a like number of nuns, who, with a number of lesser ecclesiastics
attached in various capacities to the eight chapters,
formed a body of nine hundred individuals, — that is to
say, a twenty-eighth part of the population, — whose lives
were devoted to the service of the altar.

In addition Avignon, after having had seven times
seven Popes who had reigned seven times ten years,
possessed in 1727 seven times seven things which are of
importance in estimating the attractions, the beauty, and
the moral condition of a large city.

She had seven gates, seven palaces, seven parishes,
seven collegiate churches, seven hospitals, seven monas-
teries of monks, and seven convents of nuns.

With regard to the claim put forward in behalf of " the
gentle manners of its people," as one of the elements in

the attractiveness of Avignon, by her historian, François
Nouguier, we are bound to say that it seems to be less
supported by the facts than all the rest; and on this
point alone do we take exception to his judgment, reminding him of the never-ending quarrels between the white
and black penitents, who murdered one another at every
opportunity, and divided the city into two camps which
were always well supplied with broken heads.

Of course, we have not a word to say to him of the
massacres of the Glacière in 1791, nor of the murder
of Maréchal Brune in 1815. Those were occurrences
which worthy François Nouguier, learned as he was,
could not have foreseen at the time when he wrote.

But aside from these gentle manners, which are somewhat questionable in the eyes of the nineteenth century,
Avignon exhibited herself in the beginning of the
eighteenth under conditions which were agreeable to
the eye and the mind of the traveller.

In the first place, besides the Dominicans who had
been established there since 1226, and the Cordeliers
in 1227, besides her Augustinians, Carmelites, Mathurins,
Benedictines, Célestins, Minimes, Capuchins, Recollets,
Fathers of Christian Doctrine, Unshod Carmelites,
Antonines, Priests of the Oratory, and Observantins,
Avignon had its Jesuit college and novitiate, founded
in 1587 by Louis d'Ancezune.

Now, he who spoke of Jesuits at that time spoke of
learned, affable men, who had a hand in every political,
social, or commercial movement of the age: it might be
that commercial interests summoned them to act as media-
tors in those distant, unknown seas into which flow the
waters of the Ganges and the river Bleu, the Rhone of
India and the Rhone of China; it might be that missionary zeal, urging them on to undiscovered lands,

enticed them to the vast plains of Brazil, or the mountain fastnesses of Chili; it might be that at their posts in Europe they scanned the unfolding pages of politics,— that volume without end, whose every word tells of hope blighted or ambition gratified, of a dynasty founded or a crown shattered; it might be that literature retained them, inheritors of the traditions of the Benedictines, beneath the gray arches of the cloister, between the little patch of turf with its sparse flowers, and the bright sunlight, cut off by the high walls of the college.

Avignon, that privileged city which had all that other cities have and a thousand things beside, had then her Jesuits with the rest; and it is to the chapel of the novitiate that we first introduce our reader, with the preliminary information that we are in the early days of May, 1727, and that Louis XV., now seventeen years of age, is King of France.

At the summit of a street which was called Rue des Novices, — we say "at the summit" advisedly, because the streets of Avignon, which city was built with a view to protection against the mistral and the sun, consist for the most part of steep ascents or sharp declivities, — on Rue des Novices, we say, arose the building of the novitiate, dwelling and chapel.

This building, similar in form and general plan to all those which the Jesuits have erected in France, or indeed in other countries, affected the sober and modest style which is of no special time, and can never compromise those who make use of it, since it reveals nothing to the eye materially, and one must needs be a very erudite archæologist to find the soul of a mass of stone in the works of a society of which many members deny a soul to mankind.

The Jesuits, parasitical travellers, disguised invaders,

while dreaming of conquering the whole world, step by step, were very careful, wherever they gained a foothold, that their tent, destined some day to become a citadel, should not give offence to the eye. Every parasite, when he takes his seat at table, is careful not to ape the elegance of the rich man's dress, nor to clothe himself in rags like the poor man; he would attract attention to his opulence or his poverty. Every ambitious person should assume an appearance of modesty, if not of absolute humility, ready, when the time is ripe, to stretch out his claws like the tiger, or to open his maw like the shark.

Thus it was that the Society of Jesus, in Flanders and France and Spain, where its principal houses were, had allowed the founders of these houses to make use only of the meaningless architecture of the cloister or barracks, which consisted at that time of great bare walls of stone or brick, with long windows barred with iron, a portico or two with very sober ornamentation, and here and there a half-column, — as if columns in full relief would have been too manifest an exhibition of luxury.

The same severe treatment prevailed in the interior, combined with most careful attention to hygienic conditions and the daily curriculum; the straight line prevailed wherever the fathers had to keep an eye upon the novices, but darkness and labyrinthine windings in those regions where they had to meet the public.

Further than this, we will not undertake to describe the interior of the establishment of the Jesuit fathers at Avignon; one of our actors is awaiting us in the chapel of the novices, where, in view of the importance of his rôle, we will hasten to join him.

And yet, as every drama has its *mise en scène*, we ought to say a word of this chapel to which we are about to introduce our readers, just as we have had

a word to say of the city which they have traversed with
us.

Let them stay a moment upon the threshold, then,
and they will see a circular apartment of moderate size,
with unfigured windows, which receive the light directly
beneath the cupola, and shed its full brilliancy upon the
lofty arches, but sift it gradually, so that it reaches the
flagstones of the floor much reduced in brilliancy. A long
altar, almost without ornamentation, is stretched like
a chord across the arc of the apse; behind the altar are
a few oak stalls, screened and dark, to afford greater fa-
cilities for spying or for meditation on the part of the
fathers who take their places there during the services.
Such is a description of the place in a few strokes.

It was one o'clock, and all the services were at an end;
the sun was beating down furiously upon the city, so that
the church was deserted.

At the left of the altar, however, beside a narrow aisle
which led to the stalls of which we have spoken, a
young novice, clad in the black robe of the order, was sitting in a chair against a pillar, his head half buried in
a book, which he was devouring rather than reading.

The young man was not so absorbed in his book, nevertheless, as to forget to cast a stealthy glance to right and
left every few moments; on his left was the little door
by which the fathers could enter the chapel from the
novitiate; at his right the large door which gave admittance to the faithful from the street.

Was it simple curiosity or was it absent-mindedness?
The latter surely would be a very natural failing in a
young person for whom breviary and ritual are but dry
and monotonous pasturage.

But we have said that the young novice seemed to be
devouring the pages of his book; did he thus look to

right and left to challenge the admiration of some one who was watching him, and was he a hypocrite instead of being absent-minded?

He was neither the one nor the other.

Any one who had crept up behind him and looked over his shoulder as he was reading, would have discovered that a volume of less size was concealed within the missal, — a volume of which the paper was cleaner and fresher, and of which the typographical appearance was irregular, that is to say, formed of those lines of unequal length which twenty-nine years later were to serve Master André as a criterion by means of which to distinguish betwixt verse and prose, when he measured them with a bit of string to make them neither too long nor too short.

Thus we need not wonder that the novice dreaded a surprise. It is the experience of every pupil who is hiding a forbidden book in his lesson-book. But there are forbidden books and forbidden books, just as there are sticks and sticks; there are books only slightly forbidden and books very vehemently forbidden; there are those which involve no more serious penalty than memorizing five hundred lines, and those which involve loss of liberty, — the dungeon even.

To which class did the volume belong which the disciple of Loyola was reading, and in which his eyes and his thoughts were alike deeply buried?

In order to solve this problem, the spectator would not even have required to approach him; he might have guessed the whole thing by the movement of his head, a certain mysterious inflection in his voice, — an inflection which was as far as possible from that suited to the psalmody of the church, and was marvellously like that sort of sing-song which was in vogue on the stage at this time. In fact, his suspicion would have become certainty at sight of certain gestures which imprudently disclosed to view the novice's arm and fingers,— not like the mild-mannered arm and benevolent fingers of a priest deliver-ing a discourse, but, rather, like the threatening arm and clenched fingers of an actor playing his part.

For above half an hour the novice had been chanting and gesticulating thus, when the hasty entrance of a stranger who appeared at the church door, and whose nervous, precipitate steps resounded upon the flags, inter-rupted the performer, and caused him to change his gesture from the biceps to the wrist; that joint and the patella being the only ones which the faithful might exercise within the walls of the church,— the latter being brought into play in the process of genuflexion, and the other in going through with the *mea culpa*.

II.

THE new-comer was a man of some twenty-eight or thirty years, of nervous and sickly appearance, pale, tall of stature, graceful of movement, and of distinguished bearing; well dressed, and yet in a sort of careless way which did not lack charm, and was half-way between the *déshabillé* of a nobleman and the *négligé* of an artist. Evidently very deeply preoccupied by painful thoughts, he was crushing his hat under his arm, as he passed a white well-kept hand through his hair, which was wet with perspiration.

His attractive face, sweet and tinged with melancholy, wore an expression of anxiety and distraction which the novice would have observed except for the assiduous pains he had taken to look neither to right nor left, from the stranger's first appearance upon the scene.

After hastily entering the church, and stopping for a moment to look about him, the stranger seemed to collect his somewhat anxious thoughts again, and began to pace rapidly up and down and back and forth, until his glance fell upon the novice, whereupon he made straight for him.

The novice, guessing at his course rather than seeing it, quickly closed his double book, buried his face in his clasped hands, and hypocritically feigned to be absorbed in fervent prayer.

Meanwhile the new-comer had drawn so near as almost to touch the shoulder of the novice, who pretended to return to the earth at that instant from the gulf of piety in which he had been swallowed up.

"Pardon, my brother, if I disturb your devotions," said the stranger, opening the conversation.

"My brother," the novice replied, rising to his feet, and carelessly holding the book behind him, "I am at your service."

"Listen, my brother, to what brings me hither. I desire to have a confessor; that is my reason for approaching you and breaking in upon your prayers, for which I most humbly ask your pardon."

"Alas! I am only a novice," the young man rejoined; "and as I have not received holy orders, I cannot hear confession. You must see one of our fathers."

"Yes, yes, that is what I would like," cried the stranger, martyrizing his hat more than ever; "yes, that is what I must do, — see one of the fathers. Would you do me the favor to introduce me to the presence of the one who you think would be able to grant me a few moments, or to bring him here to me?"

"It is just the dinner-hour, and all the fathers are in the refectory at this moment."

"Oh, the devil!" exclaimed the unknown, with visible dissatisfaction. "All in the refectory! oh, the devil!"

The next moment he seemed to realize that he had been invoking the enemy of mankind in the sacred precincts.

"What have I said?" he cried. "Forgive me, O my God!"

He made a quick, almost stealthy sign of the cross.

"This little difficulty about procuring a confessor

seems to disturb you, my brother," said the novice, with awakened interest.

"Oh, yes, yes, indeed it does."

"You are in great haste, then?"

"In very great haste."

"How unfortunate that I am only a novice!"

"Yes, it is unfortunate. But you are almost old enough to be ordained, and you soon will be — and then, then — Ah, my brother, my brother, how happy I esteem your lot!"

"Happy! why, pray?" asked the novice, naïvely.

"Because within a year you will have attained the goal for which every Christian soul should strive, — I mean, salvation; and meanwhile, living here in the Jesuit novitiate, you have the privilege of confessing your sins to these worthy fathers when you choose, and as often as you choose."

"Ah, yes, that is very true; when I choose, and as often as I choose," the novice returned, with a sigh which implied that he did not value at the same figure as the stranger the distinguished favor he had received from above.

"And then, too," the stranger continued with growing enthusiasm, "here you are at home; this church, this altar, these consecrated vessels, all are yours."

The novice cast upon his interlocutor a look of wonder which was not wholly without uneasiness. It was clear that he began to be apprehensive that he had to do with a man whose brain was somewhat unhinged.

But the stranger went on, becoming more and more earnest in his speech, —

"This coat is yours; this rosary, it is yours also; and this book, this holy book in which you may read from morn till night, it too is yours."

As he uttered these words in an impassioned voice, he shook the novice so energetically by the arm that the hand at the end of the arm let fall the much belauded book, at the same time that the brochure we have described fell from its hiding-place.

When he saw the two thus separated, the novice pounced upon the brochure in a frenzy of fear, and buried it in the mysterious depths of one of the pockets of his cassock; and then, still quaking with apprehension, he picked up the book.

That done, he glanced timidly at the unknown. But he had taken no note of what had happened, so absorbing was the religious exaltation to which he had worked himself up.

The eyes of the two met, and almost at the same moment the unknown grasped both the novice's hands.

"See, my dear brother," he cried, "I see that it was God who led me to your church, and the hand of Providence which put you upon my path; you inspire me with the most loving trust. Pardon this expansiveness in a man who is much to be pitied; but in truth your face gives me courage."

Indeed the novice's face, of which we have as yet said nothing, was one of the most attractive faces imaginable, and hence well deserved the eulogium which it received.

"You say that you are unhappy, my brother, and wish to confess?" repeated the novice.

"Yes, I am indeed unhappy!" cried the unknown. "Oh, yes, I would indeed like to confess."

"Is it that you have had the misfortune to commit some sin?"

"Some sin! Ah, my whole life is one long sin, — a sin which lasts from morning till night!" cried the unknown, with a sigh, which seemed to indicate that his contrition left little to be desired.

"I am speaking to a malefactor, then?" the young man asked with something like terror.

"Oh, yes, to a malefactor, a great malefactor."

In spite of himself, the young man recoiled a step.

"Judge yourself," the unknown continued with a despairing gesture; "I am an actor!"

"An actor!" cried the young man, most affably, and drawing near as the unfortunate artist drew away in his turn, as if, after the avowal he had made, he was no longer fit to touch his fellow-mortals, — "you an actor!"

"*Mon Dieu!* yes."

"Ah, you are an actor!"

The young man continued to approach.

"What!" exclaimed the artist; "you know what I am, and yet you do not shun me as one shuns a leper?"

"Why, no," said the novice; "for my part, I have no hatred for actors." And he added, in so low a tone that his interlocutor could not hear, "Quite the contrary."

"What!" the artist repeated; "you do not turn away in disgust at sight of a heretic, a man who is damned and outside the pale of the church?"

"No."

"Ah, you are so young still! but some day — "

"My brother," said the novice, "I am not of those whose hatred springs from prejudice."

"Alas! my brother," the artist rejoined, "actors are guilty of original sin, — simple in other cases, but double, triple, quadruple in mine, for I am the son, grandson, and great-grandson of comedians. If I am damned, it will be partly on account of Adam and Eve."

"I don't quite understand you," replied the novice, with much curiosity.

"I mean, my brother, that I am an actor by birth, and that I shall be damned on account of my father and mother, my grandfather and grandmother, and in short, all my paternal and maternal ancestors to the third and fourth generation; in a word, Monsieur, my name is Champmeslé!"

The novice's eyes opened to their fullest extent, their expression of profound astonishment having a slight admixture of admiration.

"What! Monsieur," he cried, forgetting the fraternal form of address customarily used in the religious orders, "can it be that you are the grandson of the famous comedienne ? "

"I am, Monsieur. Ah, my poor grandmother! A well-damned woman she! "

"In that case your grandfather was the comedian Champmeslé, who always played the kings."

"You have said aright. Marie Desmares, my grandmother, married Charles Chevillet, Sieur de Champmeslé; he had succeeded the celebrated Latorillière at the Hôtel de Bourgogne. His wife made her début in the rôle of Hermione, which had been played so superbly by La Desœuillet, whom she succeeded."

"So that your father," the novice continued eagerly,— "so that your father was Joseph Champmeslé, who played the valets, and your mother Marie Descombes, the first young woman ? "

"Just so. But tell me, my brother," cried Champmeslé, in amazement, "do you know that you seem to be pretty well posted in affairs behind the scenes for a Jesuit novice ? "

"Monsieur," replied the young man, alarmed at having thus yielded to the attraction which the conversation had for him, "although we are so far removed from the world, we always have an idea of what is going on there; besides, I was not born at the Jesuits', and my early education was given me at home."

"To whom have I the honor of speaking, my brother?"

"My name is Jacques Bannière, unworthy novice."

Champmeslé courteously saluted his new acquaintance, who no less courteously returned his salutation.

III.

ACTOR AND JESUIT.

THE conversation continued, quite naturally becoming, with each word, more interesting for both participants.

" So you desire to confess? " said Bannière, returning to the point at which Champmeslé began the foregoing digression apropos of his ancestors.

"*Mon Dieu!* yes, my brother, and these are my reasons. You, who have some acquaintance with the history of my family, are probably aware that my grandfather was a close friend of Monsieur Racine? "

" So I have understood, and of Monsieur La Fontaine too," Bannière hastened to reply, blushing as he remembered the legend which connected those two names somewhat lightly with that of Marie Desmares, wife of the elder Champmeslé.

" Although he was a second-rate tragedian, perhaps because of his limitations in that respect, my grandfather was a man of much wit, and therein had the advantage of his father, Monsieur Chevillet, of whom you may have heard perhaps? "

" No, Monsieur," returned Bannière, timidly, ashamed that his familiarity with the Champmeslé pedigree stopped at the third generation.

" Ah! but my great-grandfather, Chevillet, who was also a comedian, had all the intellectual ability of my great-great-grandfather, a very affable and pious poet, who wrote mysteries, and played in them too at need."

"Really!" cried Bannière, in amazement; "a poet and comedian at once, like Monsieur Molière?"

"*Mon Dieu*, yes! Only observe, I pray, that those words which I emphasized in speaking of him, 'a very affable and pious poet,' serve to distinguish him from Monsieur Molière, who was ill-tempered and a scoffer."

"Yes, Monsieur, I certainly will observe that distinction, and will remember it, I promise you, when the time comes for me to remember it. But meanwhile, Monsieur, why will you not take a seat? Our fathers will be at table for a quarter of an hour yet, and there is no reason why you should remain standing."

"None at all, Monsieur — pardon me, I should say 'my brother.' I gladly accept a seat and the pleasure of further conversation with you, if you are not wearied by my loquacity."

"Wearied indeed! Pray believe, on the contrary, Monsieur, that I am exceedingly interested in what you say. We were speaking of your grandfather."

"Of my grandfather, that is true; so we will return to my grandfather, and you will see that I do not indulge in meaningless digressions."

"Oh, I am sure of that!"

"I was saying that Chevillet de Champmeslé, my grandfather —"

"He who played the kings' parts?"

"Yes, the friend of Monsieur Racine."

"And Monsieur La Fontaine?"

"And of Monsieur La Fontaine, that's the man. I was about to say, then, that Chevillet de Champmeslé had known much sorrow and disappointment in his life. In the first place, the loss of his wife, who died in 1694, and then of Monsieur Racine, who died in 1699. I say nothing of the loss of Monsieur La Fontaine, who preceded both the others, dying the death of a most exemplary Christian in 1693."

"By the way, did not your grandfather collaborate with Monsieur La Fontaine, and write with him four comedies: 'Le Florentin,' 'La Coupe Enchantée,' 'Le Veau Perdu," and 'Je vous prends sans vert,' I think?"

"Monsieur, while I admire your profound erudition in dramatic matters, which continues to arouse my wonder on the part of a novice, I must tell you that my own belief is that good La Fontaine good-naturedly, and to pay a compliment to my grandfather, allowed it to be said in society, that they worked together."

"Ah, yes!"

"It was like this: my grandfather allowed him to become one of his family, and La Fontaine allowed my grandfather to get some of the credit for his work."

Bannière blushed imperceptibly.

"So you say," he rejoined, "that your grandfather had known sorrow; the death of his wife and of Monsieur La Fontaine and Monsieur Racine."

"To these sources of chagrin," continued Champmeslé, "we must add the very moderate success, I might even say, the dead failure of certain pieces, which he wrote without assistance, such as 'L'Heure du Berger,' 'La Rue Saint-Denis,' and 'Le Parisien;' a man can but be fatigued, who keeps falling from time to time, especially when his fall is in five acts, and in verse at that. In short, my grandfather, after 1700, became very moody and sullen, like Louis XIV.; he was taciturn, almost dumb, and dreamed from sunrise to sunset. The trouble came, my brother, when Champmeslé, from being a daydreamer, fell into the way of dreaming at night, and in his dreams saw La Champmeslé, his wife, and Mademoiselle Chevillet, his mother, who, with faces of ghostly pallor, leaning upon one another with a grieved and threatening expression, made each a beckoning motion with the finger, which means, 'Come with us.'"

"Ah, *mon Dieu!*" Bannière interjected.

"Monsieur, that happened on a Friday night in the month of August, 1700. This dream made so deep an impression upon my grandfather's mind that it was as if it had really happened; go where he would, from that moment his eyes always saw the sweet face of La Champmeslé, surrounded with raven-hued tresses, and the stern countenance of Madame Chevillet with its frame of gray hair, and their melancholy smile, and their mournful gesture; so that he sang incessantly on all occasions,

'Adieu, paniers, vendanges sont faites.' [1]

Now, just at that time, Monsieur, my grandfather had played Agamemnon before Louis XIV., and the king had done him the honor to say to him after the performance: 'Well, Champmeslé! you still act as atrociously as ever, do you not?' In his capacity as a man of sense my grandfather had always had a similar estimate of his own histrionic ability, and he then determined to give up the kingly rôles, and take the first comic old man."

"Allow me to say, Monsieur, that if your grandfather was really so distressed as you say by the successive blows which fate had dealt him, the moment was ill chosen to assume comic old men's parts."

"You are quite right, Monsieur; and many people who saw the poor devil in that line of parts have told me that they could imagine nothing more incongruous than the combination of such buffoonery with that despairing countenance. He wept so bitterly, in making others laugh, that his heart was broken, and he had to return to such rôles

[1] "Adieu, hampers, the grapes are gathered."

as Agamemnon, which one can always play with safety, though one be stupid beyond belief."

"Ah! then one can play Agamemnon and the like when one is stupid?" asked Bannière, innocently.

"*Dame!* my brother, look at the men who play those parts. — Ah! forgive me, I forgot that novices cannot go to the play."

"Alas!" murmured Banniere, looking up towards the roof.

"Well, then! the proof of what I say is that my grandfather played that line for nearly a year after he had the dream, and during that year was hissed only five or six times; which brings us down to 1701, and the end of my story. But pardon me, my brother, I think you are going to lose your handkerchief."

Indeed something white, which might in the half light of the chapel be taken for linen, was protruding from Bannière's pocket. It was the accursed little book which he had stowed away so carefully, but which was showing its nose again in spite of all he could do.

The novice hurriedly crushed it in his hand, and resumed, —

"In 1701, you were saying, my brother?"

"In 1701, on the same nineteenth day of August, my grandfather again saw his wife and mother in a dream, paler and more doleful than before, and persistently repeating the same sign."

"Imagination, doubtless," muttered the Jesuit apprentice.

"Not at all, but reality, my brother, reality. He awoke; he opened his eyes; he lighted his float light, his candle, his lamp; he rattled his spoon against his glass of *eau sucrée*, and still, still, despite the float-light, the candle, and the lamp, despite the noise, he saw in the darkest corner of his apartment those two women, the young and the old, bending those fateful forefingers, and saying with finger and head and smile, 'Come with us, come with us!'"

"That was frightful," said Bannière, as he felt the perspiration on his brow.

"I must tell you that it was fatal too," said the artist, assenting, as we see, to Bannière's characterization. "Monsieur de Champmeslé rose at once, and rushed off in the middle of the night, half dressed, to arouse his friends, and tell them what had happened.

"Some of them, false friends, laughingly showed him the door; others, with more consideration, used words of consolation, citing examples of dreams that never were realized, and trying to persuade him that his was of that sort; one only, a true friend he, made him pass the night with him, and talked with him till dawn of the beautiful and good Marie Desmares, and of the virtuous Mademoiselle Chevillet de Champmeslé, his mother, and succeeded in persuading him, or very nearly that, that two such estimable individuals could not possibly wish any ill to him who was the son of one and the husband of the other.

"So long as Champmeslé was in bed with his friend or in his presence, he was somewhat reassured, as we have said; but the blow was struck. He had scarcely left his comforter when the same thoughts came back to him. It was a Sunday, and they were playing Racine's 'Iphigénie,' preceded by some little piece which I can't now recall. While the latter was in progress, my grandfather, in Greek costume, was walking up and down the foyer. His helmet was pulled over his eyes, and his velvet coat of mail was all bespangled with tears, which, like liquid diamonds, were streaming down to his very buskins. And it was pitiful to hear him humming away at his eternal refrain, which grew more lugubrious every day: 'Adieu, paniers, vendanges sont faites.' Everybody who heard that doleful strain said to himself, '*Mon Dieu*, a melancholy Ulysses Champmeslé will be to-night.' "

"Ulysses is not exactly a side-splitting part at best," said Bannière, phlegmatically, although stirred to the lowest depths by this narrative.

"Side-splitting or not, Monsieur, I assure you that the part was played in an awe-inspiring fashion that day. Baron, who was playing Achilles, lost command of himself; and Sallé, who was the Agamemnon, and who had been at sword's-points with Baron for a month, replied in spite of himself when the latter asked him, —

'Seigneur, qu'a donc cet bruit qui vous doive étonner?'[1]

'Is Champmeslé ill?' "

"Whereas," Bannière interrupted, "his proper reply is:

'Juste ciel ! Saurait-il mon funeste artifice?' "[2]

"Right again. But upon my word, my brother, I find you exceedingly well informed in these matters."

"Yes, I was taught all that at home," rejoined Bannière, modestly.

"The performance at an end," resumed Champmeslé, "my grandfather had no idea of going to bed and trying to sleep. He was too much afraid that as soon as his eyes were closed, possibly while they were still open, he should see his wife and mother again. He wandered about the streets, careful not to glance into the dark corners; and in the morning, when the church doors were

---

[1] "Noble sir, what is there in this uproar to cause you astonishment?"

[2] "Great Heaven! Can it be that he is aware of my baleful stratagem?"

open, he gave thirty sous to the sacristan of Saint-Eustache to pay for a Mass each for his mother and his wife.

"'I owe you ten sous, then,' said the sacristan.

"'No, for I want you to say a third Mass for me. Keep it all.'"

"A persistent man, that grandfather of yours," said the novice.

"Ah! you will see that he did well to be persistent," the artist rejoined.

"On returning to the Hôtel de la Comédie where the players sometimes lunched before rehearsal, the first person whom Champmeslé met was Baron.

"Baron joked him upon his sinister expression. But nothing could remove the lines from my grandfather's brow; at each of Baron's witticisms he shook his head with an air which seemed to say, —

"'Ah, if you only knew!'

"Baron understood.

"'You have real cause for suffering, then?' he asked.

"'A real cause! *Morbleu*, I should say so!' was my grandfather's reply; 'the very greatest that I ever had in my life.'

"And he muttered beneath his breath, 'Come with us, come with us.'

"'After all, however great your grief,' said Baron, trying to sustain the conversation upon a level of pleasantry,

'Ta douleur, Champmeslé, ne peut etre éternelle.'[1]

"'Ah!' said my grandfather; 'it will do just that, for it will end only with my life.'

"'Come, tell me what it is; if it is such a serious matter as that, I desire to know it.'

---

[1] "Thy sorrow, Champmeslé, cannot endure forever."

" ' You wish to know it ? '

" ' Yes.'

" ' Well, I am unhappy to know that you are on bad terms with Sallé.'

" ' Ah! I should say so! A scoundrel who insists that I am growing old, and goes about telling everybody so.'

" ' He is wrong; one is as old as one seems to be, and you look barely thirty.'

" ' You see, then, that he is a villain, a scamp, a miserable wretch.'

" ' Whatever you please, Baron; but I do not want to die knowing that you two are at enmity; and as that must soon happen —'

" ' What! what must soon happen ? '

" ' My death.'

" ' Very well, then; as you say. I will make up with Sallé the day of your death, old fellow,' said Baron.

" ' Do it now, then, for it will be to-day,' rejoined my grandfather.

" And notwithstanding all Baron's *ifs* and *buts* and *fors*, for he was not easily persuaded, my grandfather compelled him to enter the cabaret.

" Sallé was sitting there at lunch.

" My grandfather compelled Baron to sit opposite his enemy, and took his place between them."

" At table," remarked Bannière, " melancholy thoughts vanish."

" Ah! young man, young man," cried the actor, sadly, " you will soon see how greatly mistaken you are! Although sitting at the same table, Baron and Sallé continued to sulk, and showed their teeth a little at first. But without relaxing his sepulchral expression for an instant, Monsieur de Champmeslé poured so much good wine into their stomachs that they finally softened.

Quick to observe that their hearts were touched, my grandfather took a hand of each, and put one in the other upon the table; then, as if his duties in this world were accomplished, and as if nothing remained for him to do on earth, he let his head fall in his hands."

"It may be," said Bannière, "that he hid himself thus because of the vision which pursued him."

"Ah! that suggestion proves you to be a youth of discernment," said the actor, "for it was just that. In the position he had assumed, my grandfather seemed to be shedding all the tears that his body could hold.

"'Good,' said Sallé; 'Champmeslé is weeping now that he has made us laugh.'

"'That's not it,' said Baron, jocosely. 'Champmeslé undertook to die if he was fortunate enough to reconcile us to one another; he has reconciled us, and now he is dying, *pardieu!*'

"My grandfather heaved a sigh which had an uncanny sound. The two friends looked at one another and fell to shuddering involuntarily.

"Then they looked at Champmeslé. His immobility, which was so absolute that there was no symptom of breathing, terrified them. His head was still between his hands. Baron took away one hand and Sallé the other, and his head fell forward, face down upon the table; his cheeks were bloodless, his eyes staring, and his mouth tightly closed. He was dead."

"Oh, Monsieur," cried Bannière, "that is a heart-rending tale!"

"Is it not, my brother?" returned the artist, sighing deeply.

"But all this," continued Bannière, who had a logical cast of mind, — "all this does not make clear to me why you want to confess."

"Why — But understand, my dear brother, I pray you, that we Champmeslés die suddenly. My grandfather, as you have just heard, died suddenly, my grandmother died suddenly, my father died suddenly; and each of the three immediately after their respective first appearances in new parts, — for this was the first time that my grandfather had played 'Ulysses,' having given up the rôle of 'Agamemnon,' to Sallé, who had long been ambitious to play it. So, you see, with every rôle that I play for the first time I quake with fear, lest I die suddenly, like my father, my grandfather, my grandmother — "

"But are you now on the point of making one of these first appearances ? " asked Bannière, timidly.

"Alas! yes, my brother," replied Champmeslé, with a despondent gesture.

"When ? "

"To-morrow."

"To-morrow, did you say ? "

"Yes, to-morrow."

"What part are you to play ? "

"Oh! a very difficult one."

"What is it ? "

"Hérode."

"Hérode! What! Hérode in Monsieur de Voltaire's 'Hérode et Mariamne!'" cried Bannière, leaping back, and clapping his hands in amazement.

"Oh, don't blame me for it, I beg! " said the artist, in a pitiful tone; "I am in despair."

"You are in despair at the idea of playing this part, and yet you play it ? " exclaimed Bannière, somewhat at a loss to explain this apparent inconsistency.

"*Mon Dieu !* yes," cried Champmeslé; "an inexplicable anomaly, is it not ? But so it is. What can I do ?

Nothing, for I have all the family superstition; sometimes thoughts come to my mind in this connection — "

"What thoughts?"

"Thoughts which I cannot put into words because
they involve casting a stain upon my grandmother's
good name."

"Tell me what you mean; I am not all the world, and
your thoughts will be sacred."

"It sometimes comes into my head that I am not
really the grandson of my grandfather."

"Nonsense!"

"It comes into my head that this rage which I have
for the stage, and the result of which is that when I am
not acting I think I am denying my birth, and when I
am acting I think I am damned, is due to the fact that
my blood is, as they say in heraldic language, in equal
parts actor and author. In the old days there was gossip
because Monsieur Racine wrote all my grandmother's
favorite rôles. There was no less talk because Monsieur
La Fontaine allowed my grandfather to write his name
beside his. Ah! if it be as I suspect, I should be damned
on other grounds, being the grandson of an actress and of
a man who wrote love tragedies."

"But," said Bannière, innocently, "there are as many
chances that you are the grandson of Monsieur La
Fontaine as of Monsieur Racine."

"That would be much worse, for then I should be
descended from an actress and a man who wrote very
immoral stories."

"This is indeed a case of conscience," said Bannière;
"but it is not for us to discuss it, and as soon as one of
our reverend fathers shall have left the table — "

"Oh, yes, a confessor, a confessor!" cried Champmeslé,
— "a confessor who will tell me the end of all this: a

confessor who will tell me whether I am the grandson of Monsieur Chevillet, Monsieur Racine, or Monsieur La Fontaine; a confessor who will tell me if one must necessarily be damned when one is the son, grandson, and great-grandson of an actor. Oh for a confessor, a confessor, a confessor; for I am going to play a new part to-morrow, and I want to confess *in articulo mortis*."

"Calm yourself, pray, my dear brother; you are not old enough to fear such a catastrophe."

"Ah! how blessed you seem to me, you holy men," cried Champmeslé; "how blessed do I esteem your lot, who have neither white nor red paint to lay upon your cheeks as in 'Pyramus and Thisbe,' nor false beard to attach to your chin, as in 'Hérode;' how blessed do I esteem your lot, who, instead of being triply descended from actors, are Jesuits all, from father to son."

"Monsieur!" exclaimed Bannière, "what's that you say? *Jesuits from father to son!* Why, you are mad, my very dear brother."

"Pardon, pardon, a thousand pardons; but you see, when I am about to appear in a new rôle, I no longer know what I do or say. 'Jesuit from father to son,' — of course I know that is not possible. Oh, permit me to give you a Christian embrace, my brother, to be sure that you forgive me."

He proceeded to embrace the novice so heartily, and pressed him so affectionately in his arms, that the famous brochure, which seemed to have an unconquerable ambition to bask in the daylight, leaped out of Bannière's pocket once more, and fell full into the hands of Champmeslé, who involuntarily read upon the titlepage the words —

"HÉRODE ET MARIAMNE.

Tragedy in Five Acts. By Monsieur Arouet de Voltaire."

IV.

THE SACRIFICE OF ABRAHAM.

THE amazement consequent upon this discovery, and the muttered comment which amazement called forth from the scruple-ridden actor, who had just laid his whole heart bare before Bannière, would have humiliated the novice beyond expression, if an unexpected event had not diverted his thoughts from what had taken place.

This unexpected event was the appearance of a Jesuit father at the end of the little passage-way which led, as has been said, from the novitiate into the church.

With this appearance all Bannière's self-possession returned.

"Silence, for mercy's sake, Monsieur Champmeslé," he exclaimed; "here comes one of our fathers into the chapel."

In order to make short work of any suspicions which the father might conceive, Bannière rushed to meet him, crying, —

"Reverend sir, if it please you, Monsieur who is here desires to be heard in confession."

The Jesuit continued to walk towards the two young men.

"Hide the book," Bannière whispered to the actor; "hide the book, pray hide it!"

Bannière forgot that it was in no way surprising that an actor should have a copy of a comedy or a tragedy in his hand.

Nevertheless the artist hastened to comply with Bannière's entreaties, and put the hand which held the book behind his back. But while he accomplished that manœuvre with the precision and address of an actor to whom all means should be familiar, he fixed his gaze with deep attention upon him who was drawing near; for that man was to become his judge.

"It seems to me that he has a good face," said Champmeslé in an undertone to Bannière.

"Oh, yes, he is one of the kindest and most indulgent," Bannière replied, "and at the same time one of our most learned professors: it is Père de la Sante."

It may be that in imparting a slightly louder pitch to his voice Bannière intended to be overheard by the priest, and in this way to disarm his wrath by flattery, — which might be esteemed the more delicate, as it was not addressed directly to the one for whom it was destined, but reached him on the rebound as it were.

Père de la Sante, upon receiving the information that the unknown who was talking with Bannière was a penitent waiting for him, turned aside from his course towards the young men, and directed his steps towards a confessional, motioning to Champmeslé to follow him.

Champmeslé bowed affectionately to Bannière, and as he did so found a way to return to him without being seen the profane volume which had so inconveniently fallen from his pocket.

But as he handed it to him, he could not forbear saying to him in a voice overflowing with kind feeling:

"Oh, my dearest brother, why do you risk the destruction of your soul when you are in so good a position to procure salvation?"

This orthodox advice, however, did not seem to have much effect upon the novice; for as soon as he was sure that neither confessor nor penitent was spying upon him, he went eagerly at his reading of " Hérode et Mariamne " once more; nor did he cease until Champmeslé, absolved and blessed, left the confessional and the church, as lightly as a cork rises to the surface of the water when relieved of the lead which had held it down.

The Jesuit followed him from the confessional; but as he very considerately coughed and expectorated before coming out, Bannière had ample opportunity to expect him, to see him coming, and to allow him to approach without endangering the precious brochure.

Let us say a word of Père de la Sante, who at this time enjoyed very high repute in Paris and the provinces; entirely scholastic, be it understood, confined within the four walls of the Jesuit colleges, and denied by the other religious orders, all of which were madly jealous of the one with which we have to do, and which had made such enormous headway in so short a time.

Père de la Sante was a fat man of florid habit, with bushy gray eyebrows which gave him a crabbed look, which was abundantly atoned for, in the eyes of the physiognomist, by the soft blue of his eyes, and the frankness of his thick lips.

He was a rare type of man, — a scholar steeped in poetry, an ancient philosopher, who, instead of studying Plato and Socrates as curiosities, took them as his masters, allotting to the gloomy schools of modern theology the restricted place in his studies which the practical man allots to elaborate theories. A good Christian withal, a zealous but tolerant Catholic, he was slow to allow himself to be provoked to harsh measures; and he saw in Bossuet, as well as in the Cardinal de Noailles, admirable subjects for Latin verses.

It was to this benignant Jesuit that Bannière, somewhat preoccupied by thoughts of his interview with Champmeslé, proceeded to offer the humble but dignified respect which every novice owes to his superior.

But Bannière had an object in view; he was anxious for enlightenment as to Champmeslé's apprehension of eternal damnation, and his desire was so eager that one might suppose that it had some other basis than his love for his neighbor simply, and that, in fact, Bannière, an obedient slave of the decrees of the Church, at that moment really loved his neighbor as himself, and more than that, — that he loved himself as his neighbor.

And so, when he had made his reverence to the Jesuit, he said, —

"It seemed to me, my father, that your penitent went away with a very light step."

"The step is always light, my child, when the conscience is light," was the Jesuit's reply.

"So, then, I may believe that you gave the poor fellow absolution."

"Yes, my son, upon performing a trifling penance which he promised faithfully to perform."

"Yet it seemed to me," Bannière persisted, "from certain words which he let fall in conversation, that this man was an actor."

"Yes, my son, so he is," said Père de la Sante, looking wonderingly at Bannière. "What then?"

"Why, then, it seemed to me, my father, that since all actors are excommunicate, it would be useless to give him absolution."

Père de la Sante, with all his learning, seemed somewhat embarrassed for a reply.

"Excommunicate! excommunicate!" he repeated; "to be sure, actors are excommunicate, except in case of conversion and repentance."

"Ah, yes," Bannière said; "and as he has repented and become converted, no doubt — "

"He gave me the impression," retorted Père de la Sante, "that he was a perfectly honest man."

"Oh, to be sure."

"Do you not agree with me, my son? "

"Indeed, yes, in every respect."

"You talked with him quite a long while, I think? " Père de la Sante asked, interrogating Bannière with his eyes.

"I cannot say just how long I talked with him," the novice replied, with that skill in evading a direct response which the least remarkable disciple of the school of Loyola soon acquires.

"At all events, however little talk you had with him, my son, you must have noticed the elevation of his sentiments? "

"Yes, my father; and yet, I always believed that excommunication made all that of no account, unless there was abjuration and repentance."

Père de la Sante scratched the end of his nose with his forefinger, a process which his intimate friends recognized as an infallible sign of embarrassment.

"There are clear distinctions in the actor's profession," he replied; "tragedy, for example, is one of the least dangerous branches."

Bannière smiled as if he saw that Père de la Sante had given him an opening to get the better of the argument.

Père de la Sante noticed the smile, no doubt, and interpreted it as we have done; for he added quickly, —

"I mean Latin tragedy especially."

"Yes, yes, tragedies like those which you compose yourself; 'The Sacrifice of Abraham,' for instance, — 'Abrahami Sacrificium.' "

"Yes, like that, my son, or like my other tragedy, 'Les Héritiers,'" said the Jesuit, with a modest blush.

"I do not know the last, my father."

"I will give it you, my son."

"It is very true," added the novice, "that in tragedies dealing with sacred subjects, composed with a pious and moral purpose —"

"And played by young men," broke in Père de la Sante, growing warm as every poet does in speaking of his own work, "to the exclusion of every earthly emotion which requires to be interpreted by the other sex."

"Besides, my father," said Bannière, "such tragedies are not really theatrical pieces, but poems."

"I have never even ventured to write iambics," continued the Jesuit poet, "lest they should too nearly resemble those of Terence and Seneca. As for the metre, my son, as for the metre — oh, well! in my judgment, such works ought to please God rather than to displease him."

"The fact is," said Bannière, seconding the poet's enthusiasm, — "the fact is, that the part of Isaac is a very beautiful one."

"If I remember aright, it was you who played it, my son."

"Yes, you were kind enough to select me from among all my comrades."

"As the one whose head was most in keeping with the part. You played that part very well, did you know it?"

"Ah, my father, that was three years ago; and now —"

Bannière made a motion of the head, which signified, "Now, it would be very different. — But then," he continued, "how could one help but recite well such lines as this,—

> ‘Si placet innocuo firmatum sanguine fœdus
>   Jungere — ’ ”

"Indeed you did not say that line badly then, but you say it better now. Ah! you have remembered my remark as to the word ‘placet.’ You pronounced it badly, like a man of the North; while you, on the contrary, are from — ”

"Toulouse, my father."

"Ah! the men of the North may play French tragedies well, but they will never learn to play Latin tragedies; for them there are no long or short syllables, no consonants or vowels; for instance, ‘placet’ consists of two short syllables, does it not? ”

"Yes, my father; for ‘si placet’ is a dactyl."

"Very well! you pronounced ‘placet’ formerly as if ‘pla’ were a long syllable. I called your attention to it, and you have corrected it. Abraham also made a similar mistake in pronunciation. But that was natural enough, for he was from Rouen. Let me see; it was in this invocation:

> ‘O qui terrarum spatia immensum Pelagusque
>   Œternis regis impertis — ’

Do you remember that? ”

" ‘Et fulmine terras,’ ” Bannière completed the line.

"Ah! you have a very good memory, my son," cried the delighted Jesuit.

"It ’s not difficult to remember such admirable lines! Oh, the part of Abraham was a fine one too! All the parts were fine. I would have liked to play all of them."

"I am very much pleased that you remember the first line, which does not lack a certain grandeur," said Père de la Sante, whose vanity was flattered; "throwing the cæsura back to the third foot in a word composed of three long syllables is an original idea, and the 'Pelagusque' is somewhat picturesque."

"It is superb!" cried Bannière.

"I do not boast of the second line as my own," continued the Jesuit, modestly; "for it is Virgil's, and I transplanted it bodily, in the first place because it came into my head, and secondly because I thought I could not improve upon it. But, to return to the misplaced accent of the young man who played Abraham, he pronounced 'regis,' which is certainly composed of two short syllables, and means 'thou commandest,' as if it had been 'regis,' meaning 'of the king,' in which case one syllable would certainly have been long, and the other doubtful. But we have gone a long way from the subject of our conversation," suddenly exclaimed the poet, whose mind, after three years, was still intent upon the false accents of his pupils. That is easily excused, happily; for a sonorous Latin verse is such a fine thing! "We were saying, as nearly as I can remember, that there is no great risk, I might even say no risk at all, in playing Latin pieces."

"Yes, my father; but this good Monsieur de Champmeslé, whom you have just confessed, does not act in Latin, but in French; he does not recite sacred poetry, but the profanest of the profane."

"That makes a difference, as the late great king used to say," rejoined Père de la Sante; "that is why I would not say that the poor devil, so long as he acts in French tragedies, can be in a state of grace; for," he added, shaking his head, "these French tragedies are a very suspicious branch of the drama, since that abominable Arouet has taken a hand in writing them!"

At these words a shudder shook the frame of the novice, and he hastily carried his eyes as well as his hand to his pocket, to make sure that it was not betraying him again.

In all probability Père de la Sante failed to notice the agitation of the novice, for he went on: —

"There's a fellow, that Monsieur Arouet de Voltaire, who is hardly in a state of grace; and yet," he added with a sigh, "with Père Porée's help, what a fine Jesuit he would have made, — that rascal Arouet!"

Bannière nearly lost his balance as he saw the crockery-ware eyes of Père de la Sante brighten up, and his eyebrows bristle.

This time his fright was so evident that it attracted the attention of the Jesuit, whose mind suddenly received a ray of light.

"But how is it with you," he said bluntly to the novice, — "you, of whom we have said nothing? Is it possible that you are dreaming about acting?"

"You do not forget, my father, that you yourself assigned me the rôle of Isaac," said Bannière, deprecatingly.

"Yes; but that was in the 'Sacrifice of Abraham,' a Latin tragedy. That is not what I refer to."

"My father — "

"Are you thinking about acting in French tragedy?"

"Oh, my father," cried the novice, "you have always been so kind to me that I should never dream of lying to you."

"Mendax omnis homo!"[1] cried Père de la Sante, sententiously.

"Every wicked man!" added Bannière, quickly; "but I am not a wicked man, and consequently am not dis-

[1] "Every man is a liar."

posed to lie. Do you mean to ask me about my inclination ? "

" To be sure."

" Well, then, I will answer frankly, my father. Since I played in your 'Sacrifice of Abraham,' since I recited your beautiful lines, and enjoyed the abundant wealth of your ideas combined with the nobility of your sentiments — "

" See how the wretch tries to cast the whole responsibility upon me ! " exclaimed Père de la Sante.

" Indeed, I do, my father; and it is no more than just. I had no thought of the stage. Who put it into my head ? You. I had no idea what a part in a play was. Who selected me to play Isaac ? You. Who superintended my rehearsals, guided me with advice, and encouraged me with applause ? You, my father, always you."

" Miserable wretch, what are you saying ? "

" I am saying, my father, that if you had written 'The Sacrifice of Abraham' in French instead of Latin — "

" Pshaw ! "

" I am saying that at this moment, instead of being performed in a poor Jesuit college, it would be given upon the stage of every theatre in France."

" Nonsense, I say ! "

" It would be given before the court at Versailles, and before the king. Oh, what noble French lines might have been made out of such Latin lines, as —

> ' Si placet innocuo firmatum sanguine fœdus
> Jungere —' "

" I have made them, wretched boy ! " cried Père de la Sante; and he began to declaim : —

> " ' S'il faut, pour consacrer la divine alliance,
> Répandre dans ce jour le sang de l'innocence.' "

But he checked himself.

"*Mon Dieu!*" cried he, "what in Heaven's name was I doing? The truth of the matter is," he continued with a sigh, "I could have composed tragedies in French quite as well as that blackguard Arouet, if I had chosen."

"In that case, my father," said Bannière, who throughout the conversation had let no favorable opening escape him, — "in that case you certainly cannot blame me, you who have written tragedies, for longing to act them. I have always heard it said that there could be no end without a beginning, no effect without a cause. You are the beginning, I am but the end; you are the cause, and I the effect."

"That, my son," retorted Père de la Sante, horrified at the turn the conversation had taken, and especially at the attempt to hold him responsible, — "that is too weighty a question for me to answer *ex abrupto,* — off-hand. To-morrow, day after to-morrow, or on some later day, we will resume our conversation."

"Pardon me, my father, a few moments more," insisted Bannière, seizing the Jesuit by the girdle.

"Not a second!" cried Père de la Sante; "two o'clock is striking, and the reverend principal, Père Mordon, is awaiting my report."

Tearing his girdle from the youth's hands, the author of "The Sacrifice of Abraham" disappeared in the passage, leaving "Isaac" Bannière in the deepest perplexity.

V.

REVEREND PÈRE MORDON.

THE perplexity of the novice was vastly increased by the word " report " which Père de la Sante had uttered.

For this report was the terror of all novices.

In brief, the name was applied to a sort of review, in which the principal received separate reports from each professor employed in or attached to the novitiate, in addition to reports from certain pupils who were more forward than the others in bringing forth into the light of grace, or the grace of light, as you choose, the works of their comrades.

The unfortunate Bannière was well acquainted with this Jesuitical function. Like the Venetian denunciations or the Portuguese inquisition, the " report " of the Jesuits appeared to its victims in the terrifying proportions of the unknown; it was a cloud which was never seen to gather, but from which at a given moment, and generally when it was least expected, thunder and hail came forth, but without either light or smoke.

The custom was, in short, that every word, every thought, every action of the novices should be reported to the implacable tribunal of the principal. The result of the " report, " for those who were compromised by it, was first of all a warning, sometimes a stormy explanation; but punishment was inevitable.

It goes without saying that every Jesuit who was interrogated by the principal was expected to give him full and explicit answers to every question, even though ne should thereby compromise those who were nearest and dearest to him, — a friend, a relation, or a brother.

Scarcely had poor Bannière, then, after being abandoned in the church, as we have seen, by Père de la Sante, returned to his cell, when a *cuistre*, as the servants of the establishment were called, opened his door, which novices were under no circumstances allowed to keep locked.

In truth, the novitiate of the Jesuits was a terrible period of trial; the object was to crush and destroy and annihilate that work of nature which we call "man," to substitute for it that slave of an order which goes by the name of "Jesuit." No means was neglected to effect that transformation, from the most intoxicating temptations to the most atrocious barbarity. So one treats wild animals whom one wishes to tame, and who, with that end in view, are deprived of the first three essentials of animal life, — light, food, and sleep.

The stoutest resistance is overborne by darkness, loss of sleep, and hunger. Suppose the novice to be sleeping the sweet, calm sleep of youth; without warning he would be roughly awakened, and with no motive, to no profit, and with no other design than to bend body and mind to passive obedience, he would be ordered to make the circuit of the garden a hundred times or to repeat the service of the Virgin. Suppose him to be at the famishing-point, and just about to sit down to a hearty dinner; as the first morsel was on the way to his mouth, the order would come for him to be present at some conference, two, three, four, or five hours long. If perchance, his longing seemed too eager to enjoy the first rays of the May sun, the first breezes of spring, which seem to come laden with life and health, as with the sweet perfume of the budding plants, they would bury him for a day, for two days, or perhaps a whole week, in some gloomy cavern, where no air blew upon him save emanations from the tomb, and that subterranean current which moans sadly around the corners of the pillars which uphold the arches of crypts.

At last, when the subjugated soul and mind had no will remaining other than the masterful will which presided over that vast and marvellous association which was called the Society of Jesus, the novice was received into the bosom of the order; and there he became, according to the degree of his ability, his intellect, or his genius, a simple block, a corner-stone, or the very keystone of the arch of the enormous structure built in darkness by black-frocked artisans, who aspired to universal domination.

When the valet appeared upon Bannière's threshold, he had not yet had time to hide his ill-fated "Hérode," and was looking with all his eyes for a corner in which he might stow it away.

The valet interrupted this important proceeding by announcing that the reverend principal had sent for him. Bannière replied only by smoothing out his pocket, and resigning himself to follow.

Two minutes later he found himself in the presence of his superior.

Père Mordon, superior of the Jesuits of Avignon, was physically and morally the most perfect contrast imaginable to Père de la Sante. Tall and thin; pale with the yellow pallor of ivory; possessed of a head which seemed to be all forehead, punctured with two staring eyes, which acquired a brilliancy impossible to endure when they were fixed for a long time upon one; and with a slit of a mouth below his long, straight, pointed nose, — a mouth which seemed to have been gashed with a razor,

so little did the lips protrude, and so closely did they
adhere to one another, — such was Père Mordon.

" Immensus fronte, atque oculis bipatentibus."

Bannière had never doted on the society of his superior; on this occasion, we say it without doing him
injustice, he had a horror of it.

The Jesuit's forehead seemed doubled in extent; his
eyes had the fatal glitter of the eyes of a basilisk; his
nose, whiter than usual, kept growing whiter still towards
its pointed end; and his closed lips seemed to turn in,
instead of protruding.

The Jesuit saw the effect his aspect had produced,
and tried to lessen the brilliancy of his eyes in some
degree by partly veiling them under their lids.

He made a sign with his finger to Bannière to approach;
Bannière obeyed, and did not stop till he reached the
table which stood between himself and the superior.

The young novice was pale and trembling; but by the
double lines in his forehead, and the drawing together of
his eyebrows, it was easy to see that he also was the
possessor of a will of his own which would not break
without a struggle.

" Bannière," said the Jesuit, sitting in his armchair,
like a judge on the bench or an emperor on his throne,
" what have you been doing to-day ? "

Bannière understood that this form of question, covering the whole day, was really intended to refer to the
time he had passed in the church.

" My father," he asked, " where must I begin ? "

" Begin with the morning, *secundum ordinem.*"

" Is it really necessary ? "

" I do not understand you."

" You only wish to question me upon one solitary point,
my father."

"And upon what point do you think that I wish to question you, pray?"

"Upon what I was doing from noon till two o'clock, for example."

"So be it!" said the priest.   "You are very clever, — good.   I will not question you at all, then.   I will accuse you."

"I await your charge, my father."

"Twice before to-day, a tragedy of that villain whose real name is Arouet, but who dubs himself Monsieur de Voltaire, has been found in your cell, — once in your mattress, and the second time under one of the flags."

"Yes, my father; and each time the book was confiscated, and I was punished."

"And each time you have bought another copy."

"It is true, my father."

"So that this morning, while pretending to read your breviary, it was really that devilish work which you were reading in the chapel?"

"I do not deny it."

"Where have you hidden this third copy?"

"I have not hidden it, my father; it is in my pocket, and here it is."

"You give it up to me voluntarily, then, with due repentance, and you promise not to attempt to procure another?"

"I hand it to you voluntarily, my father, but without repentance.   As for trying to procure another, it would be useless.   I know it by heart."

The superior crumpled the little book in his bony hand, but with undisturbed tranquillity he said, —

"You are persistent, Bannière; *pervicax.*"

"Yes, my father," rejoined Bannière; "that is a fault of which I confess that I am guilty."

"It is a good quality, too, my son, when exerted for good objects. Patience, which narrow minds prefer to it, is only a negative virtue; perseverance is well-timed activity; the two qualities in combination in one person are said to denote that that person has a 'calling;' it would seem that you have a calling."

Bannière blushed; every word that Père Mordon uttered brought a drop of perspiration to his forehead.

"Come, answer me," continued the superior, following the progress of Bannière's emotion upon his features, "is this inclination of yours for the stage a decided calling, or simply a whim?"

"My father!"

"Is it a mere whim, as I said, a caprice, a passing fancy? Is it nothing more than the fictitious aptitude of sluggards for anything except the task which they have to do? Take care, my son; for if it is that, you are nothing more nor less than a shirker, intent upon evading your duty; and shirking is by God's law to be punished."

"I am not a shirker, my father; but — "

"But what?" demanded the Jesuit, without moving a muscle of his face, or allowing a line to appear on his expansive brow.

"But," Bannière went on, "the novitiate causes me some anxiety."

"Disgust you mean, my son."

"Pardon me, my father, I did not say that."

"So much the worse for you if you did not say it," retorted Mordon, inflexibly; "for if you did not say it, I must conclude that a short time ago, when you were deceiving the watchful eyes of your superiors and the Majesty of God in our holy chapel by the ill-timed, illicit, and furtive perusal of a profane book, — I must conclude, I say, that you were simply yielding to the temptations of the Evil One, who lies in wait in the shadow for dull, thick-witted souls, and seeks to prey upon them, *quærens quem devoret ;* and in this case, as you have yielded to a vulgar temptation, easily overcome, as you must have yielded without urging, surrendered without a blow, I shall be compelled most regretfully, my son, to inflict upon you one of the most severe punishments which we have it in our power to inflict, and which will be so much the more severe as this unfortunately is not your first offence."

Bannière recoiled in terror; but his courage came back almost immediately. He realized that he was on the point of engaging in a polemical discussion, in the issue of which his whole future was involved, and that he must carry it through to the end, at the risk of final discomfiture.

"Very well, my father, so be it," said he; "I much prefer to be punished three times, six times, ten times even, confessing that I have sinned voluntarily, I might better say, instinctively, than to allow you to suspect that before I arrived at my present position I had not exhausted my strength in the struggle. Yes, my father, I have struggled; but, like Jacob, I have been again and again overthrown by the angel. I feel an irresistible impulse to read these tragedies, and find an eager pleasure in it which consumes me. Pardon me, if my outspokenness offends you; but you see I am no longer my own master since I entered upon this experience, as I have sufficiently proved by saying what I have said."

" *Vocatio vocatur,*" said the Jesuit, coldly, with undisturbed self-possession. "I admit the accuracy of that text. Now we will take that admitted text for the subject of our conversation. We will say then, my son, that you

have a calling for this art of public exhibition which is
called the 'drama'?"

"Yes, my father, and I believe in that calling."

"Very good. But simultaneously with the revelation
of your aptitude in that direction, you are studying
theology at the Jesuit novitiate?"

"My father — "

"Oh! that may also be admitted, I think."

Bannière fairly shuddered at the cold tone in which
the reverend father laid down these ominous premises;
he divined that by bringing to bear some unforeseen
argument, of which he could anticipate the force, Mordon
would proceed to floor his interlocutor, like those clever
wrestlers who allow themselves to be seized in some part
of the body, to entice their opponents, and eventually
vanquish them more easily.

Bannière, then, breathed rather than uttered these four
words, —

"Yes, it is admitted."

"Very good!" said the Jesuit. "We will say, then,
that while connected with the Society of Jesus you have
been fascinated by the actor's profession?"

"My father, I am only a novice," Bannière hastened
to say.

"A novice preparing to become a Jesuit is precisely
the same thing as a Jesuit for our purpose; for we are
reasoning by anticipation, and substituting the future for
the present."

Bannière sighed, and bent his head.

"I say, then," resumed the superior, "that you are
destined by your relatives to enter the order, but that
you are doubtless well informed in advance what are the
advantages and disadvantages attendant upon the title of
Jesuit. However, my son, as you may not be sufficiently

informed, I will briefly enumerate both advantages and disadvantages. Are you listening, my son?"

"Yes, my father, I am listening," replied Bannière, leaning upon the table to keep himself from falling.

"The disadvantages," continued the superior, "are celibacy, canonical poverty, and disciplinary humility. You understand me, do you not?"

"Perfectly, my father."

"The advantages are the association itself, the support of almost all human intellects, put in motion by a latent interest, inseparable from the existence and real welfare of each associate, our organization being of such a nature that the least member can receive no benefit, moral or physical, in which the whole society does not share. Do you still follow me, my son?"

"Perfectly, my father."

"Hence it follows that the happiness of each one is in proportion to the happiness which we procure for all the others, and *vice versa*. In the word 'happiness,' I include two words, 'well-being' and 'glory,' words which are the mainsprings of all organizations; 'well-being' of those founded upon material considerations, 'glory' of those whose aims are spiritual or idealistic. I add, then, that every Jesuit is caressed and honored by the Society in proportion to the well-being and glory which are conferred upon the Society itself through his instrumentality, and that the Society is itself prosperous and glorious in proportion as its subjects are honored and happy. Every Jesuit, then, must study to be useful in order to be appreciated; when he is once appreciated, he has his reward."

"I still follow you, reverend father," said the young man, as the superior paused, as if awaiting comment.

"Now," Père Mordon continued, "mad indeed would be the guiding spirits of a society who should overlook

the purpose for which it was founded, and should neglect
to spread out over all the branches of that fruitful tree
which brings forth happiness and glory, the diversely
skilful hands of all those who are banded together in the
holy name of Jesus. It is enough to enlighten the
superiors, who are always selected, you know, my son,
for their brilliant abilities; it is sufficient to call their
attention to the fact that all men are born with different
aptitudes, but that all, from the lowest to the highest,
have an aptitude for something or other; for nature has
ordained that everything in this world, animate or inani-
mate, is of use for some purpose. So much the worse
for those who do not use or are not used. In this way
sometimes die of inanition, of cold and isolation, those
germs capable of fertilizing or of being fertilized, which
the wind carries from the plants or trees where their
work is to be done, and deposits upon unfruitful ground.
But among us, my son, among us who are able to detect
each one's aptitude and to turn them all to good use,
among us there is no dying of inanition or cold or solitude. Every seed is good in our eyes, for we develop
the usefulness of each germ, sure as we are of making it
bring forth fruit. For my own part, who have the
guidance of a number of human souls and minds, I
declare to you that I am in no way perplexed by this
diversity of aptitudes, which I see developing in my
hands, and that I am as well pleased to observe in this
garden of intellects which has been put in my charge
the blossoming of a scholar as of a poet, of an engineer
as of a musician, of a mathematician as of an artist. You
may, since you desire it so earnestly, become a clever
actor; so be it, I give my consent; become an actor,
then, if your temperament urges you to that profession
and your calling demands it."

"But in that case, my father," cried Banniere, giddy with joy, "I am no longer a novice; I am no more a student here; I shall leave the Jesuits!"

"Why so?"

"Because the actor's life is incompatible with the life of a recluse, since the one is sacrilegious and accursed, preordained to go straight to hell, while the other is a holy personage, predestined to canonization. The choice must be made, I appreciate that, for one cannot serve two masters at once. You are so good as to leave me free, my father; very well, then! I will admit that the noble bearing, gesticulation and declamation, and constant study to make an impression upon the public, have for me an irresistible fascination and attraction."

"Good, very good, my son!"

"Therefore I will leave the Jesuits to devote myself assiduously to the study of my new profession."

"Leave the Jesuits?" repeated the reverend father, with perfect coolness; "why so, I pray to know?"

Bannière gazed at him in amazement.

"What! my father," said he, "do you wish me to live half at the theatre and half in the convent, one foot upon the stage and one in the church? It is not possible, my father! it would be rank sacrilege, it seems to me."

"But I have said nothing of the sort, my son; to leave the Jesuits would be not only ungrateful, but absurd as well."

"But not to leave them — pardon me, my father, my mind is wandering, no doubt — but in truth I do not fully understand," stammered the poor wretch, writhing on the gridiron which was being gradually heated by the crafty dialectics of the superior.

"Yet nothing can be easier than to understand, my

son; for nothing is more clear, and a few words will suffice to prove to you that the good sense of the matter is all with me. Give me a definition of the word 'actor,' I beg."

"My father," began Bannière, embarrassed beyond description, "the actor — the actor — "

"Go on, my son, go on."

"He is a man who speaks in public."

"Good. 'Who speaks in public,' remember that."

"*Mon Dieu! mon Dieu!* what sort of a trap is he setting for me?" muttered Bannière.

"Go on with your definition of an actor, my son," persisted Mordon.

"Well then, the actor, my father, is a man who utters for the behoof of those who have come together to hear him, the most beautiful commonplaces which morality can furnish, upon virtue and vice, crime and its punishment, weakness and passion."

"*Very* good," said Mordon, who had followed and repeated each word of the definition with eyes cast down, approving nods of the head, and a pantomime expressive of entire acquiescence.

"Lastly," added Bannière, "the actor is a man who in a costume calculated to set off his personal charms arouses in the public breast emotions, whose mission is to please, to instruct, and to improve."

"And that is all, is it not?" asked Mordon.

"I think of nothing else," was Bannière's timid response; for he was vastly more ill at ease under this ominous approbation than he would have been if his words had been excepted to.

"Very well, then," Mordon rejoined, "I was right, my son, in insisting that you could do all that you have described perfectly well without severing your connection with the Society of Jesus. I will go further, — with the aptitude and the evident calling which you have demonstrated, to accomplish all the results which you have yourself enumerated, it would be impossible for you to withdraw without depriving the Society of a considerable accession of glory and well-being. For that reason, my son, you will not go forth from its bosom."

"But, my father," Bannière said, alarmed at this ominous indulgence, and quite at the end of his patience, if not of his perseverance and his calling, "no one ever saw a Jesuit an actor!"

"No one ever saw a Jesuit an actor, very true," was Mordon's phlegmatic retort; "but Jesuits have been known to become preachers. Why should you not be a preacher, and a fine preacher too?"

"I a preacher!" exclaimed the thunderstruck Bannière, bearing hard upon each syllable.

"Why, to be sure; I should say that you yourself, only a moment since, were drawing the portrait of a preacher with a master hand."

"I?"

"Yes, you, to be sure."

"Of an actor, you mean!"

"Or of a preacher. Let me repeat your definition word for word.

"First. 'A man who speaks in public.' Preachers speak in public, unless I am much mistaken.

"Second. 'A man who utters for the behoof of those who have come together to hear him the most beautiful commonplaces which morality can furnish, upon virtue and vice, crime and its punishment, weakness and passion.'

"I think, my dear son, that preachers do just that.

"Third. 'The man who in a costume calculated to set

off his personal charms arouses in the public breast emotions, whose mission is to please, to instruct, and to improve.'

" There is your threefold definition; you see how well I remember it, my son, for I have not changed a word. Now, if ever a definition fitted a person exactly, this one of yours, my son, fits the preacher. And indeed, clad in his priestly costume, which is the noblest and most imposing, and the best calculated to set off the personal attractions of a handsome man (modest and decent attractions, my son, for we never think of any others, do we?), his hair well oiled, his hand half hidden within his flowing lace-sleeve, the preacher, when he has a beautiful face, as Monsieur de Fénelon had, can produce a most marvellous impression upon his audience. I do not say — note well, my dear son — that I approve of Monsieur de Fénelon's theological opinions. No, quite the contrary; but I am speaking of his appearance and manner only. Thus I have applied every part of your definition, and I await your response."

" Pardon, reverend father," said Bannière, "but I expected, in speaking to you with so much freedom, to persuade you of my calling to be an actor."

" Or a preacher, my son. I understood."

" But whatever you may say, my father, it is not the same thing."

" Absolutely the same, my son, at least according to your definition; and when the same definition applies to the two, if either is entitled to priority, it certainly is the preacher."

" But, my father," cried Bannière, "let me finish my definition, please!"

" Very willingly, my son; finish it, finish it."

" I will add, then," said Bannière, with the naïve

triumph of a young lamb who has escaped for the moment from the wolf's jaws, "that the actor is a man who plays historical pieces, — works which represent deeds of high emprise, and recall events which have changed the whole face of the world."

"I stop you there," said Père Mordon, with imperturbable calmness. "You have put the finishing touch, with a very clever stroke of the pencil, to your portrait of the preacher, and I congratulate you most sincerely upon it."

"What!" cried Bannière, at his wits' end.

"Do me the favor, I beg, to name a play, comedy, or tragedy, or drama of any variety, which can for a moment abide comparison, for style, interest of its plot, scope of its action, detail of its situations, or its final catastrophe, with the Passion of our Lord Jesus Christ. Imagine yourself standing in the pulpit, the sole actor, mark you, without leader or associates, and that you have it in charge to interpret that sublime drama, in which Heaven for the redemption of the earth lends to it the Son of its God: imagine that you are portraying the tergiversations of Pontius Pilate, the artifices of Caiaphas, the hatred of the Pharisees, the apostasy of Peter; tell me, do you know in the whole length and breadth of the drama, in the plays of Corneille or Racine, of Shakspeare or Jonson, or of the old Greek masters, a more marvellously beautiful scene, a more sublime soliloquy, than the meditation of Jesus on the Mount of Olives, or a more superb and picturesque *mise-en-scène* than the arrest of Our Lord in that same garden?

"Where can be found a grander spectacle than the judgment of Pilate, or one with greater lyric suggestions and of higher moral value than the choice between Jesus and Barabbas? Add to this the development of each separate mode of torture, with its religious and moral significance. Last of all, the progress to the place of execution, surrounded by the saintly women, — its haltings and its faintings. And the punishment itself, my son, and that marvellous narrative, compared with which, you will agree, the narrative of Theramenes or of Ulysses is hardly more than commonplace, or even the description of the battle of Salamis, in the pages of ancient Æschylus, the master of masters! There, my dearest son, there is a tragedy where human vice and passion are involved. There is a historical work, there an event which has changed the face of the world; a drama in which you may play, if you choose, the principal part, the only part, with the applause of the whole Society, and of the world, — before kings and queens, if you so desire, and with a bishopric or an archbishopric in prospect, — yes, a cardinal's baretta, to say nothing of the pontifical tiara itself, a dubious but still possible chance, upon which no actor has ever counted, so far as I am informed."

After this discourse, in the course of which the reverend father had warmed up a little as orators do for their peroration, Mordon raised his eyelids, opened his eyes to their full size, and fairly enveloped the novice in the brilliant gleams which shot from them.

But Bannière, irritated by all this resistance, and wounded by the subtle twists and turnings in which the crafty and loquacious Mordon had indulged, cried out, —

"My father, it is neither church nor pulpit, nor sermonizing, nor missionary ardor, with which my mind is occupied. I care nothing for the applause of a religious gathering; my calling, wretched, fated, accursed that I am, draws me towards profane things. I aspire to be an actor upon the boards of a theatre, where actors and actresses perform,— actors like Monsieur Baron, actresses like Mademoiselle de Champmeslé! That is what I desire, my father, that is what I ask, that is what I must have!"

"Enough, enough, my son," rejoined the Jesuit, passing his hand across his broad forehead, upon which for a moment had appeared great folds like the waves of the Mediterranean in a storm; "I believe, upon my word, that you are in error as to your pretended calling, and I tremble lest your present symptoms denote those diabolical temptations, by means of which the enemy of the human race seduces feeble souls. Happily your welfare is precious to me, my son; and to assist you in acquiring strength of purpose, I beg you to repair upon the instant to the Chamber of Meditation, where you will pass such time as may be necessary to restore those healthy mental conditions which form the basis of every education intended to promote God's glory."

As he ceased speaking, Père Mordon struck a bell, and repeated before the servant the order which he had given Bannière; and the young man, crushed to earth, flushed with shame, gasping in bitterness of spirit, with head cast down and trembling knees, followed the valet who was to conduct him to the Chamber of Meditation.

VI.

THE CHAMBER OF MEDITATION.

THE convents had their *in pace*, their prisons, and their dungeons. The Jesuits, who were too civilized to concern themselves with man's physical side alone, invented the CHAMBER OF MEDITATION.

On the first floor at the rear of the building, flanked by a corridor barred and bolted as to its windows and its doors, opened, or rather closed, a room of vast size, whose arched roof was sufficiently high to prevent the meditations of the prisoners interfering with those of the spiders who had selected the corners of the black cornices for their place of abode; sufficiently high also — and this was the most important point — to preclude all hope of those same prisoners ever reaching the window, supplied with a single pane of glass, which stared down from the roof like a Cyclopean eye, and gave entrance to an infinitesimal amount of light, much impaired by the dust and smoke on the glass.

As we have said, the light of day descended very sadly and bashfully into the depths of that forbidding cage; but we must say that Apollo, who was god of light and of meditation at the same time, could hardly have experienced the least pleasure in visiting the interior of this retreat, the four walls of which were hung with black material, plentifully sown with death's-heads and cross-bones, of some white stuff laid upon the black, and fastened with a stout thread of black and white. More than that, scattered here and there among these sinister symbols were inscriptions worked in white upon the hangings; and there again was exhibited that singular caprice of imparting to these compulsory meditations, inflicted by the Jesuits upon rebellious novices, a character quite at variance with the historic gayety of the French as a people.

All the blackest dregs which the ancient poets found in their empty amphoræ, all the most wildly despairing shrieks of the Sages, from the " O bios esti parodos skias," to the " Serius ocyus " of Horace, from the doleful verses of the " Dies Irae " to the much criticised formulas of the " Perindè ac cadaver " of the Society of Jesus, it was all spread out there in white letters upon those gloomy, black, deathly-hued hangings.

These innumerable mottoes of huge size, and in different styles of lettering, attracted the eye, like revelations standing out in relief from that black wall, as if all these stern moralists and spirit-depressing versifiers had come from the depths of the unknown world where they dwelt, to trace with invisible finger, for the benefit of the " meditating " novice, their meditations, revised, corrected, and expanded, according to the circumstances of the case.

Bannière, then, was cast into this dungeon, which was absolutely strange to him, and which he knew only from the reports of those of his comrades who had had a taste of it.

Bannière was a well-behaved novice, that is to say, he was regular in the performance of his duties as a student, liked the Latin verses, and the French ones too, of Père de la Sante, and admired to the point of enthusiasm Monsieur Arouet. So that, as we have seen, he had had two copies of " Mariamne " confiscated, and had not handed over the third to the superior until he knew all the different parts by heart, from Hérode, King of Palestine, down to Narbas, an officer of the Amorrhean kings, and from Mariamne, Hérode's wife, to Élise, her confidante.

From Bannière's enthusiastic admiration for Monsieur de Voltaire, which rebounded in gushing streams upon the two or three tragedies which the young philosopher had already published, we may infer that he did not know of the terrible failure which had been the fate of the tragedy of "Mariamne" at the time of its representation, on the 5th of January, 1724, three years before the events with which we are concerned. The failure was so complete that the tragedy was thought to be dead for good and all. But Arouet was persistent; he picked up the pieces of the poor queen, and put them together as well as it had been ill done before; he shortened the scene between Varus and Hérode, and substituted a touching narrative of the death of Mariamne for her death by poison on the stage, — a *denouement* which was enlivened, to the author's discomfiture, by the ill-timed pleasantry of a spectator, who began to shout, "La reine boit " (The queen is drinking)! And the play, thanks to these emendations and many others which the author enumerates in his preface, to which we refer our readers for fuller information, — thanks to these emendations, we say again, the play had in 1725 a success as pronounced as its failure in 1724 had been.

This does not prove that the public were strictly logical, but it does prove that the play succeeded at last after it had failed at first. Bannière had learned not only the play as it was written, but the variations inserted by the author at the end, doubtless so that not a line of that beautiful poetry, which still at this hour causes three fourths of the Academicians to faint with delight, need be lost to posterity.

Up to that time Bannière knew nothing of the rigorous discipline of the Jesuits beyond the confiscation of Monsieur Arouet's books.

His calling — a gentle, but bright light — had hitherto served to people the gloom of the novitiate with affable shades and graceful phantoms of all sorts. He had made friends among his fellows, and had compelled the respect of his masters by the originality of his character. In a word, he had enjoyed that indefinable consideration which always falls to the lot of independent and self-assertive minds in every branch of industry.

That is why, in the course of his captivity with the other black birds in the cage of the novitiate, he, more than the others, had seen friendly hands approach the bars, and had longed for air and freedom more than the others; and being, like all gentle natures, of a trusting disposition, he seemed to have fallen from such a height into the dungeon of meditation, that the only resource which remained to him was to curse the perfidious wretches who had brought about his heavy fall.

Bannière's first emotion, then, was surprise; the second, indignation.

But he was a youth of good sense; he quickly reflected that the Jesuits could not compound with actors, and that if Jesuits and actors were to make common cause, it would be unbecoming and unfair for the ones to be confessors of kings, governors and princes, and to be State Inquisitors, notwithstanding their ugly and melancholy garb, while the others not only were excluded from all places of honor, but were excommunicated, dishonored, and cast out in all their embroidered coats, velvet mantles, and feathers; that God, who is supreme wisdom and eternal justice, had given each his compensation; that the Jesuit, when once he had become accustomed to his cage,

loved it, because he gilded the bars, while the actor, on
the other hand, could not learn to become fond of cages,
not having succeeded in gilding them.

This logic led Bannière to such an immoderate longing
for freedom that he resolved to seek to procure it by every
conceivable means.

After he had read and criticised with bitter irony all
the texts which the walls recited to him, he vented his
spleen against his superiors who were persecuting him,
and esteeming the occasion a favorable one for indulging
without restraint in declamation, he began to play
"Hérode et Mariamne," all by himself.

The arches, which were accustomed to hear naught but
the complaints and maledictions of the meditators, wondered
to find themselves re-echoing the hemistichs of a tragedy.
Bannière, draped in his cassock, over which he had
thrown the coverlid of his bed by way of mantle, acted,
shouted, and groaned the different rôles, imitated the note
of the trumpet announcing the heralds, and the various
sounds emitted by the mob, — in short, carried Voltaire's
masterpiece through to the last line of the variations and
notes.

That lasted quite four hours.

During those four hours Bannière was agreeably
diverted in his triple rôle of spectator, actor, and incar-
cerated Jesuit.

But all things have an end here below; whether the
Chamber of Meditation was producing its due effect,
whether fatigue was getting the upper hand of poetry
in the wretched prisoner's mind, or whether because the
gentle Mariamne had no longer to struggle with her
ferocious tyrant, certain it is that Bannière finally fell
into a state of torpor.

Nor was that all. We have said that the Jesuits

sometimes disciplined recalcitrant novices with hunger; that which subdues tigers, lions, and elephants might well have a like effect upon Bannière. A full brain makes an empty stomach, but an empty stomach does but little towards filling the brain; at best it fills it with naught but vapors.

In short, after two hours of resistance, during which Bannière's moral force grew constantly weaker,—having no longer the strength to declaim even the smallest rôle in his favorite tragedy, nor to read with benefit the ghostly inscriptions, the prisoner lay down upon his bed, covered himself with the blanket, and began to reflect upon his present as compared with his past situation.

He did not go farther than that, the future being enveloped in such utter darkness that he did not seek even to guess at what it held.

The night, a wise counsellor of honest minds, called by the Greeks "the mother of opportunity," and used by the Jesuits as a potent auxiliary in subduing their rebellious subjects,—night came slowly down from heaven, and covered the solitary window, the dungeon's eye, with the film of blindness.

Gradually the white letters of the inscriptions along the walls faded from sight; gradually they returned to the oblivion whence they had been exhumed those moral apothegms which told of the doom of mankind, to disappear like the dust, to rot, and to bend like the reed beneath the hand of necessity.

Soon Bannière could distinguish nothing; and he lay there upon his poor couch, growing colder and more depressed with every moment. Two hours more passed away, during which he came definitely to the conclusion that the inscription affixed to the door of the apartment in which he was confined was not a mere unmeaning collection of letters, but that the place was very justly called the " Chamber of Meditation."

"Que faire dans un gìte à moins que l'on n'y songe ?"[1]

said La Fontaine.

So Bannière dreamed; and having dreamed, he went to sleep.

Night, as old Homer says, had traversed half the sky in its silver-wheeled chariot of ebony, when a peculiar, sharp, persistent noise awoke the novice from the drowsiness which hunger and meditation had produced in his brain.

This noise, a very familiar scratching, came from the hangings at his left.

Bannière opened one eye after the other, and having turned upon his bed so as to face the noise, he listened.

The strident echo continued to sing its monotonous song. There was no room for mistake; the novice recognized the sound made by the teeth of a rat. It came from a spot about twelve feet from the floor, and between the hangings and the wall.

Bannière sighed a doleful sigh.

What caused him to sigh? The thought of the contrast, alas! for in his humbled frame of mind he considered that rat very much to be envied.

Happy indeed was the little creature, to be making a hearty midnight supper upon the inscriptions of the moralists and stoic philosophers who preached abstinence and disinterestedness!

Happy indeed was he, free to glide about between the wall and the hangings, to feast upon the old cloth and old leather.

But no, it was not upon cloth, or leather either, that

[1] " What is there to do in bed unless one dreams ? "

the beast was feeding. The echo was sonorous, and indicated that the rat was at work on wood.

That was a fact of serious importance, mark well. Not for you, dear reader, nor for you, Madame, wrapped in your comfortable *robe de chambre*, with your feet on the andirons, and the soothing consciousness that you have only to say the word, to go for a turn in the Bois, or to the Champs Élysées at least; but for Bannière, the unhappy captive, in whose ear the slightest sound assumed a degree of importance in proportion to his weariness of captivity, and his longing to be free.

Thus it made a vast difference to Bannière whether the rat was gnawing wood or leather.

His reasoning was something like this: —

"That's wood! Yes, that rat is certainly gnawing wood. Now, how in the devil can he have hoisted a piece of wood to that height? and if he has accomplished that feat (which would require much long, hard labor, as he has no machine like that which Antony used to transport his galleys from the Mediterranean to the Red Sea), how does he succeed in maintaining his hold upon that surface of stone or plaster, while he tranquilly eats his supper, as he seems to be doing? Has he a hole there, or a piece of cornice or some protuberance to serve as a table?

"Perhaps he has taken a grip on the wall, and made a bridge of himself across to the hangings. He could crunch away then at his leisure, using himself as table and hammock at once.

"But no! that echo is so sonorous, and grates so upon the ear, the sound is so clearly defined, that it cannot be made upon a mere splinter of wood which the rat has detached somewhere. It surely is produced by a constant series of attacks by the little fellow upon a woody mass, immovable and having, like all solids, length, breadth, and thickness.

"There must be some woodwork up there," said Bannière to himself; and he added reflectively, "Perhaps, indeed, the whole wall is of wood beneath the hangings."

As this thought occurred to him, he rose and walked to the wall and struck it; there was no sound, for it was of solid rock.

"Very good," muttered the novice; "but that does n't prove that there's no woodwork up there. A window, perhaps!"

And thereupon Bannière built up a whole poem of suppositions.

"What is the use of that window? Why have a window under thick hangings?

"There are little wickets, called Judases, through which every meditating novice is sure of being watched by some spy whose duty it is to report to the father superior.

"There are secret doors — "

There Bannière checked himself.

"If there are secret doors," said he, "there are ways of getting out of the Chamber of Meditation."

He thereupon began to sound the wall again, and convinced himself that the door or window was in its lowest part at the abnormal height of six feet at least; for he tested the whole wall up to that height, which he was able to reach with the tips of his fingers, by standing on the tips of his toes.

"If it is a door, and that door is up in the air," was his judicious reflection, "it can be of no possible use; unless," he added, "he who proposes to use it brings his ladder along.

"It must be, then, that the woodwork is a window-frame and not a door-frame."

The window was not an unlikely supposition; so Bannière decided for the window.

But as the darkness rendered exploration difficult, he postponed further operations till the morning. The result of this postponement was that the rat passed a delicious night, and never ceased his gnawing till daybreak.

Not so fortunate as his host, the rodent, Bannière passed a most anxious night, especially tormented by internal pangs, which were outwardly expressed by the grumbling mutterings of hunger, and harmonized admirably with the gnawing of the rat.

VII.

THE PROCESSION OF HÉRODE AND MARIAMNE.

WE have said that the rat's banquet came to an end at daybreak; and at daybreak the novice's labor began.

His first care was to make himself absolutely certain that his arm and hand, extended to their utmost length, would not reach the supposititious window. But for all its lack of the conveniences of a well-furnished apartment, the Chamber of Meditation afforded all that was essential for a man who did not fear to run the risk of breaking his neck, to climb to a height of ten or twelve feet.

The materials for his scaffolding consisted of the small cot which served him as a bed, topped by the stool which took the place of a chair. These two objects, one upon the other, reached to a height of four feet, and by adding a second stool an elevation of five feet and a half was obtained; Bannière's five feet and four inches perched upon this structure made nearly eleven feet.

If it should be necessary to go higher, he could climb up on the hangings, using the white inscriptions for foot-holds. He might tear the hangings, but no matter; by the very act of tearing them he would at least find out what mysteries were hidden beneath them.

The event justified Bannière's procedure. He climbed up on the cot, thence to the first stool, and so on to the second; having reached that point, he tore the hangings to make a place for his foot, which added two or three inches more to his stature; he then struck his fist against the wall, and was rewarded by hearing a sound similar to that made by a wooden shutter when an inquisitive hand is trying to open it.

Bannière sought a support for his other foot, tore the hangings in another place, and, held up on one side by the *vanitas vanitatum* and on the other by the *connais-toi toi-même,* and his left hand grasping a death's-head, with the right he thrust aside the thick material, and discovered the very thing which his perspicacity, so highly spoken of by Père Mordon, had led him to anticipate, — that is to say, an old condemned window, closed with a shutter reinforced by an iron bar. In the days when it had done duty for an apartment, which probably had not then attained the dignity of a Chamber of Meditation, the size of the window was well suited to the task of lighting it properly; whereas, in default of it, the room received all of its light through that' dubious opening, an eye without an eyeball, which pierced the roof, and gazed dismally at the prisoner.

" A window! " cried Bannière, joyfully.

But he quickly checked himself.

" Good! but upon what does it open ? "

" Oh, head of Medusa! if I burst open this shutter, cut away the curtain, and open a prospect, what will that prospect embrace ? Shall I not find on the other side of the window either the sneering face of some spy of the superior, or it may be the mocking countenance of the superior himself ? Why may not the Jesuit have a room of his own adjoining this ? Why may he not have anticipated the effect of the rat's gnawing, and have a biting phrase all reaqy for the first appearance of my nose through his window ? "

It was horrible to think of.

"But no! a rat will always have more instinct than a superior, even a superior of the Jesuits, has of cleverness. A rat would not gnaw away all night unless he were sure that he could do it with impunity. If he selected that place, it was because he knew that he had no surprise or ambuscade to fear."

Suddenly a cold perspiration sent a chill down Bannière's back.

"Suppose that Père Mordon, who has seized two copies of 'Hérode et Mariamne,' and detected me studying a third, who has boxed me up here, and kept me without food for eighteen hours already, in order to restore his disciple's religious and moral perception,—suppose that Père Mordon, that shrewd and all-embracing genius, has lowered himself so far as to invent some machine which imitates the gnawing of a rat! Such things are known in natural history, and why should they not be possible in mechanics? Serpents whistle like birds, and hyenas imitate children's crying, to attract the attention of human beings; foxes have been seen hunting the hare as dogs do, while one of their number, himself a fox, lay in wait for him to pass. Now, a Jesuit is no more of a bungler than a serpent, no more of a fool than a hyena, and no more of a simpleton than a fox; he would surely be clever enough to draw a novice into the snare of a serious mistake, at need. What would be necessary to accomplish it? A paltry two hours' gnawing on a piece of wood."

Bannière's imaginings terrified him; but his first audacity soon returned.

"I weaken!" he exclaimed; "I, who am imprisoned and starving, recoil at the thought of one more annoyance! No, by my faith! I will open that window; it may be a window, or it may not, but in any event it is a way out of some sort, and if I find a Jesuit on the other side, and he cries, 'What do you want?' I will reply, 'Bread.'"

As if to encourage himself before the pangs of hunger became unbearable, Banniere climbed up again, drew the iron bar, and opened the shutter.

Ineffable joy! No Jesuit was on the watch behind the window; only the glorious sun, binding up his golden tresses in the azure sky, invaded the sombre breeding-place of meditation.

Through the opening he had made, Bannière breathed the delicious air of the morning, and the moist odor of the Rhone, rising in soft vapor from the river-bed to the house-tops.

He inhaled several deep breaths, and then looked about him.

The window opened on a street which cut another straight street obliquely, their junction forming a square.

Thanks to the steepness of the straight street, Bannière could see the people passing; they were scarce as yet, but he could see them.

He took his fill of that sight so dear to the eyes of a prisoner, inhaled a large stock of the air of liberty, and estimated the height of the window. It was nearly thirty feet from the street, which was paved with that sort of broken stone which is peculiar to the cities of the South.

Having taken in all these details at a glance, Bannière feared he might be discovered before he had come to any determination; so he stepped back, closed the shutter, readjusted the inscriptions, and smoothed out the hangings; after which he dragged the cot back to its place, and returned to his stool like a dog to his kennel.

Towards seven o'clock Bannière heard sounds in the corridor, and saw his door open. It was the servant bringing him a morsel of food, which seemed even less than it was, so furious was his appetite. He did not play at daintiness, however, for he thought that he needed strength, and devoured the meagre pittance to the last crumb.

Then, sure of being undisturbed until the morrow, the servant having warned him to divide his supply of food into three portions, as he should not return that day, the prisoner mounted again to his observatory.

It was the time of day when provisions are laid in, when housekeepers go to the fish-market, when the snappers of the bread and cake sellers, and the rattles of the collectors are heard in the streets.

With his chin resting on the window-sill, Bannière looked at all these agreeable sights with as much wonder as if he had never seen them before.

Suddenly he heard a great noise of drums and fifes, cymbals and Chinese bells, and at the end of the straight street he saw defile into the square a long procession of people in odd costumes, with banners and enormous placards. One of the latter bore, in black letters upon a red ground, the words: —

"Procession d'Hérode et Mariamne, Tragédie de Monsieur Arouet."

This first announcement was followed by a second poster bearing these seductive words: —

"The dramatic company of the city will to-day present the beautiful moral tragedy of Hérode et Mariamne, by Monsieur Arouet de Voltaire, as admirable for its fascinating style as for the purity of its sentiments."

Then came the actors in two lines, in their stage dress, followed by the supernumeraries, and the guards of Hérode, with their cuirasses and armor. There were Romans, Asiatics, and Jews in considerable numbers.

The long tails of the horses, the crescent-shaped standards (which indicated that the manager cared more for the magnificence of the *mise-en-scène* than for historical accuracy), and the glistening spangles made all the little ragamuffins in town shriek with delight.

At the head of the actors Champmeslé dragged himself along, sad unto death. The kind words of Père de la Sante had lost their effect, doubtless, for he was in every respect like a martyr going to the stake before his eye has caught sight of the crown which awaits him.

But, notwithstanding his deep despondency, he was so bravely attired in a red chlamys, with a helmet-turban, wide-topped boots with spurs, and a white cloak with gold stars, that the crowd devoured him with their gaze, the women especially; the result being that the glances of the men were laden with that assumed contempt which is the cloak of envy.

Again, notwithstanding his despondency, of which Bannière alone knew the cause, there was something so noble in his royal bearing, that the novice, who considered it the very acme of honor to lead such a procession and to be clad in such garb, almost forgot himself so far as to clap his hands when he passed; but just at that moment he espied, beneath her long white veil, Mariamne, surrounded not alone by King Hérode's guards, but by a crowd of officers from the garrisons of Nîmes and Orange, who had come to Avignon to attend the holiday-making which was caused by the presence of so large and important a troupe in the city. These officers, like the inquisitive heathens they were, tried from time to time to raise the veil in which the Queen of Palestine was modestly enveloped, like a sun in its recess of clouds. Suddenly the cloud opened to allow the sun to smile upon a handsome captain who had, under his uniform of the royal gendarmerie, all the appearance of a great lord; and Bannière, dazzled by the rays shed by the beautiful planet, which showed its face for a moment (for the behoof of another than himself, it is true, but which he had chanced to see), forgot the necessity of holding on, and losing his balance, which his hands alone had enabled him to maintain, he pitched headlong down into the Chamber of Meditation, carrying with him a great piece of the hangings which he had seized as he fell, and leaving the wall quite bare.

Whatever the moving cause of his resolution may have been, Bannière had sworn not to remain captive in a city where such miracles were taking place. So he went gayly back to the assault, and hung his chin upon the window-sill once more, just as the last of Hérode's guards, whose enormous halberd was visible some seconds after the man had disappeared, passed out of sight in the street to the left.

"Good!" thought Bannière; "this evening I will tear off a piece of the hangings, tie it firmly to the window-frame, let myself down along the wall, and go, happy and free, to see this piece played at the theatre by real actors and actresses.

"The fathers will make a great outcry; let them do it, I don't care. They will have me followed, — all right; they will catch me at it, — that is perfectly certain; but *ma foi!* I shall have seen the play; and if they punish me for it, why, upon my soul, I shall suffer for something."

VIII.

THE ACTORS' LOBBY.

BANNIÈRE did as he had resolved, step by step. When the light began to fail, he tore down great pieces of the hangings, and made a cord twenty feet long, with knots placed at intervals; to that cord he intrusted himself, dropped the six or eight feet which remained between him and the ground when he reached the end of the cord, took to the pavement, and ran at headlong speed, like an intoxicated or insane man, in the direction of the theatre, which was situated opposite the Ousle gate, and was easily located by the shouts of the door-keepers and the notes of the fife.

It was just the hour when all the fair ladies of Avignon were arriving at the theatre, and the long lines of carriages, sedan-chairs, and Bath-chairs began to crowd the square.

Bannière, cast into the midst of this concourse of people, was decidedly shamefaced, and oppressed by his novice's garb. It is very true that custom then permitted ecclesiastics, and Jesuits in particular, to attend dramatic performances. But Bannière was not the proprietor of a single sou. He might, indeed, have requested some pleasant-featured person,— and they are always very numerous at the door of a theatre,— to take him into his box with him; but his infernal dress would attract all eyes, and if among those eyes there happened to be two

in the service of Père Mordon, he was lost. He might
have taken off his wretched cassock; but if he had done
so, it would have left him in his shirt-sleeves, and how
could he gain admittance in his shirt-sleeves, except to
the most crowded galleries?

He was in very great perplexity; the minutes were
rapidly passing by. Hidden behind a pillar, he saw,
with a painful swelling of the heart, the prettiest little
feet under the whitest of skirts trip lightly by him, while
from the carriages and chairs alighted such plump legs
and slender ankles that all the inscriptions in the Chamber
of Meditation would have failed at that moment to supply
the poor Jesuit with sufficient philosophy.

Suddenly Bannière perceived two of the Jesuit fathers
in their black carriage, awaiting their turn in the line of
carriages with saintly patience. Having reached the
door, their conveyance halted; to enter, they must pass
within four paces of Bannière.

Tormented by the triple demon of curiosity, longing,
and fear, Bannière took the moment when the carriage
stopped to effect a skilful retreat; he began by placing
a pillar between himself and the fathers, and keeping in
its shadow as he moved away, he finally darted into the
actors' lobby.

But he had no sooner taken refuge in that gloomy and
dusty corridor which was feebly lighted by a single evil-
smelling candle-end, than he felt himself pushed roughly
back by two strong hands which came very near throwing
him off his balance, so preoccupied was he. But he was
young, active, and strong; if he fell, he ran the risk of
showing his torn breeches; so he clung fast to the impertinent individual, who had a way of making room for
himself, so strangely out of harmony with the polite
manners of that period.

It was a man; and as he turned about, Bannière found himself face to face with him.

"Let me pass, death of all the devils!" he cried, trying to force Bannière against the wall.

"What! you, Monsieur de Champmeslé!" exclaimed Bannière.

"And you, my little Jesuit!" cried Champmeslé.

By the sickly light of the candle-end they had recognized each other.

"Ah, Monsieur de Champmeslé!" said one.

"Ah, my dear Bannière!" said the other.

"It is really you?"

"Alas! yes, it is I."

"Pray, whither are you rushing off like that? Are you in need of something for your costume?"

"Ah, yes, my costume! I don't care for my costume."

"Yet it was very handsome," said Bannière, enviously.

"Yes," said Champmeslé, bitterly; "it is so beautiful that I shall wear it in hell."

"In hell! what do you mean?"

"Nothing; let me pass."

"But one would say that you were running away, my dear sir."

"Indeed I think I am running away."

"But the performance?"

"Ah! the performance; that is just the reason I am running away."

"Oh, yes, I understand."

"Let me pass then, I tell you."

"Always the same fancies?"

"More than ever. Do you know what has happened to me?"

"You terrify me."

"Monsieur," said Champmeslé, with haggard eyes, "I dined at noon, did I not?"

"I have no doubt of it."

"After dinner I took my nap."

"Very sensibly."

"Very well! my brother, during my nap —"

Here he looked uneasily about on all sides.

"During your nap?" Bannière repeated.

"I had a vision, myself."

"Oh!"

"Such a vision as my father and grandfather each had."

"What sort of a vision, *mon Dieu?*"

"Only mine was even more terrifying than theirs."

"How so?"

"I saw myself, my dear brother —"

"You saw yourself?"

"Yes, in hell, upon a red-hot gridiron, in my Hérode costume, and turned by a devil who was as like Monsieur de Voltaire as two drops of water. Oh, it was frightful! Let me pass, let me pass!"

"But, my dear Monsieur de Champmeslé, you don't mean it."

"On the contrary, I do mean just that; let me pass!"

"But you will make the whole play a failure!"

"I prefer to have it a failure, rather than to be turned on a gridiron, in the dress of King Hérode, for all eternity, by a devil who looks like Monsieur de Voltaire."

"But you will ruin your fellow-actors!"

"On the contrary, I shall save them and myself, and with myself all the poor wretches who would be damned for coming to see us. Adieu!"

This time Champmeslé joined his wish and his motion so successfully that he twisted Bannière around three times, and meanwhile had passed him and was off.

" Monsieur de Champmeslé! Monsieur de Champmeslé!" cried Bannière, following him a few steps.

But in vain did Bannière cry after him and follow him, for the actor had heard steps approaching on the stairway which led into the theatre, and at the sound he had darted away like a stag which scents the pack.

Bannière was left alone, bewildered to stupefaction.

But the voices and steps, which Champmeslé had heard as if by intuition, began to be very audible on the rough stairs.

The steps were very hurried, and the voices were crying, " Champmeslé! Champmeslé! "

There were both male and female voices.

Suddenly the door opening from the stairway into the lobby flew open, and there burst upon Bannière's sight an avalanche of frightened actors and actresses in tragic costumes, shouting with all their strength in woe-begone tones and with gestures of despair, —

" Champmeslé! Champmeslé!"

The whole rout surrounded Bannière, shrieking: " Champmeslé! Champmeslé! Have you seen Champmeslé?"

" Yes, Messieurs," said Bannière, " to be sure. I have seen him."

" What have you done with him then?"

" I? Nothing."

" Well, then, where is he?"

" He has gone."

" Gone! " cried the women.

" You let him go?" shouted the men.

" Alas, yes, Messieurs; alas, yes, Mesdames. He has fled."

Bannière had no sooner uttered that word than he was pounced upon, seized, pulled hither and thither in ten different directions by ten pairs of hands, — some soft and charming, others rough and almost threatening.

"He has fled, he has fled!" cried actors and actresses in unison. "The Jesuit saw him go. Monsieur le Jesuite, is it really true, is it absolutely certain, that Champmeslé has fled?"

Bannière could not answer them all. They who questioned him appreciated that. So the orator of the troupe, he whose business it was to make a speech to the public on great occasions, raised his voice and requested silence, and silence ensued.

"And so, my brother," he asked, "you saw Champmeslé go away?"

"As plainly as I see you, Monsieur."

"Did he speak with you?"

"He did me that honor."

"To tell you — "

"That he had had a vision."

"A vision — a vision — is he mad? what vision?"

"He saw himself damned, and being cooked upon a gridiron, which was being turned by Monsieur de Voltaire dressed as a devil."

"Ah, yes, he spoke of it to me also."

"And to me."

"And to me."

"But where has he gone, anyway?" the orator asked.

"Alas, Monsieur, I have no idea."

"When will he return?" asked the duenna.

"Alas, Madame, he left me in ignorance upon that point."

"But this is terrible!"

"It is unworthy of him!"

"It is downright treachery!"

"He will be late for his *entrée!*"

"He will disgust the audience!"

"Ah, Messieurs and Mesdames!" cried Bannière in a doleful voice, well calculated to prepare his hearers for most terrible revelations.

"Well, what is it?"

"If I dared to tell you the whole truth — "

"Tell it, tell it!"

"I should announce to you that you will not see Monsieur de Champmeslé again."

"Not see him again?"

"Not this evening, at all events."

At these words the lobby was filled with exclamations of despair which penetrated into the stairway, and thence spread through the upper corridors.

"But why — why is it?" the question arose on all sides.

"Why, Messieurs, I have told you, and, Mesdames, I tell you once more, — because Monsieur de Champmeslé is possessed of a timorous conscience, and fears that he shall be damned if he plays this evening."

"Monsieur," said the orator of the troupe, "we are in a bad place to talk about our affairs; we can be overheard. The rumor of Champmeslé's flight may get about before we have found means to lessen its effect. Do us the honor, Monsieur, to ascend to the green-room."

"To the green-room!" cried Bannière, "the actors' and actresses' green-room!"

"Yes; there you can give us all the details which you cannot give here, and it may be, Monsieur, some good advice."

"Yes, yes, come," said the women, hanging on Bannière's arms; while the balance of the troupe divided into two parties, one of which went ahead, pulling him along, and the other pushed him behind.

IX.

THE GREEN-ROOM.

BANNIÈRE, to his credit be it said, resisted like a hero; but unfortunately he was the weaker party, and they dragged, or rather carried, him to the green-room to testify to the truth of the fatal news.

There before the whole troupe, all ready to begin the play, Bannière was compelled not only to narrate a second time all that had taken place in the actors' lobby ten minutes before, but, as a preface to the woful catastrophe which had brought despair upon the company, he found himself describing the visit of Champmeslé to the chapel of the novitiate the day before, and the conversation that ensued.

This narrative, delivered with a degree of emotion easily imagined, for the novice was in a fever of excitement with his flight, and intoxicated by the bright glare of the lamps, and by the touch and breath and subtle perfumes of the actresses, who surrounded him with an atmosphere beside which the blasts of hell so much dreaded by Champmeslé would have seemed like cool breezes from Lapland, — this narrative, we say, produced a most dismal effect upon the assemblage.

"Well, the money will have to be returned, that's sure," exclaimed the orator, letting his hands fall despondently.

"We are ruined!" said the first old man.

"The theatre will have to close!" cried the duenna.

"And to think that the whole city is in the hall!" added Mariamne's maid, a young soubrette of eighteen, who spoke as if she knew the whole city.

"And Monsieur de Mailly, who has provided a supper for us and sent word that he will come to eat it with us!" said the orator.

"And Olympe, who has no Hérode now!" the first old man added.

"Does she know what has happened?"

"No, she is still in her dressing-room; she is just finishing her toilet. I heard Champmeslé, as he passed not five minutes ago, call 'Good-evening,' to her."

"Well, let us tell her," said several voices among the women, forgetting their selfishness in the face of this public catastrophe.

Immediately there was a grand rush for the door; and Bannière, deserted for the moment, seized the opportunity to take his station modestly in a corner.

Suddenly the crowd at the door separated.

"What is it? what's the matter? what do you want?" said a young woman who made her appearance on the threshold. She was exquisitely beautiful, and came majestically forward, clad in a regal costume of great magnificence, with skirts ten feet in circumference and a towering head-dress, and followed by two maids of honor, bearing the train of her cloak.

Her eyes were black, and shone the blacker for the powder around them; her cheeks were full and oval-shaped, rosy even without rouge; her teeth as white and transparent as porcelain, her lips lusciously red and inviting; she had the arm and hand of an Oriental queen, and the foot of an infant.

Bannière, as his eyes rested upon her, leaned against the wall for support; had it not been behind him, he

would have fallen again, as he fell in the Chamber of
Meditation. It was the second time that day that he had
been overwhelmed by the gorgeous beauty of that woman.

"The matter is, my poor Olympe," said the orator,
"that you can go back to your dressing-room, and
undress."

"Undress! and why so?"

"Because we do not play this evening."

"Indeed!" she retorted, with the pride of a veritable
queen; "we do not play this evening! Who will prevent
us from playing, please?"

"Look around you, dear friend."

"I am looking."

As she spoke, Olympe's eyes made the circuit of the
green-room, embracing in their itinerary Bannière with
the rest, but resting no longer upon him than upon the
others. Only, when these two stars passed before the
novice, each of them let fly a spark. One of the sparks
put his brain in a whirl, the other set his heart on fire.

"Are we all here?" the orator asked her.

"Why, yes, I should say so," replied Olympe,
thoughtlessly.

"Look carefully; one of us is missing."

Olympe removed her eyes from her corsage where she
was adjusting a piece of lace, and turned them again
upon her companions.

"Ah! yes," she cried, "Champmeslé! Where is
Champmeslé, pray?"

"Ask Monsieur," said the orator.

He seized the novice by the hand and shoulder, and
pushed him towards Olympe.

It was a curious sight to see the Jesuit scholar, all
black and squalid, face to face with this queen of beauty,
all white and gold.

The young man's lips moved, but to no purpose; he could not articulate a word.

"Well, Monsieur, speak!" said Olympe, imperiously.

She fascinated him with a glance from her wondrous eyes.

"Madame," stammered Bannière, passing from deep crimson to the pallor of a corpse, — "Madame, pardon me; I am only a poor student of religion, and I am not accustomed to such sights as I see at this moment."

The orator in a few words acquainted Olympe with all that had taken place.

"You mean to say that all that you tell me is true?" said she.

"Ask Monsieur."

She turned again towards Bannière, and questioned him with her queenly glance.

"It is true," said Bannière, bowing as if Champmeslé's fault weighed heavily upon him.

Olympe remained for a moment mute and thoughtful, with contracted eyebrows, while her eyes were still fixed absently upon Bannière.

Suddenly she said with increasing irritation, —

"No, no, Champmeslé's departure must not and shall not prevent the performance."

Every one looked at her in amazement.

"No," she repeated, "no, it is out of the question for me not to play this evening, and I will play."

"All by yourself?" queried the orator.

"Why, nobody is missing but Champmeslé, so far as I can see."

"That's quite enough. Who will play Hérode?"

"Why, some one must—"

"What?"

"Read the part."

"Read the leading part at the first performance! It is impossible!"

"Come, come," said Olympe; "there is no time to lose; the audience is waiting, and will soon lose patience."

"But," muttered several of the actors, "we cannot have a part of such importance read! When the announcement is made that somebody will read the part of Hérode, the audience will demand their money back."

"But I tell you I *must* play this evening, nevertheless!" cried Olympe. "I must!"

"Why not tell the audience something now? Why not pretend that somebody is ill? In that way we can gain half an hour, and meanwhile we can chase after that damned devotee, bring him back, willy-nilly, even if we have to choke him, put on his costume in spite of him, and push him onto the stage. Come, let us make an announcement at once!"

"But suppose you fail to lay hands on him?" suggested a voice.

"Very well; then the audience will be prepared. We can say that the sick man is much worse. We will catch him during the day to-morrow, and have the success to-morrow night which we ought to have to-night. With the assurance of a performance to-morrow, perhaps the people will not ask for their money, but will be satisfied with an exchange of tickets."

"No, no," said Olympe, "it is to-day, not to-morrow, that I propose to play; not to-morrow night, but to-night, that I mean to make a hit. Either the part will be read to-day, or I will not play to-morrow."

"What are your reasons, pray?" the orator asked her.

"My dear fellow," was Olympe's reply, "my reasons are my own; if I should give them to you, you might

possibly not find them satisfactory, while to my mind
they are unanswerable. I propose to act to-day, to-day,
to-day! "

Having expressed her will in this peremptory fashion,
Olympe began to tap her foot on the floor, and open and
shut her fan with that degree of haste and excitement
which in a nervous woman indicates the approach of a
terrible paroxysm.

Bannière had followed every one of the beautiful
queen's movements, his eyes devoured her, he hung
breathlessly upon each word that she uttered, and he
felt a sympathetic twinge of the nervous irritation from
which she was suffering.

"Why, Messieurs," said he, "do you not see that
this lady will be ill and faint, and perhaps die of grief,
if you do not read the rôle of 'Hérode'? *Mon Dieu!*
Read it for pity's sake! Is it so very difficult to read a
part? Ah! if I only were not a Jesuit! if I only were
not a novice! "

"Well, suppose you were n't a novice," cried the
orator, "what would you do, pray? "

"*Parbleu*, I would play the part," cried Bannière,
carried beyond himself by the emotion which Olympe's
growing impatience aroused.

"What! you would play it, — you? " exclaimed the
orator. "You are joking! "

"Why should I not? " said Bannière, proudly.

"In the first place you need to know the lines."

"Oh! if that is all, I do know them."

"What! you know the part? " cried Olympe.

"Not only Hérode's, but every other in the play."

"You know Hérode's lines? " repeated Olympe, taking
a step towards him.

"To prove what I say," said Bannière, stretching out

The Green Room of the Avignon Theatre.

Drawn and etched by E. Van Muyden.

OLYMPE DE CLÈVES, I. 89.

his arm, and strutting as tragedians strutted in those days, "here are Hérode's entering words."

And he began to declaim: —

"Eh quoi ! Sohême aussi semble éviter ma vue ;
Quelle horreur devant moi s'est partout répandue ?
Ciel ! ne puis-je inspirer que la haine et l'effroi ?
Tous les cœurs des humains sont-ils fermés pour moi ?
En horreur à la reine, à mon peuple, à moi-même,
À regret sur mon front je vois le diadême.
Hérode, en arrivant, recueille avec terreur
Les chagrins dévorans qu'a semés sa fureur.
Ah ! Dieu ! "

All the actors, lost in amazement, crowded around Bannière, who would have gone right through to the end of the scene, had not Olympe interrupted him. "He knows it! he knows it!" she cried; and the actors applauded enthusiastically.

"Well, well!" exclaimed the orator, "here is a lucky chance!"

"My dear Monsieur," said Olympe, "you have n't an instant to lose. Take off that shocking Jesuit's robe, which makes you ugly enough to frighten one; get into the costume of Hérode, and to the stage — quick, quick!"

"But, Madame — "

"You have the calling, my young friend," Olympe continued, "and that is all that is necessary; the rest will come later."

"To say nothing of the fact that you will never have such another fine opportunity to make your début," added the orator.

"Come," said Olympe; "make an announcement, and bring Champmeslé's clothes at once. Just look at him! Oh, he is a fine-looking fellow, — not a calf's head like

Champmeslé. There's an Oriental Monarch for you! there's a physique and a voice that are worth while! Oh, be quick, be quick!"

Bannière uttered a cry of inexpressible alarm. He felt that at that moment his whole destiny was in the balance. He would have resisted, but Olympe seized his hands. He would have spoken, but Olympe laid her pink fingers upon his lips. At last, bewildered, with brain whirling like a drunken man's, he allowed himself to be carried off by the dressers, who made a King Hérode of him in ten minutes in Champmeslé's own dressing-room.

Olympe, standing at the door, hurried on the costumers and the hairdressers, maintained her power over the novice by words of encouragement, and kept up an incessant tattoo on the floor, crying, "Come! come!"

Bannière saw his despised monkish garb thrown into a corner, as it was taken from him piece by piece; and ten minutes later he emerged from his dressing-room, in magnificent and radiant attire, really beautiful in face, transfigured, and as superb as the queen herself, who completed her subjugation of his heart by embracing him.

From that moment Bannière, utterly vanquished and subdued, did not utter a single word; he pressed his hands upon his wildly beating heart, and let them lead him into the wings, where he was just in time to hear the following deliverance of the orator to the audience:

"Messieurs, our comrade Champmeslé, who had shown some signs of indisposition during the day, has been attacked with a sudden chill. The attack is so serious that we have some apprehension that he may be lost to us and to the stage. Fortunately one of our friends, who knows the rôle, has consented to undertake to act it in his place, so that the performance may not fall through;

but as it is his first appearance on any stage, and he is entirely unprepared for this début, he bespeaks your kindest indulgence."

Fortunately for the débutant, Champmeslé was not a public favorite; and so the whole assemblage, who had felt that something out of the common was happening on the other side of the curtain, applauded with great vigor.

The applause had not entirely died away when the signal was given for the curtain to rise, so that the enthusiasm of the audience might not have time to cool; and amid perfect stillness and breathless expectation, the play began.

Let us now explain why it was that Mademoiselle Olympe de Clèves persisted so obstinately in playing "Hérode et Mariamne" on that particular evening.

X.

OLYMPE DE CLÈVES.

MADEMOISELLE OLYMPE DE CLÈVES, who was called
"Olympe" for short in the dramatic company, — the lovely
creature whose face we have already seen on two occasions,
once in the street procession and again upon the threshold of the green-room, and who had produced so acute an
impression upon Bannière at each appearance, — Olympe
de Clèves was a young woman of good family, who had
been carried off from her convent by a musketeer lover
in 1720, when she was barely sixteen.

This musketeer, after remaining faithful to his mistress
for a year, — an almost unheard of circumstance in polite
circles at that time, — left her one fine day, and she
never saw him again.

Olympe thus deserted, and with no hope for the
future, — for she did not dare to return to her family, and
did not choose to go back to the convent without any
dowry, — sold the few jewels which she still possessed, and
after a year's study made her début upon the boards of a
provincial theatre.

She was so lovely that she was hissed. She appreciated the truth of the paradox that when Nature had
done so much for a woman, it was more than ever necessary that Art also should do much for her. She set to
work, in good earnest this time; and after another year,
appearing at a different theatre, she was as heartily
applauded for her talent as she had been, as we have
said, hissed for her beauty.

Gradually, and passing from one troupe to another, Olympe had mounted to the level of the theatres in the large cities, and she enjoyed a twofold reputation as an excellent actress and a virtuous woman, — a living enigma to lovers and men of wealth.

It was not so much that Olympe was naturally virtuous, but she had learned to hate all men from her experience of one man; and as wounds sink deeper in the most loving hearts, there was still an open, bleeding wound in the heart of the forsaken fair one, even after five years.

Abbés, officers, financiers, actors, and fops, — Olympe trod them all under her feet for three years.

At last, on a certain day, or evening, at Marseilles, Olympe noticed in the wings a man of great personal beauty and most distinguished bearing. He was dressed in the uniform of the Scotch guard, and wore the insignia of a captain.

Olympe had been playing a small part in which she had made a great hit, and as she left the stage she was surrounded by a great number of men.

At least twenty gentlemen, of the highest distinction, came up and said to her, —

" Mademoiselle, you are charming; " or, " Mademoiselle, in my eyes you are adorable. "

The cavalier whom we have mentioned drew near, and said to her with the greatest respect, before the whole company, " Madame, I love you. "

Then, without another word, he saluted, stepped back a few paces, and mingled with the crowd of Olympe's admirers.

This sentence, thrown at her so bluntly, annoyed Olympe at first blush by its oddity, and afterwards by the effect produced upon those who were present.

She asked of the young people about her the name of that extraordinary disciple of Cupid.

She was told that it was Louis Alexandre, Comte de Mailly, Seigneur de Rubempré, de Rieux, d'Avecourt, de Bohard, du Coudray, etc., captain-lieutenant of the Company of Scottish Guards.

"Aha!" was her only comment; and she returned home alone, as her custom was.

She had at that time an engagement of eight thousand livres per year. She had received from an elderly relative, who had remained her friend notwithstanding the escapade of the musketeer and her adoption of the dramatic profession, about thirty thousand livres, which she was spending at the rate of six thousand a year, being thus assured of an income of fourteen thousand livres for at least five years, while waiting for a better engagement.

She sometimes received in her own apartments, and did it very handsomely too. In fact, her receptions gradually acquired some little celebrity in the provinces; so that every fashionable man's first care was to obtain an introduction to Mademoiselle Olympe. No aspirant had ever failed.

It is true that all the gallant things which had been invented to say to the fair hostess had been so much time thrown away; everybody was welcome, but no one was favored above the others.

A still more extraordinary thing was that no one boasted of having been so favored.

Upon returning home on the evening in question, Olympe found herself involuntarily thinking of Monsieur de Mailly.

"He will adopt the usual course," she said, "and I shall see him here my first reception day,—that is to say, the first day that I am not in the cast."

But she was mistaken.

The Comte, who did not miss a single play in which

she took part, came behind the scenes to salute her after each performance. But he did so without saying a single word, or taking any more definite step.

This course of proceeding was very surprising to Olympe; she could not doubt that the Comte was deeply smitten with her. Love never fails to manifest itself unmistakably in every movement of the true lover.

Was he bashful, then, this captain of gendarmes? It was hardly probable.

Then why, after having declared his sentiments so frankly, was he waiting? For what was he waiting?

"I wonder if he imagines, by any chance," thought Olympe, "that because I am only an actress, I hold him in sufficient reverence, as a grand seigneur, to seek him out and reply to his declaration with a similar one of my own."

She waited for the Comte to make some further venture; but the Comte made no move.

Olympe then adopted the plan of turning her back upon him when he came to make his regular nightly salute.

It was an heroic, perhaps dangerous step. Monsieur de Mailly, a man of thirty-three at this time, holding a good place at court, a worthy gentleman in his own right, very highly connected, possessed of social and military rank, was gladly welcomed everywhere by both sexes. The insult of an actress might not only wound and disgust the Comte himself, but many other people who were connected with him.

But she was a daring creature, this same Olympe. She allowed Monsieur de Mailly to approach, looked him full in the face, and when he had made his customary obeisance, she coolly turned her back without acknowledging it in any way.

The Comte felt the blow; he flushed to the roots of his hair, straightened up, and took his leave, without seeming to notice the commotion excited among Olympe's courtiers by the rebuff she had administered.

The next day Monsieur de Mailly appeared again. Many people had in the mean time cautioned Olympe that she was incurring considerable risk by her impertinence.

But she cared so little, the hothead! that when Monsieur de Mailly approached she turned away from him before he saluted her at all.

The Comte was not disconcerted. On the other hand he walked straight up to her, and said to her abruptly, but with perfect courtesy, —

"Good-evening, Mademoiselle."

As he spoke, he placed himself so that she could not avoid him.

Every one was looking on at this little comedy with an interest easily understood.

Olympe made no reply.

"I had the honor, Mademoiselle," said Monsieur de Mailly, "to bid you good-evening."

"And you did wrong, Monsieur," she retorted in a loud voice, "for you should have guessed that I would not reply."

"If you were an ordinary actress," continued Monsieur de Mailly, "and should put such an affront upon me as I have received, I would write a note to the governor of the city, requesting him to punish you for your impertinence; but as you are not an actress simply, I forgive you, Mademoiselle."

"But if I am not an actress and nothing else, what am I, pray, Monsieur?" demanded Olympe, fixing her great, wondering eyes upon the Comte.

"This, I think, is not the place to tell you, Mademoiselle," replied Monsieur de Mailly, maintaining the exquisitely courteous address which had been his strong arm of defence; "the secrets of the nobility are not to be thus cast to the winds of the wings."

Olympe had heard too much not to desire that Monsieur de Mailly should say more; so she walked resolutely to a corner of the stage, and beckoned to him to follow her.

He obeyed.

"Now speak," said she.

"Mademoiselle," he began, "you are a young lady of family."

"I?" said Olympe, in open-mouthed amazement.

"I know it to be so, and to that is due the respect which I have always shown you, even when you have insulted me, and for no earthly cause; I know, I say, your whole life, and nothing can make me regret my conduct towards you, not even your harsh treatment."

"But, Monsieur —" Olympe began, deeply moved.

"Your name is Olympe de Clèves," pursued Monsieur de Mailly, imperturbably, "You were educated at a convent on Rue de Vaugirard. My sister was there at the same time. You left the convent three years and a half ago, and I know under what circumstances you left it."

Olympe turned pale; but as her cheeks were still covered with rouge, only her lips became white.

"In that case, Monsieur," she rejoined, "you were making sport of me the other day when you said —"

Olympe checked herself.

"When I told you that I loved you?" continued Monsieur de Mailly. "No, Mademoiselle, I was not making sport of you; on the contrary, I was telling you the truth."

Olympe made a gesture implying doubt.

"Allow me to smile at a speechless passion " — Mon‧
sieur de Mailly raised his hand — " or at one which speaks
but once, I should say," said she.

"Mademoiselle, you did not understand me, I see very
clearly," replied Monsieur de Mailly. "I saw you and
knew you; I knew you and loved you; I loved you and
told you so, I told you so and proved it."

"Proved it! " cried Olympe, thinking that at last she
had her adversary at a disadvantage. "Proved it! You
mean to say that you have proved that you love me ? "

"Certainly I do. When one loves an actress, one says
to her: ' You please me exceedingly, Olympe, and, upon
my word, I will love you, if you choose.' But when one
pays his addresses to a lady of quality, to Mademoiselle
de Clèves, one says to her nothing but this: ' Mademoiselle, I love you.' "

"And when one has said that, as I admit that you
have done," retorted Olympe, with a disdainful laugh,
" one waits for the lady of quality to bring her reply in
person."

" One waits not for what you suggest, Mademoiselle,
but one waits until a woman who has suffered on account
of the desertion of her first lover, and has never consented to listen to a second because of her hatred of all
mankind, — one waits, I say, until that woman, transformed and disarmed by the respectful conduct of a
refined man, brushes away her hatred little by little to
listen to words of love. That is what one awaits,
Mademoiselle."

"It would have been better, then," said Olympe,
trembling with emotion, " it would have been better, it
seems to me, to say nothing at all to that woman."

"Why so, pray, Mademoiselle ? The respectful hom-
age of a gentleman cannot be distasteful; and in the first

place it proves his delicacy, secondly, it tells of hope of better days to come, and lastly, it indicates that the woman upon whom it is bestowed might make a worse choice. That is all I undertook to prove to you, and I am only too happy if I have succeeded."

She lowered her eyes for a few seconds, and then raised them to his with the light of affection shining in their depths.

The Comte did not need that she should speak. He took her hand.

"Have I made myself understood?" he asked.

"Ask me that in a week," was Olympe's reply. "And when I am used to the thought, ask me if you are beloved."

With these words she raised her hands to the Comte's lips and was gone, leaving him trembling with joy.

The Comte, instead of following her, inclined his head respectfully, and walked back towards the officers, who questioned him about the explanation they had had.

"Was it tempestuous?" said one.

"Did it hail?" asked another.

"Was there thunder and rain?" was the jocose inquiry of a third.

"Messieurs," replied the Comte, "Mademoiselle Olympe is in very truth a most adorable creature."

With these words he left them. They watched his exit wonderingly; but a few days elucidated the mystery.

XI.

A FIRST APPEARANCE.

THREE years have passed since that revelation. Olympe having been separated from her lover three or four times by the exigencies of war or garrison duty, had felt the bond which united them grow gradually weaker. In 1727 Monsieur de Mailly was still in garrison at Marseilles, while Olympe was playing in comedy and tragedy at Avignon.

For two months she had not seen the Comte; it was only the night before that he had sent word to her that, being compelled by the duties of his new office of commandant of gendarmes, to which he had just been appointed, to go to Lyons, he proposed to take Avignon in his way, and attend the first performance of "Hérode et Mariamne."

The reader may ask, perhaps, why Monsieur de Mailly, wealthy and amorous as he was, had allowed Mademoiselle Olympe de Clèves to remain on the stage. We will reply that the matter did not depend upon him. He had indeed suggested to the actress that she should abandon the profession; but having become an actress by necessity, Olympe had allowed to enter her empty heart a passion which was as consuming as the other, in a different way, — the love of her art. So she had frowned upon every suggestion of the sort, declaring that nothing in the world would tempt her to renounce her freedom of action; she had accordingly continued to spend her fourteen thousand livres yearly, accepting from Monsieur de Mailly only such gifts as commonly pass from lover to mistress, and clinging to her profession as a resource against evil days.

Twenty times had the Comte renewed his entreaties to that effect; twenty times had Olympe rejected them. We know that Olympe wanted what she wanted very badly, and was especially wilful in respect of not wanting what she did not want.

Now she had replied to the Comte's letter that he could pass the following day tranquilly at Avignon, and that "Hérode et Mariamne" would be given in the evening. That was a Thursday; so it was absolutely necessary that "Hérode et Mariamne" should be performed on that Thursday. This explains why Olympe had so obstinately persisted that the part should be read, and had embraced Bannière when he agreed to act it.

It may be that Olympe depended upon the success she was likely to make in this part to rekindle her lover's affection, in which she had thought for some time that she could detect a slight abatement; it may be, on the other hand, that we are supposing her to have a desire which she had not, and that she had no ulterior object, — for black darkness prevails in the female heart in regard to all matters connected with the mysteries of love.

We left Bannière, dressed for the rôle of Hérode, at the moment when the three strokes of the bell announced the rising of the curtain.

Monsieur de Mailly, with all his staff, was in the large box opposite the stage. He had shared with the rest of the audience their anxiety as to the state of affairs in the wings; every one was asking, "Will there or will there not be a performance?" The assemblage, which was a large and brilliant one and bursting with impatiɜnce, breathed freely when they heard the signal and saw the curtain rise.

We cannot undertake to say whether it was fortunate or unfortunate for Bannière that he had no part in the first and second acts; but we do know that after each act he was sadly in need of the encouragement afforded by the presence of Olympe, who, to keep him in good heart, came behind the curtain to rehearse the principal scenes with him.

The cause of the gravest anxiety and preoccupation to the wretched novice was not the Pope's legate, who was present at this solemn function, nor Monsieur de Mailly and his staff, nor the municipal authorities, who sat in the front row: it was the two Jesuit fathers who weighed heavily upon his conscience; for he was as sure that they were there as if they had come expressly to watch for his appearance, and who could say that they would not recognize him despite his beard and his royal cloak?

So it was that Bannière was seized more than once with an irresistible desire to take to his heels. But two things prevented,— the attraction which bound him to Olympe, and the close watch which was kept upon him. There was not a soul, from the leading actor to the lowest supernumerary, who did not know that he was making his début almost by surprise, that he had exchanged the frock of a novice for the costume of Hérode; and as, all things considered, he might very naturally be attacked with remorse like that which had got the best of Champmeslé, they did not choose that the same cause should lead to a similar result, and that the play, which had come very near not beginning, should be exposed to the danger of not being played through after it was once begun.

Therefore Hérode was actually guarded by his guards,

who left their places and followed his every step in the wings as unremittingly as we have since seen the guards of Monsieur de Nangis follow their sovereign lord, in the drama of "Marion Delorme."

At last the curtain which had fallen upon the first and second acts rose upon the third; the fateful moment was at hand. Bannière, more dead than alive, heard the lines flow on one after another, and at every line that was recited he felt his own doom approaching. Although the actors on the stage spoke in the ordinary time, it seemed to him as if they were hurrying like madmen; the scenes succeeded each other before his eyes, like those dismal mists which the tempestuous westerly wind blows up beneath a lowering sky. At last came the third scene of the third act, which immediately precedes Hérode's entrée. Like a rising sea, the unhappy Bannière watched the moment for him to enter draw near; soon there were but four lines between him and that supreme moment, — soon again but two, but one! With the last measure Bannière's brow was bathed in cold perspiration. A sort of dizziness came over him, and he looked about to see if there was any opening for him to make his escape; but even as he turned, he saw the smiling face and enheartening glance of Olympe. He heard around him a whisper of "Come! come!" He felt a little hand, mightier than the hand of a giant, push him from behind, and a sweetly modulated voice whisper, "Courage!" The breath with which this word was uttered burned his cheek. He took a step forward and found himself before the footlights, before the great chandeliers, before three thousand rays gleaming from the eyes of the spectators, among which eyes, shining with infernal brilliancy, he fancied he could recognize those of the two reverend Jesuit fathers.

He entered slowly, gasping for breath, bewildered, and ready to pitch forward headlong at each step on the gradual slope of the stage.

But he was so handsome and well-made, his face wore such a gloomily melancholy expression; he had so well-turned a leg, and an eye so full of fire that a perfect thunder of applause, intended partly to encourage him and partly as an acknowledgment of his obligingness, arose throughout the great audience, who moved hither and thither, impelled by the attraction of curiosity, as a field of grain bends and waves beneath a summer wind.

The effect was instantaneous; the film which covered Bannière's eyes passed away, the blood which hummed in his ears ceased its surging, and, electrified by the bravos as the race-horse is by a word of praise or by the spur, he gallantly attacked his opening lines.

He was absolutely sure of one thing, — his memory, — but he was by no means sure of his personal appearance. The latter made an excellent impression, and half the battle was won.

Stimulated by the applause, Bannière acquired renewed strength; he said to himself that after all he was a man like other men, the equal in intelligence of the people in the hall, and very possibly the superior in talent of those upon the stage.

The result was that he delivered his tirades almost as confidently upon the stage as he had done in the green-room. In default of science, he had force; in default of by-play, he had fire; and as Olympe said to him in a low tone, " Good! good! " several times during her first scene with him, he acted very well indeed; for he acted as he might have done in the Chamber of Meditation, without realizing the danger.

As for Olympe, who had long been at home on the

stage, and who, instead of two malevolent Jesuit fathers among the audience, had Monsieur de Mailly and a whole staff of adorers there, she allowed herself to be carried away by her part, as she never would have done with Champmeslé perhaps, and did not let slip a single opportunity to score a point, sustained as she was by the approving murmurs of the whole hall and the noisy bravos of the garrison.

It was a capital performance. Bannière not only made no mistake himself, but he actually gave their cues to nearly all the others. The reader will remember that he knew the whole piece by heart.

So it was that after his first entrée he was overwhelmed with congratulations by the whole company, men and women alike. But after his second entrée, he had for him only the women, who, it must be said, remained faithful in their admiration to the end of the play.

When the end arrived, Olympe did not embrace Bannière again; she thanked him.

Bannière was too giddy to notice the distinction; the man who is tipsy from drinking poor wine, no longer appreciates the bouquet of choice vintages.

Bannière, then, was congratulated, flattered, and made much of; he tore himself away from all this adulation, for he still retained in a vague way the hope of returning to the novitiate, and took refuge in the dressing-room where he had changed his clothes.

He had much difficulty in finding it, but succeeded at last.

The first thing he discovered on entering the room, was a bath. As if to wash the stain from his body with water at the same time that he cleansed his soul by confession, Champmeslé was accustomed to take a bath after each new rôle that he played. Bannière eyed the bath

enviously; he thought that since he had taken Champmeslé's part, he might justly take his bath too. From
deduction to deduction he soon succeeded in convincing
himself that he had every right to the bath, while
Champmeslé had not one.

He removed the Hèrode costume, and stretched himself out luxuriously in the bath.

He had been there ten minutes, rubbing himself vigorously with Champmeslé's soap, and passing in review, as
in a dream, all the incidents of that eventful performance,
even to the least detail, when some one knocked at his
dressing-room door.

Bannière started nervously in his bath, like a thief
caught in the act.

"Well, what is wanted?" he asked. "You can't
come in."

Bannière was modest to the last degree.

"I do not wish to come in, Monsieur," replied the
voice of the hair-dresser. "King Hérode is wanted."

"Where?"

"In the green-room."

"What do they want of King Hérode?"

"Monsieur le Comte de Mailly is giving a supper to
the gentlemen and ladies, and says that the party would
be incomplete without King Hérode, as Queen Mariamne
attends."

Bannière did not reply for a moment; but then he
reflected that he had no other clothes to put on than his
Jesuit suit, and that he would cut a sad figure at this
joyous banquet in such sombre guise.

"Say that I thank Monsieur le Comte de Mailly with
all my heart for the honor he has done me," replied
the novice, "but that I cannot accept, having no coat."

"What, no coat?" said the hair-dresser; "have n't

you the costume of King Hérode, all ermine, silk, and velvet?"

"Yes," said Bannière; "but that is a costume, not a coat."

"Why," said the hair-dresser, "everybody is in costume; indeed, it is one of the conditions of the supper."

"Mademoiselle Olympe too?" Bannière ventured to ask.

"In full costume. She has merely taken off her paint and plaster, and taken a bath; that is why they are not yet at table."

A supper with Monsieur de Mailly; a supper presided over by Olympe; a supper where he should see her once more, where she would tell him that he had acted well; above all else, a supper at which he would make his appearance, not in the filthy novice's frock, but in the magnificent Hérode costume! In all those considerations there was more than enough to determine Bannière to postpone his return to the novitiate two hours more. Besides, they either knew of his escape or were still in ignorance of it; if the latter, two hours would make no difference, whereas if they already knew of it, the punishment would be so fearful in any event that two hours more could scarcely increase it.

Bannière was in the position of a man condemned to be hanged, and who for the sake of an hour of delicious enjoyment risks being torn on the wheel. Since death is death, Bannière desired to indulge first in such pleasure as only the gods know.

So he replied quite nonchalantly, —

"Very well, then, say to Monsieur de Mailly that I shall have the honor to accept his invitation."

He emerged from his bath, radiant and exhaling perfume. To the stage paint had succeeded the deep brown

tint of the skin which is the distinguishing mark of the
men of the South; in place of the flowing wig appeared
the waving black locks, to which the water had imparted
the glossy bluish tint of the crow's wing. He viewed
himself in Champmeslé's mirror, and for the first time
realized that he was handsome.

But at the same moment he said to himself with a
sigh, —

"Ah! and she, too, is very beautiful."

He then made the best of his way to the main foyer,
where the feast was spread.

XII.

THE SUPPER.

OLYMPE, as the hair-dresser told Bannière, had gone down to the green-room. But there a surprise awaited her. She found Monsieur de Mailly and his officers, in travelling-dress, booted and spurred. During the ten minutes which Olympe had passed in her dressing-room, the Comte and his staff had effected this rapid change of toilet.

With the most melancholy air that he could command, the Comte then informed Olympe that during the play he had received an express from the king; that his Majesty demanded his immediate presence at Versailles, and that he should have set out at once upon receipt of the express, in accordance with the respect which he owed to the king's command, had he not given to his respect for his mistress the preference over his respect for the royal person; that he had consequently, as soon as the curtain fell, given the word to his officers to prepare themselves for a journey, and had allowed them only ten minutes in which to do it.

They were all there, as we have said, in the green-room when Olympe entered.

Having saluted her, the Comte turned to the other ladies.

"Mesdames," said he, "accept our salutation and seat yourselves at the table."

It was at this moment that Bannière appeared at the door. Upon hearing the cry of surprise uttered by two or three of the actresses, Olympe turned about.

Bannière, in truth, deserved the tribute of admiration which his presence evoked; it was impossible to imagine a handsomer or more distinguished-looking youth than he.

Olympe uttered no sound; she simply looked at him in astonishment, that was all.

Monsieur de Mailly nodded carelessly.

Bannière crossed his hands upon his chest, as Orientals and Jesuits do, and bowed low. He found it quite natural to make one of the most respectful and most courteous salutations imaginable.

Monsieur de Mailly addressed a few complimentary words to the young man, while Olympe smiled her approval. Then he took a glass, filled it with champagne, and handed it to Olympe, poured out a second glass for himself, and said as he held it aloft, —

"To the king's health, Mesdames and Messieurs."

The officers had followed their commander's example, each of them, glass in hand, first holding it aloft, and then draining it to the king's health.

Monsieur de Mailly then turned to Olympe.

"And now, Madame," said he, "we drink to your grace and loveliness."

This toast, as we can easily conceive, was drunk with acclamation by the whole company except Bannière, who had not the courage to drink a second glass, although he had found the first very good.

It was not that Olympe was not in his eyes as fair as Venus herself, but the toast was proposed by Monsieur de Mailly, albeit with perfect courtesy, yet with a certain tone of proprietorship which tore poor Bannière's heart.

Monsieur de Mailly, who had, on the other hand, the best of reasons for drinking, placed his glass on the table after he had drained it to the last drop, and taking

Olympe's hand in his, said to her as he pressed a kiss upon it, —

"Farewell for a little, dear heart."

Olympe made no reply; it seemed to her that there was something peculiar in the Comte's manner towards her. So she contented herself with letting her eyes follow him as far as the door; then her glance returned to the company and fell upon Bannière.

He was very pale, and was leaning upon a chair, as if without that support he might fall.

"Come, my king," said Olympe to him, pointing to the chair at her right, "take the seat which the Comte should have occupied. Honor to whom honor is due."

Bannière obeyed mechanically, and seated himself, trembling like a leaf.

At this moment they heard the footsteps of the officers' horses galloping off on the Lyons road.

Bannière breathed again, while Olympe could not repress a sigh.

However she took her place at the table; and as her self-control was very great, she seemed to banish her preoccupation with a toss of the head.

The supper was at an end; the ladies and gentlemen, freed from the restraint of the officers' presence, found the occasion much more enjoyable. Bannière, above all, had seen Monsieur de Mailly take his departure with a satisfaction for which he could hardly account, but which he did not take the trouble to conceal.

Actors, especially those whose lot is cast in the provinces and who do not eat every day, generally have excellent appetites; and Monsieur de Mailly's repast was done full justice to.

Bannière, seated beside Olympe, ate and drank, but in a most nervous and embarrassed frame of mind: he said

not a word, and while he devoured the eatables and
drinkables with both hands and mouth, — we must
remember that he had had nothing to eat for thirty-six
hours, — he devoured his lovely neighbor with his eyes.

She, like a sensible girl, did not seem to regret the
departure of the officers; she did the honors of the feast
with admirable grace; she even carried her good-humor
so far as to make all the men gloriously tipsy by doubling
the number of bottles ordered, and having the extra
supply charged to her.

Every moment added to the exaltation of Bannière,
for at every turn his eyes met his fair neighbor's eyes,
and his hand met hers. And so, towards the close of the
banquet, he was no longer an ordinary mortal; he called
himself Roscius, Baron, the genius of Comedy.

The trouble was that he was over head and ears in
love, and slightly tipsy. His pale and melancholy beauty
had become transformed into beauty of a more brilliant
cast. From his eyes shot all the flames of love and
wine.

It then became Olympe's turn to lower her eyes; and
the modest queen understood that it was time for her
to leave the table; accordingly she rose, courteously
wished her comrades much pleasure, said good-night, and
left the room, without any signs of anger, but with
perfect dignity.

She had had only water to drink.

When they saw her rise and prepare to take her leave,
the men undertook to get on their feet and return
courtesy for courtesy; but at least half of them, who had
had great difficulty in retaining a sitting posture, as soon as
they tried to execute the other movement, stumbled and
fell over the other half, whose legs were protruding from
under the table.

The women did as Olympe had done, with this variation: as they withdrew, they passed in line before the
young man, and each gave him a farewell kiss, as if they
were about to part forever, since Bannière was going back
to the convent.

As the last one performed this ceremony, Olympe, who
was just crossing the threshold, looked around and saw
the bashful Joseph wiping his lips.

She smiled and disappeared.

Thereupon Bannière, left alone amid these topers who
cumbered the floor of the green-room as uprooted trees
cumber the ground, fell a victim to despondency
unutterable.

In short, with Olympe's departure, the dream had
ended, and stern reality had supervened.

Reality! That is to say, instead of the golden heaven
in which he had lived for two hours with gods and goddesses, the convent where he should see none but black-
robed mortals; instead of the green-room, brilliant with
many lights, where the acclamations of the audience and
the clinking of glasses could still be heard, the Chamber
of Meditation, with its dry bread and clear water, and its
dismal inscriptions.

All this was not very seductive to the imagination, and
yet he must needs go and submit to it all again.

Slowly he crossed the supper-room, walking carefully
to avoid stepping upon the bodies of the unlucky com-
batants, who had succumbed to the rattling storm of
chambertin and champagne. He was as sad at heart as
a victorious general visiting the battlefield where he has
left half of his army. One would have said it was Pyrrhus
after the battle of Heraclea.

He returned to the room where he had dressed; the
lights were dying out: he revived the almost extinct

flame, and began to search for his novice's clothes which he had left in a corner.

To his utter amazement they had disappeared.

At first he thought that his dresser must have thrown them behind a door or into some wardrobe; he felt behind all the doors, and opened all the wardrobes, but to no purpose.

After fifteen minutes' search, he gave it up and went downstairs again. The concierge alone was left in the theatre; dressers, coiffeurs, and wing-boys, all had gone.

The concierge eyed him narrowly.

" Did those things belong to you," he said, — " a black cloak, black breeches, and a hat like a quartern loaf?"

" Yes, they did belong to me."

" Well, well! but they would not become you so well as the costume you are wearing at this moment."

" Have you seen them, pray?" said Bannière, anxious for an explanation.

" Certainly I have," was the reply.

" Where?"

" *Pardieu!* on the back of Monsieur de Champmeslé."

" What do you say? on the back of Monsieur de Champmeslé?"

" Yes! He came back to his dressing-room; as he went in, he saw your clothes, and he at once made the sign of the Cross."

" Without speaking?"

" Oh, no! He said: 'Beyond question, it is the will of God, since he sends me not only the inclination, but the very dress of a monk.'"

" And then?"

" Then he removed his civilian garments, and put on your novice's suit."

" But what became of the clothes he took off?"

"He gave them to his dresser, on condition that his wife should say five Paters and five Aves a day for him for a week."

"Is it long since he went away?"

"Oh, it 's more than an hour."

It was enough to turn the poor fellow's head, and Bannière was completely bewildered by this development.

If it were a serious matter to return to the novitiate at two in the morning in the garb of a Jesuit, it was vastly more so to appear at that hour with the costume of King Hérode.

However an idea suggested itself to him. It was not an hour likely to be selected for parading the streets, even when dressed as a Jesuit; and Champmeslé must have gone home.

"Where does Monsieur de Champmeslé live?" he asked.

"On Grande-Rue, opposite the statue of Saint Bénezet, next door to Mademoiselle Olympe."

"Mademoiselle Olympe!" Bannière could not help repeating the name, with a sigh. "Mademoiselle Olympe! Ah!"

As he still showed no purpose of moving, the concierge said,—

"Come! what do you propose to do? I must lock up here; it is high time. You can sleep in your bed all the forenoon to-morrow, while I must be up and at work again at six o'clock."

Bannière smiled bitterly.

Sleep in his bed all the forenoon! There was considerable doubt about that!

"Well, well," the concierge repeated; "did n't you hear me? Monsieur de Champmeslé lives on Grande-Rue, opposite Saint Bénezet's statue, and next door to Mademoiselle Olympe."

"All right, I hear you," said Bannière, "and I will prove it by going there."

Like a man whose mind is made up, he darted bravely into the street, still clad in the Hérode dress.

The concierge closed the door behind him.

XIII.

IN WHICH CHAMPMESLÉ CAUSES BANNIÈRE SERIOUS EMBARRASSMENT.

BANNIÈRE took the direction indicated by the concierge. He found the statue of Saint Bénezet, and directly opposite was a house which he judged to be that of Champmeslé.

But the house was as dark and gloomy as the remorseful and fearful heart of him who dwelt therein. All the shutters were closed except one, through which one could see that all was dark within as well as without.

The house beside it, on the other hand, — the one which the concierge had described as Olympe's, — was alive with that pleasant, cheerful light which indicates that no lonely vigil is being kept, although its inmates are yet awake. The blinds were drawn on the first floor, it is true, and that was the only floor which seemed at the moment to be occupied; but one could see through the interstices a rose-colored light, which, softened by curtains of silk, indicated the boudoir, or the bedroom perhaps, of a pretty woman.

Bannière-Hérode looked at that lovely rose-tinted light, sighed, and knocked at Champmeslé's door.

But to all appearances, the deserted aspect of the house did not belie it, for to Bannière's three vigorous blows there was no response.

He struck six blows. Still silence.

He struck nine blows.

Up to that time Bannière had adopted the plan of
doubling and trebling the number three, which the gods
like, as is well known; but receiving no response to his
three times three, he lost his patience, and began to beat
a tattoo on the door, which soon aroused the dogs in
three or four neighboring houses, and they began a concert in which all the deep and shrill tones of the canine
gamut were represented. Undoubtedly the hammering
and the concert which it evoked, produced a more or less
disagreeable impression upon the tenant of the next
house, for one of the blinds with the beautiful rose lining
opened, and a young maidservant, the typical Marton of
the comedy, with her blue cap over her ear, put her
head out through the opening, and in a bitter-sweet little
voice asked, —

"Pray, who is making such an uproar at such an
hour ? "

"Alas, Mademoiselle Claire, it is I," Bannière
replied.

He had recognized one of Olympe's maids; and as
Olympe had called her by name before him, and he had
not forgotten a syllable that Olympe said, he remembered
her name.

"Who are you ? " asked the girl, trying to pierce the
darkness with her bright eyes.

"Bannière the débutant."

"Ah, Madame," cried the giddy soubrette, turning to
speak to her mistress, who was still invisible, — "ah,
Madame, it is Monsieur Bannière ! "

"Monsieur Bannière, do you say ? " asked Olympe.

"Yes; and — and — oh, Madame, forgive me if I can't
help laughing, but the poor boy is still in his costume of
King Hérode."

"Impossible ! " cried Olympe, who could not conceive

any emergency which would compel Bannière to parade
the streets in such guise.

"But it's so, it's so," insisted Claire. "Isn't it
true that you are still dressed as Hérode, Monsieur
Bannière?"

"Alas, yes, Mademoiselle," said the unhappy novice.
"But Madame will not believe me."

A ray of hope entered Bannière's mind.

"She has only to come to the window," said he, "and
she can make sure of it with her own eyes."

Bannière brought into play, in uttering this sentence,
the most pathetic notes of which his voice was capable.
They went straight to Olympe's heart; and she, half
inclined to laugh and half touched, approached the window, where Mademoiselle Claire respectfully made way
for her, although, to gratify her curiosity, she remained
close behind her mistress, standing on tip-toe and peering
over her shoulder.

"Is it indeed you, Monsieur Bannière?" Olympe
began.

"Yes, Mademoiselle."

"What are you doing there, pray?"

"Why, you see, Mademoiselle: I am knocking at
Monsieur de Champmeslé's door."

"But Monsieur de Champmeslé is not at home."

"Alas, I fear you are right, Mademoiselle."

"What do you want of Monsieur de Champmeslé at
this hour?"

"I want him to return my clothes, Mademoiselle."

"What clothes?"

"My novice's clothes, which he found in his dressing-
room, put on his own back, so it seems, and went off
with."

"Oh, you poor boy!" murmured Olympe.

Bannière did not hear the words, but he saw the gesture which accompanied them, and understood it.

"Madame," said he, "Monsieur de Champmeslé has not yet come home, but he must come home sooner or later."

"Surely he must at some time or other."

"I am convinced of it, Madame; but I cannot wait for him at his door in such a costume as this."

"Why not?"

"Why, because the day will soon be here, Mademoiselle; it is at least three o'clock, and if I am seen in this costume, I am lost."

"Lost?"

"Yes, lost in order to do you a service."

"How are you lost?"

"Because I am a novice at the Jesuits."

"Ah, so you are, poor fellow!"

"Madame," Bannière ventured to say, "if you would allow me to come into your house?"

"I beg your pardon?"

"I would gladly wait wherever you choose, — in your dining-room, or parlor, or reception-room."

Olympe turned around to consult Claire.

"Dame!" exclaimed the maid; "I say, Madame, that a woman must have a very hard heart to leave such a fine fellow at the door."

"Ah, indeed!"

"I thought that Madame meant to ask my opinion. I beg pardon if I have given it without being called upon."

"No, no; on the contrary, you did just right, for I did mean to ask your opinion, and it agrees with mine."

"Madame," Bannière asked at this point, "what have you decided to do with me?"

"Show him up, Mademoiselle," said Olympe to her maid; "and let him come into the adjoining room."

"Madame realizes that that room is mine."

"Very well; when he is in your room, we will decide what to do."

Claire darted to the door to execute the order. Olympe cast a last glance at poor Bannière, who was holding his arms out to her as a shipwrecked sailor might to the lighthouse on the shore, and closed the window.

For a moment Bannière lost courage. In making his request he had feared that he was a little over-bold, so that when that rose-lined blind was closed upon him he thought that he was shut out beyond recall.

In his very natural despair he set to work again upon Champmeslé's door, and was hammering away furiously, when he heard the next door open very softly.

The same head with the coquettish blue cap appeared; and Bannière saw, so to speak, the word "Come" issue from two rosy, smiling lips.

He did not wait for the word to be repeated; he rushed into the hall, and Mademoiselle Claire closed the door behind him; then, as he found himself in utter darkness, a little hand sought his, and having found it, drew him gently forward, while the same sweet voice, which sounded to Bannière's ears like that of a messenger from heaven, whispered, "Follow me."

Nothing could be easier than to follow when this charming, perfumed guide went before. Bánnière found a staircase with a sharp turn in it at the end of the hall; but he was forewarned by a pressure of the hand of every obstacle. Thus it was out of the question that any mishap should befall him.

Arrived at the top of the stairs, he was shown into Mademoiselle Claire's bedroom. Only a single door, but that fastened with a double lock, separated him from Olympe's apartment.

Claire went to the door.

"Here we are, Madame," said she.

"Very good, Mademoiselle," replied Olympe, who was listening on the other side of the door. "And are you there too, Monsieur Bannière?"

"Yes, Madame," said Bannière, "and very grateful for the favor you have granted me."

"That's of no consequence. So you say that you lack the proper clothes in which to go back to the convent, and that it would be difficult for you to go back in the character of King Hérode?"

"I think it is not possible, Mademoiselle."

"Very well; then I will give you others."

"Clothes?"

"Yes."

"The devil!" muttered Bannière, who was rapidly losing his anxiety to go back to the novitiate; "that's not what I want."

He added aloud,—

"I thank you most sincerely, Mademoiselle."

"What! do you propose to accept the clothes?" Claire interrupted in an undertone.

Bannière, delighted to find his own inclinations seconded, made a sign with his hand, which meant, "Never fear."

"By the way," he continued, "I left the convent in a curious way."

"How was that?" Olympe asked.

"I came out by the window."

"By the window?"

"Yes. I ought to say, Mademoiselle, that I was a prisoner in the Chamber of Meditation."

"For breaking the rules of the order?" queried Olympe, laughing.

"For learning the tragedy of 'Hérode' by heart, Mademoiselle."

"Ah! really?"

"I discovered that the chamber had a masked window; I unmasked it, and through the window I saw — ah! Mademoiselle, it was what I saw through the window which led me to destruction."

"What was it that you saw, in God's name?"

"I saw the procession of Hérode and Mariamne. I saw you raise your veil to salute Monsieur de Mailly; and—"

"And what?" Olympe persisted.

"And you seemed to me so beautiful, Mademoiselle, so beautiful, that I swore I would see you act that same evening."

Mademoiselle Claire made a wry face.

"Ah! really?" exclaimed Olympe again.

"So I made a sad wreck of the hangings of the Chamber of Meditation, let myself down from the window, ran like a madman toward the theatre without thinking that I had no money to pay for my seat. Suddenly I saw two Jesuit fathers on their way to the play. I sought shelter in the lobby, and there met Monsieur Champmeslé, who was running away; behind him came his comrades running after him. As I was the only one who could give positive information about him, they dragged me off to the green-room; there I told the whole story. You came in; I saw that you were in despair at the idea of postponing the performance, and I thought you more beautiful even than in the procession. Your despair tore my heart, I forgot everything under the spell of your radiant presence. I said, 'I shall be ruined, to be sure;

but no tear shall dim those lovely eyes;' and I am ruined, Mademoiselle. That's the whole story."

"Oh, the viper!" muttered Claire.

"Is it really true?" rejoined Olympe, in a voice deeply moved; "did things really happen as you say?"

"Upon my honor, Mademoiselle."

Something like a sigh was audible on the other side of the door.

"After all," said Claire, joining in the conversation, "it seems to me that Monsieur Bannière's affairs are not so desperate as he says."

"Explain yourself," said Olympe.

"Monsieur came out through a window."

"Yes," said Bannière.

"It was dark when you came away?"

"Almost dark."

"Your flight is probably not yet discovered."

"Probably not."

"Very well, then, just get back through the same window."

"Yes, indeed," said Olympe, "let him go back through the same window that he came out of."

These words were accompanied by another sound resembling a sigh.

"That is just where the difficulty lies," said Bannière.

"Difficulty!" repeated Olympe, quickly; "how so? Tell me."

"The window is very high."

"Oh, well, you can find a ladder," said Claire.

"A ladder? where?" asked Olympe.

"Even so, it will have to be a very long one," added Bannière.

"We have a very long one in the garden," said Claire.

"It must be at least thirty feet in length," said Bannière.

"Oh, it's fully that."

"Yes; but a ladder of that length requires at least two men to carry it, put it in position, and hold it."

Mademoiselle Claire had no answer ready for this argument.

There was silence for a moment on both sides of the door.

"Well," said Olympe at last, "I fear it will be very hard for you to get in by the window, if the window is so high."

"Oh, it is even higher than I said," Bannière hastened to add.

"What are we to do then?" said Olympe.

"Madame," said Bannière, "you will not be so cruel, I hope, after giving me a moment's shelter, as to turn me out of your house, and leave me exposed to the chilly air, and the anger of the Jesuits."

"Monsieur Bannière cannot stay here, however," said Mademoiselle Claire, sourly; "for this is my room."

"You are both right," said Olympe, opening the door; "you are right. Mademoiselle Claire, show Monsieur into my dressing-room."

As she spoke, she pointed to a door on the other side of her apartment, opposite the one which led into Claire's quarters.

"There is a couch there," she added; "and a night is soon passed when it is half-past three in the morning in the month of May. Go on!"

Mademoiselle Claire had not a word to say; the imperious, yes, royal gesture which accompanied the last word admitted no rejoinder. Bannière, too, instead of following Mademoiselle Claire, went on ahead this time.

He walked across the room with a step light as air, scarcely touching the floor, bowed low before the beautiful fairy, who had made a different man of him in half a day, and disappeared in the dressing-room.

Claire followed him, and when she reached the door, —

"Well, Madame," she asked, "what is to be done now?"

"Why, the bolts are to be thrown on my side of the door, and you are to come and undress me. It is time, I think, is it not?"

Mademoiselle threw the bolts, and returned to her mistress, who held out the sleeve of her peignoir that she might assist in taking it off.

"But, Madame," said Claire, as she performed this office, "suppose Monsieur de Mailly should come back as he said?"

"Well, suppose he should come back?"

"What shall I say to him?"

"You will tell him just the truth, that's all."

She finished taking off her peignoir with her own hands, and dismissed the maid with a gesture. Claire withdrew with lowered head, and going through an expressive pantomime which meant, —

"*Ma foi!* I don't know what to make of this."

XIV.

THE CABINET OF MEDITATION.

ONCE in the cabinet, Bannière had fallen into a luxurious easy-chair, on the seat and back of which lay various articles of clothing which Mademoiselle de Clèves had but just laid aside.

The pleasant warmth which exhaled from them seemed to have permeated the cabinet from floor to ceiling, impregnating the atmosphere with a subtle, intoxicating perfume.

Bannière, in a state of nervous exaltation, tremulous and feverish, buried his face in his hands, and asked himself if all that had happened to him was not a dream, like one of those infernal dreams which the mocking adversaries of the Holy of Holies used to visit upon the unhappy monks in their cells in the early days of Christianity.

He passed it all in review: the procession of Hérode and Mariamne, his flight, the slender ankles and diminutive feet of the ladies of Avignon, the actors' lobby, the green-room, the performance, the supper, the kisses which the ladies of the play had bestowed upon him, the chambertin and champagne, the wilderness of plump white shoulders which had surrounded him; and then Olympe's eyes, her nervous white hand pressing his arm, her teeth,— those pearls to which God had given so beautiful a setting, — her lovely teeth, hidden to be sure, but which shone upon him in a sudden smile at the beginning of the feast!

And oh! the flitting across that lovely rose-colored chamber, the gilded bedstead with lace coverlid standing in a satin-lined recess; the rose-tinted light, the intoxicating perfume, everything in short that he had seen and felt in five short seconds; Olympe in a simple peignoir, her hair free from powder, and falling about her shoulders, — all this, in combination with the tirades of Hérode, the bravos of the audience, and a feeling of dread which from time to time made Bannière's heart stand still, made such a hurly-burly in his brain as would have driven the most sober-minded of men mad.

He heard Olympe dismiss her women; he heard the rings of the bed-curtains slide along their golden rod; he heard the dainty bed creak beneath the weight, light as it was, of the body which intrusted itself to it.

Then he looked about him for the first time.

An alabaster lamp, suspended from the ceiling by a silver chain, lighted a fascinating dressing-room, in which the mirrors and consoles, as well as the ewers and basins, were all of Saxon manufacture; in Bannière's eyes, after a hasty glance around, it had no defect except the lack of transparency of its walls.

As we have said, the tempest of emotion evoked in Bannière's brain by his recent extraordinary experiences and his present situation amounted to frenzy, and became almost insupportable under the additional incentive of his overmastering passion for her who was so near at hand, and yet as far away as if the ocean rolled between them.

He rose from the easy-chair, and began to pace madly up and down in his narrow quarters, muttering incoherently to himself, and recklessly regardless of the objects which lay in his path. The existence of such objects was soon brought home to him, however, with embarrassing distinctness, and the melodrama was near becoming roaring farce, when his foot came in contact with a foot-warmer, and he fell heavily against the door which communicated with Olympe's apartment.

The noise of his fall brought him to himself, at the same time that it aroused some apprehension in his mind, for it was an absurd noise.

But it was still worse when he heard Olympe's voice asking, —

"For Heaven's sake, what are you doing in there, Monsieur Bannière? Are you tearing down the partition?"

"Oh, Mademoiselle!" replied the unhappy youth in a woe-begone voice, which gave to his exclamation all the force of a sigh.

"Well, what is it? You are not ill, are you?"

"Oh, Mademoiselle," he repeated with the same inflection, "I am on the rack."

"Poor Monsieur Bannière!" said Olympe, in a tone of mock sympathy, "what has happened to you? Do tell me."

"It is very hard to tell, Mademoiselle."

"Bah!"

"One thing I do know, however, and that is that I am damned, for certain."

"What! Just because you have acted in one tragedy? Nonsense! I have acted in more than a hundred, and have strong hopes of salvation, notwithstanding."

"Ah! it's a very different matter with you, Mademoiselle; you are not a novice at the Jesuits."

Olympe began to laugh at his dolorous accent, and her apparent scorn increased his despondency tenfold; he expressed it by long-drawn sighs, which became absolutely heart-rending where they had been simply melancholy.

"Come, come, my dear comrade, we must go to sleep," said Olympe, quite seriously; "it will soon be four o'clock."

"Impossible, Mademoiselle, impossible! I had some champagne to drink, and my head is in a whirl. I saw your eyes, and my heart is on fire."

"Oh, *mon Dieu!* that is a downright declaration."

"Mademoiselle!" exclaimed Bannière, clasping his hands as if he could be seen on the other side of the door.

"I begin to be of your opinion; you certainly will be damned, Monsieur Bannière, if you don't look out," continued Olympe.

"Mademoiselle," cried Bannière, in a frenzy, "do not laugh at me. I am freezing and shivering and burning up all at once. Oh, I verily believe that this is what is called being in love, mad with love!"

"Is it not rather what is called being tipsy, my poor fellow?"

"Oh, no! If you but knew! My head is calm, comparatively speaking. It is my heart, my heart, my heart, which beats more and more madly. When I hear your voice, when I hear— Ah me! I feel as if I were dying."

"Go to sleep, go to sleep, dear Monsieur Bannière."

"Mademoiselle, ever since the first moment I laid my eyes on you I have felt that I had ceased to be my own master."

"My dear Bannière, every letter I receive — and I receive a great many — begins with just those words."

"Happy they whom you have allowed to demonstrate the truth of what they have written, Mademoiselle."

"Poor boy! do you happen to have a ray of intelligence about you, dear Monsieur Bannière?"

"Alas! I don't know, Mademoiselle."

"Oh, well! I pity you with all my heart, if what you say is true. Go to sleep."

"Oh, you pity me, Mademoiselle," rejoined Bannière, noticing only the first phrase, and ignoring that humiliating imperative which had already been injected into the conversation three or four times,—"oh, you pity me; but that proves that you have a kind heart."

He shook the door by way of peroration.

"My dear friend," said Olympe, laughing, "you prove to me in return that you have strong hands."

"Ah! there you begin to make sport of me again," said Bannière. "If you only knew how small a thing it would take to comfort me; only one kind word, and I am sadly in need of it. You have no idea how mad I must be to speak to you so boldly. No, I am no longer master of myself, I am demented."

"Let the door alone, Monsieur Bannière, or I call my women."

Bannière obeyed, and leaned against the door instead of shaking it.

"I tell you that I am a madman," he continued. "God is already chastising me for the sin into which the devil led me. Love! alas, it is not for me that yours is reserved; what am I, after all? A mere clod, a speck of dirt, a poor miserable wretch! Oh, I am lost irrevocably, I assure you!"

"Monsieur Bannière," said Olympe, in her most serious tone, for she began to realize that there was real suffering underneath this farcical scene,—"Monsieur Bannière, you are all wrong to excite yourself so. There is in you the stuff of a good fellow, and a clever fellow too; more than that, I believe that you possess a kind and honest heart."

"Oh!" exclaimed Bannière.

"You have an attractive face, too," continued Olympe; "you will get along famously with the ladies, believe me."

"You only in all the world do I care to please,—only you, only you."

"But you are a novice at the Jesuits."

"Ah! yes."

"And so long as you have not cast your frock to the dogs—"

"Oh, Mademoiselle, it has already been cast to the dogs, or soon will be, if—"

"If what?"

"Oh, what's the use? With or without my frock, she whom I aspire to please will never look at me."

"She whom you aspire to please is myself, is she not?"

"Oh, yes, Madame, you, you!"

"Thanks! for you say that in a way that leaves no room for doubt; and believe me a woman is always grateful to the man who truly loves her. To such a man she owes, if not a love equal to his own (for a woman is not always mistress of her affections), at least the whole truth. Well, dear Monsieur Bannière, my heart is given to a worthy gentleman, one Monsieur de Mailly."

"Alas!" sighed Bannière, who felt that that was indeed an insurmountable obstacle.

"And as I wish to steal nothing from any one, Monsieur Bannière, and as our mutual promises are as binding as an honorable man and woman can make them, I beg you, for your own sake, to think no more of the subject now occupying your mind."

"Occupying my mind!" cried Bannière, humiliated, crushed,—"occupying my mind! she calls this torture 'occupying my mind'!"

"You heard what I said, my dear neighbor," said Olympe, firmly; "in ten minutes you have learned more about me than any other will learn in ten years. Now, dear Monsieur Bannière, take this torture of yours more philosophically, stretch out on your cushions, and go to sleep."

"Good-night, Mademoiselle," replied Bannière, dismally enough; "I have to ask a thousand pardons for all the embarrassment I have caused you, all the foolish things I have said to you, and the absurd annoyances I have subjected you to. At last, Mademoiselle, I realize the whole extent of my misfortune. So from this moment, have no fear, Mademoiselle, you shall have nothing more to reproach me for. Sleep, Mademoiselle, sleep; my despair now is speechless,— the most cruel of all for him who experiences it, but less burdensome for her who causes it."

Olympe made no reply to this discourse; she composed herself once more to sleep; and the noise made by her bed-curtains drowned another noise, which Bannière, if he had heard it, might have taken for a sigh.

He, poor fellow! buried himself in the easy-chair, and resigned himself to the anguish of immobility.

He had just fallen into a state of torpidity rather than sleep, when he heard a loud knocking at the street door.

Bannière started up, and listened with all his ears; every sound was an event, in his state of mind.

He heard sounds in the adjoining room which indicated that Olympe too was listening.

After a moment's interval the street door opened and closed; then Bannière heard the door of Olympe's room open, footsteps on the floor, and the rattling of the bed-curtains.

It was a terrible blow for Bannière, who thought he saw in the incident proof that she had lied to him, and was false, too, to her sworn fidelity to Monsieur de

Mailly, galloping along the Lyons road. His courage gave out; he slid from the chair to the floor, rolled himself up in the Herodian cloak, and lay like a dead man.

Never had he suffered so intensely.

Suddenly he heard an exclamation of surprise in Olympe's room.

With the cowardice of all lovers who are jealous, he listened with all his ears.

"Who brought this letter, pray?" demanded Olympe.

"Good! it is only a letter," thought Bannière.

"A dragoon, Mademoiselle; he came at full gallop, and as soon as I had the letter in my hand he was off as fast as he came."

"Mademoiselle Claire's voice!" exclaimed Bannière; "better and better."

"This is an extraordinary proceeding!" said Olympe, with a quiver in her voice.

After a pause, she added, —

"Go back to bed, Claire."

"Very well, Madame."

Claire took a step or two toward the door.

"One moment — " said Olympe.

Claire stopped.

"Unlock the door of that dressing-room."

"The room where the Jesuit is?" queried Claire, with an accent of most profound astonishment.

"Yes."

Claire unlocked the door, and Bannière rose to his feet in a flutter.

"What next?" asked Claire.

"Assist me to dress," said Olympe; and after a few moments of hasty movement, she added, —

"Beg Monsieur Bannière, if he is not asleep, to do me the favor to come and speak with me a moment."

Bannière, it is needless to say, was on his feet before the words were uttered.

Claire opened the door behind which the poor novice had shivered and suffered so much. She saw Bannière standing before her.

"He is not asleep, by any means," Claire told her mistress.

"So much the better," said Olympe; adding in the next breath,—

"Be kind enough to come here, Monsieur Bannière, I beg you."

"Mademoiselle —"

"That is to say if you have no objection," said Olympe, smiling.

Bannière stepped into the room with a pale face and wildly beating heart.

In a low chair by the bedside, in the soft rays of a float-light burning in perfumed oil, Olympe, clad in the same simple peignoir, seemed to the bewildered novice as fair as Venus rising from the foam of the sea.

Near her stood the femme-de-chambre, in a charming negligée, fit to break the heart of the most devout of novices.

Olympe's cheeks were flushed, her forehead and eyebrows were knit, her eyes flashed fire. She held an open letter in her fingers, which were as rosy-tipped as Aurora's own.

"Come here, Monsieur," said she.

"Umph!" thought Bannière, "she is going to show me the door. The letter is a command to that effect from Monsieur de Mailly. I am at the end of my tether."

"You may go, Mademoiselle." said Olympe to Claire.

Claire stood a moment in mute amazement; then, at a sign from her mistress, she bowed and left the room, with the air of one who makes up her mind to obey, without comprehending.

Bannière, finding himself standing alone by Olympe's side, was seized with downright vertigo; under sentence of death and bound to the stake, he could hardly have been more ghastly or more tremulous.

"She has sent her maid away so as not to humiliate me before her," he said to himself. Oh, poor Bannière!

Olympe raised her eyes, still gleaming with anger, to the novice's face.

"Monsieur," said she, "read that letter, please."

"Here we go," thought Bannière, trembling as with the ague.

However he took the letter, and read: —

MY DEAR OLYMPE, — Everything has an end in this world, and love is no exception. You love me from sentiment, and on my side I reproach myself with having no longer that ardent passion for you which you deserve to inspire. But my friendship has survived my love; and the king, by recalling me, has shown me how deep and earnest that friendship is, by the regret with which I leave you.

You would have been the woman to wait for me forever, for you are loyalty personified. I myself break the bonds which may be a source of vexation to you.

Open your wings, beautiful dove!

I have left in your secretary two thousand louis, which I owe you, and a ring which I beg you to accept.

Do not wonder at my writing to you. I should never have dared to say such brutal things to your face.

Au revoir, and without ill feeling.

COMTE DE MAILLY.

"Oh, *mon Dieu!*" cried Bannière, in the first impulse of his heart, after he had read the letter. "Oh, Mademoiselle, how unfortunate you are!"

" I ? " retorted Olympe. " You are mistaken. I am free; that 's all."

Before Bannière had time to readjust his emotions, there was a second knocking at the street door, quite different from the first and much more vigorous.

XV.

THE JESUITS AT THE PLAY.

BEFORE divulging to our readers the identity of the latest intruder upon the privacy of our hero and heroine, it is indispensable, in our opinion at least, to return for a few moments to certain personages, who, although undoubtedly of less importance, ought not, nevertheless, to be altogether neglected, being considerably interested in this portion of this veracious history.

We refer to the Society of Jesus, which we have slighted somewhat during the last three or four chapters. Particularly we refer to Père Mordon and Père de la Sante, who are, in our judgment, of too much importance to the plot to have their rôles thus cut.

We have said that the Jesuits went to the theatre; at this time abbés and priests were permitted to go, in order to judge of the literary merit and the moral tendencies of the play. It was an established fact that the preacher might properly borrow from the histrionic artist some of his gestures and tricks of elocution. Whatever redounded to the glory of God was looked upon as fair game, especially by the Society of Jesus.

" Ad majorem Dei gloriam " was the Society's motto.

It might therefore be of the utmost consequence to the glory of God that the reverend fathers Mordon and De la Sante should go to listen to the periods of that heathen Voltaire, declaimed by those renegades of actors.

Doubtless Père Mordon in one of his sermons, and Père de la Sante in one of his sacred tragedies, would make good use of some morsels of gold found in that dungheap. *Margaritas in sterquilinio.*

This explains why Bannière, hidden behind his pillar, had seen two Jesuits, at the hour for the play to begin, alight from their carriage at the door of the theatre, after devoutly taking their place in line.

We have said that at that apparition Bannière was so terrified that he lost no time in seeking a place of refuge in the lobby. His terror was so great that he had only taken time to espy the ends of their robes, and the crowns of their hats. These two extremities of the vestments of the reverend fathers were enough to make him quit his position with the utmost haste.

It would have been quite another matter, of course, if he had been able to guess at the identity of the illustrious persons by whom those robes and those hats were worn.

As for the good fathers, they did not see so much as the hem of the robe, and the hat-brim of Bannière; and with all our confidence in their penetration, we venture to say that, even if they had seen them, they would have been a long way from divining that among the three hundred young people in their charge, the one who darted off so quickly before them was the captive of the Chamber of Meditation.

Thus the worthy fathers entered the theatre without a thought of Bannière, and took possession of a little box with a grating in front, — a battery whence they could fire hot shot at Voltaire, and gather the spoils in tranquillity, thereby doubly benefiting the cause of religion.

Père de la Sante, who had confessed Champmeslé the day before, anticipated a certain degree of pleasure in seeing his penitent yielding to his weakness, and committing the sin he so abhorred; and although the

confessor had been indulgent, the critic threatened to be
correspondingly severe.

Just as his eyes beneath their thick black brows
were beginning to glitter with hostility, which in this
excellent man had a touch of good-humor, the orator of
the troupe disturbed his pleasant anticipations by announcing the indisposition of Champmeslé and the obliging
offer of a substitute.

The good fathers grumbled a little; but they, like all
the others, had to submit patiently, and becoming interested during the progress of the first two acts, where
much is said about Hérode, but he does not appear, they
had almost forgotten the substitution when the Syrian
King made his entrée in the third act.

This entrée, which we described in its proper place,
made as deep an impression upon the two reverend
fathers as it had done upon the rest of the audience; but
after a few seconds, strange thoughts began to pass
through the minds of both.

The voice, the gait, and what could be seen of the
face (the beard and the wig, it will be remembered, concealed a large part of it), — all these reminded the Jesuits
of some person of their acquaintance, but so vaguely and
indistinctly, and it was such a far cry from Hérode clad
in silk and velvet to Bannière in his black robe and
sugar-loaf hat, that both exhausted the whole list of
their acquaintances without thinking of Bannière. But
all of a sudden, by a gesture, the pronunciation of a
word, or a familiar mannerism, the débutant betrayed
himself to each of them, so that each said to himself
instantaneously, but still under his breath, for neither
dared to put in words so absurd an idea: "It is
Bannière!"

The result was that a few seconds after that ray of

light had shone in upon their minds, Hérode having by a bit of fine declamation and an impassioned outburst won the admiration of the pit, and aroused a tempest of applause, Père de la Sante, so far carried away by his artistic temperament as to join in the demonstration so sweet to an actor's ear, cried aloud, —

"That rascal played Isaac altogether too well not to make a good Hérode some day!"

This exclamation fell in so well with the thought which was springing up in Père Mordon's mind, that he turned his blazing eye upon Père de la Sante, and demanded, seizing him by the arm, —

"Is it not he?"

"I confess," replied the writer of Latin tragedies, "that if you refer to a resemblance — "

"Extraordinary, is it not?"

"Miraculous."

"Between this actor and little Bannière?"

"Between this actor and little Bannière, yes."

"It strikes you then as it does me?"

"That is to say that I would swear to it, if — "

"So would I, if I were not silenced by a doubt."

"What is it?"

"Why I locked Bannière up in the Chamber of Meditation."

"Yourself?"

"Myself."

"Well?"

"Well," said Mordon, smiling, "you know, my brother, that there are excellent locks on the doors of that apartment."

"That is a good reason," muttered Père de la Sante; "and yet — "

"And yet?"

"It is so exactly his voice, his step, his gesture; and I am so familiar with them too, for I made the rascal rehearse — "

"Do me a favor, my brother."

"At your service, reverend sir."

"Go to the novitiate and find out."

Père de la Sante made a wry face. To be disturbed in his pleasant occupation was not agreeable to him; and his conviction that Hérode and Bannière were one and the same person began suddenly to weaken perceptibly.

"The more I consider, reverend sir," said he, "the more I think that we are mistaken. Look again at the fellow on the stage."

"I am looking at him," said Père Mordon.

"Well, that man is a consummate actor, while little Bannière has never walked the boards in his life."

"Except under your direction."

"Oh, a college performance is not enough to educate a man for the stage."

"Very true; and yet — "

"Look again, sir; this man before us has command of gesture, majestic bearing, and real eloquence; little Bannière could not have all that."

"Hum!" rejoined Père Mordon, "a true calling gives to some what long practice sometimes denies to others."

"Agreed, agreed! but just see how the eyes of that actor devour Mariamne! see how languishing and affectionate is Mariamne's manner toward this Hérode whom she ought to abhor! I, who confess many lovers, can assure you those eyes have long known one another."

"Very well; but why should not Bannière, who is so perverted, have known this actress for a long while?" demanded Père Mordon.

" Because if he knew her, I should have heard of it, " said Père de la Sante.

" You would have heard of it ? "

" To be sure, for I am his spiritual director. "

With this the discussion came to an end, and the Latin tragic poet was left to contemplate the French tragedy in peace. After a subdued exclamation, which told of suspicion almost dispelled, Père Mordon also began to attend to the action of the play once more; but his remaining doubts were more openly displayed, because he had no reason to conceal them.

These doubts lasted as long as the play.

When the curtain fell for the last time, the two Jesuits hurried back to the novitiate.

Everything was quiet about the house; there was no indication of that commotion which is always caused among those in authority by the discovery of an escape or a scandal.

Nevertheless this appearance of security only half reassured Père Mordon, who could not banish the thought that Hérode and Bannière were the same man. He was no sooner in the porch than he began the solution of his doubts.

" Has supper been carried to the novice in meditation ? " he asked.

" Why, my father," replied the person addressed, " your Reverence did not so order. "

" True enough.   Is there some one in the corridor ? "

" The watchman, as usual. "

" A lantern, and let some one light me thither ! "

The attendants obeyed.

When he saw the locks all in position, and the door quite intact, Mordon smiled, and De la Sante rubbed his hands.

"We were mistaken," said the latter: "*induxit nos diabolus in errorem.*"

"When one escapes," rejoined Mordon, less easily reassured, "it is seldom by the door."

"But there are no windows in the Chamber of Meditation," said Père de la Sante.

"*Fingit diabolus fenestras ad libitum,*" retorted Mordon.

"Bannière!" called Père de la Sante. "Bannière! Bannière!"

Each time that he called he raised his voice a tone.

But Bannière could not reply.

The two Jesuits looked at one another, as who should say, —

"Oho! Will Hérode and Bannière turn out to have been the same man, after all?"

The question must be decided one way or the other; and by order of Père Mordon the door was opened.

Then the sad spectacle of the unmasked window, the torn hangings, the lacerated and maltreated inscriptions, burst upon the sight of Père Mordon and Père de la Sante.

"It was indeed he whom we saw as Hérode," said the former, with an angry ejaculation. "I suspected it not only from the way he declaimed his lines, but because I heard him prompting all the others. The villain when he handed me the copy of the play admitted that he knew it all by heart."

"Mea culpa, mea culpa!" cried Père de la Sante, beating his breast.

"Here's another villain," said Père Mordon, "who would like to escape us as that accursed Arouet has."

"Oh, so far as that goes," rejoined Père de la Sante, "you need have no fear. The villain — and he is a villain indeed — has only one resource; rabbit or fox, he must come back to his hole. Very well, teach him to play such tricks again by taking away his rope; he will be at his wits' end, for he reckons doubtless upon getting in the same way he went out. Cut these strips of tapestry, and the fugitive will be compelled to knock at the door, shamefaced and contrite."

"Take away his rope!" cried Mordon, eagerly. "Why, you are mad! rather than take it away, I would substitute for it a silken ladder with steps, if I could find one. The only question is, will he come back?"

"For God's sake, what do you suppose will become of him?" asked Père de la Sante, unfeignedly dismayed at the thought, then first occurring to him, that Bannière might have taken wing forever.

"I don't know what may become of him," retorted Père Mordon, "but I do know that he ought to be here before this."

"Perhaps he sees our light," said the other, "and it is that which alarms him."

"Yes, that may be so; and yet — But no matter, put out the light."

The light was put out, and they waited nearly a quarter of an hour, during which time Père Mordon did not vouchsafe a word in reply to the impatient suggestions of his companion.

Finally he said, —

"Well, he will not return at this hour: we have only one chance, and that is that he has passed the time we have been waiting here in exchanging his profane garb for his Jesuit's suit. Will you go to the theatre, Père de la Sante?"

"I?" said the father; "that seems hardly judicious."

"Why so?"

"Because they will recognize me and put him on his guard."

"You are right. Send the two servants; only let them not lose an instant."

The two fathers left the Chamber of Meditation, and found the two servants in the corridor.

"Go at once to the theatre," said Mordon; "ascertain whether the Jesuit who entered by the actors' lobby has or has not come out. If he has, return here; if he has not, hide in the lobby, seize him when he passes, and bring him here; gag him, if necessary, but bring him at all hazards."

Père Mordon uttered these words with the incisive brevity of a judge pronouncing a sentence which he wishes to have carried out without delay and without variation. The two servants were off at the word, and ran at the top of their speed to the theatre.

They arrived as the last stage-lights were being put out; and having learned from the concierge that he had not seen the novice who had come in go out again, they ambuscaded themselves in the lobby through which the actors usually emerged one by one, and there, hidden in the shadow, they lay in wait for their prey.

XVI.

A SOUL SAVED FOR A SOUL LOST.

BUT it was written on high, in the book of small causes and great results, that that day was to witness as many incidents, burlesque or tragic, as it contained hours.

During the last act of the play — just as the curtain fell, in fact, and when the whole company were crowding around the débutant to congratulate him — a man of sombre mien, pale and dishevelled, had passed through the deserted lobby, slowly mounted the rough stairs, and, without looking to right or left, or before or behind, guided by the mechanical instinct which makes it natural for one to do, without any effort or participation of the will, such things as one is accustomed to do every day, he had reached the corridor upon which the actor's dressing-rooms opened.

This man was Champmeslé himself, weary and crestfallen, worn out by wandering like a madman through the darkest and loneliest streets of Avignon; Champmeslé, who had gone up and down more than two thousand steps perhaps during the evening, and who, having come to the end of his dreams and fears and prayers, and of his strength as well, had made up his mind to return to the theatre, — in the first place, to find out what had happened; secondly, to ask pardon of his comrades for the wrong he had done them in compelling them to submit to a pecuniary loss; and thirdly and lastly, having obtained their forgiveness, to go to sleep,

and receive when he awoke, with mind refreshed, some
inspiration from above.

It is true that he could hear in the distance, in the
direction of the stage, the clamor of many voices; but
they had no very definite character, and might pass for
murmurs of discontent as well as for applause : so Champmeslé continued to walk toward his dressing-room.

Actuated by such sentiments as we have described, and
more disposed than ever to do penance, he entered that
room, the very tabernacle of his iniquity.

He was hardly within the door when his eye fell upon
the clothes of the Jesuit lying upon a chair, neatly
folded, and forming a sort of pyramid, upon which was
the regulation sugar-loaf hat, carefully brushed by the
theatre-boys.

At this sight Champmeslé uttered a cry of surprise.
He could not believe his eyes; he looked at the things
more carefully, and touched them; finally, convinced
that they were not painted but real clothes, as they say
in theatrical parlance, he raised his hands to heaven and
fell on his knees.

These garments which had been substituted for his
Hérode costume, and were waiting for him there in his
dressing-room, seemed to Champmeslé nothing more nor
less than an indication from on high of the path he was
to tread.   He remembered nothing of his encounter with
Bannière in his Jesuit's dress, and he was very far from
imagining that Bannière had been carried off by force
to the green-room, and led in leash by the bright eyes
of Mademoiselle Olympe, to play the part of Hérode.
He took no steps to ascertain, and asked no questions.
This coat was in his eyes the proof of his calling, the
symbol of God's will; a Jesuit's robe descended from
heaven into the dressing-room of an actor, was a much

more convincing revelation than a dream. Providence in
dealing with him had improved upon the hereditary
visions of the family. No more doubt, no more hesitation! The coat! the coat!

From that moment he forgot his fatigue, his hesitation vanished. In the twinkling of an eye he threw off
his own clothes; he donned Bannière's frock and breeches,
put the novice's hat upon his head, and went forth with
an air of exaltation, while his former comrades were on
their way to the green-room to do honor to Monsieur de
Mailly's banquet.

But Champmeslé had barely taken ten steps in the
dark corridor, reciting the five Paters and five Aves
which Père de la Sante had imposed upon him as a
penance, when the hirelings of Père Mordon, seeing a
Jesuit approach them in the half light, and reasoning
that there could be no other Jesuits than themselves and
Bannière abroad at midnight, cast themselves upon him,
one forcing his hat down over his eyes, while the other
tied a handkerchief across his mouth, and both uniting
in dealing him divers vigorous blows in the ribs; then
they carried him off, as two hawks might do with a
sparrow they had been hunting in company.

Ten minutes later they reached the novitiate, without
having attracted the attention of passers-by, who were
very few at that late hour.

As they were expected, the door opened and closed
again behind them almost before they had knocked; and
at the same instant the triumphant exclamations of the
two servants and the porter announced that Bannière
was taken, and was once more within the walls of the
novitiate.

"Who is it?" asked Père Mordon from the threshold
of the door where he was waiting.

"It is he, Bannière, the fugitive!" cried eight or ten voices at once.

"Good!" said the superior; "take him up to the Chamber of Meditation."

Père Mordon's commands were obeyed to the letter; and the unhappy Champmeslé, still mistaken for Bannière, was carried bodily to the Chamber of Meditation, and deposited upon the floor, after performing which operation the servants withdrew, at a sign from the superior, carrying with them a smile and an approving word.

Meanwhile the sufferer, bound and gagged, and with his hat jammed down over his eyes, was no sooner released by his tormentors, than he rolled over on the floor, gasping for breath, and trying to get rid of the handkerchief which was suffocating him. De la Sante, who was soft-hearted at bottom, did his best to assist him; and the hat was first removed, then the handkerchief.

"It's not Bannière!" cried the superior.

"It's Champmeslé!" cried De la Sante.

They both stood, lost in wonder, gazing at the actor, while he, sitting on the floor, with haggard eyes, arms hanging by his side, and knees almost up to his nose, looked from one to the other, recognizing neither, ignorant whither he had been carried, utterly at a loss to comprehend what had befallen him, and vainly asking himself who these two persons were who had done him a good and a bad turn.

At last he recognized the dress; from the dress he went on to recognize the men, and thence the house. God was still manifesting himself to him, since he had brought him by force to the very place to which he would have been only too glad to come, if he had been sure of a welcome. He leaped to his feet, and then fell back to a kneeling posture, with the facility of an acrobat, seizing a hand of each of the fathers.

"Oh, God be praised," said he, "for bringing me to your arms!"

At this apostrophe Mordon and De la Sante crossed themselves, exchanging a look of mute interrogation.

As the most obscure things in the world, even Spanish intrigues, are always explained in the end, the two Jesuits at last disentangled the complicated web of this affair. They left Champmeslé in the Chamber of Meditation, with the doors wide open, with no fear of his running away; and while De la Sante remained behind with full powers in case of emergency, Père Mordon hastened to the governor of the city to have official bloodhounds with keener scent than those of the novitiate put upon Bannière's trail.

The magistrate, who had been much entertained at the play, was still more entertained when he learned who the leading actor was; and his orders to seize Bannière wherever he should be found were accompanied with shouts of laughter.

The governor was welcome to cause Bannière's arrest laughing or not, for aught Père Mordon cared, provided only that Bannière was arrested; so he thanked the governor for his compliance, and was politely shown to the door by him, still in high good-humor.

Thus at the hour to which our story has advanced, everybody had succeeded according to his desire. Bannière was by Mademoiselle Olympe's side, Champmeslé was making great strides in the way of salvation, and Père Mordon was in a fair way to recover his novice. The governor laughed his heartiest as he set his archers on the culprit's track; so that Voltaire, the moving cause of all this turmoil, would have cried, if he had seen it.

as he cried twenty years later, that everything was for the best in the best possible of worlds.

The first to find himself at odds with that maxim was poor Bannière.

The gentle reader will remember that we left him radiant with happiness in Olympe's boudoir, with dilated eyes and clasped hands, and on the point of falling upon his knees, when a sudden and violent blow upon the door made him jump.

This interruption evidently portended something serious. Olympe jumped too, and signalled to Bannière with her hand to listen.

A second blow, more vigorous than the first, followed it almost immediately.

Olympe ran to the window; while Bannière, divining instinctively that this nocturnal visit had something to do with him, remained like a statue in the posture in which the first blow of the knocker had surprised him.

Olympe raised the shade, softly opened the window a little way, and peeped out between the cracks of the blind.

Through the open window Bannière could hear a confused sound as of measured steps, and words spoken in a low tone.

Olympe, without speaking, beckoned to him to come to the window; and with three steps he was at her side, looking out through the same opening.

Beneath the window were some ten or twelve men, some armed and some unarmed, while a carriage drawn by two horses stood in the shadow of a *porte-cochère*.

"What do you say to that?" asked Olympe of Bannière, in a voice so low that he guessed at her words from the breath which he felt on his face, rather than from any sound.

"Alas, Mademoiselle!" said Bannière, with a sigh. "I say that all those fellows have the appearance of wishing no good to King Hérode."

"Yes, that's so," returned Olympe; "they can smell a Jesuit a league away. Tell me, have you the least inclination to return with those miserable black-coated fellows?"

"Oh, Mademoiselle," cried Bannière, somewhat louder than was prudent, "I would go to the end of the world to escape them!"

"'Sh!" whispered Olympe; "they heard you."

Indeed, a commissioner, easily recognized by his stiff assumption of authority and the ill-temper he displayed at having been disturbed in his sleep, — a detestable commissioner in black, flanked by two acolytes in gray, — raised his head, and, leaving the group, came under the balcony.

"Come, come," said Olympe, "we have no time to lose; it is indeed you whom they're after. Luckily the door is a stout one, and we have at least ten minutes before us, before they will burst it open."

"Do you think that they will burst it?" asked Bannière.

"They certainly will; but in ten minutes one can do many things; that is to say," added Olympe, looking at Bannière, "when one does n't lose one's head."

"Mademoiselle," said Bannière, "only one thing could make me lose my head, and that thing is the misfortune of displeasing you; but, assured of your approval and sympathy, I would face the whole world."

"Well said!" Olympe rejoined. "Come."

"But it is my costume which embarrasses me," said Bannière, pointing to King Hérode's magnificent cloak.

"Go and change it then," said Olympe, hurrying Bannière back into the dressing-room.

She opened a great wardrobe, hidden behind the hangings, and Bannière found himself in presence of a complete outfit.

"Dress yourself without losing a second," said Olympe, "and I will do the same. You have five minutes for your toilet."

As she spoke a third blow, more vigorous than the others, resounded upon the door; and the solemn words were heard, —

"In the king's name, open!"

XVII.

FLIGHT.

THESE words were a sharper spur to Bannière than Olympe's injunction had been. In five minutes his toilet was finished, and he was just about to return in triumph to Olympe's apartment, when a charming little cavalier appeared on the threshold.

Bannière made an exclamation of surprise, for he did not recognize Olympe in her male garb until a second glance.

"Oh," he cried, "how lovely you are!"

"You shall tell me that later, my dear Bannière, and I will listen to you with great pleasure, I confess, for that sentence is one of those of which a woman never grows weary; but for the moment we have no time to lose in compliments. Come."

"Where?"

"How do I know? Wherever it shall please chance to lead us."

"To lead *us*, did you say? Pray, are you coming with me?"

"Certainly I am," replied Olympe.

"You love me then?" Bannière asked.

"I don't know whether I love you, but I do know that you are going to leave this house, and so am I. Come, are you ready?"

"Oh, am I!" cried Bannière; "I rather think I am!"

"Then," said Olympe, "not a word; do as I do, and follow me."

She went to her secretary and opened it. Monsieur de Mailly's two thousand louis were there in neat piles, — one thousand in rolls of one hundred louis each, and one thousand in notes payable to bearer.

"Take the gold," said Olympe, "and I will take the paper;" and while Olympe was stuffing her pockets with paper, Bannière was stuffing his with gold.

"Is it all right?" said Olympe.

"Yes."

"Now, take this."

"What is it?"

"My jewel-case; be careful of it."

"Never fear; but what are you looking for now?"

"A ring."

"Oh, yes!" sighed Bannière, "Monsieur de Mailly's. I think I saw it on the chimney-piece."

He ran his hand along the marble slab. "Here it is," said he.

"Give it to me," said Olympe; and she slipped it on her finger.

"Listen!" said Bannière.

"What! quickly! quickly!" cried Olympe; "the door is yielding."

"What shall we do now?"

"Do as the door is doing," said Olympe, with a fascinating smile.

She seized Bannière's hand and drew him along.

"But you don't mean it, do you?" asked Bannière in terror; "we are going right toward them."

"Trust to me," said Olympe; so he followed her into a corridor at one end of which was the staircase. A cabinet opened upon the corridor; and into it Olympe pushed Bannière, following close upon his heels.

They were hardly in the cabinet, when the staircase

re-echoed the hurried steps of the commissioner and his archers, who, arousing the entire establishment, called forth shrieks of terror from Claire and Olympe's other women.

But the hurricane passed without pausing at the door of the cabinet; and Olympe, having locked the door through which they had entered, opened another door giving access to a narrow stairway which led into a dark passage, and that in turn to a garden.

The fresh air blowing upon his face of itself made Bannière breathe more freely.

The two runaways glided under the lime-trees, until they came to a gate, and found themselves on the slope of a deserted street, through which Olympe hurried her companion.

Both were running too fast to make conversation practicable; but as they were hand in hand, they talked with their hands instead of with their mouths. Through street after street they passed, and from square to square, still running, until they came to the Ousle gate, which remained open all night.

Once without the gate they found themselves on the bank of the river, whose proximity was made evident to them by the coolness of the air even before they saw the pearly gleam through the dark trees of the promenade.

Bannière was darting off in the direction of the wooden bridge; but instead of following his lead, Olympe drew him off to the right, and began to climb down the bank like a school-boy on a marauding expedition.

Bannière followed her passively. Poor Bannière! With a silken thread she could have led him to the seventh circle of hell.

The two young people, then, were within a hundred paces of the river-side. Olympe went straight to a small boat, the padlock of which she unlocked with a key she had been careful to take with her. They took their places in the boat.

"Do you know how to row?" she asked the young man.

"Luckily, yes," said Bannière. "When we used to go upon the river, I always did the rowing."

"Good!" said Olympe, laconically. "Row away, then."

Bannière took an oar in each hand, and bent manfully to his task.

It was no child's play, — the Rhone is broad and swift at the point where our two fugitives undertook to cross it; but Bannière had said no more than the truth: he was strong and vigorous, and also had a certain measure of skill in the management of his oars.

Sweating, and breathing hard, and with blistered hands, he accomplished the passage, without allowing his bark to drift too far down stream.

Nothing had appeared behind them to make them think that they were pursued.

Arrived on the opposite bank, Olympe, who had acted as pilot during the voyage across, fastened the painter to one of the posts of a little pier which she recognized, leaped ashore with the aid of Bannière's hand, and started off at a run again in the direction of Villeneuve-les-Avignon.

Bannière ran by her side, without asking any questions.

However the two fugitives were not obliged to run all the way to the village which could be seen, shining white in the darkness, on the hillside. Olympe, some two hundred paces from the first straggling houses, halted, quite breathless and exhausted, but still smiling, before a picturesque little cottage half covered with spreading vines.

Bannière halted beside her.

"Knock at that shutter," said Olympe.

Bannière's one thought was to obey. He knocked hard enough to bring the walls down.

"Call, 'Père Philémon!'" continued Olympe.

And Bannière shouted in stentorian tones, "Père Philémon!"

An old man's voice answered within.

"There he is! Wait!" said Olympe.

She sat down upon a wooden bench against the wall.

Soon another sound was heard within the house,—the sound of the heavy step and shuffling sandals of Père Philémon.

At this sound Olympe struck three light blows upon the shutter.

"Ah, is it you, Mademoiselle Olympe?" said a tremulous voice.

"Yes, it is I, Père Philémon," replied Olympe.

"All right! I will open the door."

"It isn't worth while. Just wake Laurent, and tell him to saddle the two horses without losing a minute."

"And you?"

"Oh, I will wait here."

"Very well," replied the old man.

And the sandals went scuffling back toward the interior of the house.

"Olympe, Olympe," whispered Bannière, breathing for the second time only since the archers had knocked at the door, "what has happened to us, *mon Dieu!* and what is that secret passage through which we succeeded in making our escape from the house?"

"Why, it is a hidden door, that's all, my dear Bannière."

"The existence of the door was unknown, then?"

"Yes, except to Claire, Monsieur de Mailly, and myself."

Bannière sighed.

"And the boat on the river?"

"That boat belongs to the little Cabaret de la Berge,— a place little known to novices, I fancy, but very familiar to lovers, who go there to dine under the green arbors, and use the boat after dinner for a little turn on the river."

"Then you used to go on the river?" said the novice, whose heart sank deeper and deeper at each revelation made by Olympe.

"Yes, Monsieur de Mailly was very fond of this excursion," replied the young woman, tranquilly.

"And Père Philémon," said Bannière, humbly; "would it be indiscreet to ask you who Père Philémon is?"

"Not the least in the world. Père Philémon is an old servant of Monsieur de Mailly, who gave him this pretty little cottage, two acres of vineyards, and two horses, which we used from time to time in our excursions, and which we will use to-day for our flight."

Bannière sighed again, more deeply than ever.

"Well, what is it?" Olympe asked.

"Oh, well," rejoined Bannière, looking gloomily at his sleeves, "I know, of course, that I have no right to sigh about that, when all that I have, even to the clothes on my back, belongs to that gentleman."

As he spoke, Bannière looked at Olympe, as if to say to her, "Yes, everything, everything, even my clothes, even you!"

Olympe frowned, as if to plough in her own mind a furrow as deep as that which jealousy was ploughing in the heart of the novice.

But Bannière saw the cloud gathering on her brow,

and gave her no time to reflect, throwing himself at her feet with real ardor.

"Olympe," he cried, "whatever happens, receive the vow which I make you. You have sacrificed everything for me, and my life belongs to you. If you love me, — which I do not dare to hope, in truth, for in what way have I been able to attract you? — but if you love me, I, for my part, worship you! Even when you should no longer love me, — and that day would be the most wretched of my life, — you would none the less be in my eyes a divine being, the queen of my whole existence. You have drawn me up to your level; I will be worthy of you, and you shall not regret, I swear to you, the exchange you have made of the handsome, refined gentleman for the poor novice."

"The handsome gentleman who abandoned me," said Olympe, gently, giving Bannière her hand to kiss. "Have no anxiety," she continued, "and consider yourself bound in the future only by your love. You are under no engagement with me, and on the day when, like Monsieur de Mailly, you cease to love me, like him you will be free. Be sure of this, my dear Bannière; you have attracted me, I think that I love you, at all events I hope that I shall love you. While Monsieur de Mailly remained my master, you could never have been aught to me. Now I am free. Love me if you wish, love me as much as you wish; that can do no harm. I consider you a clever, lovable fellow, and accept you as such. All that you do not know of the world, of men and things, you will soon learn. If, when you are more knowing, you are not a still better fellow than you are now, I shall be much mistaken, it will be my own fault, and the punishment will fall on me. It is enough. Let us talk no more of these paltry

things. The life of two lovers ought to date only from
the day when they first met; before that they did not
exist, because they did not know each other. The past
then is wiped out. Look! see what a beautiful, mild
day it is going to be; it will be the first day of our life.
As they say on the stage, all the rest has been put far
behind us. Let us not raise the rear curtain behind
which all the broken scenery and useless stage properties
are thrown. Do you hear the horses neighing? They
are in the courtyard. Give me your hand and look at
me. Good! you love me. Let things take their course,
— when you no longer love me, you will not need to tell
me so."

Bannière grovelled at Olympe's feet, kissed them and
her hands a million times, while Père Philémon, opening
his shutter and his door, appeared in *déshabillé*, and
offered Olympe a glass of Cahors wine and a piece of
cake, smiling hospitably the while.

Then he extended the same courtesy, except that the
glass and the cake were both larger, to Bannière.

Olympe asked Bannière for one of the rolls of gold
with which his pockets were lined, opened it, put a
double louis in Père Philémon's hand, a louis in
Laurent's, leaped fearlessly upon her horse, while Bannière mounted his rather timidly; and the two, fully
informed as to the road, took that which ascends the
right bank of the Rhone and leads to Roquemaure, after
they had arranged with Père Philémon as to the inn at
which they should leave the horses.

While they are galloping along lovely roads which the
summer has not yet had time to turn into mere gutters of
dust, lovely roads bordered with sloping banks of turf,
silver-leaved olive-trees, and blooming gardens; while
they are joyously inhaling the fresh, free air of the

morning, and hastening toward the unknown future which is always eluding one's grasp and vanishing like a phantom, we will devote a few lines of hypocritical compassion to the poor archers and unlucky commissioner, who were vying with one another in rummaging about in cabinets and bedrooms and wardrobes, in stairways, cellars, attics, and stables, in courtyards and gardens and sheds, and who finally, happily an hour too late, stumbled upon the secret door, — a discovery which evoked cries of rage, imprecations, and oaths strong enough to scandalize the Jesuits even, in whose interest they had undertaken this disagreeable task which succeeded so ill.

It is almost useless to add that the governor, when he learned of Père Mordon's discomfiture, laughed more heartily than ever.

A very delightful character was this governor of the catholic, apostolic, and Roman city of Avignon.

XVIII.

REST.

LET not our readers be astonished at the speed with
which our lovers — even Bannière, who was by no means
at home in the saddle — left the leagues behind them in
the early morning hours.   It was of the utmost importance to them to get beyond the limits of the jurisdiction
in which the offence had been committed as quickly as
possible; for the evasion of a novice was an offence subject to severer penalties at Avignon, a Roman city, than
elsewhere.

Olympe and Bannière rested awhile at Roquemaure,
where they left their horses at the inn agreed upon with
Père Philémon; they then crossed the Rhone to Orange,
and thence set out in a comfortable post-chaise for Lyons,
— a city of considerable size, and sufficiently populous and
liberal to enable two well-to-do and happy lovers to abide
there without being disturbed or disturbing others.

Olympe, who was well used to breaking camp and
pitching her tent in a new place, went in search of lodgings, and succeeded in finding, in the very heart of the
city, near the Place des Terreaux, made memorable by
the execution of Cinq-Mars and De Thou, a little
house furnished throughout, which was waiting for
wealthy tenants, with wood in the cellar, wine in the
bins, and linen in the linen-chest; a house, indeed, made
expressly, not for a grave, devout, old-fashioned hermit,
but for two lazy, joyous hermits, fond of good cheer.

The price of this house, all furnished, just as it stood, with its doors thrown hospitably open and spits turning before the fire, was four thousand livres per year. Olympe informed Bannière, who was stupefied at the enormity of the sum, that it was the very best of bargains for the tenants, and the very worst for the owner, and that she could hardly believe that such a prize had really fallen at the first attempt into the hands of two reprobates, whom the Jesuits did not hold in the highest consideration, and whom they ought certainly by their maledictions to have involved in the everlasting disfavor of Providence.

They paid the rent for two quarters in advance; they paid for the wine and wood, for everything, in short, that was necessary to insure them six months of undisturbed happiness; and when Bannière saw another gold louis make its way from his store into the pockets of a stranger, — which was happening every moment we must say, — and when he would follow it with his eyes as far as possible, Olympe would say laughingly, —

"What we bought was necessary, was it not?"

"Why, yes," would be Bannière's reply; for he did not know what it was to have a different opinion from Olympe.

"And whatever is necessary contributes to our happiness, does it not?"

"To be sure," Bannière would reply again, gazing at Olympe in a way to demonstrate to her that she was necessary to him beyond everything else.

"Happiness is the end which man ought to seek here on earth?"

"And we have found it!" Bannière would cry.

"Very well, then, so long as we are happy, what are you worrying about, my friend?"

"Ah! I am worrying about the duration of our happiness."

"You do wrong, then; you admit that you are happy, — and that is a thing which human beings rarely admit, — thank Providence for it, and ask nothing more."

"You are my Providence!" Bannière would whisper.

He was an apt scholar, with abundant inclination to learn; and in the course of a week he had mastered Olympe's whole system of philosophy, — had mastered it so thoroughly that at the end of the week she had nothing more to teach him, whereas he began, in his turn, to lay a hand upon the money, and to spend it as freely and with as keen an eye to the necessities of life as his mistress.

In Bannière's eyes (we must give him due credit), the great necessity of life was the adoration of his love, — absolute, idealized, noble.

At first he wanted to cover Olympe with jewelry and ornaments. She reminded him that her jewels were as beautiful as those of any woman on earth. Nevertheless Bannière persisted, until she threatened to buy for him twice as much as he bought for her.

"Very well," said Bannière, "no more buying. I like jewels, but only for you. If I had jewels, I would like to have them from you. Give me only that ring which you have on your finger."

"Which ring?" asked Olympe.

"That one," said Bannière, pointing to the ring which Monsieur de Mailly had left with the two thousand louis, and which Bannière, in all the hurry of the flight, had seen glistening on the chimney-piece.

It was a superb ruby, surrounded with diamonds.

Bannière pointed to it in a dogged way which indicated something more than the mere wish for the ring as such. His hand was already held out to receive it, for Olympe had never refused him anything. Surely she would not refuse the ring; for what was the paltry ruby which Bannière desired to her?

It must be said that during the month they had been together not the shadow of a cloud had passed across the pure azure of their heaven.

Bannière was much surprised, therefore, when he saw Olympe's eyes seek his at this request, and she asked, —

"Why do you want that ring, my friend?"

Bannière was so unprepared for the question that it disconcerted him.

"Why, because —" he stammered.

"That's no reason," said Olympe, with a smile.

Bannière smiled back at her, and replied, —

"I think it's the best reason I can give you, dear Olympe."

"Do you want a ring?"

"I should like one, but it must be like that."

"Very well! this ring is worth about a hundred louis; take a hundred louis, my friend, and go and buy one like it."

"*Mon Dieu!*" he exclaimed, "that ring is very precious to you, is n't it? It's easy to see that it came from Monsieur de Mailly!"

He pronounced the last words with an angry intonation, and awaited the result.

But she said very coolly, —

"To be sure, it came from Monsieur de Mailly What then?"

"Why, then I can understand that you will not give it to me; but I cannot understand why you wear it on your finger which so often touches mine."

"As to that, my friend, you are perfectly right," said Olympe.

She drew the ring from her finger, and put it away under the false bottom of the box in which she kept her jewels.

Bannière saw the ring disappear, and immediately began to regret that he had provoked so uncomfortable a scene between himself and his mistress, and a scene which was decidedly lacking in tact, since it awakened the hardly vanished memories of her earlier passion.

She sulked, and he sulked. Bannière's situation was absurd; so he took his hat and his sword, and went out for a turn on the quays in the fresh evening air.

As for Olympe she undressed and went to bed, after locking her door and stationing Claire before it as sentinel. Claire had been informed by Père Philémon, at Olympe's request, of her mistress's new domicile, and had succeeded in reaching Lyons in peasant costume without arousing the suspicions of the Jesuits.

When Bannière returned, he had invested in a huge emerald which cost one hundred and twenty louis; his reflections had driven him to that, for the lovesick wretch was for the moment in quest of a ring, and wished to make Olympe forget her ruby.

At the same time he wished to make her forget, and above all to forget himself, some words she had said upon Père Philémon's bench, — words of unfathomable depth, in whose mysterious darkness his restless love could see only ominous meaning.

"If, when you are more knowing," Olympe had said, "you are not even a better fellow than you are to-day, I shall be very much mistaken; it will be my own fault, and I shall have to pay for it."

Since those words were spoken, Bannière had become

deeply versed in the science of life; had he become a better fellow? He feared greatly that Olympe's conscience or her keen insight would reply in the negative.

"I am a poor wretch, then," he told himself, "I am a vulgar fellow, and am deserving of her in appearance only; she is deceived in me, and it may well be that after she has gone on for some time believing me to be of pure gold, she will recognize me some day as being as false as a counterfeit coin, or a piece of jewelry of base metal. When that day comes, she certainly will cease to love me."

He had therefore bought the emerald to prove to Olympe that he had a good disposition, and would be the first to seek a reconciliation.

But, as we have said, Claire was on guard. Bannière found her on the threshold; and she forbade his entering, because her mistress was asleep.

At once furious and ashamed, and almost in despair, Bannière shut himself up in his own room, where he passed half the night writing letters and tearing them up.

At last, worn out with fatigue, we had almost said with remorse, he went to sleep, with his elbows on the table and his head resting on his hands, while his unsnuffed candle trickled down the sides of the candlestick.

About two o'clock Olympe crept into his room, saw the torn letters, the guttering candle, and the sleeping Bannière.

She gazed at him a moment, graceful as a shadow in her white peignoir; she stooped over him, breathed a kiss upon his brow, which was furrowed even in his sleep, and without waking him sat down beside him in an easy-chair.

It happened that the sleeper, waking at daybreak
shivering with cold, chilled to the bone, generally miserable and cursing his unhappy fate, stumbled against
the easy-chair in which he proposed to finish his night's
sleep, and saw the smiling face of Olympe.

Straightway he fell at her knees, weeping bitterly and
beating his breast as he cried, —

" Oh, yes, she is better, a hundred times better,
than I ! "

Olympe accepted the emerald, and wore it for a while
upon her finger ; then she said to Bannière, —

" Your little finger is just the size of my third finger ;
I give you this emerald, and do you wear it for love
of me."

Bannière forthwith strutted like a peacock, and proceeded to dazzle all the females who took the air on the
grand Mall.

The next day after the nocturnal incident we have
described, Olympe noticed that Bannière was very deeply
preoccupied.

" What 's the matter ? " she asked.

Bannière looked up at her timidly.

" You have something to ask me," said Olympe.

" Yes," he replied, " I want to ask you if you will be
my wife."

Olympe smiled ; but the smile vanished at once, and
her face assumed an expression of the utmost seriousness.

" You are a dear fellow, Bannière," said she, " and I
do not for a moment doubt that it is with the firm purpose to make a happy woman of me that you ask me to
marry you ; but, fortunately or unfortunately, what you
ask is impossible."

" Why so ? " asked Bannière.

" If the lover was jealous of Monsieur de Mailly's

ring," said Olympe, "the husband might be jealous of something different."

"Olympe," cried Bannière, "I swear —"

"No oaths, my friend," said Olympe. Putting her hand over his mouth, she added, —

"Let us remain as we are; we are well enough so."

Bannière would have replied; but Olympe raised her finger with a smile, and everything was said. The question of marriage was not raised between them again.

What a fascinating life is that of lovers who are real lovers! How well they can do without any third person; how skilfully they brush aside all the dust and dried leaves and insects which threaten to fall into the nectar of their happiness!

During the first six months of their residence at Lyons Bannière and Olympe did not see a single strange face in their house. It is true that they had some reluctance to be seen, lest they might be recognized; but their principal reason for hiding themselves, if the fact were known, was their wish to be alone.

And then, too, Olympe had endless expedients which aroused Bannière's enthusiastic admiration; she conceived the idea of having musicians play symphonies in her antechamber during the hot weather, while she and Bannière remained invisible.

She loved riding, and to make little excursions of two or three days' duration in the neighborhood, in a comfortable carriage well stocked with provisions and cushions.

She loved whatever amused Bannière; and everything that she proposed amused him.

After six months of schemes for enjoyment each more ingenious than the last, our lovers, while seeking one day for a new one in the common purse, discovered that their store was reduced to a hundred and fifty louis.

That was barely enough to maintain the gait of the last six months for one month more.

Bannière looked at Olympe, and Olympe looked at Bannière; the latter, weighing the gold in his hand, remarked, —

"One hundred and fifty louis make three thousand six hundred livres."

"I was just making the same calculation," said Olympe, smiling.

"That is what many happy, yes, very happy people spend in a year. We have had, therefore, in our six months of happiness six years of such happiness as they have."

"Very true," said Olympe.

"But we have only one month of the same happiness left," continued Bannière.

"That might be so," said Olympe, "for lazy folk, but not for people who work!"

"Who work!" exclaimed Bannière, with surprise. "Do you propose to work, pray?"

"Indeed I do."

"At what, *mon Dieu?*"

"At my profession. Am I not an actress? Are you not an actor? Are there not two theatres at Lyons? Are there not a hundred theatres in France, if the two at Lyons want none of us? Finally, have n't we an income of twelve thousand livres ready to our hands in the parts of King Hérode and Queen Mariamne?"

"Death of my life! You are an enchantress!" cried Bannière, delirious with joy; "and everything you touch changes to gold."

"Then, too," added Olympe, "life is beginning to be a little stale; we are growing fat."

"That is true, upon my word!"

"Think of it! — travelling from city to city, changing one's residence continually, the applause, the study, the fascination of the art, the excitement — "

"You electrify me, Olympe! "

"And here we are economizing; idleness is ruining us; we lose all that we spend and all that we do not earn."

"Yes, we do indeed! "

"To-morrow morning, Bannière, go and find the manager of the theatre and bring him to me."

"I will, my dear."

"And meanwhile let us have a good time this evening, — a concert on the water all to ourselves, and — "

"And our love," cried Bannière. "Oh, how rich we are! "

XIX.

LIFE IN THE PROVINCES.

THE manager of the theatre came on the next day but one to call upon Olympe, whom Bannière had pointed out to him upon the promenade.

Our readers must not picture to themselves the manager of the period which we are trying to describe, as the autocrat with whom we of the present day are familiar, having his seraglio, his police, and his bullies.

In the seventeenth and eighteenth centuries to be the manager of a theatre was to be the constitutional arbiter of the destinies of an enterprise maintained by the combined talent of a dozen or more wandering artists, sometimes including a poet who was attached to the society.

A manager was then purely and simply the leading actor of his theatre, — so far as his responsibility was concerned.

Bannière had seen enough of actors; he had heard enough from Olympe, and had a sufficient store of natural cleverness and Bohemian instinct, to know what line to adopt in this great enterprise of alluring a theatrical manager.

He was careful not to tell him that Olympe was an actress who had already made her mark. He represented her as a girl of good family, who was stage-struck and ready to drop, head downward, into the managerial snare.

He did not lay stress upon Olympe's personal beauty and distinguished mien; he simply took him to the promenade, as we have said, and pointed Olympe out to him.

The manager saw her, was presented to her, saluted her, made an appointment, and made his appearance promptly at the hour named, — a sign of interest which very properly seemed of good augury to our lovers.

The manager, well used to such stories as Bannière had told him, believed as much of it as he chose; but when he was ushered into the sumptuous establishment of the two young people, when he was buried in the luxurious easy-chair they offered him, when he found himself amid flowers and the sweet perfumes of a boudoir, when from the boudoir he passed to the dining-room to refresh his inner man, when he perceived the silver plate and the crystal, when he had tasted the exquisite wines and toothsome sweetmeats, — he was so astounded that he made up his mind at once that the would-be débutante had not an idea about acting.

So he conceived the scheme of taking his fill of the pleasant odors, cheering himself up with the good wine, in short, enjoying a good hour of material felicity, and after the interview thanking with all his heart the generous hosts who were mad enough to dream of treading the boards when they had such soft carpets.

But Bannière and Olympe were as shrewd as he; they allowed him to indulge in such fancies as he chose, and then at dessert, when he was in comfortable trim, they begged him to listen to a specimen of the science of the new aspirants to dramatic renown.

The actor, at that proposal, bridled up, emptied his glass, and prepared for the conflict with a contemptuous smile.

Olympe saw the smile, interpreted the contempt, and patiently bided her time, sure of victory.

"Well, I will give you the cue," said the artist, in a sonorous voice. "What do you know?"

"What do *you* know?" asked Bannière.

"I! Oh, I know everything; I play the leading rôles. Select your best piece, and let 's see what you can do."

"Do you know 'Hérode et Mariamne'?" Olympe asked him in her mildest tones.

"Parbleu!" ejaculated the half-tipsy actor.

"Well," said Olympe, "begin where you choose."

"And I will prompt," said Bannière.

"Have you the prompt-book?" asked the manager.

"Oh! I don't need it; I know the whole play by heart."

"Very good," said the guest; "I will play Hérode."

"My part," interjected Bannière, with a smile.

The actor seemed in no wise disturbed at Bannière's announcement, and thundered out his lines in a hoarse voice.

Olympe replied.

But she had not recited ten lines before the old fellow began to open his ears.

"Oho!" he exclaimed.

"What is it?" asked Olympe, modestly; "have I made a mistake?"

"No, no, quite the reverse; keep on."

The manager leaned his elbows on the table, and fixed his eyes, glowing like coals, upon Mariamne, who resumed the thread of her part.

"Aha!" said he, "you have acted before now, have n't you?"

"Occasionally, yes," replied Olympe.

"Where?"

"Oh! here and there," Bannière answered for her, to avoid the necessity of lying.

"But do you know that you are simply superb, Mademoiselle?" shouted the drunken old fellow, with the deepest admiration; "upon my soul! you remind me of La Champmeslé!"

"Did you ever act with her?" asked Olympe, with a smile.

"Oh, I was employed at the theatre," said the manager.

"And you, Monsieur?" he resumed, addressing Bannière.

"You wish to hear me?"

"Yes."

"That's no more than fair."

With a deep voice and the terrifying wealth of gesticulation which characterized the old school, Bannière began the lines which accompany the *entrée* of Hérode.

The old actor listened in uncompromising silence; when he had concluded, he said, lengthening his lip, —

"Monsieur is not bad, but he still has much to learn."

"I will learn then," said Bannière.

"And to study."

"I will study."

"Not bad?" interrupted Olympe, coming to the rescue of her friend's self-conceit. "Come, come, my good friend, it's easy to see that you play the same parts."

"Besides," added Bannière, a little piqued, "we were only speaking about Madame, I think."

"You are mistaken, my dear," said Olympe, quickly; "on the contrary, we are speaking about both of us. He who has me will have you, or else he will not get me."

"Ah!" said the manager, "that complicates matters."

"Do you mean it?" asked Olympe.

"Yes, I must consult my associates. If only Madame were concerned, I would come to terms on my own responsibility, for our leading lady, La Catalane, is not strong enough; but as to Monsieur's line of parts, — the devil! that's a different matter."

"Is it your line?" asked Bannière.

"Call it our line," said the old fox.

"Well, what about your line?" Bannière persisted.

"Our line is already divided among three, and I must consult with the others."

"Listen!" said Olympe, who knew actors well from her long experience with them; "our bottles are empty, it is true, but the wine-cellar is not far away. Go and find those of your associates whose consent is indispensable; bring them here, for we can come to a better and more speedy understanding all together than separately. Besides, it is dinner-time, — we will dine together."

Bannière seized the occasion to open a screened door, through which floated treacherously such a delicious odor of roast meat, such a savory hint of *volaille farcie*, that the actor, his hesitation at an end, left the house, inhaling deep draughts of the seductive emanations from the kitchen, through nostrils whose abnormal dilatation plainly signified, "I will return."

And he did return, flanked by four leading members of his troupe, — three men and a woman.

The three men were pale, threadbare, and out at elbows; as old as their costumes: they were the financier, the noble father, and the first servant.

The woman was of Olympe's size, but less distinguished-looking, and with these further differences, that Olympe's eyes were blue, and hers black; Olympe was a blonde, and she a brunette; Olympe's complexion was fair and rosy, hers a dull brown; in every respect she was of the true Catalan type, to which fact, doubtless, she owed her name, La Catalane. In addition she had lovely hands and a figure which was excelled in grace by none but Olympe's.

Olympe received them all as comrades, put them at their ease with a word, seated them at table, and joined without the least ceremony, in the theatrical slang which was so foreign to her refined taste.

She asked the name and line of each one, smiling even more sweetly when she addressed the solitary female than when she addressed the men.

"La Catalane," she replied, showing a double row of little white teeth.

Olympe recommended La Catalane to the attention of Bannière.

The dinner was of the liveliest; everybody got a little tipsy except Olympe, who as she stooped to pick up her napkin at dessert saw one of La Catalane's tiny feet upon Bannière's foot, while with the other she was tapping that of her neighbor on the other side. Olympe blushed. She felt something like a serpent's tooth at her heart. But as she rose and glanced at innocent Bannière, she knew by his calm face that he was unconscious of his good fortune. She contented herself with holding out her hand to him; and Bannière rose with the greatest eagerness, and hastened to imprint a kiss upon it.

Under the influence of the good dinner, they recited verses and acted scenes of all sorts. At last Bannière brought pen, ink, and paper, and Olympe drew up a contract which the five associates signed.

She stipulated for a fixed salary of twelve hundred livres for herself, and an eighth of the profits for herself and Bannière. Her modest demands enchanted the whole party, and they separated most affectionately.

Olympe noticed that La Catalane kissed Bannière five times, while Bannière counted ten kisses bestowed by the actors upon Olympe.

When they had all gone, " You see, dearest," said she, without referring to the quintuple caress, but confining herself to the success of their project, — " you see that we are almost sure of six thousand livres a year."

" Yes; but they were too lavish with their kisses," retorted Bannière.

A last word which abundantly satisfied Olympe that she would do very wrong to harbor any malice against La Catalane.

From that moment Olympe thought only of her rôle and her début, which had been fixed for the following Thursday by the council of six.

XX.

IN WHICH A NEW CHARACTER APPEARS UPON THE HORIZON.

PROSPERITY, unfortunately, is one of those goddesses of uncertain temper and inconstant character, whose wings no mortal can flatter himself that he is able to bind, — a difficult operation, which no conqueror, except Cæsar, has ever succeeded in accomplishing with the Goddess of Victory.

Now it came to pass that Olympe made her début;

That she made a very successful début in a piece by an unknown author;

That there was a good deal of talk about her début, and that the talk brought crowds to the theatre;

That the coming of the crowds made the receipts very large.

It came to pass, in short, that Monsieur and Madame de Bannière as they were called, produced a very favorable impression upon the people of Lyons.

Hence they became famous, while formerly they had only been happy.

But their celebrity naturally led them to spend much more money than they had spent formerly.

They had to hold receptions, and to make some display, whereas up to that time their life had been absolutely secluded.

The end of the louis came at last. The receipts were very slow of passage from the purse of the partners into

that of Monsieur and Madame de Bannière. At the
end of every month there was interminable wrangling.
To judge from the remarks of the associates, the engagement of Olympe and Bannière was a burden to the
company.

Aside from these little difficulties, things went along
after a fashion. At the end of every month Bannière
solved the trouble by showing his teeth; and the men
paid because those teeth were so solidly set, and the
women because they were so white.

But it happened about this time that the king fell
sick, that his illness made a deep impression throughout
France, and that all forms of entertainment were arrested
by the news; and the theatres being the places of entertainment *par excellence*, they became more and more
deserted in proportion as the churches filled up.

Matters went on thus for two or three months, and
then, after an agonizing death-struggle, the troupe became
insolvent.

The contract of association was rendered null and void.

Then, when the theatres had recovered a little vitality
with the king's convalescence, the partners, once more
masters of the situation, dictated terms to Olympe and
Bannière to which they had to submit.

The doors were opened once more.

Olympe had become habituated to the life again, and
went back to the theatre with that ardor which real
artists bring to their work. Bannière, too, had nibbled
at the delights of applause, and, unsatisfying as that food
was compared with the juicy roasts which had courted
the manager's sense of smell, on the day of his first call
upon Olympe, he devoured it. Rather than not play
at all, they played for the wretchedly small salaries
which the association, a free corporation, accorded, in its

strict impartiality, to the artist who stood above the line, and the common strolling player, in equal portion.

Pecuniary embarrassment, with veiled face and uncertain step, crept into the establishment of Bannière.

Bannière perceived the privations which Olympe inflicted upon herself; accustomed as she was to living in luxury, narrow circumstances were a real hardship for her. He saw black rings gather around her eyes, her lips grow pale, and her hands fall listlessly at her sides.

As Olympe had predicted, Bannière had lived quickly, so to speak, and learned a great deal in a short time. In a year he had lived a whole lifetime. He knew the exact weight of joy in the heart, and he knew too how many joys a single sorrow can cause to wither.

Then from time to time jealousy bit savagely at Bannière's heart,— jealousy utterly without cause; but every one knows that the most terrible jealousies are those which have no reason for being.

This happened when Olympe was reaping a harvest of bravos and smiles upon the stage. He sometimes would be standing in the wings, and he would count the exquisites who were crowding around the fair creature.

And he would shudder to think that among all those red-coats he might encounter another Monsieur de Mailly, with his rouleaux of gold, his servants, his houses, his horses, and his love, at every turn.

If such a mishap ever should befall, what would become of him, Bannière, a mere puffed-up atom, magnified to the statue of a giant by that microscope of the soul which is called love?

Many times, while the adorable and adored creature was bowing her thanks for the flowers and shouts of applause, Bannière would ask himself how all those fine fellows who were parading about her came to be richer than he.

He remembered that he had read somewhere that
maxim which is none the less alluring for being all
wrong, —

"Those whom Providence forgets have the right to try
chance; he who has not God on his side is a great fool
not to make friends with the devil."

He remembered a complete system of philosophy which
he had thought out in the gloomy days of the novitiate,
a complete theory of free-will which he had thought out
in the cloudy days of his theatrical experience.

He said to himself that so long as a man could dispose
of his own skin, that man was as good as another; that
the skin was as good a stake as anything else; that, given
a louis, a man might risk the loss of that louis, with the
right to pay with his skin a second louis which he has
not, in order to win back the first louis which he no longer
has.

So Bannière took the only louis which was left in his
house, and went off to risk it at the gaming-table. He
won, as fresh hands always do win. One of the axioms
which Bannière was ignorant of, perhaps because it was
true, was that the devil has no snares set except for
novices in sin.

With his louis Bannière won fifty louis, which he carried away in triumph; and Olympe, marvelling greatly,
found them, on her return from the theatre, in the drawer
of her chiffonnier in place of the single louis she had left
there, and which she did not expect to find, having told
Claire to take it to pay expenses for the next two days.

We can understand how such a beginning drew Bannière on. And yet while the fifty louis lasted, and he
had no absolute need to play, he abstained. True it is,
that although he kept away from the gambling-house, the
game ran incessantly in his head. On the stage he heard

the clink of the gold, and would get confused or neglect his cue. Two passions cannot exist on good terms in a man's heart; one must consume the other in time. The passion for play consumed the passion for acting; Bannière was hissed, and went to the gaming-table for consolation.

In three months Bannière had become a regular stand-by and pillar of the gambling-house.

Olympe meanwhile continued to work for her associates; she worked for the valets, she worked for the financiers, she worked for the noble fathers, who bought wine and fuel with the price of her labor. She worked for La Catalane, who, thanks to Olympe, received over and above her earnings outside the theatre two hundred livres a month, upon which she dressed herself handsomely.

Olympe's toilet, on the other hand, suffered correspondingly. What was luxury for La Catalane was next door to poverty for Mademoiselle de Clèves. They still continued to maintain some outward show of prosperity, but real plenty had disappeared from the household. Olympe said to herself, with perfect truth, that solitude was the crowning point of wretchedness; and she kept the house full of people, so that their chatter might drive care away.

She invited people to the house because she saw that Bannière was being drawn away from her, because she felt lonely, and she knew that to invite people to her house was the surest way to recall him.

She hoped that Bannière would be jealous, and that the gambler, having won the battle with the actor, would in turn succumb to the lover.

It was a hard fight, and victory was uncertain. Bannière had become a gambler by profession; he brought

to the exercise of the trade all the skill which a man of
intelligence devotes to the success of what he undertakes;
he did not win more than another might have done, to
be sure, but he lost less.

Olympe also had been jealous. Perhaps, she had
thought, this gambling was only a pretext to cover up
some love-affair. So she had summoned Mademoiselle
Claire, and told her to bring the male costume in which
she had fled with Bannière. She had sadly put it on
once more, and followed her lover, almost ashamed of
what she was doing.

It was really to the gaming-table that he went. Olympe
hesitated a moment about following any farther; then she
made up her mind, and darted behind him into that hell
on earth.

When, after watching for half an hour, hidden in a
window-recess, she had seen what gambling was, she
made her escape, with pale cheeks and anxious heart.

So it was that when Bannière returned, instead of
receiving him coldly as she had done of late, she took his
hand, sat at his feet, and said to him in a tone as endear-
ing as a lover's, and as fondly persuasive as a mother's, —

"You have been gambling, dear."

"*Mon Dieu!* yes," said Bannière.

"And you have lost?"

"No!" he cried.

"But you have not won?"

"Oh, I ought to have won a thousand louis."

And he explained to her, with the feverish enthusiasm
of the gambler, all the grand coups he should have won
if luck had not been against him.

"Poor boy!" said Olympe, after listening to him attentively, and with the deepest pity; "such a world of
emotion and calculation and struggling and suffering!"

Olympe was always the same, — kind, loving Olympe; the tears came to his eyes.

"Go on," said he.

"Oh, *mon Dieu!*" said Olympe, "the conclusion is very easily reached. "You say that you neither win nor lose; so it's just as well not to play at all. Come, is it agreed? Don't go there and get your blood so heated; you will at least be economizing your vital force."

Bannière was about to cry, "It is for you;" but he checked himself.

He was still in love; so he was still generous and thoughtful.

Olympe went on: "We are not yet at the end of our resources; we still have jewels which we can sell."

"Oh," cried Bannière, "before the jewels, I should say the plate had better go."

"The plate? Oh, no!" said Olympe. "I can very well dress and go about without jewels; but without plate we can no longer receive."

"What! whom do you want to receive, in God's name?" said Bannière, who, as he was seldom at home, returning only when everybody had gone, did not know that Olympe received.

"I have a plan of my own," said Olympe. "You will not remain a gambler any longer than you remained an actor. Variety is a necessity for you. From a novice you became an actor; from an actor a gambler; from a gambler you will turn into a man of the world, a man of the sword perhaps, — how can I tell? And so you will continue until you have accomplished the last transformation of all, and become a magnificent butterfly."

"Alas!" rejoined Bannière, "up to this time, poor

Olympe, I have scarcely been more than a caterpillar beside you."

"My dear boy," said Olympe, "you have intelligence, education, and good manners; you are an eminent logician; you speak well —"

"What possible good will all that do me, if I have no one to give me a lift?"

"That's just it, my dear Joseph; some one will give you a lift."

"Who, for instance, might that some one be?"

"The Abbé d'Hoirac."

"The Abbé d'Hoirac?"

"Don't you know whom I mean?"

"No, upon my word, unless it's that hedge-priest who was always prowling about the wings on nights when you played, and was forever treading on my feet."

"That's the very man."

"What! that little wretch who is always fluttering about, humming and singing like a crazy cockchafer?"

"Indeed, that's a very good description of him," said Olympe, laughing heartily.

"Do you mean to say that I must seek the patronage of that half-fledged creature?"

"Ah, now you are unjust, Bannière; a goose, I grant you, but not half-fledged. Take him for all in all, the abbé is a fascinating little dandy, and it is plain that you have not noticed him carefully."

"But one would say that you had taken a good deal of notice of him, to make up for my neglect," retorted Bannière, who hardly knew how to take Olympe's pertinacity.

"What! more nonsense!" said Olympe.

"How in the deuce do you know him?"

"In the same way that I know quantities of people

whom you do not know. Every evening you go off to your game, and every evening the Abbé d'Hoirac comes to pass an hour or two at chess with me."

Bannière shook his head gloomily.

"You have convinced me," said he, "of the futility of my attempts to make our fortune at the gaming-table. To-morrow I will play chess with the Abbé d'Hoirac."

"And at that game, my dear, you will win instead of losing; I will answer for that."

"Is this Abbé d'Hoirac such a perfect creature, pray?" said Bannière, somewhat piqued.

"He is not perfect, my dear fellow, for there is no perfection in this world. But since I am reduced to the company of Claire and my hairdresser on days when I do not act, the society of this crazy cockchafer, as you call him, has not seemed to me a thing to be altogether despised."

"It is curious," said Bannière, "that I have never detected the striking merit of Monsieur l'Abbé d'Hoirac. To be sure, I have not paid much attention to him except when he has trodden upon my feet."

"You persist in harping upon the abbé's awkwardness, my friend; however, it is very natural. The abbé is near-sighted, so much so that he can't see the end of his nose. How can you expect him to see his feet, which are much farther from his eyes than the end of his nose is?"

"You are right, Olympe," said Bannière; "and the first time I meet the Abbé d'Hoirac I will look him in the eye."

"Very well, you will see a very pretty doll," said Olympe, coolly, passing into her dressing-room.

"When will Monsieur l'Abbé be here again? This evening?"

"No, I act this evening."

"To-morrow, then?"

"Yes, to-morrow."

"At what time?"

"At six o'clock, as usual."

"Very well, Madame."

Olympe looked askance at her lover, shrugged her shoulders, and put herself in the hands of her maid.

XXI.

THE ABBÉ D'HOIRAC.

THE evening arrived, and with the evening Madame de Bannière's usual guests.

Bannière did not go, as his custom was, to the gambling-hell. He proposed to make the acquaintance of this Abbé d'Hoirac, of whom he had heard so much.

He saw him come in as the clock struck six; it was his regular hour.

This delightful creature caused his presence to be announced, in the first place by two servants, and then by a delicious odor of musk, which ascended to the first floor as soon as he put his foot on the first stair.

Behind the abbé came two more imposing lackeys, bearing an enormous salver, laden with flowers, rolls of music, and confections.

The abbé made his *entrée* very gracefully; he walked, to be sure, with his arms stretched out in front of him as if he were playing blind man's buff, but this uncertainty of gait was not without a certain charm.

He had an attractive face, plump and rosy, great eyes fringed with long lashes; the eyes lacked brilliancy, but the incessant activity of the pupils gave to the eyeball all the play of color and transparency which the movement of the fingers gives to a dull opal.

The abbé closed his eyes and opened his lips, hid his eyeballs and showed his teeth; he knew how to smile very cleverly, so as to give a roguish expression to his turned-up nose, which would have been simply ugly in a

gentleman of less polished manners or of less illustrious
family than he.

Faithful to his custom, he saluted Olympe by kissing
her hand, as a hand was kissed in those days at Versailles; and still adhering to custom, he proceeded to
tread with both feet upon both Bannière's feet, — that
gentleman being near at hand, engaged in surveying him.

"Monsieur de Bannière, the master of the house,"
said Olympe, hastening to present the ex-novice to the
abbé, in order to cut short the bad humor of the one,
and assist the bad sight of the other.

"Ah, Monsieur, a thousand pardons!" cried the abbé;
"I am a most unfortunate man."

"I assure you, Monsieur, that you did n't hurt me at
all," said Bannière.

"Oh, no, Monsieur, no; it was not, by any means,
for my involuntary awkwardness that I begged your
pardon!"

"For what was it then, please, Monsieur?" said Bannière, surprised and hardly daring to wipe his buckles.

"Why, Monsieur, it was because I did not know I
was to have the honor of seeing you, and so took the
liberty of offering Madame de Bannière a few flowers
and sweetmeats."

"Lovely flowers they are, and the sweetmeats could
not be better," said Bannière.

"It may be so, but such as it is not proper that another
than you should offer Madame," cried the abbé.

"Monsieur—"

"That is why, with your leave, my two servants will
at once throw them all into the street."

"Oh, Monsieur!" exclaimed Bannière, "that would
be downright wicked."

"Throw them out, throw them out!" said the abbé.

The lackeys did as they were told, and actually emptied the salver, laden with the offerings of their master, out of the window.

Bannière marvelled much at this performance, the magnificence of which humiliated him.

Olympe simply smiled. She had followed the flowers with her eye as they were launched into space, and had seen a paper fall out of one of the nosegays.

Bannière made several obeisances to this abbé who was so polite and so pompous at once, whose cue it was to be forever speaking and forever smiling. He sang duets with Olympe, he sang solos, he played on a violin which his servant had brought; in short, he furnished the entertainment of the evening, with assiduous courtesy to Bannière, by which the latter was much embarrassed.

As for Olympe, she yawned very frequently during the evening. Frequently, too, she gave her hand to the "master of the house" to kiss; in a word, she reassured Bannière as a worthy, honest woman can reassure her lover.

It may be that she was more successful in that direction than was advisable; for there are certain hearts whose fidelity depends always upon the state of fear or subjection in which they are held.

When the abbé had fluttered about the salon for three hours, and had broken the strings of his violin and his voice, he remarked, —

"Really, Madame, I must introduce you to a very worthy man."

He began to laugh.

"Of what man are you speaking?" asked Olympe.

"You, especially, must know him, Monsieur de Bannière," continued the abbé, still laughing.

"Who is the man?" asked Bannière, in his turn.

"Are you very devout, Monsieur de Bannière?" asked the abbé.

"I?"

"Yes; are you very scrupulous?"

"Why,—moderately so. Why do you ask such a question?"

"The worthy man I spoke of —"

"He whose acquaintance you wish us to make?"

"Yes — is a Jew." Still the abbé laughed.

"What do you say, Abbé?" exclaimed Olympe. "A Jew! *Mon Dieu*, how can he serve us?"

"A Jew a worthy man!" said Bannière, with a smile a little forced. "You must be a very holy man, Monsieur l'Abbé, to have seen such a miracle."

"If you only could see the lovely pearl he sold me this evening, and for a mere nothing, really!"

"Ah! let us see it, Monsieur l'Abbé," said Olympe, with that childish eagerness which women always exhibit when jewels are in question.

"I no longer have it," said the abbé.

"What have you done with it?" asked Bannière; "can you tell before a lady?"

"*Mon Dieu!*" said the abbé, innocently. "I think that I fastened it to one of those bouquets, and it probably must be somewhere down there in the gutter."

The abbé said all this with the same charming smile.

"Monsieur l'Abbé is either a Gascon or a millionaire," was Olympe's comment.

"Both," replied the abbé, calmly. "I was saying that I would bring my Jew here some day; and if he does not find a way with that golden tongue of his to sell you ten thousand crowns' worth in an hour, I will discard my name d'Hoirac, Madame. He is a man without a rival."

"That pearl!" Bannière was thinking, "that pearl! There are men, then, who are wealthy enough to throw pearls out o' window in that fashion. Cleopatra at least drank hers."

He looked at the abbé's *retroussé* nose, this time with some admiration.

D'Hoirac spread his wings and took his leave about ten o'clock.

"You may perhaps think," said he to Olympe, "that I am leaving you very early to-day; but I promised La Catalane to take her to supper with Messieurs d'Abenas: they are two gentlemen from my part of the country who are recommended to me by their great kinsfolk, and whom I am launching in the world."

While he was speaking, Olympe was gazing contentedly at the impassive countenance of Bannière, who would have given a thousand drops of his blood if the chatterbox would only go, and give him an opportunity to hunt for the pearl.

But, alas! Madame's hairdresser had overheard what the abbé said.

This hairdresser — a sovereign, despotic oracle, who often worsted Claire in argument when the discussion turned on matters theatrical — was ordinarily admitted to all the councils; and when she was not admitted, she supplied the omission by listening at the doors.

It was enough for her, then, to hear what the abbé said; she knew that the street was deserted after six o'clock. If she were to seek, why should she not find?

Bannière saw her go out, although, like a person of theatrical training, she would have dissimulated her proceeding. He realized that, despite his prayers for the abbé's departure, it would come too late.

The reason for our opinion that the abbé postponed

his departure too long, is that, while Bannière was undressing that same evening, the hairdresser handed Olympe a letter which she said she had found in the street, and which was no other than the one Olympe had seen fly out of the bouquet.

It may be that Olympe would not have been put out with the letter (such an extraordinary organ is the female heart!) if the incident of the pearl had not spoiled it all.

While she was reading the letter in her dressing-room, Olympe heard Bannière stealthily open the door of his chamber.

She guessed that his purpose in opening it was to go downstairs, and that his purpose in going downstairs was to look for the pearl.

She conceived a bad opinion of him for that.

"Where are you going, my friend?" she asked, crumpling the letter into the pocket of her peignoir.

"I?" said Bannière. "Oh! nowhere. I was going out."

"Going out bareheaded as you are? What are you going out for?"

"To get a breath of air," said Bannière.

"Better stay in the house, then, my friend," said Olympe. "Really, if the abbé should see you in the street to-night, he might think you were looking for his pearl."

Bannière blushed as if his own conscience had reproached him from Olympe's mouth.

He returned to his chamber and went to bed, but slept very ill. All night long he tossed and turned in his bed. Poor Bannière! he was dreaming of pearls and diamonds.

The next day, however, Bannière sought out the abbé

upon the promenade, where he was to be met with every day.

After the customary salutations and a few aberrations of the abbé's feet upon those of Bannière, the latter asked,—

"Were you not with your Jew friend a moment ago?"

"No, indeed."

"Excuse me! I thought—"

"I was with the Sardinian ambassador."

"Ah! no one but myself would make such blunders. To think of mistaking an ambassador for a Jew!"

"Possibly you are in need of him?"

"Of the Sardinian ambassador?"

"No, of my Jew."

"Well, I may as well admit it, for I can hide nothing from you," said Bannière.

"Yes, the fact is that in spite of my near-sightedness, perhaps because of it, I am reasonably keen-witted. Do you happen to want the address of this Jew, dear Monsieur Bannière?"

"If you would kindly give it to me, you would do me a great favor."

"Jacob, Rue des Minimes, opposite the Golden Willow."

"The Golden Willow?"

"Yes, a great tree of gilded wood which projects from the shop of a—of a dealer in toys; yes, I remember the billiard-balls and snuff-boxes."

"Thanks!"

"Do you desire to buy something for Madame de Bannière?"

"Yes; but, hush!"

"Pardieu!" exclaimed the abbé.

Then a sudden thought came to him.

"Have you a chair ? " said he.

"No; but I will hire one on the square."

"Take mine."

"Oh, Monsieur l'Abbé — "

"Pray take it, my dear fellow.   Ho there, my bearers ! "

Bannière allowed himself to be forced into the abbé's fine chair, and its owner gave a signal to the servants.

The husband safely boxed up, the abbé set out on the run to seek the wife who was rehearsing at the theatre.

As he turned a corner he experienced a violent shock which made him cry out with pain; but having recognized the man with whom he had collided, he uttered another cry of surprise.

"Jacob! you clown! why don't you look where you 're going ? "

"Pardon, Monsieur l'Abbé! I was much preoccupied myself; I was turning a corner, too, and had n't the honor to see you."

"What! you had n't the honor to see me ? "

"No, Monsieur l'Abbé."

"And you know very well, you villain that I have the monopoly of blindness ? "

"Monsieur l'Abbé will forgive me. I had no idea of getting in his way, but it was this chest which made me stoop."

"What is there in the chest, pray ? Silverware, I will wager."

"Silverware, yes, Monsieur l'Abbé."

"Which you are going to sell ? "

"No, which I have just bought, on the other hand."

"Go home quickly, you wretch! I have sent you a customer.   Keep him there as long as you possibly can

He is a friend of mine who is likely to buy as much as this chest will hold. Wait a moment! that's a very pretty chest, it seems to me."

"I think it is; just look at it. By changing the cipher, the chest would be the very thing for you, Monsieur l'Abbé."

He raised the chest to the level of the abbé's eyes.

"What is the cipher?" the abbé asked; "an O and a C?"

"Yes, it is doubtless the cipher of some adorer, who presented the chest to the actress."

"To the actress, do you say? Did you buy the chest of an actress?"

"Yes, Monsieur l'Abbé, of Madame de Bannière."

"Oh, Jacob, what's that you tell me? What! Madame de Bannière selling her silverware?"

"As you see, Monsieur l'Abbé!"

The abbé took the chest from the Jew's hands, and nearly let it fall, so heavy was it.

"How much did you pay for it?" he asked. "Now, don't lie."

"Two hundred pistoles, Monsieur l'Abbé."

"Villain! you stole half of it; there are four hundred pistoles' worth of silver in this chest. Send it to my house."

"Do you purchase it?"

"For three hundred pistoles."

"Three hundred pistoles will hardly do it, Monsieur l'Abbé; you yourself valued the chest at four hundred."

"Impudent scoundrel!" exclaimed the abbé. "I give you a hundred pistoles profit right in your hand, and you are not content!"

"Oh, the times are so hard!"

"Come, carry the chest to my house."

"I will do so, Monsieur l'Abbé;" and the Jew made a movement as if to take his leave.

"But first wait a moment."

"I am waiting, Monsieur l'Abbé;" and the Jew halted.

"Tell me how you made this lady's acquaintance."

"Through her hairdresser."

"Ah, so there's a hairdresser! I haven't seen her yet; to be sure, I don't see anything. Keep my friend a good long time. Off with you!"

He pursued his way towards the theatre, saying to himself, "Jew, hairdresser, husband, silverware sold, and jewelry bought; everything goes as if it were on casters."

XXII.

M. DE MAILLY'S RING.

BANNIÈRE had nothing to buy at the establishment of Jacob, the Jew; but he had much to sell there.

He sold all the jewels Olympe had given him, and all those that he had given her as well.

He sold them for five hundred louis, which he put in his pocket.

He had discovered a plan of play, sure to succeed, — a sort of alternating double or quits, which was infallible; but in order to work it to the best advantage he must have eight hundred louis at his disposal, and he had but five hundred.

With eight hundred louis he would have been perfectly sure of winning two millions. Reduced to twelve thousand livres, he sighed as he thought that he should win for his dear Olympe only a paltry eleven hundred thousand.

It was a small matter; but after all, small as it was, the sum of eleven hundred thousand livres would run the household nicely for a lustrum or two, without the assistance of abbé or hairdresser or theatrical partners.

That was the way they reckoned time before the invention of the metric system.

Bannière said to himself that, after all, eleven hundred thousand livres was a very pretty sum, and in gold would more than fill the hats of ten abbés, which are the largest of all hats.

When he had won that amount,—that being the least difficult part, since his calculations could not fail,—he would pack it on the back of a sturdy commissioner, two if need were, and would have the sacks carried to Olympe's boudoir; there he would cut them open in her absence, strew the carpet with the contents, and make her bathe her pretty feet up to the ankles in this cold bath with shining yellow waves.

There was a large gathering at the gambling house on that evening. Bannière took his seat distractedly in the first vacant chair; his bag of louis was at his hand.

He took a card, and began to prick out his plan. All his calculations made, he began to play.

His calculations were accurate apparently, for he won. Just as he was raking in twenty louis, an exclamation in a woman's voice attracted his attention. He looked up, and recognized La Catalane opposite to him, punting against him.

This woman laughed if she won, laughed if she lost,—laughed all the time, in fact.

She was exactly like the abbé, except that she laughed louder than he.

Bannière continued to win, and La Catalane to punt. Bannière had already won fifty thousand livres, and La Catalane had lost her last sou.

She borrowed ten louis from her neighbor, and proceeded to lose the ten louis with undiminished good spirits. Then she borrowed ten more louis and lost them, while Bannière kept on winning.

She changed her place in disgust, and came and rested her two plump little hands upon the shoulders of Bannière, who took no notice of her.

She shook him and teased him, and almost embraced him.

But Bannière was as cold as the yellow coins which the croupier kept sadly pushing over to him with his rake.

There came a coup upon which Bannière expected to win three hundred louis. He reckoned that the black would win, and staked upon the black.

Red turned up.

La Catalane laughed aloud.

Bannière looked up at her.

"You disturb me, my dear," he said, with some temper; "pray be careful."

The following coup he lost again.

That made six hundred louis at two strokes.

He doubled his stake, and lost upon a coup of which he felt absolutely certain.

Then he shook his shoulders to dislodge La Catalane's hands.

"Go to the devil!" he exclaimed; "you have brought me your bad luck."

The fair creature recoiled a step, in high dudgeon.

Twice more Bannière lost. It was an unparalleled run of ill-luck.

He had a hundred louis left, risked them all on one coup, and lost again.

"Lend me a louis," said he, pale as a ghost, to the actress.

"A louis?" said she; "why, if I had a louis left, I would play with it. It's half an hour since I had a sou."

Bannière rose with pallid brow, face bathed in perspiration, and head in a whirl, and went out of the room to breathe.

His head was burning hot. He went home to Olympe, who sat waiting for him at the window.

From Bannière's way of repelling La Catalane, one

would have said he was passionately fond of Olympe.
From his way of receiving Olympe's questions, one would
have said he was in love with any other woman.

Observing his mood, Olympe asked him with her
accustomed gentleness, —

"Are you thirsty, my dear?"

"Thirsty! why should I be?" shouted Bannière, like
a madman. "Am I a drunkard, pray?"

"Gamblers are not generally drunkards," replied
Olympe; "but they gamble, and in gambling their dis-
positions change, especially when they lose. You have
been losing, have n't you?"

Bannière dropped into a chair, with his head in his
hands.

"Oh, you know it very well!" said he.

Olympe made a sign to Claire, who left the room. As
for the hairdresser, who was in the dressing-room, she
kept perfectly still, so that her mistress forgot that she
was there.

After the words which had been exchanged between
the lovers, there was silence for a time.

This silence weighed upon Bannière, and yet he dared
not break it.

He adopted a middle course; he rose and paced the
floor.

"How much have you lost?" Olympe asked calmly.

"Sixty thousand livres!" said Bannière, grimly, reckoning in the sum he had won and calling it all loss.

"Oh! oh!" said Olympe; "where in heaven's name
did you get sixty thousand livres to lose? and if you had
them, why did you stake them, I should like to know?
It is such a fine thing to have sixty thousand livres! I
appreciate the value of it, I assure you, — I, who in my
most prosperous days never had more than half of it."

"That's right," cried Bannière, jumping at the pretext, "say hard things to me, reproach me with having impoverished you!"

"I did nothing of the kind, my friend; but if I should do it, I might not be altogether wrong, especially if the reproach would teach you better."

"Oh, well, Madame!" retorted Bannière, weeping with rage, "if you should be too unhappy, Monsieur l'Abbé d'Hoirac will console you; if you find yourself too poor, Monsieur l'Abbé d'Hoirac will heap riches upon you!"

Olympe coughed that little, dry cough which in a nervous person is commonly the symptom of extreme irritation restrained by the will alone.

"Why Monsieur l'Abbé d'Hoirac?" she asked.

"Because he was here this evening."

"By what do you see that?"

"I don't see it; I smell it in these odors which poison the air."

Bannière opened a window and a door.

"It is curious," said Olympe, laughing, "that you have a grudge against poor Abbé d'Hoirac because you have lost sixty thousand livres. And, apropos, you don't explain where you could have got so much money."

"Madame!" shrieked Bannière, "if ever the Abbé d'Hoirac puts his foot inside — "

"Threats, Monsieur?" said Olympe, with a majestic air which terrified Bannière.

She rose to her feet.

"My friend," said she, "you don't know what you are saying; your loss has entirely turned your brain."

"Madame!"

"Have you anything left to stake?"

"Oh, she believes it is the gambling!" he muttered; "she does not understand that I am jealous."

Olympe did not hear him.

" I see, " said she, " you must have something to stake or to break. Must I let you break my heart? No, Bannière, I prefer to lose my last pearl rather than my last illusion. I would offer you my silver plate, but I sold it to-day to pay our half-yearly rent."

" Well, and then? " demanded Bannière.

" Then, I have Monsieur de Mailly's ring left. It is the last souvenir of a man who loved me dearly, adored me at times, and never wounded me. That ring I refused to give you; but I offer it to you to-day. Take it, pray, and give me peace of mind in return."

It will be remembered that the first jealous quarrel which had disturbed the happiness of the lovers concerned this same ring.

" No! " cried Bannière, stopping the young woman, as she was about to carry out the offer she had made; " no! "

" Yes, yes! " replied she.

" No, dear Olympe, no! " said Bannière, clinging to her; " no, I implore you! Do not look for that ring! "

" Why not? " Olympe insisted; " it is worth a hundred louis; you will stake them, and lose them, and then you will have the satisfaction of having lost sixty-two thousand four hundred livres like a blue ribbon."

As she spoke, she tore herself from Bannière's grasp and ran to her jewel-case, despite his pressing entreaties, his efforts to hold her back, and his broken words which she did not choose to hear.

Olympe had a strong will and physical strength; she threw the young man off a second time, and opened the box.

Bannière emitted a stifled cry.

Olympe, without noticing the cry any more than the rest, pressed upon the spring which held the false bottom in place, and the hiding-place was revealed.

It was empty.

Her surprise, her sudden pallor, the strange gleam which shot from her eyes and changed from rage to contempt before reaching Bannière, — these are details which neither painter nor poet can depict. Spectacles of that sort are seen once in a while, but never analyzed.

Olympe let the cover of the box fall, and her hand fell upon it.

Little by little her glance lost its fire; something seemed to die within her.

Bannière threw himself at her feet, which he seized and embraced, weeping bitterly the while.

"Forgive me, Olympe, forgive me!" he cried. "I took the ring as I took your other jewels and my own too. Besides, I always hated that ring; it made my life unbearable, for jealousy is harder to bear than poverty."

Olympe made no reply; like Dido, she kept her eyes fixed on the ground, and turned her head away.

"Oh, pity me!" said the poor wretch. "Do you believe that I took the ring to sell, and enjoy myself with the proceeds? No, I sold it for the sake of gambling. Why did I play? To win, — to win so as to enrich Olympe, my divinity, my life! I would have liked to win a crown to make you a queen, Olympe. I believed that I should win, because nothing seemed to me capable of resisting my love and the will founded upon it, — not even fatality. Oh, have pity on me! Chance is a statue with an iron pedestal against which the mad hopes of its worshippers hurl themselves and are beaten

back. Olympe, if you only knew! I had already won
sixty thousand livres. I should have won five hundred
thousand. In four hours I should have won a million.
Oh, my dear life! if you had seen me just now, scarcely
an hour since! I had in front of me a heap of gold and
the vein of good luck, and I was going to make that
heap into a mountain; it was so fine when it kept on
growing, — growing all the time! Suddenly a breath
passed between me and the fairy world in which I saw
my fortune awaiting me. The door with the golden
pillars disappeared; the treasure cave was hidden from
my sight. I lost sight of the good spirit who was leading
me, I no longer knew how to read my destiny; everything became black and sombre, as when the curtain falls
after an exciting performance. Then I relapsed into the
cold and shivering misery of the common mortal, — the
mortal who fears and doubts: all my gold flew away,
flake by flake, as a cloud dissolves in the sky, as snow
melts away beneath the warm April sun. With every
piece that abandoned me, I felt a hope, a joy, a blessing
depart. When all was lost, I realized my wretchedness
for the first time; for what I had really lost was not
gold, nor hope, nor joy, nor happiness: I had lost you,
Olympe! — you, yes, you! for it is plain to me now that
I have lost you!"

At the sight of this suffering, which in its very exaltation found such profoundly eloquent expression, at the
sight of this despair writhing at her feet, Olympe raised
her head, and opened her heart to generous forgetfulness.

She was convinced that the man who had committed
that base deed was guilty of nothing but love.

Always noble, always above petty motives and calculations, Olympe took Bannière's hands, pressed them to
her heart, and embraced him most affectionately.

At this symptom of returning tenderness, the hair-dresser violently slammed the door of the dressing-room and went out without disguising her ill-humor; but it made no impression on either of the two young people, who had just found one more bright page in the fast-darkening volume of their love.

VOL I. — 14

XXIII.

THE PAGE IS TURNED DOWN.

But everything has an end, even the good which evil
brings forth.   Within a fortnight Olympe discovered
that her lover loved her more than ever; but she discovered at the same time that Bannière was a more
inveterate gambler than he had ever been.

To use a distinctively modern expression, which we
employ because it expresses our meaning so exactly,
Bannière had become impossible.

No more theatre, no more quiet talks at home.
Bannière was either dreaming or sighing when he was
not at the gaming-table, or imploring with clasped hands
the pardon of his beloved for some new offence.

While he was thus working out his own destruction,
the abbé, conscious of the superiority of his position,
was every day throwing a stone into his rival's garden of
beautiful dreams.

Olympe one evening found her silver plate in its usual
place.   She could not repress a joyful cry; for some days
her philosophy had been unequal to the task of accustom-
ing herself to do without it.

She called Claire to know who had brought the plate
back during her sleep or her absence from home.

Claire did not know what she meant.

She then summoned the hairdresser.

The hairdresser insisted that the silver chest had
never left the sideboard.

"Why, I sold it," cried Olympe, — "sold it to Jacob, the Jew."

"That cannot be, Madame," the woman replied; "Madame cannot have sold it, since it is where Madame always kept it."

"Jacob!" muttered Bannière, beneath his breath; "the man to whom I sold the jewels and the ring, the purchaser or dealer in ordinary of Monsieur l'Abbé d'Hoirac!"

A shudder and a suspicion invaded Bannière's heart at the same moment; but he put the curb on his imagination, which was all ready to run amuck, not wishing to yield at once to his bitter fancies.

"Olympe had some money hidden," he thought, "with which she has bought back the plate. Indeed, who knows that she really sold it? May she not have tried simply to make me think she was forced to that sacrifice? Women like to be pitied."

This sophistry sufficed, not to put his suspicions to sleep, but to abate them for a while.

That evening, as usual, the abbé came to take a hand at tric-trac, and to exercise his musical talent. He was extremely well received by both Monsieur and Madame de Bannière.

A marvellous fellow was this abbé for always having a new idea. Always restlessly craving novelty, without any great natural wit, he succeeded, by dint of searching, in picking up the wit which he had not.

Besides, he had a delightful way of doing everything; give him a simple promenade for a text, and he would conjure up halting-places for refreshments, games, dancers, performing-bears, merry-go-rounds, and fortune-tellers. He knew how fish should be dressed in every country on the globe; he had eighteen ways of cooking eggs; he could scent out good wine and comfortable lodgings a league away. He did not give a flower, even, as any other man would give it; he seasoned it always with some gift which made the flower valuable; if he had lived in the time of Augustus, he would have invented bouquet-holders which the Roman ladies might have used for the flowers which Lucullus brought from Asia, whose sticky, corrosive juice stained their patrician hands yellow.

The abbé never entered a room that he did not bring with him some novelty or some new suggestion for the entertainment of the company.

On the evening in question he won a louis from Olympe, and said to her, —

"That makes it only one hundred and ninety-nine louis, Madame Bannière."

"What do you mean?" asked Olympe.

"Yes, what do you mean, Monsieur l'Abbé," echoed Bannière, "by the hundred and ninety-nine louis which remain?"

"I mean," rejoined the abbé, stumbling over Bannière's feet, as his custom was, "that if you keep the louis you have just lost, I shall have one hundred and ninety-nine more to bring you on Monday."

"What?" said Olympe, blushing.

"What?" said Bannière, turning white.

"Ah! to be sure, you do not know!" said the abbé.

"Do not know what?" asked both the young people, in the same breath.

"You do not know," continued the abbé, calmly, "that I have made an addition to your benefit performance for Sunday."

"How so?" asked Olympe, in amazement.

"In this way. Baron comes to Chalon this week. I had my secretary write to him, to urge him to extend his journey to Lyons, and play at your benefit."

"Well?" said Olympe.

"Well, he replied that he would very gladly act with you and for you, Madame."

"But all this does not explain how you will owe me just two hundred louis on Monday."

"Listen!"

Bannière's face became more serene; Olympe's alone retained its anxious expression.

"As soon as I had my reply from Baron," continued the abbé, "I made a little speculation."

"A speculation, you!" exclaimed Olympe. "Oh, you don't seem to me to have much of the appearance of a speculator."

"Nevertheless it is as I have the honor to tell you, Madame."

Olympe shook her head; but the abbé, being near-sighted, did not see the movement.

So he continued : —

"Judge whether I was far-sighted. I began by hiring the whole hall at a very low figure, for nobody knew what I proposed to do. At the first syllable which I allowed to escape me as to the extraordinary attractions of the performance, I had applications for three times as many boxes and stalls as the place contains. I multiplied the prices by three, — nothing but that; and the performance will bring in four hundred louis. As the idea of the benefit originated with me, you and I will divide it. It may be worthy of an Arab, a Turk, a Moor, a Jew, or a Genoese trader, I know all that; but understand that he who originates an idea deserves something for it. Now, I reckon that something at a half; and as the idea was worth four hundred louis, there will be two hundred for me, and two hundred for you."

Olympe gazed admiringly and thoughtfully at him.

Bannière saw no hidden meaning in the words. He rubbed his hands and embraced the abbé.

"I will wager," said the latter, trampling upon Bannière's feet again, "I will wager — I *beg* your pardon, dear Monsieur Bannière — that Madame Bannière will outshine Baron, and that Baron will at once procure her an engagement at the Comédie-Française, so that we will all go and earn millions at the capital."

"Fie, flatterer!" said Olympe.

"Come, am I not right, Monsieur Bannière?"

"Right a hundred times over, Monsieur l'Abbé!" said Bannière, enthusiastically; for he anticipated three months of happiness with Olympe from the two hundred louis to be derived from the benefit.

"So long as she wants nothing," he said to himself, "or so long as she can have what she wants, I am sure that she will love me more than anybody else."

Alas! poor Bannière was not at the end of his woes.

From that moment the abbé busied himself about the performance as if he were the manager of the company. He arranged the scenery, distributed the parts, set the tailors and embroiderers at work, superintended the decorations, and attended every rehearsal.

Never did crowned head have such a body-guard as that which followed at Olympe's heels until the happy Sunday arrived.

Thanks to this body-guard, who seemed to be also a sort of genie with a magic wand, she had not even to express a wish; and if she did express one, it was gratified on the instant.

The result was that Bannière, observing the abbé's

assiduous attentions, became jealous again. He indulged in divers critical remarks upon the scenery and the abbé's taste.

But the abbé was wise in his generation, and received Bannière's spiteful flings without the least temper.

He pretended not to hear those which were evidently intended to be disagreeable.

"How lucky you are to have good eyes, dear Monsieur Bannière!" he would say. "Half the foolish things I do are chargeable to my bad eyes."

At last the day of the performance arrived.

For that day the abbé constituted himself leader of the claque.

Decidedly the abbé was able to turn his hand to anything; like Bannière, he had missed his vocation, and yet his black coat, his little cloak, and his neck-band went so well with his plump white hands, his rétroussé nose, and his cheeks fresh as a peach, that it would have been a great pity to see him in any other costume than his own.

He led the claque, then, and regulated the applause so that Baron was satisfied; but Olympe was enchanted.

The flowers and wreaths and applauding friends interested him much more than the receipts.

But Bannière was interested in the latter point, which was by no means a side issue with him as it was with the abbé. In the first place he abstracted twenty louis from the receipts to go and play double or quits a little while, with the purpose, of course, of realizing a hundred thousand livres or so of clear profit while they were applauding Olympe at the theatre.

But one cannot win on all sides at once. The twenty louis did not last an hour. When the twentieth vanished, he rose and looked about for his evil genius, La Catalane.

Luckily she was not there; if she had been, he would infallibly have wrung her neck, to be rid of her for good and all.

While Bannière was running off to gamble away the twenty louis he had borrowed from the receipts, the abbé was making himself conspicuous at the head of the applauding spectators, and assuring Olympe's triumph over Baron.

It was no simple thing to do, although at that time the famous tragedian, on the point of withdrawing not only from the dramatic stage but from the world's stage as well, was seventy-seven years of age. That fact did not, however, prevent him from playing Achille in "Iphigénie."

The performance ended, Baron, who was a gallant old fellow, placed upon Olympe's head the wreath which had been tossed to her; but he refused to sup with his com- rades, alleging the weakness of his digestive organs as an excuse.

Olympe sought everywhere for Bannière.

She was uneasy at not seeing him, and especially so in view of the disappearance of the twenty louis, which indicated that, despite his oaths, — regular gambler's oaths, — he had flown back to the gaming-table.

The loss of twenty louis was nothing to her; but these successive failures of delicacy on her lover's part were much to her.

From time to time, in the midst of her triumph, she sighed as if she foreboded misfortune.

We have said that Bannière looked about to see if La Catalane was near him.

He did not see her, but he did see a fellow-gambler who was in funds and loaned Bannière twenty louis more.

Bannière returned to the fray with ardor.

XXIV.

THE SERENADE.

BANNIÈRE's second twenty louis, or rather his friend's, being more carefully husbanded than the others, lasted four hours.

At the end of that time, after having twenty times been within an ace of winning the hundred thousand livres, to which his ambition was perforce limited, Bannière lost the twenty louis.

He left the place in a passion which we will not attempt to describe; it was complicated by all the agony of wounded self-esteem.

With the remembrance that he had been already laughed at and humiliated, and above all pardoned for a similar offence, he slunk home as shamefaced as a pickpocket after he has broken his oath to steal no more.

Despair possessed his soul; as he passed over a bridge, he almost determined to drown himself.

But Bannière was too much in love to drown himself. In his heart love overbore all other emotions. What has honor to do with a madman?

So Bannière did not jump into the river, but returned to Olympe with lagging steps.

"Poor girl!" he said to himself, "I am the only one who will have been missing at her triumph; I am the only one who will not have applauded and congratulated her. She is probably waiting for me, as she was the last time, and will begin to reproach me. But I will submit to her reproaches, I will grovel at her feet, and she will forgive me once more. She will see that I must be accursed; and then after this I will make no more attempts to better our condition. No, they succeed too ill. Olympe is showing me the way; she is working hard, and I will follow her example. This fortune which we have been pursuing and which has thus far eluded us, will drop into our hands, perhaps, when we cease to seek it."

Bannière passed his icy hand across his burning brow.

"A thousand livres!" he cried; "two months' supply eaten up in four hours! But this time, at all events, Olympe cannot charge me with having ruined her, for I took only twenty louis of the hundred which were surely coming to us from the receipts of the performance. To be sure, I owe twenty others. Bah! those twenty others I will repay from my first winnings. One cannot lose forever."

Thus we see that in less than ten minutes Bannière had sworn never to play again, and had also promised himself to repay the money he had borrowed from his first winnings at play.

Revolving such thoughts in his brain, Bannière approached his place of abode.

It was a gloomy night; one o'clock was striking on the clock of the Carmelite Church, whose towers limited the view from Olympe's balcony.

When the last vibrations of the brazen tongue had ceased to disturb the air, Bannière still listened; it seemed to him that the music of the bells was continued by another, different sound.

He was not left long in suspense.

The sound was produced by musical instruments accompanied by a passably melodious voice.

Bannière, as he walked along, had the privilege of listening to a complete symphony; and having heard it through, he sought the symphonists.

They were drawn up in line under the windows of Olympe's bedroom.

Bannière at that moment cared little for anything under heaven, and for music least of all. Indeed nothing could have had a more irritating effect upon his nerves than the mournful, plaintive tones of the flute and violins, which accompanied the guitar of the principal performer.

The guitar itself accompanied the voice which Bannière had noticed as he entered the street,— a voice which he was quite sure that he had heard somewhere or other. In fact, as he drew nearer, he recognized in him who filled the triple functions of guitarist, vocalist, and leader of the orchestra, the Abbé d'Hoirac, arrayed *en cavalier*, putting on the most languishing airs and assuming languorous attitudes as he twisted his neck toward the balcony.

The air was a long and difficult one, and it must be said that the abbé sang it very well.

Behind her half-raised blind, Olympe — easily recognizable, as she made no attempt to conceal herself — was to be seen dressed in white; and although Bannière could not distinguish the expression of her face, he had no doubt that she was smiling.

The force of imagination, especially a jealous imagination, is so strong that Bannière actually saw the smile through the blind.

Blind rage flowed into his heart, as the music flowed into his ears.

At last the difficult morceau came to an end with these words, —

"Belle Phillis, dis-moi, 'Je t'aime!'
Et je n'ai plus rien à chanter." [1]

The Abbé d'Hoirac, having in accordance with universal custom repeated the last two lines of the finale a dozen or fifteen times, ceased his warbling with a blast which put the finishing touch to Bannière's exasperation.

He rushed upon D'Hoirac, and shouted in thunder-tones, —

"Ah, you have nothing more to sing! Very well, dance then! "

With that he seized him by the throat.

The abbé could not see clearly, and had besides the disadvantage of being taken by surprise, which did not prevent him, for he was a courageous little fellow, from defending himself valiantly with his guitar against this enemy of harmonious sounds, who seemed to come out of the bowels of the earth.

The symphonists undertook to come to the assistance of their leader; but Bannière had as many arms as Briareus. He broke two or three violins, and twisted five or six flutes out of shape, whereupon the musicians immediately took to their heels, — for your ordinary musician fears more for his instrument than for his skin.

Aided by the shrieks of Olympe, the abbé finally recognized Bannière. He charged him gallantly with his guitar, for the abbé was sufficiently well to do not to worry about his instrument; but Bannière tore it from his hands and broke it into a hundred pieces on his head.

"It's very lucky for you," said the abbé, as he received the blow, " that I have no sword."

[1] " Lovely Phyllis, say to me, ' I love thee !'
And I have nothing more to sing."

"Ah, don't let that trouble you," retorted Bannière; "you can get one in ten minutes."

"Triple beast!" replied the abbé, "triple dolt! you know very well that I will not fight with you."

"Why not?" roared Bannière; "tell me, I say, tell me!"

"In the first place, because I should kill you, blind as I am, for you have never handled a sword."

"Who told you so?"

"*Parbleu!* that's easy to see from your countrified manners; and then, too, you know very well that I am an abbé, and consequently have no right to wear the dress in which you insult me, so that if I should kill you or should have justice of you in any other way, I should be condemned twice over, — by the religious as well as the civil tribunals. That's why, Monsieur Blackguard, you have acted like a boor and a coward. But, never fear! I'll be even with you."

Bannière realized that he had been over-hasty, and, fearing the threat, vain as it was, he released his hold of the abbé, who hurried away.

The few windows appertaining to the houses on the street had been opened in consequence of the uproar Bannière made. Lights were lighted, and there was considerable shouting and questioning.

That might mean the patrol and arrest. In fact, it was not long before the cross-belts of the archers emerged from the dense darkness at the corner of the Carmelite Church, and Bannière had no more than time to glide into the house through the door which was held open for him by the terrified Olympe.

The patrol, following immemorial precedent, arrived some minutes too late; they found upon the field of battle nothing but some débris of violins and flutes and the neck of a guitar. The worthy officials got entangled in the catgut, cursed a little, and that was the end of the matter.

But, his safety being assured, Bannière's rage became more violent than ever. He who had been seeking some means of moving Olympe to pity ten minutes before, had found a pretext for accusing her.

Being safely within doors, he assumed the most majestic attitude of which he was capable, folded his arms, and began to cross-examine her.

Olympe, whose first impulse had been to inquire affectionately for his welfare and if he were wounded, ceased abruptly the expression of her interest in the madman, and turned her back upon him as soon as he began to show his teeth.

Bannière was much more angered by this contemptuous silence than he would have been by an energetic reply. He ran after Olympe as she was returning to her room, and seized her roughly by the arm.

The beautiful creature turned pale from pain and shame combined, and uttered a cry like a wounded lioness, which brought her women running to her.

Bannière would have given his life to pulverize those three frail creatures who stood there before him, apparently ready to defy his wrath.

Olympe's cry was succeeded by the most profound silence, during which she raised the sleeve of her peignoir, and disclosed the red mark, already turning purple, of Bannière's fingers on the arm above the elbow.

The hairdresser threw herself weeping upon the lovely, maimed arm, which she covered with kisses, bellowing imprecations at Bannière the while.

Bannière disappeared within his own room, overwhelmed with shame. remorse. and terror.

Until ten o'clock on the following day the most absolute silence reigned in the house.

At ten o'clock Olympe rang for Claire, who hastened to her, accompanied by the hairdresser, who had left the house after the scene we have described, but had returned in the morning.

Claire was told to have lunch made ready. The hairdresser remained alone with her mistress, who asked indifferently what had become of *him*.

"Oh!" replied the hairdresser, " *he* went away this morning."

Olympe thought that her reply was given with peculiar emphasis, that she had given strange prominence to the word *he*, and she thought that the word, used as a demonstrative pronoun, was not sufficiently demonstrative.

"Of whom are you speaking?" she asked coldly, "and whom do you mean by *he*?"

The hairdresser saw that she was on the wrong road, and that the Abbé d'Hoirac was not yet the one *he*.

"I mean that Monsieur has gone out," she replied humbly. "But," she continued with animation, "it is very generous of Madame with her beauty, her talent, and her success, to allow herself to be made so unhappy."

"Who told you that I am unhappy, my friend?" said Olympe, disdainfully.

"What! is it not very evident, Madame?"

"From what?"

"Because you have wept all night."

"You are mistaken."

"Your lovely eyes have lost half their brightness,— eyes which are the admiration of the whole city."

Olympe shrugged her shoulders.

"Do you doubt it, Madame?" the temptress continued.

Olympe made no reply by word or motion.

"You must know, then," the hairdresser resumed, "that there are people who would lose their life willingly to obtain one glance from those eyes which you seem to despise."

"Oh," murmured Olympe, whose ear was tickled, sensible as she was, by the flattery, or rather by the praise,—"oh, as I have little belief in so great power—"

Praise is like perfume; wheresoever it comes from woman can always detect it afar and appreciate it.

"If you wish to make the trial, you would not be long in doubt."

"Trial of what?"

"Come, Madame, consider a little. Is he worthy of you, of an artist of your merit, a woman of your beauty? Is he worthy the having to go in a chair to the theatre, to live in this out-of-the-way quarter, to go without diamonds, and to wait till the day after a benefit performance to buy three dresses?"

"That is none of your affair, my dear."

"That's right," whimpered the hairdresser, pretending to weep; "make it a crime for me to love you, and to hate those who stand in the way of your happiness."

"I forbid your saying any ill of them, do you hear?"

"Forbid them, then, to blacken your lovely body; forbid them to steal your money for the purpose, not of gambling,—that would be nothing,—but of spending it with God knows whom!"

"Who keeps you so well posted?"

"People who know what they are talking about, Madame, never fear."

"The same who would give their life to obtain one of my glances, are they not?"

"And who are ready, besides, to lend Madame ten thousand livres a month to help her to maintain her position, — something more substantial that, and consequently harder to find."

"Ten thousand livres a month," repeated Olympe, concealing her disgust; "so you are making a proposition to me, are you?"

"Official, yes, Madame," replied the hairdresser, emboldened by what she took to be an indication of surrender; "yes, a hundred and twenty thousand livres a year, payable quarterly, — that 's all. The first quarterly instalment is all ready; I have seen it."

Olympe rose, drew her beautiful blond locks from the woman's hands, and said to her, —

"Mademoiselle, this is so delicate and important a mission which has been intrusted to you that you must have been promised a handsome recompense. Go and claim it then, I beg, without losing a moment. Go!"

"What?" asked the hairdresser, in surprise.

"You do not understand me, I presume?"

"Why, no."

"I tell you to leave my house, Mademoiselle, and never show your face inside it again."

"But, Madame," said the wretch, in an undertone, "Monsieur is not hidden there, he has gone out."

"Oh, yes, you cannot understand how any one can refuse seriously a hundred and twenty thousand livres, payable quarterly," said Olympe, sadly. "For what do you take me, I should like to know?"

"Why, Madame, according to what Claire has told me, you received from Monsieur de Mailly — "

"Whatever I asked him for, Mademoiselle, and I asked much of him because I loved him much; and I refuse much to keep Monsieur de Bannière, because I am very fond of him. Consider that as settled, Mademoiselle, and leave my house."

The hairdresser, pale with anger, tried to defend herself.

"It's no use; I understand you," Olympe interrupted. "Your principal fear at this moment is of losing the reward which was promised you. I owe you something, then, by way of recompense. Take these ten louis, and — adieu!"

The hairdresser at first held out her hand to take them, but suddenly her wrath got the upper hand.

"What sublime virtue," said she, "in a woman who ran away a year ago with a man whom she had known scarcely an hour!"

"Yes, I understand," said Olympe; "I can imagine your chagrin, my friend, for they offered you twenty times the paltry sum I can give you. But take it, nevertheless, and go offer your services to La Catalane. They will bring you in more money there with less difficulty."

The hairdresser's eyes shone with sudden fire.

"Ah!" said she, "you turn me out, and put such ideas as this in my head! Very good, I will profit by them."

Throwing the ten louis upon the carpet, she hurried off at headlong speed to La Catalane, who lived in the neighborhood of the theatre.

Olympe congratulated herself, when the woman had gone, upon not feeling the least regret for having done a worthy action.

XXV.

HOW HAIRDRESSERS EARN THEIR WAGES.

LA CATALANE, to whom Olympe advised her hair-dresser to offer her services, was not very well disposed toward Mademoiselle de Clèves.

It seldom happens that a woman casts an envious eye upon another woman's lover, without considerable hard feeling against that other, even if she has succeeded in stealing the lover away; never without deadly hatred if the lover has declined to allow himself to be stolen. It is true that she may visit a little of her enmity upon the too faithful swain.

We are about to see what Mademoiselle de Clèves's feelings were, as interpreted by La Catalane, after which we will lay bare La Catalane's reflections upon the subject.

"I 'll wager that I know what you have come for," said she.

"You know!" cried the hairdresser.

"Yes."

"What do you think?"

"That Olympe has turned you out of doors."

"How did you guess that?" asked the amazed hair-dresser.

"Oh! there was nothing difficult about it. You received the Abbé d'Hoirac this morning, and he is madly in love with Olympe. If he came to see you, it was not on your own account, was it? So it must have been on hers. If he came to see you, he did n't go away without giving you money — you sigh — well, without promising it to you, then. That is why I think you probably tried to-day to convey his declaration to Olympe; and as you are as red as a turkey-cock, and sulky, it must be because you did not succeed."

"Can you imagine such a thing?" cried the hairdresser, seating herself without ceremony, and without objection from La Catalane.

"What reason did she give for her refusal?" asked the latter.

"An incredible one."

"What was it, pray?"

"She says that she loves Monsieur Bannière, the vagabond."

"Oh, he 's a fine fellow, Agathe."

"I know him well."

"You tell me that she can still love Bannière, and yet — "

"*Parbleu!* that makes no difference."

"Mademoiselle Agathe," said La Catalane, with a laugh, "your morals are as lax as if you were a duchess; take care!"

"Do you know that this virtue of hers has cost me two thousand livres, — yes, more than that, — a hundred louis?"

"What would you have, my girl? You must prove that you have a great heart; you must prove that you despise money; you must take the loss philosophically."

"I lose a hundred louis which I almost had in my hand!" cried Agathe, opening wide her glassy eyes, which the hope of gain had brightened up; "oh, never, never!"

"I don't imagine, however, that you expect to compel

Olympe to become madly in love with the abbé, especially if she does n't choose to do so."

Agathe emitted a great sigh of anger, which might have passed for a very respectable roar.

"You would have preferred to deal with me, would n't you?" La Catalane asked, laughing. "I am not the woman to cause my friends so much annoyance. But what would you have? Certain heads attract good fortune, as the magnet does a needle. I have no chance, you see; and yet, if one looks closely at me — "

"Or even if one goes into details," said Agathe.

"At all events, I have a well-shaped head of my own," said La Catalane.

"And your neck, too," said Agathe.

"And this foot," said La Catalane, "is not very large or ill-shaped."

"And then your hands," said the hairdresser, "and your figure, and your waist! Ah, Mademoiselle, in my opinion one woman is as good as another."

"What! you see that that is n't so, Agathe, since the abbé offers Olympe what he does not offer me. How much did he offer her, by the way?"

"Ten thousand livres a month!" cried the hairdresser.

"The devil! that is a snug little sum, though, — one hundred and twenty thousand livres a year! What a pity that the little fellow, who is near-sighted, is n't stone-blind!"

"Why so, Mademoiselle?"

"Because then you would bring him here, as if you were taking him to Olympe; because I would assume my silvery, flute-like voice, — Olympe's voice, in fact, which I mimic so well in the green-room as to make everybody laugh, — and I would say to the abbé sentimentally, as Olympe would say, "Monsieur, what is asked of me I sometimes refuse; what one does not expect, I give.""

"Oho!" said Agathe.

"And as he would be blind — "

"Well?"

"Well, stupid! I would have my ten thousand livres, that's all."

"What?"

"And you would have your twenty-four hundred livres."

The hairdresser grasped her hair with both hands, and almost tore it out.

"Don't despair," said La Catalane; "put his eyes out."

"Ah, Mademoiselle, you have the heart to joke."

"What the deuce would you have me do, — jump overboard, or hang myself, or suffocate myself?"

"Oh, no, I would have you do nothing of the kind, it would be too great a sin; but I would have you get angry because a Bannière prevents us — "

"Prevents *you*, you mean; confess that it's the twenty-four hundred livres which sits especially heavy on your mind."

"Now look here!" rejoined Agathe, her eyes blazing with wrath and cupidity; "if I were in your place, I would not like to be worsted in this little scheme of ours; and to induce Mademoiselle Olympe to yield to the Abbé d'Hoirac, I would — "

"What would you do?"

"Well, if I were La Catalane, I would steal Mademoiselle Olympe's lover away from her."

La Catalane burst out laughing.

"Yes, yes, yes," the hairdresser went on; "I tell you that is the way, the true way. She will very soon find it out, for her friends will tell her; furthermore, if her friends fail to tell her, you can tell her yourself. She is as proud as Roxana, and will never forgive unfaithful-ness, and from very rage, perhaps, she would put me in a way to lay hold of our twenty-four hundred livres."

"You keep saying *our ;* why don't you say *my ?* "

"I say *our*, because if you take up with Monsieur Bannière, I will share with you what Monsieur l'Abbé gives me. Make the attempt, I beg, I implore you, to take Monsieur Bannière away from Olympe; that will be so easy for you, especially as he is such a fine fellow, as you just said yourself."

"What!" cried the giddy creature, laughing louder than before, "do you fancy that to-day is the first time I have discovered the attractions of that young man? Why, for six months I have had my eye on him."

"Oh, well, then," said the hairdresser, delightedly, — "oh, well, then, it's as good as done."

"You idiot!" retorted La Catalane, "as I have had my eye on him for six months, it would have been done six months ago, if it could be done."

"Why has it not been done, pray?"

"Because there is a more serious difficulty. We are just in the position of Harlequin desirous of marrying Columbine; the wedding would come off, if it depended on Harlequin only. Unfortunately the consent of Columbine is necessary, and Columbine will not give her consent."

"Nonsense!"

"It's as I tell you, my dear, — Columbine Bannière has no use for Harlequin Catalane."

"Have you made eyes at him?"

"I have tried him with every variety of languishing glances. Joseph was less innocent and more venture-some than he."

"He paid no attention?"

"Not the least in the world."

"Then I am lost," cried the hairdresser, despondently.

"Ah, *dame!*" retorted La Catalane; "if you are clever enough to bring him here to me some evening, or to take me to Olympe's quarters, I will answer for it that we could carry it through."

"Oh, that would be admirable!" exclaimed the hairdresser, in deep thought.

"Admirable is the very word; and for my own part, as I am a generous body, and what I want before everything else is Bannière, if we succeed, I will take him and make no claim on your hundred louis."

"Hum! how can we do it?" muttered Agathe.

"*Dame!* that's your affair. Select some evening when Olympe is to act, and when she will be delayed at the theatre by some social gathering; invent or create some means of postponing her return; meanwhile I will step into her room."

"But suppose she should return and surprise you?"

'Oh, well, then there would be just what we want, — trouble and scandal."

"What then?"

"It will be much worse than if Bannière were enticed here, for the poor wretch will be in his own and Olympe's house, — in the conjugal domicile, so to speak. That will be enough to make mischief between them for the other world as well as this. Come, what are you thinking so seriously about?"

"Ah, I am thinking that this scheme that you propose will be very difficult to carry out."

"Very well, my friend," said La Catalane, "if you choose to give up your share in it, I propose to carry it out on my own account. Since we have been talking about it, I have become enthusiastic for it."

" And — "

" And I will try it, at all events."

" Ah, *mon Dieu!* " suddenly exclaimed the hair-dresser.

" What is it, pray ? "

" Oh, such an idea! "

" Are you going mad ? "

" Oh, Mademoiselle, indeed it is a most excellent idea."

" Tell me what it is, then."

" Yes, that's the thing to do, Mademoiselle; it's all arranged."

" I am to have Bannière ? "

" Well, no."

" What am I to have, then ? I warn you that I pro-pose to hold out for something."

" You will have the ten thousand livres."

" You are losing your wits."

" Not at all, not at all."

" What are you doing, pray ? "

" I am turning the matter over in my mind."

" Well, I am all at sea myself."

" Have you any decided dislike for poor Abbé d'Hoirac, Mademoiselle ? "

" I, for the abbé ? "

" Yes, for the abbé. Ah, he's a very good fellow, after all."

" Well, suppose I have a decided liking for him, what has that to do with it ? "

" Oh, you will see, you will see."

" Well, I ask nothing better than to see; but you don't show me anything."

" Instead of surreptitiously introducing you into Olympe's house, which presents a thousand difficulties and would lead to nothing, or at least to nothing of any account — ”

“ What! nothing of any account ? ”

“ No. For suppose that everything turns out as you wish, may it not be that Olympe will forgive Bannière, after all; may it not be that an investigation will put us to shame; last of all, may it not be that even though she believes Bannière unfaithful, Olympe will resist as stoutly afterwards as before ? ”

“ Do you really believe her virtuous, then ? ”

“ Alas, yes.”

“ Indeed, it is very possible that it would be as you say,” said La Catalane; “ but even so I shall have lost nothing.”

“ Very true, but on the other hand I shall have earned nothing. No, no, no! I have a better plan than that. I have a plan to give you the ten thousand livres without prejudice to Bannière.”

“ Ah, a golden plan that, my girl! ”

“ It is this.”

“ I am listening.”

“ The abbé, when he sent me upon the mission which you know about, gave me full powers in case of success; that is to say, he directed me to hire a well-furnished house for the use of Olympe, who might be expected, perhaps, in the early days of this new arrangement, to retain sufficient scruples concerning the former one to forbid her throwing Bannière over at the very first; the abbé, too, has precautions to take, for he is married to Mother Church.”

“ Oh, our abbés, notwithstanding that nuptial bond, have adopted since the regency so general a custom of living like bachelors — ”

"No matter; I know what I am saying, and I see where I am going."

"Go on, then."

"Where was I?"

"You were at the house."

"Oh, yes; instead of telling the abbé that Olympe refuses, I will tell him that she accepts."

"Be careful!"

"Don't interrupt me."

"But what about Olympe's virtue?"

"That's just what I'm getting at; it is with that same virtue that I am going to make my trap. I will surround the affair with all sorts of rebuffs and volleys and sorties, just like what happens in besieging strong fortresses; if necessary, I will use up a week in saying 'yes' to the abbé,— nine days, perhaps; that will be three days for each letter."

"Upon my word!"

"Then, when the house is rented, and everything all ready, I will say that the fair one will consent to nothing but a mysterious, secret interview."

"Good, again; but how will you get out of it at the last moment?"

"Why, at the last moment you will be there, of course."

"I?"

"Didn't you tell me that you have no feeling of repugnance for the abbé?"

"I have no repugnance for anybody; that is, I am not a stand-offish, affected fine lady like Olympe."

"Very well, then; the appointment being made, you will keep it."

"Oh, yes!"

"That's a good plan, I think, eh?"

"Magnificent for half an hour."

"But why not for more than one half-hour? Is n't the abbé as blind as a bat?"

"Just because of his blindness," said La Catalane, with a sigh, "he will want to see better than those with the most perfect sight."

"Well, what is there to worry about? The conditions will be made; and if worse comes to worst, and you are discovered, you will have your ten thousand livres, and I my twenty-four hundred."

"Yes; but the abbé will make a great noise over it, and shut us up in some For-l'Évêque."

"The abbé will keep quiet; his interest will lie wholly in doing so. How can you suppose that an abbé who swallowed Bannière's blows with a guitar without a word, will go blathering about concerning such a palpable deception as that? No; he will swallow the exchange even more mildly, depend upon it!"

"Upon my soul, it is marvellous,—the way you have thought out all that."

"Why should I not? But what do you say,—will you or won't you?"

"The most piquant thing about it," said La Catalane, maliciously, "and the most interesting, is that if we should content ourselves with one experience, and the fraud should not be discovered at the time, the abbé would be furious with rage, and would disclose the whole thing, and everything would point so clearly to Olympe's guilt that she would not know how to justify herself."

"That very prospect is tempting to me, I admit; and in addition to that, when the disclosure is made, Bannière, who is a sensitive fellow too, will abandon Olympe, and you will have him at your mercy."

"That 's very possible, I think myself."

"Does that decide you?"

"Yes, it does, indeed."

"Shall I put the irons in the fire?"

"In with them!"

"Do you give me *carte blanche?*"

"I give you *carte noire*, which is much better."

"On your word of honor?"

"*Foi de Catalane!* I have no desire to deceive you."

"Give me your hand."

"Done!" cried La Catalane, clapping her little hand vigorously against the broad, rough palm of the hairdresser.

XXVI.

LOVE AND MYOPIA.

ONCE the plot was laid by these two female demons, it only remained to put it in execution.

It was a simple matter.

The abbé, upon receiving the hairdresser's agreement, had ordered her, whom he had constituted at once his factotum and ambassadress, to hire and furnish suitable apartments for Olympe's reception on the day when, besieged like Danae by a shower of gold, she should strike her colors.

The go-between was too shrewd either to tell the abbé of the absolute check she had met with, or to arouse his hopes too suddenly. She represented to her employer that she had been repulsed, to be sure, but that she had, as she withdrew, carefully studied a certain advantageous position, which she thought she might gradually carry, and which, when once she had carried it, would inevitably assure the victory which had eluded her once, but was not lost forever.

Furthermore, the abbé might have his suspicions, for he had had a taste of Olympe's virtue, — Olympe, who was so gentle when she was left in peace, but was so quick to bristle up at the least alarm; and it was necessary that his suspicions should be allowed to die away gradually as his passion grew. The hairdresser was like the expert fisherman who does not pull on his line until the fish has taken a good bite.

Thus a series of imaginary operations was carried on around Olympe, like those which take place about a besieged town. Progress was duly reported to the abbé, as to Louis XIV. at Nimeguen, and like Louis XIV., he saw for himself very little of the progress of the siege. To-day they had drawn the line of circumvallation, to-morrow work would begin in the trenches, day after to-morrow the sappers and miners would be called upon, and on the following day the mine would be exploded. And the abbé listened to all this, like a vainglorious general or a blind lover, — which two types have many points of resemblance.

A month passed in siege-operations. The general became more and more impatient, the lover more and more madly in love.

At last, one fine morning, the hairdresser called upon the abbé with a radiant visage. Olympe's virtue, she said, was beginning to sound a parley and to talk of surrender; but it wished to surrender with all the honors of war.

So long as Olympe surrendered, the abbé cared little for the terms, and there was no haggling over them.

Only the night before the abbé had said (and the hairdresser had used his words as the inducement to the proposed capitulation), —

"If she will listen to me, and I can please her, though it be but for one moment! I shall be the happiest man on earth."

"The happiest man on earth, if you can please her, though it be but for a moment!" the hairdresser had repeated after him.

"Why, yes!" he had replied testily. "*Parbleu!* I know perfectly well that in her heart she loves that blackguard Bannière."

" Alas! it is her one fault."

" But," the abbé had continued, " I expect nothing
more from her than the gratification of a mere caprice.
I have no ambition for her love."

A rare lover's prospectus that; but as everybody
knows, subscriptions are still obtained to-day upon the
strength of prospectuses.

The hairdresser reported, then, that Olympe had
assented to the abbé's prospectus. The terms of sub-
scription remained to be settled.

They were discussed for three days.

On the third day the female flag of truce brought the
actress's ultimatum.

She was to appoint the days of meeting.

Agreed.

Those days would be nights, since it was at night that
Bannière gambled as a rule, and Olympe was not free at
any other time.

Agreed.

The meetings were always to take place in utter
darkness.

The abbé cried out at this.

The hairdresser fell back upon the fable of Psyche and
Cupid; only the parts were reversed, — the abbé had the
rôle of Psyche, and Olympe that of Cupid.

If the abbé undertook to make use of the least glim-
mer of light, were it a lamp, a dark lantern, or a match,
Psyche would fly away, like Venus's son, forever.

This condition was discussed for thirty-six hours; but
the hairdresser, claiming to act for Olympe, would not
budge.   At last the abbé yielded; but he said, as he did
so, that he was induced to accept that humiliating condition only because of his near-sightedness, which made
it less important for him than for most people.

Article three, then, was agreed to as the others had been.

Olympe alone was to have the key of the apartments. She was never to make appointments in writing, letters being a weapon invented by the devil himself for the benefit of injured husbands and jealous guardians; on those days, or nights rather, when Olympe was willing to receive the abbé, she would send him the key, and he would know what it meant.

This article was agreed to like the others, with the added condition that the key should be returned on the following day, or the day after that at the very latest.

Three days later, the abbé, who gasped at every stroke of the bell, received the key from the hand of the hairdresser, with no other comment than these words, —

"This evening at eleven."

The abbé leaped for joy, took the key, kissed it, and began to dance around his room, singing an air from a comic opera.

When the hour arrived, the vanquisher of hearts, in his smartest attire, perfumed, and intoxicated with delight, issued forth, glided with beating heart into a little hall of the mysterious house, ascended to the first floor, and found in the anteroom the hairdresser, who led him as unerringly as Ariadne's thread to the heart of the labyrinth, whence he did not emerge until daybreak.

If the proposition had been made to renounce the meetings promised for the future, and accept in exchange the cross of an archbishop or a cardinal's hat, he would certainly have refused. Moreover we must remember that the abbé's ambition did not lie in the direction of ecclesiastical preferment.

It goes without saying that Monsieur d'Hoirac, most

near-sighted of men, had triumphed over the scruples of
La Catalane, scented with vervain, which was the perfume most affected by Olympe

In accordance with the terms of the treaty, the abbé
left the key in the door.

But his passion had reached such a height that he
began the very next morning to persecute the hairdresser
with demands that the key which he had left in the
door should be sent back to him. He urged especially
that he was anxious to give his dear mistress some proofs
of his esteem for her. Above all, he was ashamed of
her impoverished state, which was due to that wretched
Bannière.

He went on at great length as to the use he expected
to make of his wealth, and the prosperity which he had
in mind for Olympe, and in which, of course, her confidante would share.

Less than this would have been necessary to convince
the hairdresser. La Catalane, too, was equally desirous
of money and revenge. So the two impostors agreed to
have the meetings at regular intervals, their frequency
to be governed by the generosity of the Abbé d'Hoirac,
and to enjoy such tranquillity as the imprudent actions
he would not fail to commit would leave at their
disposal.

A second rendezvous was granted at a reasonable interval from the first. Its result was to change the abbé's
passion to delirium, and to transfer to the hands of La
Catalane the ten thousand livres, and to those of the
hairdresser the two hundred louis, so impatiently
expected.

But it can readily be understood that these nocturnal
meetings were multiplied to no purpose, for they brought
only a vague and incomplete happiness to the abbé's

heart. It was much like the happiness of a thief; it
surely was not that of a lover; and so he passed the day
seeking the society of Olympe, who was so imperfectly
his, since she was his only one night out of five or six,
and even then he was not allowed to see her face.

Love is distinguished from simple desire in this, — that
it is developed by the continual presence of the beloved
object. So, after three weeks or a month of these meetings, a love had grown up in the abbé's heart which
Olympe's whole life would have failed to satisfy.

As for Bannière his days were passing in happiness
and content. One day, when he had nothing more to
sell or pledge to Jacob, he ventured to ask him for a
loan upon his simple note of hand; and the Jew concluded to let him have it at ten per cent, which was
dirt-cheap, considering Bannière's financial condition.

This unexpected supply of credit came, as will be
imagined, from that golden spring called the Abbé
d'Hoirac. Olympe, as he supposed, had told him that
she was free when Bannière was playing; and the abbé,
in order to facilitate his meetings with Olympe, did his
best to make easy Bannière's road to the gambling-hell.

Poor Olympe was the only one who reaped no advantage from all this, except in the greater loneliness of her
life; the Abbé d'Hoirac had ceased to visit her, and
Bannière never left the gaming-table.

Meanwhile each meeting, while it increased D'Hoirac's
passion for Olympe, put a fresh restraint upon it; for
the false Olympe demanded, as a condition precedent to
each, that he would make no attempt to see her except
in secret.

D'Hoirac, as we have seen, began by promising; he
was too much in love not to promise whatever was asked,
and as he renewed the promise every time he was called

upon, and kept it too, he assured the success of the
schemes of the two plotters in the interval.

He had even been instructed to maintain toward
Olympe, when chance threw them together, the attitude
of a man who had been repulsed and shown the door,
and was crushed thereby. They had made him swear
that he would hardly bow to her on the public promenade, that he would never approach her unless invited,
that he would never-show himself at her house, either
in person or through any intermediary, and above all,
that he would never write to her.

We have noted above the joint theory of La Catalane
and the hairdresser on the subject of letters.

He had bowed very slightly to her when they met.

He had often hung about her, but had never visited
her, either at her home, in her dressing-room at the
theatre, or in her chair.

He had ceased sending her flowers and letters and
messages.

Everything, in short, was working to the perfect satisfaction of La Catalane and her prime minister, the
hairdresser.

But an occurrence, as simple as most of those which
upset plans and fortunes and empires, came very near
foiling the clever combination of these two worthy
females.

XXVII.

A WOMAN'S HEART.

OLYMPE had said nothing personally to the abbé; but in turning the hairdresser out of doors in consequence of the insulting propositions she had made to her, she had effectively turned the abbé out as well.

Now, since he had been thus ejected, the abbé, believing himself, as we have seen, to be the happiest man on earth, had borne himself with a degree of consideration, reserve, and delicacy which Olympe was very far from attributing to its true cause.

Indeed, his manly way of supporting a blow which must have borne hard upon his self-esteem as well as upon his passion, touched Olympe to some extent.

She had gone so far as to reproach herself for having closed her doors upon a civil fellow who had been brutally treated by Bannière, and to whom she owed some kindly consideration rather than such extreme harshness.

For indeed the worthy man had been guilty of nothing more than a little gallantry.

So it was that whenever she saw him avoid her, draw aside to let her pass at the theatre, turn about to escape her in the street, and all this with humble salutations and reverences, and a respectful submission fit to bend the hardest heart; whenever at the accustomed hour she — the poor, deserted creature, so ill repaid for her virtue — failed to see him come into her parlor, coquettish and airy and clever, with his bouquets and his music, — she

felt away down in her heart an emotion which almost
resembled remorse.

It was not that Olympe had the least symptom of
caring for this youth. Oh, *mon Dieu!* no. But a
woman never forgets a wealthy, attractive, and civil
young man who has cared for her.

Besides, as we have said, to her mind the abbé at
this crisis was apparently bearing himself toward her
with a noble and dignified pride which commended itself
to her.

This astonished her, and, beginning there, decidedly
attracted her, especially as she might have looked for
unpleasant reprisals in view of his somewhat boastful
and extremely noisy disposition. How many men in
D'Hoirac's position would have made a great noise about
their former friendly relations, and have exchanged their
love for hatred, their servility for insolence, and their
gifts for hostilities!

For a week Olympe had thoroughly expected to be
hissed, and pestered to death, as is so often the case after
such execution as she had done.

Was the abbé keeping quiet only from fear of Bannière?
That was hard to believe, notwithstanding the adventure of the serenade. She knew the little man to be as
brave as he was near-sighted; she knew, too, that he had
enough gentle blood in his veins, and consequently must
be stout-hearted enough to hold his own against hotter
heads and more dangerous swords than the head and
sword of Monsieur Bannière.

His reserve and his modest demeanor, then, could only
be attributed to his delicacy of perception and his noble
heart.

Olympe was moved by all this,— so moved that she
would not allow any one in her presence to speak deri-

sively of Monsieur d'Hoirac; so touched that she promised herself to make reparation to the worthy man, one day or another, as occasion might offer.

Alas! it is the misfortune of husbands, and of lovers too, that the occasion always does offer, to those who seek it, to make reparation to worthy folk whom they have insulted.

Bannière spoke one afternoon of going partridge-shooting with two friends of the green cloth. Olympe suggested that she should bear them company as far as the outskirts of the city.

The plan was carried out; and Olympe in her carriage did not leave the gentlemen until they were outside the walls, and the dogs had begun to rummage around in the long grass.

She was driving back alone, at a foot-pace, lost in thought, and listening abstractedly to the occasional distant reports of Bannière's gun, when she espied at the corner of a street the Abbé d'Hoirac, dressed *en cavalier* and astride an excellent horse.

He was followed by a servant who carried his sword.

Seen thus, with his good looks and his smart attire, the abbé had quite the air of a well-to-do gentleman, or even of a prince in disguise. Riding erect in his stirrups, as the English do, he was managing his mount very cleverly, upon my word! But with all his address the abbé was none the less the most near-sighted of men; and he would have passed very near Olympe without seeing her, if she had not suddenly, watching her opportunity, thought that she would never have a better one, and so cried out in her high treble, —

"Oh, Abbé, Abbé!"

The abbé recognized the voice; and although he saw hardly more than a cloud, albeit a cloud which, like those of Virgil, enshrouded a divinity, he dug his spurs so deep into his horse's flanks, as he turned in the direction of the voice, that he very nearly made him leap over the carriage.

"Is it you," he cried, "is it you who call me? Where are you, Madame, where are you?"

"I was obliged to call you," said Olympe, "since you were passing by so proudly without noticing me."

"Well," said the abbé, smiling, "have I anything else to do than obey your orders, and have you not forbidden me to approach you?"

"There, there!" said she, somewhat startled by the aspect of those mild eyes which, for all their myopia, seemed to say, by the flames that shot forth from them, so many things which she could not understand, — "there, there, now that we are face to face, can't we get along like good friends without quarrelling or speaking of love? No, let us be staid and dignified, and all will be well."

"Madame, you enchant me," said D'Hoirac, feeling for the hand which Olympe held out to him. "What! am I to have the privilege of seeing you, not only as I see you now, but *also* at your own house?"

Olympe failed to comprehend the force of that "also," and was about to request an explanation; but a gambol on the horse's part interrupted her. She gave a little shriek as she saw the abbé apparently at the mercy of the spirited animal's antics.

He mastered him, however, for the abbé was an excellent horseman, but it was too late then; they were approaching the city, and Olympe contented herself with saying:

"Leave me now, for people will talk if they should see me go out with Monsieur Bannière and return with Monsieur d'Hoirac. Leave me and come to see me when you choose."

" Oh! " exclaimed the abbé.

" But only on one condition," said Olympe.

" Tell me what it is."

" That you are never to say a word which Monsieur Bannière, of whom I am very fond, would not like to hear."

The abbé made a wry face; but still, even on those conditions, he considered the game worth the candle.

" Thanks, thanks! " said he; " I promise."

He rode off, beaming with satisfaction, across the fields, while Olympe re-entered the city.

The abbé lost no time in telling his happiness to the hairdresser, who ran off to La Catalane with her embarrassment.

" We are lost," said La Catalane, " if those two creatures meet; for they will spoil all as soon as they speak. They must not meet."

" It is impossible to prevent it since he has Olympe's permission; but as soon as he goes back there, I must go too."

" How can you fix it? "

" I will think it over."

" Reflect also that love has nothing whatever to do with her taking him back out of friendship."

The hairdresser began by seeking out D'Hoirac, and informing him that he had obtained leave to call upon Olympe again through her influence. But the leave was granted only upon the most severe conditions: he must never allude in the most distant way to anything that had taken place at the secret meetings; he must never betray, by too much animation of word or gesture, the degree of familiarity which they had reached; only his eyes were at liberty to speak: the eyes can say many things, but a woman is always at liberty to maintain that she does not understand their language.

The abbé understood the situation perfectly, and placed in the hairdresser's hands an oath drawn up with sacramental formality.

Armed with that document, the hairdresser wrote to Olympe.

Her letter was a perfect model of humility; she resorted to every known form of supplication. Since she had had the misfortune to harbor the bare idea of becoming a dishonest woman, everything had gone ill with her. She had lost her best customers in the city; her theatrical customers did not pay her, and she said that she had an enormous account against La Catalane, and could not collect a sou of it. Her only hope was that Olympe, so kind and lovely, would forgive her; with disgrace misfortune had come upon her, with pardon good fortune would return.

Olympe was proud, for she had chastised the abbé and his go-between, and both, instead of scheming against her, were at her feet.

She thought that it would be inconsistent to forgive one and not the other; so, for consistency's sake, she forgave both.

Sometimes it is a very dangerous thing for a woman to be too consistent.

The hairdresser was readmitted to Olympe's abode, just an hour before the abbé was to make his reappearance.

There had been another matter to be arranged before that reappearance was permitted. It was necessary to reconcile Bannière to the prospect; but during the two or three months that the abbé had stayed away, Bannière had been completely reassured by observing his continued respectful bearing toward Olympe. Still more was he reassured by her well-known loyalty. He had pommelled the abbé, on the occasion of the serenade, much less because he was jealous than because he had been losing at play.

The poor abbé, reinstated as a welcome guest at the house and supported there by the presence of the hairdresser, devoted himself from morning till night to that conversation with the eyes which alone his oath permitted him to hold with Olympe, — manœuvres which indifferent observers call mere flirting, but interested participants, amorous languor, — a sort of radiation from the whole person of him who loves toward the beloved object; Olympe naturally understanding nothing of it all, and greeting with harmless merriment the tender and melancholy contortions of the charming dandy.

D'Hoirac, like all those who are thoroughly deceived, and are manfully trudging along the wrong road, believing themselves to be going right, was lost in admiration of the prudence, the firmness, the sweet and modest reserve of this lovely creature. He was considerably disappointed to find that she was so afraid of Bannière; but he had not assumed sufficient authority to justify him in daring to combat openly against a custom of longer standing than his own.

It is easy to understand how thoroughly and vigilantly the hairdresser, having won her way back into Olympe's good graces by her humility, watched over poor D'Hoirac, and moderated his excitement; he was always ready to rush in headlong, like young dogs in the hunting-field, at the first scent or sight of the quarry.

She was convinced that, despite his plighted word, the first *tête-a-tête* of any length would be employed by our turtle-dove in cooing and assuming airs of proprietorship which would astonish Olympe, and lead to embarrassing explanations.

Now, to allow an explanation before the bird was thoroughly plucked, and before injured self-interest and wounded self-esteem had been thoroughly avenged, was a blunder which two such birds of prey as the hairdresser and La Catalane would have blushed to make.

The hairdresser indeed played her part admirably; she had returned to Olympe's service as the abbé's enemy, and in that capacity she naturally became very friendly to Monsieur Bannière. In this twofold character, the object dearest to her heart was to maintain absolutely unsullied the dearest possession of our actor, which was constantly assailed by the gestures and the eyes, if not by the tongue, of that accursed Abbé d'Hoirac.

Nothing therefore was more in accordance with Olympe's wishes, and at the same time more convenient for the woman herself, than her continual presence, or incessant going and coming in the room where the abbé and Olympe used to sit; so that the infernal adroitness of the woman had actually effected the removal of all obstacles to her success by the very people who were most interested in her failure.

But the abbé was not the man to waste his strength in vain struggles. He made a study of the hairdresser's tastes, and thought that she seemed to be particularly enthusiastic on the subject of maraschino.

He sent her six bottles by his servant, whom he directed to put them into her own hands; and about an hour later he stealthily rang the bell very softly, stole by Mademoiselle Claire, slipping five louis into her hand, and glided into Olympe's boudoir, with a feeling of additional security because he thought that he saw the hairdresser, through the half-open door of the kitchen, drinking maraschino out of the bottle.

Alas! one cannot anticipate everything. Even the marten, shrewdest of animals, sometimes walks into the trap; and the hairdresser, shrewdest of females, was for once as unwary as the marten.

Bannière had gone to play as usual; D'Hoirac accordingly found Olympe alone, and began operations by taking her hand and kissing it affectionately.

Olympe was in very good humor. She did not notice how flushed the abbé's face was, or the nervous twitching of his hands, or how his blue eyes rolled around under their black lashes, — eyes which, notwithstanding their defective sight, seemed to give forth electric sparks.

The fair Célimène had heard from Claire of the maraschino he had sent, and at first she joked him upon the quantity.

He looked about, and making as sure as he could with his poor eyes reinforced by glasses that there was no one in the room, he said, —

"You are quite alone?"

"Why, yes, I think so," replied Olympe, astonished at the question.

"Then I may speak to you frankly."

"There is nothing to prevent."

"Oh, how jealous I am!" cried the abbé.

"Jealous! of what?" she asked.

"Can't you guess?"

"Upon my word, no."

"Why, jealous of him who takes my happiness from me, of him who steals my very life!"

"Come, come!" said Olympe, "so that nonsense has taken hold of you again?"

"But it has never left me."

"Well, then, you propose to begin again?"

"But since we are alone, my dear heart!"

Olympe exclaimed in amazement. She thought she must have heard amiss.

The abbé stopped, gazing at her with his great eyes.

"Did I understand you to say *my heart?*" demanded Olympe.

"Why, yes," said the abbé, "you are my love, my life, my heart!"

Olympe fairly shouted with laughter.

The abbé, stupefied at her behavior, looked about to see if there were not some person in the chamber whom his myopic eyes had not detected.

"How many jugs of maraschino did you keep for yourself, dear Monsieur d'Hoirac?" said Olympe, in a tone of raillery.

"Come now," said the abbé, imploringly, "let me talk sense to you a little while."

"I certainly have no objection, for so far you have talked nothing but the veriest nonsense."

"For Heaven's sake, Olympe, drop this mask, which deceives me in spite of myself."

"This mask?"

"If you knew how **much** suffering it causes me."

"What mask?"

"Oh," cried the abbé, rising to throw himself down at Olympe's knees, "it is impossible for me to see you playing such a comedy any longer; and — "

He had not finished his sentence, he had not executed his contemplated movement, he had not touched Olympe with the end of his finger, when the hairdresser, flushed, dishevelled, and gasping for breath, rushed into the room, and almost fell between the near-sighted abbé and her mistress.

Olympe's towering wrath, the victorious yet suppliant attitude of the abbé. told the hairdresser that she had arrived in the nick of time, and that it would have been all up with the secret a moment later.

Olympe, seeing her frightened appearance, could not help laughing.

"You called me, Madame?" cried the woman.

"No; but I was just about to call you," Olympe replied, with a withering glance in the direction cf Monsieur d'Hoirac.

The abbé made an attempt to justify himself.

"Monsieur," said Olympe, "you know, I think, on what conditions I receive you at my house."

"What then?"

"What then! Why, you have broken them, that's all."

"Ah, my dear!" cried the abbé, dismayed at the tone in which she addressed him.

"Again!" said she.

"But it's before nobody but her!" cried the abbé, in despair, — "before your confidante! so it's exactly the same as if we were alone."

"Are you mad?" exclaimed the hairdresser, seizing him by the arm and twirling him around.

"Show the abbé out," said Olympe, "and request him not to drink any more maraschino on the days he proposes to come here."

The hairdresser hastened to drag out Monsieur d'Hoirac, rather than show him out.

Olympe observed her zeal and misunderstood it, as the whole world would have done, La Catalane alone excepted. She laughed so immoderately that the abbé could hear her mocking cachinnations in the ante-chamber.

The hairdresser had no sooner got him out of Olympe's presence than she began, —

"Oh, you wretched man, you will ruin everything."

"What was the matter?" asked the near-sighted fellow; "was there some one hidden there, after all? Why did n't she tell me so at first?"

"No, there was no one."

"Then why all this fuss, if we were alone?"

"Oh, how stupid men are!"

"But in what! Tell me, or I 'll curse myself."

"Was n't I there?"

"Suppose you were! Are you not the echoless wall which hears our vows, the deaf partition which sees our kisses? Does she hide herself from you, pray, — you, our go-between and confidante?"

"Stupid! stupid!" muttered the hairdresser, delighted with the word, which drove the abbé mad. "Stupid! not to appreciate all that woman's delicacy!"

"But it was the same thing before you came, when we were entirely alone."

"But, Monsieur, don't you know that there are secrets which a woman cannot confess even to herself?"

"Truly you exaggerate, my girl; and when one has a lover — "

"When one has one lover," retorted the hairdresser, "one does not act the same as when one has two."

This reply closed the abbé's mouth. It was, in fact, a rude blow for a jealous man; but woman generally prefer to deal with such by brutality rather than by persuasion.

The abbé sighed.

"Why does she have two lovers, then?" said he, gloomily.

"Pshaw! I thought you were a clever man," said the hairdresser; "but I see you are an idiot like all the rest."

"Oh, one does really get tired at last."

"Monsieur l'Abbé, I warn you that you are becoming intolerable.   Pray remember the beginning of all this."

"Ah!"

"What did you ask for then? — a simple act of charity, nothing more."

"Well, I don't deny it."

"To-day it is that no longer; to-day you make demands, and you are amazed!"

"Why has she another lover?"

"Great God! what has that to do with you?   Attend to your own affairs."

"That's what I am doing, I should say."

"Yes, in a way to ruin them forever."

"How so?"

"*Pardieu!* you will weary her, and she will dismiss you."

"Ah, indeed!"

"She will be bored to death."

"But I simply tell her of my love; how can it bore her to listen?   I ask no more than that."

"No more than that?   Really, you are very moderate in your demands!   Of course she will listen to you, but not here, — not in Monsieur Bannière's house, not in that room where everything recalls her spring-time of love, not upon that sofa where she has dreamed so many times of the poetic King Hérode."

"Pshaw!   Does she dream of Monsieur de Mailly too, I wonder?"

"Ah, now you are an ungrateful, ugly beast!   The idea of your reproaching the poor woman with her lovers when she has been kind enough not to turn you out of doors!"

"That's true, I am wrong."

"Ah, I 'm very glad that you admit it."

"Come, what will you say to her ? "

"I ? Nothing."

"Will you not speak to her of my grief ? "

"Never."

"Then how shall we be reconciled ? "

"That remains to be seen."

"Will it be soon ? "

"If you are sensible."

"What must I do to be sensible ? "

"Be governed by circumstances, and above all by the locality.   Here you are Monsieur l'Abbé d'Hoirac calling upon Mademoiselle Olympe, mistress of none but Monsieur Bannière.   Do you understand me ? "

"Indeed, only too well ! But you must agree that this is an extraordinary state of things beyond anything ever known."

"Bah ! if you were not near-sighted, you would have seen other things much more extraordinary than this, and would n't be surprised at anything."

"It may be so.   But you are interested in me, are n't you ? "

"I should think so ! If I were not interested in you, do you suppose I would preach to you as I do ? "

"Well, then, make my peace with Olympe as soon as possible."

"When do you wish it to be, — this ' soon as possible ' ? "

"To-morrow, my girl."

"*Peste !* you are in a hurry ! "

"I am in a fever, you see."

"Very well, then, to-morrow.   I will do my best; but it is difficult."

"Here are twenty louis."

"Yes, I will do my best."

"Oh!" cried the abbé, "when you speak like that, I could embrace you."

"If I were only more attractive."

"Bah! I am near-sighted."

"That is to say that you are an impertinent scamp."

"Do you think so?"

"Yes; but I forgive you because I should n't want you to be seen embracing me."

Saying this with a bitterness which she tried in vain to conceal, the hairdresser dismissed the abbé, who went out by the little door.

The human mind is so strangely constituted that the abbé when he went away was better pleased with the incident than if it had resulted according to his wishes.

So, instead of returning home, he went and woke up Jacob, and bought from him, among other jewels, Monsieur de Mailly's famous ring, which Bannière had filched from Olympe and sold to the worthy Israelite.

XXVIII.

THE ANNIVERSARY OF "HÉRODE AND MARIAMNE."

THE hairdresser kept her word to the Abbé d'Hoirac.

All hands were so much interested in having the clandestine meetings begin again, that the spurious Olympe's severity could not long endure.

The following evening a commissioner came to the abbé's domicile with a message which he could but understand; it was the key of the mysterious house which, by the terms of the treaty, he left in the door after every interview, so that they might have the pleasure of sending it to him again.

The abbé, having made his preparations, arrived ten minutes before the appointed time, his heart swelling with joy.

He was compelled to wait until the hour struck, when the rustling of a silk dress on the floor announced the arrival of her whom he was so impatiently awaiting.

To dart toward her, gain possession of a plump, cool hand, slip upon the finger the ring purchased from the Jew, fasten his lips upon it, and sue for pardon, — such was the abbé's preamble.

The conversation turned upon the episode of the preceding evening, La Catalane of course having been thoroughly posted by her accomplice as to all that had taken place. So the false Olympe, almost as well informed as if she had been the person she claimed to be, reproached the abbé in the most natural way for having conducted himself most unworthily, and explained

to him that in that house — that is to say, under
Monsieur Bannière's roof — certain subjects of conversation were prohibited which were perfectly legitimate in
their present location, — that is to say, under the roof of
Monsieur d'Hoirac.

Thus made acquainted with the details of his wrong-
doing, the abbé appreciated its enormity, and admitted
it, asked pardon for it once more, and obtained it.

He had very good reasons to give too.

"I needed some balm," he said, "for the suffering
caused by separation. To speak to Olympe only in
secret, in utter darkness, and in a strange house, could
hardly be called the summit of earthly bliss, could it?"

It was suggested that light and darkness were as one
to his defective vision.

He replied that he would waive his demurrer to the
darkness, but that the matter of separation was another
affair.

The false Olympe exclaimed at the word " separation."

But the abbé's wit was keen; he retorted that there
was a physical and a moral separation, and that the
latter variety was the most painful of all.

A little laugh was the only reply.

"Is n't that true?" asked the abbé.

"Oh, no, by no means!"

"What! this Monsieur Bannière, this absolute master,
this unworthy master —"

"Let's hear no more about Monsieur Bannière, I
beg, at Monsieur d'Hoirac's, than I hear of Monsieur
d'Hoirac at Monsieur Bannière's."

"But I shall rebel finally!" cried the abbé. "So
when you are in that house, you love this Monsieur
Bannière? Upon my word, I shall be compelled to get
rid of him."

"I do not love him, you know very well," was the soft reply.

"In that case," retorted the abbé, "why not break with him altogether?"

"Oh, there, there! we shall come to that."

"Yes, and meanwhile I am dying."

"You are a trifle impatient."

"Is n't it natural?"

"No; for if I listened to you, it would be necessary to turn the poor boy out."

"What does that matter, if you no longer love him?"

"For shame!"

"I am jealous."

"What! now, you ungrateful wretch?"

"I don't say that I am at this moment; but I shall be to-morrow, or as soon as I am no longer with you."

"What must I do, pray?"

"This: promise me that you will treat this Bannière so contemptuously that he will feel that you no longer love him."

"That's easy enough to do.   There! does that satisfy you?   Do you feel better?"

"Yes; but later, I shall be less tolerant."

"Oh! oh!"

"Because I shall be still more in love."

"Very well, then!"

But this promise was no sooner made by the false Olympe than the true one hastened to break it, as we shall see.

While the affairs of La Catalane and the abbé were going forward thus, the affairs of Olympe and Bannière were proceeding as usual, — that is to say, with considerable irregularity.   Olympe had given up catechising Bannière; but he had not given up loving Olympe, nor struggling to retain her love, so that from time to time after he had driven her to despair he would still succeed in arousing her love or her indulgence again, obstinate as she was.

Olympe's obstinacy, in fact, was all on the surface; at bottom her disposition was kind and yielding. Kindness is strength in man, but weakness in woman.

So it happened, after La Catalane had entered into an engagement with the abbé that Olympe should never be sufficiently demonstrative of affection for Bannière to arouse the jealousy of her other adorer, that Olympe and Bannière, who had not been let into the secret, executed a new lease of love in token of the anniversary of the first performance of " King Hérode."

The unlucky abbé happened to drop in upon the two lovers just at the dessert stage of the feast which they were giving in honor of their love.

The feast had been prolonged because Olympe did not act that evening, — La Catalane was creating a new part; so that, as if everything had been arranged in advance to bring about a catastrophe, the hairdresser was at the theatre to attend to her professional duties.

D'Hoirac, then, made his appearance at Olympe's door at a time when he was least expected after what had taken place two evenings before.

It must be said that he, on his side, was not expecting to find what he found there.

At that hour Monsieur Bannière was almost always at the card-table. The abbé knew that every event has its anniversary, but he did not know of the anniversary of this great event in the lives of Olympe and Bannière.

Entering the house with his customary heedlessness (the lovers too had been heedless enough to leave the key in the door), the abbé started to walk through a mirror in the anteroom which he took for a door, and in which he saw the reflection of Olympe and Bannière, a glass of champagne in the hand of each.

The abbè stood as if stupefied, staring at this tableau.

A single servant, whose attendance they had dispensed with, was picking over the remains of the feast in the kitchen.

The abbé, in a towering rage at what he had seen in the mirror, turned upon his heel, and rushed into the dining-room, not as if impelled by friendly interest, but like a jealous madman, — like a master and not a visitor.

He made a noise with his voice and a noise with the doors, and appeared before the two lovers like Calchas, with pale face and hair on end.

At this apparition Olympe and Bannière, whom the anniversary and the champagne had combined to put in high good-humor, uttered exclamations of unbounded surprise in different keys, and followed them up with roars of laughter, which raised the abbé's wrath and confusion to the highest possible point. Surely such cruel mystification was never before visited upon a man so deeply in love as the abbé, and who had been so thoroughly reassured by the interview of the preceding evening.

So he turned again and made for the door with clinched teeth, and revolving in his brain all sorts of projects of vengeance, — projects which had no form or coherence in the chaos of his rage, but which might well be ground into shape by the mill of reflection.

But just as he was putting out his hand to seize the knob, Bannière stepped in ahead of him, and took him by the hand.

"Come, come," said he, "are you so unworldly that you are scandalized by the sight of a happy lover at the side of his beloved ? "

D'Hoirac shivered from head to foot; he awaited a word from Olympe.

"Oh!" said she, "Monsieur l'Abbé cannot have any great horror of a happiness which he knows by experience, I fancy."

"Come, my dear," said Bannière, "see if you cannot make our peace with Monsieur d'Hoirac."

And, having exchanged a significant glance with Olympe, he went out, leaving her alone with the abbé in his despair.

His first word was a curse.

"Oh, what infernal wretches women are!" he cried, bringing his hand down heavily upon the table.

Olympe straightened up, as if she herself had received the blow.

"What do you say, Monsieur?" she cried, deeply offended; "is it for my ears that you speak thus?"

"For whose ears should I speak, pray," snarled the abbé "if not for yours?"

"You forget yourself then, I think."

"I do not forget myself; I am in a rage."

"Indeed!" said Olympe, contemptuously, "you are having another attack of madness, apparently."

"Madness, if you choose to call it so! Yes, madness, but ungovernable madness; so beware!"

He struck a second blow upon the table.

"Look out, Abbé," said Olympe, "or you will break the table and the glasses."

"Oh, yes; lovely trifles! One can buy new tables and glasses with money, but nothing will buy back the derided love and the lost illusions of a man of honor."

"Do you know," said Olympe, frowning angrily, "that I fail to understand a single word of all this nonsense, Monsieur?"

"Oh, have done with your dignity, Madame, or rather with your comedy, which consists in putting a gag in my mouth when I undertake to complain."

"You complain! complain of what, I pray to know?"

"What did you promise me? Tell me that."

"I?"

"Yes; had n't I the right to rely upon you?"

"Do you mean to say that I promised you anything?"

"I know what reply you will make; I know very well that here I am not on my own premises, but on Monsieur Bannière's."

"That's very true."

"But you must agree that patience has a limit; and my anger — "

"Your anger! Monsieur," interrupted Olympe, "your anger will eventually arouse mine; and when our two angers are face to face, I warn you of one thing, and that is that mine will request yours to leave the house."

"Madame," said the abbé, raising his voice, "you break your promises; permit me to remind you of them."

"Do so, I beg you, Monsieur; remind me of them, and you will greatly oblige me."

"You permit me to do it then?"

"I beg you to."

"Well, then, was it not agreed that you should never give me reason to be jealous?"

"Jealous! you! and of whom?"

"What!" cried the abbé, lowering his head, and stretching out his arms; "I find you *tête-à-tête* here with Monsieur Bannière."

"Upon my soul," cried Olympe, as if speaking to herself, "the man is mad!"

"Oh, if you forget so quickly," said the abbé, passing

from hot wrath to melancholy, "oh, I foresee a world of misery!"

Olympe shrugged her shoulders; it was clear that the abbé's melancholy was as insane as his anger.

"The other day," said she, "it was the maraschino; but to-day there really is no excuse whatever."

The abbé turned toward her with hands clasped.

"Come now, Olympe, be serious."

"Olympe!" cried the young woman, leaping to her feet; "you call me Olympe? — you!"

"Ah, indeed, this is too much!" shrieked the abbé, whose face was absolutely colorless, from having contained or rather devoured himself so long. "To the devil with your shilly-shallying, your agreements, and your conscientious scruples! I throw them all over, since you are so prompt to forget your word. Yes, here I am on Monsieur Bannière's preserve, it is true; but since you force me to it, I will speak here as I speak at the other place."

"The other place! what do you mean by 'the other place'?"

"Oh, yes, play the innocent, Madame; but this time I will not leave you till I have told you the whole truth to your face."

"What 'other place,' Monsieur?" Olympe again demanded.

"That other place where Monsieur d'Hoirac is on his own premises, Madame; that other place where you reverse Penelope's process, and put together in the evening what you unravel here in the day; that other place where I am weak enough to love the one who deceives me everywhere else."

Olympe uttered a cry which told of violent wrath to come, — a cry like that of a wounded lioness.

It warned the abbé that he had gone too far perhaps; so he passed from threats to suggestions of compromise.

"Come, come," said he; "the time has come for us to speak with perfect frankness. Let us adopt a course which will release us from this equivocal position; let us play with our cards upon the table,— no more ambiguity."

"Yes, that's it, with cards on the table," said Olympe, listening intently to see how far this insane freak would carry him.

"Very well! I have behaved like a miser, have I not?"

"On what occasion, pray?"

"You are not satisfied with what I have given you?"

"What does that mean?" said she. "You seem to be passing from insolence to indecency."

"One moment," said the abbé; "come, dear Olympe, let us talk business once for all, never to recur to the subject again, and our love will run the smoother for it."

Without taking alarm at the horrified looks of Olympe, which by the way he could not see, perhaps, on account of his bad eyes, he continued, —

"I suggest, then, that you have discovered that you have not enough of that which the hairdresser has asked of me in your name."

"The hairdresser — in my name!" And Olympe took her head in her hands, as if it were she who was going mad.

"Oh, don't interrupt me, please!" cried the abbé; "I know all that you would say; but I, as well as you, must have positive assurances. Let us agree upon them together, with equal advantages. Here are the articles which I propose — "

Olympe had made up her mind to listen to the end; she wished to get to the bottom once for all of this extraordinary mental aberration, which persisted in representing itself to her as a real conviction.

"Well," said she, falling back in her chair, "let 's see the articles."

"Article first: you will leave the stage — "

"I — I leave the stage?"

"Just wait."

"I am waiting, as you see. Only hurry up, for I may not have the patience to wait very long."

"You will leave the stage, because your life, so long as it belongs to the public, does not belong to your lover."

Olympe folded her arms as if to confine her wrath within her breast.

"Now," the abbé went on, "once you have ceased to be on the stage, nothing will be easier than to leave the other."

"The other?" repeated Olympe, more astounded than ever. "Who? what other?"

"What? No need to name him, my dear. Is n't he back of all our thoughts, — the wretch?"

"The other, the other, who is back of all our thoughts? Look here, my dear abbé, upon my word you will end by frightening me. Pray, is this a regular joke of yours, to play the madman thus? For my own part, I warn you that I am terribly afraid of madmen; so if you have a variety of jokes, please select some other, and don't go any farther with this one."

"But I am not joking; I — I am — Well, let us pass to article second."

"Go on."

"Article second: the other to be dismissed; we will give him a pension — "

Olympe moved uneasily.

"With a memorandum, drawn up by a notary, something like this: 'Monsieur Bannière shall receive annually —'"

Olympe clapped her hands.

"Aha!" said she, bursting into laughter; "ah, this is delightful! So Bannière is 'the other,' is he?"

"*It is thou who hast named him!*" replied the abbé.

"Monsieur, I prefer that you should not 'thee and thou' me, even when quoting Monsieur Racine's lines," said she, her nostrils dilating with all the pride of her nature, and all the wrath she had been nursing, since the interview began, in her scornful, irritated heart.

"Article three," the abbé went on: "you to receive yourself two thousand louis cash to settle all outstanding debts, and any forfeitures you may incur; and in addition a stipulated income of six thousand livres charged upon the estate of D'Hoirac, which was entailed upon me by my late father."

Olympe walked straight up to the abbé.

"The man who prates thus of money," said she, "is not so mad, after all. This bargain you are giving me the figures on, — who is the object of it? Myself, am I not?"

"Why, yes."

"It is myself whom you wish to purchase, then?"

"And to pay for; that is to say, if one ever can pay for an inestimable treasure."

"And you will pay in advance?" she asked ironically; "are n't you afraid of being cheated?"

"Oh, with the promises you have made me," said the abbé, "I don't see that I have anything to fear."

The words were scarcely out of his mouth when two doors were thrown open simultaneously.

One was the door of the cabinet, directly opposite the abbé.

Bannière emerged with livid countenance and trembling lips.

The other was the door of the anteroom.

The hairdresser appeared there, in dire dismay; for two words had been enough to explain the whole situation to ner.

XXIX.

IN WHICH THE ABBÉ JUST MISSES BECOMING REALLY MAD.

THE abbé was evidently thunderstruck at Bannière's appearance; his short-sighted eyes were equal to the task of observing the change which had taken place in his face, and the signs that a tempest was imminent.

He had no time to explain away his words.

"Monsieur l'Abbé," said Bannière, hardly able to produce an intelligible sound, so tight a grasp had anger taken with its iron hand upon his throat, "do you happen to remember that I once broke a guitar over your head?"

The abbé gnashed his teeth at the reminder.

"You do, do you not?" continued Bannière; "and yet at that time you were guilty of nothing worse than dinning wretched music into Madame's ears."

"Monsieur!"

"Calm yourself,— I should say, reserve your wrath for another time; I will give you an opportunity to vent it before long. This time, Monsieur, it is not music which you have forced Olympe to listen to, it is an insult."

"An insult?"

"Yes, a veritable, well-rounded insult. Oh, I heard it all."

The abbé put his hand to his hip in true knightly fashion.

"I will show you what it is," said he, "to listen behind doors."

"Madame knows very well," retorted Bannière, "that I have not been listening behind the door, because I have been to the theatre to see La Catalane in a new part and report how she played it. Having returned sooner than I expected, I heard loud voices, and in spite of myself overheard the offer you have dared to make to Madame."

"I do not feel insulted by such a trifle," said Olympe, who saw an angry flush rising in the abbé's face, and who knew that the best way for a woman to defend the man she loves is to take his side openly, — a manœuvre which always disconcerts the enemy.

"You do not feel insulted, Olympe," said Bannière, "because you are perfection itself; but I am insulted, I take the insult to myself, and I inform Monsieur l'Abbé that on two occasions his cloth has saved him from my wrath; but I would not answer for myself another time, and to spare him so great a calamity, and myself so great cause for regret, I beg Monsieur l'Abbé to keep away from my house in future."

The abbé thought he saw his chance. He was too bitterly humiliated not to have lost his head entirely; he fancied that this woman, of whose affection he felt assured, would not dare to turn against him for fear that he might compromise her by tearing off her mask.

This was not a generous idea, and it was the poor abbé's ruin.

"Madame," said he, "Monsieur Bannière speaks of his house. Are you not under your own roof here?"

"Yes, Monsieur," said Olympe.

"Madame, is it not true that, having been once forbidden this house, on account of the ungovernable passion

and bad taste of Monsieur Bannière, I was invited here
again by yourself? Tell me, pray."

Bannière opened his eyes in alarm. He feared that he
was about to hear something that boded ill for his passion.

The two men were really hanging upon the lips of this
woman whose dominion over both was unbounded.

Olympe smiled, for she saw the trap, and began to
despise the abbé. Addressing her words to him, she
replied composedly, —

"It is true, Monsieur, that I thought you a gentleman;
it is true that I was sorry to see your friendship, which
was a little exacting but honorable nevertheless, in danger of changing to hatred, which your high standing
would have made a real misfortune to me; it is true, in
short, that I committed the error, through being too tender-hearted, of interesting myself in soothing your touchy
disposition, of pardoning your acts of folly, and finally of
reopening my doors to you, after Monsieur Bannière had
very justly closed them upon you."

"The error, Madame!" cried the abbé, who was sufficiently sure of eventual triumph to cavil about words
and haggle over the phraseology of the apologies which
he expected.

"I said THE ERROR," repeated Olympe, "and I will
add the *unpardonable* error, for I can never forgive
myself for it."

"Go on," said the abbé, roughly, for his hopes were
based upon what was coming next.

"Very well, Monsieur," and Olympe's brows contracted: "I go on, and conclude by begging you to comply with the orders of Monsieur Bannière, who is master
here."

"You understand that Monsieur Bannière shows me
the door?"

" Precisely."

"And, consequently, you do the same, — you! "
shrieked the abbé, beside himself with rage.

" Even more firmly than he," replied Olympe.

" Madame! " cried D'Hoirac, making ready to rein-
force his *Tu quoque* with a *Quos ego*.

He stepped, with an insulting toss of the head, toward
the door.

But there he found the hairdresser lying in wait for
him; and she put her hand over his mouth, and hurried him away with an amount of zeal which touched
Olympe, but seemed somewhat equivocal to Bannière.

Notwithstanding the presence of the hand upon his
mouth the abbé tried hard to speak.

" Keep quiet, for heaven's sake, you blind fool! "
hissed the hairdresser in his ear, " or you are lost
forever."

" What, the devil! I want to explain," said he,
struggling to free himself.

" Well, well, you can explain later."

" At the other place ? "

" Yes."

D'Hoirac, confused, giddy, and cast down, suffered himself to be led to the door, like Harlequin surprised with
Isabelle.

During the entire distance to his own home he was
muttering between his teeth, —

" *Morbleu!* I will give the man who will fathom that
woman a hundred thousand crowns and a magician's
certificate."

Meanwhile Olympe, proud of her own performance,
went up to Bannière and offered to kiss him as soon as
the door closed behind the abbé.

But Bannière repulsed her; then, throwing himself
into his chair. he said. —

"Come! I have had enough of doubt and consequent suffering; there must be an end of this."

"Why, the end has come, I should say," said Olympe.

"Far from it!" cried Bannière; "for something has just begun to which all the powers of the earth will not reconcile me."

"What do you mean?"

"Olympe!"

"Well?"

"You invited that abbé, when I had forbidden him the house, to come here again?"

"I have admitted it."

"Yes, when you were driven to it, when you had no way of avoiding it."

"Do you suspect me, pray?"

"Do I suspect you, Madame! It seems to me that words have been uttered here which give me the right to do so."

"What has been said? Repeat the words."

"It was said, Madame, while I was listening unseen, that you have received presents from Monsieur l'Abbé d'Hoirac."

"Call him back, and make him tell you what presents I have received."

"Useless!"

"Why useless?"

"Why? Because I prefer doubt to certainty," said Bannière, in a tone of utter despondency.

"Oh, indeed! you prefer doubt, do you?" said Olympe, with bitter sarcasm; "thanks, you are very good!"

"Ah!" said Bannière, "I am not like him or like you: I am not a patrician accustomed to deal with patricians; I am not Venus, accustomed to being worshipped."

"I don't understand you. What do you mean?"

"I mean that I have not passed from the hands of one prince to those of another of the same kind."

"Beware, Monsieur Bannière," said Olympe, with the pride of a queen, "for you are dangerously near insulting me yourself."

"Yes, you are right, Olympe; yes, I am only 'Monsieur Bannière,' nothing more than the dust which can be destroyed with a breath; yes, I am the culprit, escaped from the convent at Avignon; I am the fugitive who, on Père Mordon's mandate, may be cast into a dungeon, as a vagabond, and guilty of sacrilege and apostasy.   Oh, do not heap any further insults upon me, poor, abandoned wretch that I am, who have, or had, nothing under heaven but your love!   Oh, do not cast me off, for without you you know well that I am lost; you know that I will go and give myself up to those who are seeking me; you know that, deprived of you, I will cast myself into the arms of death, — my last and sole remaining love, who will surely not deceive me!"

"Hush, you madman!" cried Olympe, rising hastily and placing her hand upon Bannière's mouth. "Suppose any one should overhear you!   Are you insane to shout in that way!"

She ran to the door and opened it, to see if any one was in a position to have overheard that unfortunate disclosure.

But she saw no one; she only heard a door close at the foot of the stairs.   She was uneasy about it, and was about to make inquiries.

"Don't take that trouble," said Bannière.   "You have only one means of saving me."

"What is that?"

"Oh, *mon Dieu!* it is to tell me that you love me."

"You have but one way to make me love you, and that is never to doubt me."

"Let me tell you the truth, then."

"Say on."

"Don't be angry, for your eyes when you are angry are flames which set despair alight in my heart."

"Never fear, I will not be angry; go on quickly."

"Well, then, this man, who tried to bargain for your love, said that he had received an acknowledgment that he had won it."

"Yes, he did say so; but he lies."

"Swear it."

"Upon what?"

"Upon something sacred, upon something in which you have faith."

"I swear to you that he lies," said Olympe, "upon my mother's honor."

"But why did he say it, then, believing you to be alone with him? Why did he act out that comedy with you, with himself?"

"I have no idea."

"Oh, there is a mystery under all this which somebody must be able to elucidate."

"Who?"

"Question your hairdresser."

"My hairdresser?"

"Yes, a woman capable of anything."

"Do you think so?"

"Yes, I assure you that it is so. She is a friend of La Catalane, your deadly enemy. You discharged this woman?"

"Yes, I did."

"Why did you take her back, in God's name?"

"How can I tell! Why does one ever do evil, believ-

ing one's self to be doing good? But these are things
which I would rather not suspect even; it is time thrown
away. The abbé has gone; let it rest at that. The hairdresser is here, — do you want me to turn her away
again?"

"I cannot deny myself that satisfaction."

Olympe rang, and the man-servant appeared.

"The hairdresser?" Olympe asked.

"Madame, she has this moment gone out," the man
replied.

"Was it not she who closed the door at the foot of the
stairway?"

"Yes, Madame."

"Where was she coming from then?"

"I think that she came from Madame's apartments."

Olympe and Bannière exchanged an anxious glance.

"You may go," Olympe said to the servant.

"She was listening," said Bannière, when they were
alone once more.

"Yes; and why should she have listened?"

"On account of our quarrel."

"Alas! we quarrel so often that that alone can no
longer interest any one," replied Olympe; "but no
matter, — the hairdresser will end her service here this
evening, since you wish it."

"No, no! I no longer wish anything; absolutely
that is so! I am mad with love, you see, — mad because
I am poor, and a burden to you. I would give my life
for one year with a hundred thousand livres at my
disposal."

"Don't gamble any more then, for you always lose.
Hoard up what you have already lost, and what you will
lose if you keep on, and in that way, *mon Dieu!* you will
soon have something much better than the hundred

thousand livres; you will have peace of mind due to the certainty of my love, and then you will be rich indeed, for I shall owe my happiness to you."

As she said these words, Olympe kissed Bannière so fondly that the abbé if he had been present would surely have died of rage.

XXX.

WHEREIN IT IS DEMONSTRATED THAT THE HAIR-
DRESSER HAD OVERHEARD EVERYTHING.

BUT the abbé could not see; he was running with all
the strength of his little legs.

The hairdresser, too, was doing her best in the same
line, and she arrived at the domicile of La Catalane in a
state of breathless excitement.

The actress started up as she saw her.

"All is lost!" the hairdresser began.

La Catalane fairly leaped into the air.

"How is that?" she demanded.

"That Bannière has kicked the abbé out of the house."

"Well, what then?"

"What then?"

"Yes."

"It is impossible that there should not be a clear and
unequivocal explanation between Olympe and the abbé,
and it may come at any moment."

"Never! if we use our wits."

"How can we prevent it, I should like to know?"

"It's a very simple matter: there is only one way in
which the abbé can really be undeceived, and that is to
see me in the light when I impersonate Olympe at the
little house. That way he may adopt, if he has any
suspicions, and then we should really be lost. So from
this time we must decide not to receive the abbé there
any more, — no more traces; nothing can ever be discov-

ered.   It will be in vain that Olympe will struggle and
deny and rage, D'Hoirac will not believe her innocent."

"Yes, but he will bring me into it too," said the
hairdresser. "He will call upon me for my evidence,
and I shall have to give it."

"Very well! you give your evidence, and it is that
which ruins Olympe."

"Yes? and how, pray?"

"Oh, pshaw! that's very difficult, isn't it? You
will maintain that you hired the house for Olympe; you
will swear that Olympe has been there, and you will be
believed,—for scandal is always believed, especially when
it concerns actresses."

The hairdresser shook her head.

"We shall get ourselves into trouble," said she.

"Bah! have you trusted our secret to any one?"

"I? Never!"

"Are you afraid of Olympe, then?"

"No; but I am afraid of Bannière."

"What do you think he'll do to you?"

"Bannière? He will kill me!"

"Oh, no! I will wheedle him so that I shall appear a
veritable Minerva in his eyes from the moment that he
believes Olympe guilty."

"He will kill me, I tell you, and you with me."

"Bah! we will make the abbé defend us."

"He will kill the abbé too."

"You think so?"

"Oh, you don't know him," said the hairdresser,
thoughtfully.

"Why, is he such a terrible fellow, this Bannière?"

"Oh, indeed he is!"

"Dear boy!"

"Listen to me," said the hairdresser: "this is no time

to joke. You propose to satisfy a caprice, and give yourself the pleasure of robbing Olympe of a lover; that's about your idea, is n't it?"

"To be sure."

"Well, the abbé is the only one you will steal from her?"

"Why so?"

"It is written that Bannière will not play Olympe false."

"Again I ask you, why?"

"Because if you do not ruin the man, I will ruin him myself."

"What do you mean by ruining him?"

"Well! imagine this."

"Imagine what?"

"That I know a secret about him which is sufficiently compromising to make him disappear."

"Oho! Has he been cheating at play?"

"Better than that."

"Tell me quickly."

"No, you are too fond of him. I will attend to my matters myself."

"What do you mean? Do you propose to ruin the poor fellow?"

"Yes, and at once; for if I don't do it to-night, he will wring my neck to-morrow, and I object to that."

"You are frightened at nothing."

"Let me tell you how things will turn out. At this very moment, either I am an old fool, or Olympe and Bannière are reconciled. To-morrow the abbé will make his peace with Bannière. Men are always like that; when you think they are hacking at one another's throats, they are hugging one another."

"That's true enough."

"Well, then, Bannière and the abbé being reconciled,
I shall be sacrificed; the abbé is rich and powerful, and
will have me sent to the workhouse."

"That would be no more than right."

"You, in the mean time, will have pocketed the profits.
More than that, when I am safely in the workhouse,
you will find some way of making up with Bannière too.
Women are always like that; when one thinks them
friends, they are lovers."

"Upon my word, I had no idea you were such a
moralizer. Have you, by chance, any of Monsieur de La
Rochefoucauld's blood in your veins?"

"No; but, failing that, I have invented something else
to prevent my being victimized, and in its execution you
may assist me, if you please."

"What is it?"

"You will assist me, or I will do it by myself."

"State your wishes, my girl, go on."

"The abbé is going to call upon the counterfeit
Olympe."

"Oho! you didn't tell me that, and I am *en
déshabillé.*"

"Make your toilet. He will come in a furious rage
with you for having allowed Bannière to turn him out."

"I will soothe him."

"Eleven o'clock is just striking; he will be there at
half-past."

"Do you think so?"

"I am sure of it."

"*Peste!* we have no more than time enough. Help
me to dress, pray."

"Come, come! let us go into your dressing-room, and
listen to me. You are about to learn the secret of my
method of arranging matters, so that in three hours you

will have two thousand louis more, and I one Bannière less."

They entered the cabinet, and the door closed upon them, preventing us from hearing their paltry plotting and indecent schemes upon the purse and the honor of their enemies.

XXXI.

THE abbé, promptly on hand at the time appointed, though he was in a furious rage, had not long to wait for the spurious Olympe.

As for that damsel, she made her appearance just as she was on all other days, wasting but little anxiety on the storm of reproaches which Monsieur d'Hoirac had in store for her.

"Ah!" he cried, when he heard the door open, "at last the moment has arrived to take my revenge for all the affronts which the most perfidious of women has made me endure."

La Catalane stopped at the threshold of the room where he was waiting, and asked calmly, —

"What affronts?"

"Why, those which I swallowed this evening, wretched woman!"

"Where?"

"At your house."

"At Monsieur Bannière's, that is to say."

"Oh, the devil!" cried the abbé, seeing the drift of her words; "there you go again intrenching yourself behind that paltry rampart of the distinction between Monsieur Bannière's house and Monsieur d'Hoirac's."

"That is my fortress."

"I know that well enough, *parbleu!*"

" There was a certain treaty signed, if I remember. "

" Yes; but there were other stipulations, too, which you violated. "

" You refer to the affection which Monsieur Bannière so often shows me ? "

" Well, what have you to say on that score ? " said the abbé, with redoubled fury.

" Nothing. "

" What! Nothing ? "

" No, nothing, except that I could not prevent him. "

" What! You could not prevent him, in my presence ? "

" Is it my fault ? Poor boy! He doesn't know of your rights, and thinks he has some of his own. "

" It is outrageous, I tell you, and I will not put up with such torture any longer. "

" Quite right, too, Monsieur l'Abbé. "

" Ah, indeed! that 's very lucky. "

" So I have made this appointment to see you for the last time. "

" What! the last time! " exclaimed the abbé.

" To be sure. "

" Then I am a dupe ? "

" How so ? "

" Why, because when you have to choose between Bannière the actor and Monsieur l'Abbé d'Hoirac, you choose Monsieur Bannière. "

" *Dame !* "

" And so, after having abandoned everything to me, you take it all back again. "

" But your persistent importunity, Monsieur ? "

" My importunity is that of a man whose love is increased by every hour that passes. Oh, you have never been jealous, that 's very plain. "

"Pray, what am I to do to satisfy you?" asked La Catalane, with a woe-begone expression.

"If you can find in your heart no means of satisfying me, I have nothing more to say."

"What!" cried the false Olympe, "do you think it is so easy in this world to reconcile one's inclination with one's true renown?"

"Your renown! Why, Madame," said the abbé, somewhat reassured, "do you not consider that it is as glorious to belong to Monsieur d'Hoirac as to Monsieur Bannière?"

"Oh, of course; but —"

"Everything that you can say is a pitiful reason, Madame. If you loved that man a little less, and me a little more —"

La Catalane pretended to weep.

To the abbé's mind it was Olympe who was shedding these tears, yet he did not waver.

"You ought to understand one thing," said he.

"What is that?"

"That I am at the end of my patience."

The impostor's sobs were heart-breaking. One of the great points of La Catalane's dramatic power was her ability to weep to order.

"Come, come! what's the matter?" said the abbé, beginning to be a little touched.

"Why, you can see, Monsieur, that I am weeping."

"Weep if you please, but come to some decision."

"Oh, it's all decided, Monsieur, — on your part at least. Leave me, leave the woman who has given up everything to you, as you said just now."

"Leave you, leave you! I know very well that it is your wish that I should leave you," said the abbé, gradually assuming the defensive.

"My wish?"

"Yes, to be sure. Indeed, this whole scene you are favoring me with is the result of a mere whim."

"A whim?"

"I mean it."

"Does poor Bannière deprive you of anything more to-day than yesterday?"

"Indeed he does; for he deprives me of the faith I had in you."

"Oh, indeed," said La Catalane, "if you have lost faith in me, I am most unhappy."

And her tears flowed more freely than ever, with a running accompaniment of sobs.

The abbé held his tongue.

"Well," she cried, "what do you order me to do?"

He approached her in order to soothe and cure her wounded pride with the balm of affectionate pardon, but she pushed him away.

"Oh, no," said she, "you are a hard-hearted wretch."

"And you — are you not as hard-hearted, yes, a hundred and a thousand times more than I?"

"Oh!" cried La Catalane; "pray understand this, — that I choose to deal with a friend and not a tyrant."

"Speak, then."

"No; it is for you to dictate your terms, since you came for that purpose, and I will see whether I ought to accept them; I will see whether I am dealing with a man who really loves me, or a man who simply claims to dictate every act and word of my life."

"God forbid!"

"And yet —"

"Why, you know very well that your pleasure is my only happiness."

She shook her head in the darkness; but the abbé divined the gesture.

"You have proved it to me so many times, have n't you?" said she.

"Your pleasure, then, consists in having that actor caress you in my presence," cried the abbé, with renewed irritation.

"Oh, you are a spiteful fool," La Catalane retorted, "and you don't know what you are saying."

"But I should say that I saw it."

"Saw it?"

"Yes, saw it."

"Nonsense! you saw nothing of the kind."

The abbé leaped up from his sofa.

"Well, upon my soul, that's a little too much!" he cried.

"No, you saw nothing," continued La Catalane; "otherwise you would adore me at this moment."

"That's a good one too. I did not see him showering kisses upon your cheeks? I did not see him pressing you to his heart? Oh, no, I saw nothing of all that!"

"No; for if you had seen it, you would also have seen all the signs I was making to you, and all the smiles I was lavishing upon you, to induce you to take the fooling patiently."

"I saw nothing of all that; at all events, that is not what you promised me."

"Well, and did you promise to come and offer me, in 'stand and deliver' fashion, two thousand louis, and six thousand livres a year? Did you promise me that during all your fond speeches and your interesting proposals, while you were pressing my fingers and kneeling devoutly at my feet, Monsieur Bannière, green with jealousy, would be hidden in the next room? Did you promise me that from that point he would hear every word you said,

and see everything you did? In short, did you promise
to bring this horrible lesson upon yourself, and this
disagreeable scene upon me?"

"You ought to have warned me," said he, somewhat
mollified.

"But what did I do, blind bat that you are?"

"Do you mean to say that you warned me?"

"I mean that I nearly broke my jawbone muttering
cautions to you; I dislocated the arch of my eyebrows
rolling my eyes at you; my toe is all black from kicking
against your chair to keep you from coming too near."

"And I saw nothing of it!"

"You are the stupidest or the blindest of mortals.
Everything that has gone wrong has been through your
fault."

"Alas!"

"Yes, and now groan,— that's very nice; reproach me,
— that's very kind. And I meanwhile am suffering
keenly."

"You are suffering?"

"Can you doubt it? Do you imagine that after you
had gone, Bannière did not give me a fine dressing down?
Do you think he is deaf and blind like you? If he is
deaf and blind, he hasn't lost the use of his arms, I can
tell you."

"Oh, *mon Dieu!* did he threaten you?

"Threaten, indeed! You are very good! He beat
me."

"Beat you? — my poor angel, that blackguard beat
you?"

"Fortunately he vented his anger upon me, violent
though it was. I was terribly afraid, I promise you, that
he would take it out of you. He would have killed you
on the spot. He's a violent fellow."

"Thank God! I have arms."

"Yes, but no eyes; whereas he has arms and eyes and a sword."

"Do you think I'm afraid of him?"

"Oh, no, I don't think you're cowardly. Besides, you are not exposed to the danger; I'm the one."

"I will protect you. Ah! you shrug your shoulders."

"*Parbleu!* begin by protecting yourself."

"My dear, you seem to forget what I am."

"I do not forget, but I know also that your cloth requires you to adopt many precautions which a man of the sword might neglect. If you were a dragoon like Monsieur de Mailly, you would give me more confidence with one look than the Abbé d'Hoirac can give with a whole army."

"If I can't avenge myself, I can at least take care of — "

"What pretext have you for injuring an honest man, who is only defending his own property?"

"His property, his property! Why, you're not his wife."

"No; but I was his mistress."

"He is an actor."

"Well, I am an actress, if you come to that."

"At all events, I don't propose that he shall frighten you and beat you."

"He will care little for anything you can say; and if you cry too loud, he will cry still louder. So much the worse for you then; an actor has nothing at stake compared with an abbé."

"By that reasoning, Madame, it seems that you propose to put up with that fellow forever."

"Oh, no, no!"

"Why not? Why do you say no?"

"Because, you see, I have a way of getting clear of him when he embarrasses me too much."

"Really, then, why don't you put it in operation, for it seems to me that we are pretty seriously embarrassed."

"The devil! he's so headstrong!"

"Confide it to me."

"Never."

"Then you don't love me? And you propose to subject me forever to the brutality of that villain?"

"I do not say that; but there's a great difference between simply turning out of doors a man who bores you, and utterly ruining a poor wretch who has trusted in you, and whose secret you know."

"Aha! so there's a secret."

"A fine one, I tell you!"

"Tell it to your little friend."

"No, no, there are no friends —— "

"You deny that I am your only friend, do you?"

"Am I wrong in doing so?"

"It seems to me —— "

"Pray what have you done that I should call you my friend? Is it because you are my lover?"

"But — Olympe —— "

"That's no proof at all. A friend is one whose devotion is so absolute that one cannot possibly doubt him."

"I should say that I had given myself to you absolutely."

"Body and goods?"

The abbé rose to the bait.

"As to the body, I have nothing to say. As to worldly goods," said he, "make your demands; I have already put my proposals in due form; I don't know that there is any Bannière in the closet here."

"Mon Dieu!" said the spurious Olympe; "that's a

very delicate and important question to discuss, Monsieur
l'Abbé; however a woman must make up her mind some
time when her independence is at stake."

"Your independence will never be assured, my dear,"
said the abbé, quickly, "so long as you live with this
Bannière; therefore you would better give him up."

"That point can hardly be considered as at issue
between us, Monsieur."

"The question to be settled is whether your apprehension will prove to be stronger than your scruples."

"Precisely."

"Well, then! how about the two thousand louis which
I offered you?"

"Oh, how bluntly you talk about money!" said La
Catalane, delighted beyond measure.

"I am compelled, in order to induce you to make up
your mind, to prove to you that while you will be less
pinched for funds, you will be more at liberty. It is
essential, too, that you furnish me with the means of
depriving Bannière of the power of injuring you which
he seems to have; I will use them in case he abuses that
power, and in that case only."

"I shall never make up my mind to do that."

"Listen!" said the abbé, becoming more earnest, as he
felt her resistance growing less; "if you love me, you will
put that man in my power."

"No, no; don't require that."

"You accused me just now of not being your friend; I
propose to show you that you are wrong. A friend — I
quote your own definition — is one whose devotion is
absolute, and includes body and goods, given beyond
recall. I am yours, my wealth is yours, and my hand
should be yours if I could marry."

"That's talking," said La Catalane.

The abbé proposed to strike the iron while it was hot.

"I have the two thousand louis here in a chest," said he. "I wanted to find out whether you would be as generous as I."

"What do you call generosity, please?"

"I mean that I wanted to find out whether, in consideration of a paltry sum which would assure you comfort, you would consent to leave the stage, and give your whole life to me alone. Here are the two thousand louis; take them, and give me the reward I ask."

The abbé held out the notes to La Catalane, who seized them with eager fingers.

He took advantage of her proximity to steal a kiss, which was not denied him.

When the shameless creature felt this unhoped-for and to her eyes fabulous wealth within her grasp, a strange process took place in her heart; the abbé became dear and sacred to her, while Bannière possessed no further attractions. She pressed the poor dupe to her heart, and in a tone expressive of more real affection than she had ever felt in her life, she said, —

"You have a good heart, and you deserve that I should do, for love of you, what nothing else could have induced me to do. You deserve that I should set your mind entirely at rest. You deserve to have in your power the only man whom you have any occasion to fear. And as you dread the rivalry of this Bannière, as you would not perhaps be the stronger in a contest with him, I will show you my weapons; they are deadly. Persuasion, esteem, and love take him from my hands, and place him in yours."

The abbé opened his ears, and closed his arms.

"Know, then," said she, "that Monsieur Bannière is a runaway from a Jesuit novitiate."

The abbé shuddered.

"From what place?" said he.

"Avignon."

"The principal of that college is a friend of mine; his name is — "

"Mordon, is it not?"

"That's it."

"And he is seeking by land and sea and mountain the fugitive whom I have hidden in my arms to this day."

"Merciful Heaven!" exclaimed the abbé, wild with joy.

"You understand," resumed La Catalane, "that I confide this secret to you as a man of honor. You understand that otherwise, and if I did not know you well, the poor wretch would be lost."

"Oh, yes!"

"A Jesuit novice, in short — "

"To be sure."

"A Jesuit novice, who turns actor."

"The devil!"

"A Jesuit novice, who, after turning actor, lives with an actress, and heaps indignities upon ministers of religion like you!"

"Yes, yes!"

"The poor boy doesn't know what the result of that will be."

"Nobody knows," said the abbé, fairly trembling with joy.

"So then, my dear D'Hoirac, I place in your hands a weapon which you will never use unless Bannière should threaten you too freely and too loud."

"Thanks, my soul!"

"I have suffered agony, you see, to see you at daggers drawn with that hot head to whom your profession and your cloth forbade you to reply, as your heart and your name would incline you to do."

"Oh, yes, I have suffered too," said the abbé, fiercely; "but—"

"But henceforth," continued La Catalane, "you are on guard and well armed. Now have the virtue of the strong, and be patient."

"Never fear."

"I beg you, do not let your anger get the better of you about a trifle; remember that in putting this poor youth in your hands, I have abundantly proven that you have nothing to fear from him; and as for myself—"

"I will do as you suggest, in every respect."

"Thanks! you are as generous in your dealings with men as with the ladies. How can one help loving you—what do I say?—adoring you?"

The abbé, happier than any pope, did not perceive that that evening he was adored for his forty-eight thousand livres.

La Catalane had nothing more to get out of him, and she knew it. Like a true courtesan, she thought only of herself. The abbé, young, handsome, and wealthy, had only one defect, his near-sightedness,—a defect to which La Catalane owed the success of all the talent she had brought into play since their acquaintance began.

Having thus skilfully steered her threatened bark into port, the unblushing impostor, with the aid of her confederate, had her money and was beyond fear of detection. The abbé, with the aid of his money, had had some hours of illusion.

Let us see what Bannière was to have.

XXXII.

MONSIEUR DE MAILLY'S RING.

THE unfortunate Bannière was in utter ignorance of the
fine scheme that was being concocted against him. He
did as children do when they are playing with powder,
and hold the powder in one hand and fire in the other.
He had resolved to avenge himself for all his self-inflicted
suffering, upon Olympe, — that is to say, upon the only
person in the wide world who really loved him.

He had suffered the pangs of jealousy; therefore he
had resolved that Olympe should suffer in the same
way.

The insensate fool, at the risk of breaking that noble
heart, chose to punish her for mere imprudence; and that,
too, when the only imprudent acts which she had committed had their origin in the very nobleness of her
heart.

The day after the scene with the abbé, when Olympe
thought the whole affair had passed from Bannière's
mind, as it had from hers, he attended the rehearsal at
the theatre, where he found all the company assembled.
La Catalane was laughing as usual, and the hairdresser
was studying the faces from behind the wings.

Olympe, like all great artists, was accustomed to rehearse with great gravity. On this particular day she
went through her part even more seriously than usual.
The poor woman had reached that first phase of discouragement which is exhibited by habitual melancholy.

No more gayety, no more pleasure, either in the accomplishment of one's duty or in such matters as in former days were diverting and agreeable. The eye is dull, the heart can do naught but sigh, and the wound which cuts so deep monopolizes its strength so entirely that it can hardly find enough to beat regularly.

Olympe then was rehearsing her part. La Catalane was teasing this one or that in the wings.

Bannière went directly to her, and grasped her hands. He was very handsome that day, with the beauty which Nature had given him, and even more with the animation which a living thought evokes upon the features of man or woman, even though its purport be the doing an injury to one's nearest and dearest.

Bannière began to fool with La Catalane, and before long she had to defend herself against his assiduity. Indeed she not only defended herself, but she experienced an emotion which much resembled terror, when he approached her.

Her conscience reproached her for having been the instrument of his approaching ruin. It was as if she saw walking and talking and laughing before her a condemned man, ignorant of his doom.

It may be, too, that the actor's contemptuous demeanor which had endured so long, had wounded her.

But Bannière appeared to notice nothing. He was indefatigable in trying to win smiles and pleasant words from La Catalane; indeed, so fertile in expedients is revenge, he exhibited an extraordinary, coquettish vein, which nobody would have supposed him to possess.

La Catalane, be it said, was not a young woman of remarkable intelligence; on the other hand, hers was not a bad nature.

She would have loved Bannière dearly if he had loved

her. We know that she had shown herself at least as
tenderly inclined as this new Joseph had shown himself
indifferent.

It seemed very strange to her that this disdainful
youth should seek her out at the very moment when she
had decided to break with him forever.

However slight an admixture of philosophy a woman
may possess, the most commonplace has an instinctive
delicacy which is worth as much as the quintessence of
all the huge treatises on psychology.

She began then, as we have said, by keeping Bannière
at arm's length; then, seeing that he persisted, she
yielded so far as to let him speak, although continuing
to act on the defensive.

A vague idea came to her at first that Bannière wanted
to make use of her in some way. The idea was short-
lived, however; for if he suspected anything, he would
surely employ neither gentle nor temporizing means to
avert such imminent peril.

No, Bannière could know nothing; he came back
because he came back; he was attracted by naught but
the magnetism of her lovely eyes and the charm of her
beauty.

It was a little late, no doubt; but the hour had struck
at last. She could see passion speaking in his every
look; in every act of his she could see an apology for
his past disdain.

The little performance was observed by Olympe as by
all the others. Bannière's shouts of laughter interfered
with the rehearsal several times, and drew upon the
offender a stern impatient "Hush!" from Mademoiselle
de Clèves.

Then they withdrew into a dark corner, where they
could be heard whispering and giggling together, — a

variety of torture which is insupportable to a jealous person.

Olympe bravely put force upon herself, that she might not appear to notice Bannière's unseemly conduct.

La Catalane gently succumbed to the fascination of being courted by a fickle lover.

The rehearsal at an end, Olympe left the theatre without a sign of consciousness from Bannière, and went home without him.

La Catalane was very well content to be the cause of her rival's chagrin.

In the evening Bannière returned to the theatre, Olympe not being in the cast. When she saw him leave the house, she frowned, and said nothing.

But anger triumphed over dignity. Olympe during the evening appeared behind the scenes, where Bannière, who fully expected to see her, was making more violent love than ever to La Catalane, whose part that evening was as charming as her costume.

Bannière, by his energetic advances, had altogether convinced her that she had reason to repent having put his liberty in jeopardy just when he was ready to love her.

Why, it was her own property upon whom the bloodhounds of the law were to be let loose; it was, as a great diplomatist has since said, worse than a crime,—it was a mistake.

When she saw Olympe come to the theatre, contrary to her custom,—when she saw her, Olympe the haughty, enter the lists to fight for her lover, — La Catalane suddenly felt an inordinate desire to win.

So she took advantage of a moment when Olympe was looking darkly at them both, to say to the young man,—

" You say that you think me beautiful ? "

" Yes."

"And that you love me?"

"Madly."

"And that you are sorry you have not told me before?"

"I said so, and I say it again."

"Then I must forget how ungrateful and rude you have been."

"Forget it, I implore you."

"Then I must forgive you."

"I crave your forgiveness."

"Well, then, in order that you may not believe that I depend on the breath of your caprice, in order that you may know that my affection is deep and sincere, — deeper and more sincere, be assured, than many passions which are paraded — "

Here she cast a malevolent glance in Olympe's direction.

Bannière shuddered.

"In order to prove that to you," continued La Catalane, "I beg you to come and take supper with me. We have very serious matters to discuss."

"That's a curious way of inviting a fellow," said Bannière, trying to joke. "You invite me with a sort of threat."

"Just look, pray, at those two pieces of cannon, under fire of which I am speaking to you."

"Poor Olympe!" thought Bannière, involuntarily recoiling a step.

"You accept, do you not?" asked La Catalane.

"Do I accept!"

"Oh, I know you. I know all the power which others have over you; I know that to avoid displeasing certain other people of whom you are afraid, you wouldn't mind breaking an appointment."

"Here is my word and my hand on it," said Bannière.

"At ten o'clock," said La Catalane.

"At ten o'clock," he repeated.

He had no time for more; Olympe fell like a thunder-bolt between them.

Bannière, completely out of countenance, slunk away behind the side scenes.

La Catalane clinched her fists, like a woman deter-mined to defend herself.

Olympe, pale, but calm and collected, after a fleeting, contemptuous glance which was lost upon Bannière, began to survey La Catalane from head to foot.

"You have a lovely costume," she said, in a mild voice, "and you are marvellously beautiful to-night."

La Catalane was expecting insults and an assault; she was almost speechless with amazement.

"Do you think so?" she stammered.

"You are beautiful enough," continued Olympe, "to make women jealous and lovers amorous. I strongly suspect my own lover of having fallen in love with you; but as I do not choose to be jealous, I beg you to tell me frankly if he really loves you. Oh, tell me, tell me in all sincerity; in my eyes you are so fair that I can under-stand that you have the remains of my affection."

La Catalane, satisfied and humbled at the same time, was preparing to reply; but at the first movement that she made Olympe uttered a cry terrible to hear.

She had seen on her ring-bedecked hand the ruby which came from Monsieur de Mailly, which Bannière had sold to the Jew, and the Jew to the Abbé d'Hoirac, and which La Catalane had received from the last-named.

Olympe pounced upon the hand, looked at the ring closely, recognized it, breathed a feeble sigh, and fainted.

The noise of her fall upon the boards recalled Bannière, who was as unable to understand the occurrence as La Catalane herself. But, beside himself with grief, he forgot all his schemes, seized Olympe in his arms, and carried her home, weeping bitterly and tearing his hair in his despair.

When he had succeeded in recalling her to consciousness, when, as he knelt beside her, he met the first glance of the poor girl, he was terrified at the wrath and hatred which it expressed.

"What is the matter? For God's sake, what is the matter, dear Olympe?" he said.

She extricated herself from his arms.

"What is the matter?" she replied. "You know very well; don't make me repeat it. The matter is that you promised me your love, and that now you offer me your compassion."

"Oh, you don't think it."

"But now you were offering your love — a contemptible love, I know — to that Catalane; now that my weakness has betrayed me, and you fear that you have wounded me too deeply, you cast off La Catalane for my benefit, just as you cast me off for hers."

"Never! never!"

"Oh, don't lie about it! Have at least the courage of honor. You know that I can no longer love you; try to retain my esteem, if nothing more."

"Olympe, those terrible words freeze my heart with terror; would you have so little indulgence for a poor, sick spirit, sick with jealousy?"

"Jealousy! — you!" said she, with supreme disdain.

"Oh, when I saw you receive that dandy, that idiot, that Abbé d'Hoirac here, when I saw him at your feet, when I heard his insulting offers, I thought that he could not be there without some encouragement from you; I suspected you, I wished to show you what they suffer who suspect. I know that I committed a fault, a crime if you will; but pardon me. I have pardoned you."

"Yes!—for you, who only suspected, it was easy to pardon. Besides, you knew very well that I was not guilty. But, as for myself, can I doubt? Have I not the proof before my eyes?"

"The proof,—you have the proof!" he cried; "you have the proof, and of what?"

"I saw you."

"You saw me flirting and fooling and lying, and smiling artificial smiles at that woman, solely to annoy you, while I watched you closely to observe the effect of my wretched scheme,—that's what you saw."

"And the supper at ten o'clock?"

"It is ten o'clock now, and I am here at your feet."

"And that makes you a man of honor, does it?" she said with unutterable scorn; "but there is still another matter which you overlook, but which is quite enough to dishonor you in my eyes."

"What is it, Olympe, for God's sake?" he asked in terror.

"Do you dare to ask?"

"I implore you to tell me!"

"Decency would require that the woman to whom you sacrificed me should be, like myself, a refined and faithful person; decency would require that she should be content to keep your love-tokens carefully put away in her jewel-case, so that no one might recognize them as henceforth belonging to her."

"What do you mean by love-tokens," said he, "and by jewel-case?"

"Yes, go on with your lying, or trying to lie!"

"I do not understand."

"Oh!" said she, with a contemptuous elevation of her shoulders, "what a paltry, feeble nature you have, Monsieur Bannière, and how little you deserve to be loved by such a heart as mine! Do you really believe, then, that I should have been alarmed and should have fainted because I discovered that you were making an appointment with that woman? Make appointments with all Lyons, if you please; I should hardly care."

"Pray whence came the trouble, then, which had such an alarming result?"

"From your cowardice, your dishonor."

He started up, and raised his head.

"You insult me," he said, "for a trifling bit of folly."

"Trifling! Ah! you call by that name the 'bit of folly' which if related by me to the police would lead to your being shut up at Pierre-Encise within two hours."

"Would they shut me up for accepting from La Catalane an invitation to supper which I did not attend?"

"I am not talking about your appointments," said she, in a rage.

"What are you talking about, then? You will end by driving me mad."

"Better that I should drive you mad than denounce you as a thief."

"Thief!" he cried, with bloodless face; "oh, beware, Madame!"

"Yes, indeed! after stealing from the women, you strike them! You will strike me, and then go boast of it to La Catalane."

"Olympe! Olympe!"

"And then some day her turn will come, and you will steal from her and strike her for some other's sake."

"Olympe, I am growing blind! Take care, for I can't answer for myself!"

"There 's a ring which will have travelled a good deal up to the time when it will figure at the police court as a piece of damning evidence."

"The ring!" he muttered, "the ring! To be sure, I had forgotten that!"

He threw himself at Olympe's feet, and beat his head against the floor.

"Oh, you disgust me!" said she. "Only this hateful poltroonery was lacking. Rise, Monsieur, and go; I am no longer either grieved or angry. Go and find her with whom you have an appointment; tell her that she may henceforth show herself fearlessly with my ring, and that I will not tear it from her finger."

Bannière raised his head; his cheeks were wet with tears.

"Olympe!" he murmured, "what did you say?"

"I said that I give that woman the ring you have already given her after stealing it from me. I release both of you from your remorse and fear of the galleys."

Bannière stood erect, trembling and in disorder.

"I gave your ring to La Catalane,— I!" he exclaimed.

"And she wears it on her finger with the rings of her other lovers; she might at least have done you the honor of wearing it alone. The ruby is worthy the distinction."

"You say that La Catalane wears your ring on her finger?"

"Monsieur de Mailly's ring; yes, Monsieur Bannière."

"Olympe, we will send for La Catalane to come here. Olympe, if she has that ring on her finger, we will make her confess where she got it."

"Oh!"

"Olympe, I swear to you by everything sacred in this world; I swear by my love for you — that disgusts you! by religion — you smile! — I am stifling with rage and grief and pity! I swear to you by your mother that I never gave that ring to La Catalane!"

"Who has it on her finger! Swear now that you never stole it from me!"

"I did steal it from you! Yes, I stole it! That word is not degrading enough. I am a thief! Olympe, it is true; but I did it that I might sell it, and gamble with the proceeds, in the hope of gaining riches for you. Olympe, I cannot lie any more; what would be the use? The proofs are accessible. I sold the ruby to Jacob the Jew; he will tell you so. I never so much as thought of that woman. Give her your ring! Oh, I would have much preferred to die!"

"You were offering her your love."

"Olympe, don't think it. But then, what am I! Nothing but a poor, miserable wretch. Give her your ring, Olympe! Never, never!"

Olympe shook her head with an icy look which irritated Bannière.

"You don't believe me?" said he.

"No."

"Don't be so obstinate; you will regret it later. In half an hour the proof will be here. I will run to the Jew's now. Oh, no, I will not go, for you would think I had patched up a story with him. I will stay here, and do you go, Olympe, or better still, write him, for you are not feeling well and cannot walk. *Mon Dieu!* have mercy on me! You see that I am not lying! To take the ring from you was a crime, but not a theft. I had no profit from the money, much less did it go to benefit that woman. Oh, don't overwhelm me! I hated the ring; it was a souvenir for you, — an agreeable one, perhaps, but hateful, hateful, hateful to me! Olympe, I implore you to lay aside that freezing demeanor; Olympe, do not drive me to despair! You accuse me, and I deny the charge. Look to the proofs; it will be time enough to condemn when you have the proof at hand."

"What's the use?" said she; "something has died within me since you have been talking. I have done my utmost to rekindle in my heart a spark of sentiment, but I find nothing there. Love? — oh, it is dead! Pity? — dead! Between the two extremes what a galaxy of illusions! Don't defend yourself, it is n't worth while; I saw the ring on La Catalane's finger."

"Why could n't she have bought it from the Jew?"

"That's weak; find something else, Monsieur Bannière."

"But suppose it's true, nevertheless!" exclaimed the poor fellow, in a paroxysm of grief. "Suppose they tell you so, and prove it; suppose — "

"If the Jew were here and should say so, if La Catalane should grovel at my feet and say so, I would not believe them."

"*Mon Dieu!* Olympe!"

"This is the worst of this sort of thing. Blind is she who has never been deceived as I have been. Confidence and Distrust both wear bandages upon their eyes, — the one because she does not wish to see what is evil, and the other because she does not wish to see what is good."

Bannière, at his wits' end, his arguments and words alike exhausted, approached the window for a breath of fresh air.

Olympe remained where she was, sombre and impassive. Just as Bannière, after looking upward as if to ask of

heaven an inspiration, was turning again toward Olympe
to make a final effort, a shout came up from the street,
and nailed him to the spot.

"Do not stir, Bannière," said a voice, "or you are a
dead man!"

XXXIII.

THE ARCHERS.

BANNIÈRE heard the strange injunction which was laid upon him, and leaned out to look into the dark street.

Olympe trembled. Bannière was threatened with serious danger, and love was not so extinct at the bottom of her heart as she herself believed.

By leaning out, Bannière could see the cross-belts and bayonets of soldiers glistening along the wall opposite the house.

The movement he made was almost imperceptible and in no wise resembled flight, but the gun-barrels were aimed at him.

"Do not stir," the voice repeated, "or we fire on you."

Olympe forgot all that had gone before. She ran toward him.

"What is it?" she cried in affright.

"In the name of the king!" said the voice of a commissioner, who was just entering the house, the door having been opened to him; "in the king's name, I arrest you!"

"*Mon Dieu!* what does it mean?" exclaimed Olympe, clinging to Bannière's shoulder.

"Oh, these are doubtless the soldiers whom you asked the police to send to arrest your thief, Olympe," said Bannière, unable to repress the nervous trembling which seized him, and maintaining his position only by clinging to the window-frame.

Olympe had not even time to protest. The door of the room flew open, and the terrified lackey showed the way to the commissioner and two fusileers.

"That's Bannière," said the magistrate; "I recognize him."

"What is your business with me, pray?" feebly muttered the poor wretch.

The commissioner came forward, pointing him out with his finger to the soldiers, and repeating the same words he had said before, —

"In the king's name, I arrest you!"

"But what has he done?" cried Olympe.

"That's the concern of the judges who will have to try Monsieur. I only know that I have a precept, and I am serving it."

They dragged Bannière away; and Olympe, forcibly separated from him, fell fainting upon a couch.

Bannière had already disappeared in the grasp of the soldiers. He had disappeared more firmly convinced every moment that Olympe was the moving cause of his arrest. He was wrong, however; for since the discovery she had made of Bannière's infidelity and the whereabouts of her ring, she had had neither time nor means to notify the police.

But the Abbé d'Hoirac had had twenty-four hours since La Catalane's revelation; he had made use of them like a man in haste to obtain revenge and liberty.

He had himself gone to the authorities, and laid the case before them. Was it not shameful that a man should have broken his vows and promises, and have left the Church for the stage, in defiance of all law, divine and human?

" In the King's name, I arrest you !"

Drawn and etched by E. Van Muyden.

OLYMPE DE CLÉVES. I. 312.

The vicar of the archbishop seemed deeply impressed, as may be imagined, by the problem thus laid before him.

He replied that to break the vow taken by the novice was a crime.

The Abbé d'Hoirac, delighted to find his opinion thus subscribed to, went on in the same line.

"Is it not true," said he, "that the scandal is the more hateful when caused by those who are looked to to set a good example?"

The archbishop's vicar replied that he was happy to find Monsieur d'Hoirac, who was reputed to be somewhat addicted to worldly pleasures, so devoutly disposed.

The abbé bowed with beaming face.

"You have some disreputable priest to denounce?" the vicar asked.

"Yes, Monsieur," replied the abbé.

"And this priest has gone on the stage?"

"Yes, Monsieur."

"Our powers are much circumscribed by the Parliament," said the vicar; "but we still have the right of inquiry."

"Ah," said the Abbé d'Hoirac, "I forewarn you that you have to do with a villain who has a sharp nose, and during the inquiry he will get scent of the chase and disappear."

"What is his name?"

The abbé hesitated about naming him. An evil action never issues readily from the heart of an honorable man, although such actions sometimes do issue from such hearts.

"It is he who plays the emperors at the city theatre," said the abbé.

"Aha! it's Bannière. then?" said the vicar. who

was well posted in matters theatrical, like many ecclesiastics of the time.

"Precisely."

"Indeed, he does n't act badly," said the vicar. "I
like his declamation very well; he has a fine delivery and
a well-modulated voice."

"Oh, yes, I have nothing to say against him in that
respect."

"And you say he is a runaway novice?"

"Yes, from the Jesuit college at Avignon."

"I will write to Père Mordon to send and reclaim
him."

"That's very well; but as I had the honor to say,
when Père Mordon's reclamation arrives, Bannière will
have fled."

The vicar scratched his chin a moment.

"I see what you would like," he said; "a provisional
arrest, — what we call officially a precautionary seizure."

"For the greater glory of morality," said the abbé.

"Yes; *ad majorem Dei gloriam!*" said the archbishop's vicar, laughing. He was nursing a little inclination toward Jansenism, and was not sorry to have his
little joke at the Society of Jesus, when opportunity
offered.

D'Hoirac's lips parted in a smile which disclosed his
even, white teeth.

"You are still interested in the Jesuits?" asked the
official, smiling too, but with no teeth to show, alas!

"I like all kinds," replied the abbé; "and in that
respect I follow the example of my respected relative the
archbishop, who is more of a shepherd than a pastor.
You of the old school are more exclusive, and don't
understand that. If the late king were alive, you would
be charged with Arnauldism or Port-Royalism; while I,

a Jesuit, like the bee of which Horace sings, gather the honey of orthodoxy from every flower."

"Even though they grow on the stage," said the official, with his most cunning smile.

"Everywhere, I said, Monsieur le Vicaire," replied D'Hoirac. "I need not write myself then to my uncle's friend, Père Mordon; and you are obliged to me, are you not, for leaving the credit of the capture with you in his estimation?"

"Very much so, my dear Abbé. I am extremely glad to be useful to Messieurs the Jesuits, when they are endeavoring to be agreeable to us. Reverend Père Mordon is a man of intellect, and will repay the service I am about to do him."

"And now," asked D'Hoirac, "when will you execute this precautionary seizure?"

"Whenever you think fit, Monsieur l'Abbé!"

"Will this evening do?"

"This evening?"

"Yes."

"Is it practicable?"

"Perfectly."

"This evening, then. Have you any choice as to the manner of arrest?"

"Oh, no! Let there be no public scandal, that's all."

"Shall we arrest him at home, then?"

"I think that will be the best plan."

"Where does he live?"

"I'm sure I don't know."

The abbé preferred not to seem familiar with Bannière's abode, for then he must show that he knew Olympe's also.

"Oh, the devil!" said the vicar; "you don't know?"

"You can have inquiry made at the theatre," suggested D'Hoirac.

"You are right; that shall be done, Monsieur l'Abbé."

"One last question."

"Put it."

"Explain to me, I beg, Monsieur le Vicaire, the progress of an affair of the variety we are discussing."

"That's very easy."

"I am listening."

"Precautionary seizure, formal arrest, incarceration."

"Provisional."

"It is all provisional. Of course, Monsieur l'Abbé, you must know that it can be nothing more than provisional in such a case. Incarceration,— I had got so far,— reclamation by the reverend principal, argument, provisional return of the novice to the convent, and private examination of the case before the proper official."

"Ah, before the officials at Avignon?"

"Oh, no! before the official of the place where the fugitive has been living and was arrested."

"Very good! at Lyons then."

"At Lyons, yes; perhaps that will be disagreeable for you?" the vicar asked slyly.

"By no means, Monsieur. And then?"

"Then, as I was saying, the trial."

"An ecclesiastical trial is a long-winded affair, is it not?"

"Oh, it has no end, especially when some influential person is interested in having it continue."

"And meanwhile will the poor wretch be kept always in confinement?"

"No. When he is restored to the Jesuits, he becomes

their pupil again; and as the reverend fathers are extremely clever in keeping their grip upon those who do not desire to stay with them, and as they can make themselves very disagreeable to those who resist, it is almost certain that within two or three years the novice will make his profession, and accept orders with very good grace."

"Ah! who knows?" said the abbé, whose thoughts were so full of Olympe that he was little inclined to believe that any one could forget her, having once known her.

"In any event," continued the vicar, who saw that something was tormenting the abbé, and was anxious to reassure him,— "in any event, whether prisoner or Jesuit, our shameless novice will not be able, for a long time hence, never indeed, to scandalize society with a repetition of the disgraceful performances which have so justly offended your devout disposition."

The abbé thanked the official and took leave of him, determined not to make his appearance at Olympe's house until after the disappearance of the principal obstacle to his happiness.

As the vicar had promised, the armed force, led by a commissioner, had taken Bannière into custody that same evening, upon his requisition, as was narrated in the last chapter.

Père Mordon received the letter containing the news the day after the precautionary seizure.

The Jesuit, enchanted at the thought of recovering his lost lamb, forwarded his formal reclamation to the magistrate at Lyons; this reclamation, intrusted to the college courier, an intelligent fellow, who, like the mule of Phèdre, knew how to trot and to gallop when necessary to accomplish the ends of the order, and always

ad majorem Dei gloriam, reached Lyons two days after
the little squad had hurried Bannière off to prison.

Bannière evinced no particular disposition to rebel.
He was buried in such black despair that except for the
automatic action of his legs, obeying the impulse given
from time to time by blows with the butt end of a musket,
one would have thought the poor boy turned to a pillar
of salt, as Lot's wife was for her fatal curiosity.

The archers were hurrying along behind the commissioner, and the commissioner gathering up the skirts of
his robe so that he might travel more quickly, when the
escort, at a street corner, ran plump into another party,
just turning in from the adjoining street.

A dragoon with a lantern came into collision with
the commissioner, to whom, not recognizing his quality,
he administered a violent blow, accompanied with these
words, —

"Well, you sot, don't you see my officer?"

The commissioner would have asserted his dignity and
entered a protest if it had been a mere lieutenant; but by
the rays of the lantern he recognized the uniform of a
colonel; so he restrained his ill-humor, and made way
for the others to pass.

The party then disclosed itself as consisting of three
dragoons, two of whom were a little distance in the rear,
and an exceedingly handsome cavalier, with lace at his
wrists, and perfumed with roses.

Behind the dragoons was a small valet bearing his
master's sword and cloak.

The colonel, looking askance at the commissioner and
his henchmen, said to the lantern-bearer, —

"Aha! show a light here, Laverdrie; there's game
behind the commissioner, I think."

"Yes, Monsieur le Colonel," replied he of the black
robe, humbly.

"Very well, very well, do your duty," replied the colonel, with a disdainful accent. "By the way, what street is this?"

"Rue de la Réale, Monsieur le Colonel."

"Oh, that's not what I'm looking for. Is there not a Rue Montyon about here?"

"You are within reach of it, Monsieur le Colonel; it's the street we just left."

"Very good, thanks."

"The first to the left, Monsieur le Colonel."

"Go on, Laverdrie."

"Yes, Colonel."

"And do you," said the officer to the valet, "see if you can discover the residence of Mademoiselle Olympe de Clèves."

The valet quickened his pace, and preceded those whom he had been following.

At the name of Olympe, Bannière seemed to awake as from the sleep of death. He opened his eyes, saw the lantern, the epaulettes, the uniforms, heard the clashing of spurs and the sound of voices.

The consequence was that he seated himself upon a stone, unable to take another step.

"Oh, *mon Dieu!* oh, *mon Dieu!*" he muttered again and again.

Meanwhile the dragoons and their colonel had gone on.

"Oh, *mon Dieu!*" still the same refrain.

"Well, well! are we going on or not?" the commissioner demanded.

"Monsieur, the prisoner will not move," replied an archer.

"Strike him with your muskets, strike him!"

"We have struck him, Monsieur."

"Prick him with your bayonets, then."

" We have pricked him too, Monsieur. "

The commissioner approached in a rage. The worthy
man had never seen such a thing! The blows with the
musket sometimes failed to overcome resistance, but the
pricking never.

Bannière sat there on his stone, pale, dishevelled, and
suffering agony. His glassy eyes were fixed obstinately
upon Rue Montyon, at the spot where he had seen the
last of the valet, the lantern-bearer, and the two dragoons
following the colonel, who was on his way to Olympe,
without doubt.

" Oh, *mon Dieu!* " he groaned; " this explains it all.
She was expecting a new lover, and had me arrested to
get me out of the way. Oh, *mon Dieu!* "

The fact is that such an idea was enough to tan the
hide of any man in love, however sensible he might be,
to such a point as to render it impervious to gunstock or
bayonet.

The commissioner employed the last means which the
law left open to him. He caused Bannière to be laid
upon a couch of interlocked muskets, and the poor boy
was carried in that fashion to the *maison de ville*, where
he was deposited in a cell.

The archers suffered even more than he, for they found
him very heavy.

XXXIV.

MONSIEUR DE MAILLY.

OLYMPE had not begun to recover from the grief and alarm caused by the arrest of Bannière, when she heard more strange voices at her street door, and the next moment in her reception-room.

The servant, still trembling from the effects of the visit of the archers, did not hesitate to introduce without preliminary announcement a fresh arrival in uniform, accompanied by several others.

Indeed the honest fellow would have shown in a whole army in the same way, if it had presented itself at his mistress's door.

Olympe, hastening to the door to know the cause of the sounds, and hoping vaguely that they were bringing Bannière back, suddenly recoiled, exclaiming, —

"Monsieur de Mailly!"

It was, in fact, the colonel, who entered the room, with his lantern-bearer in his wake, weary of asking if Mademoiselle de Clèves was visible, and out of patience at receiving no reply.

"Yes, Madame," said he; "it is I, no other. You have a remarkably silent servant there."

"Monsieur de Mailly!" said Olympe, again; her mind, weakened by the recent excitement, made no attempt to face this new storm.

"Well — but — I seem to produce all the effect of a ghost here, — the effect of a husband!" said the colonel, smiling.

"Pardon me, pardon me!" stammered Olympe.

The dragoon and the servant withdrew when they saw the colonel take her hand.

She seated herself, half dead with conflicting emotions.

"I either terrify you or incommode you," said Monsieur de Mailly, courteously, "whereas I claim that I ought to produce neither effect upon you, — no more when I am by your side than when I am far away."

Olympe made no reply; she was suffocating.

"We are still friends, I suppose," continued Monsieur de Mailly. "I came here to have the honor of seeing you, and I hope that there is no one who can possibly be offended by the presence in your house of a friend who presents himself with civility."

Olympe stammered out a few words interrupted by sobs.

"I prefer to withdraw rather than cause you the slightest embarrassment," said the colonel. "I came here the bearer of what in my mind was a bit of good news; but I fear now that it may be bad."

Olympe at last ventured to trust herself; she raised her eyes to Monsieur de Mailly's.

"Good news, Monsieur le Comte?" said she, with a sad smile.

"But not finding you free," pursued the colonel, "I hesitate."

"Free!" she repeated.

"Oh, I know that you are not free, that you have bartered away the liberty which I restored to you."

"Monsieur —"

"I restored it to you, Mademoiselle; of course you were at liberty to make whatever use of it you chose. Believe me when I say that I should not think of reproaching you in any way. I have understood that you were dearly loved and very happy."

"Very happy!" cried Olympe, bursting into tears; "you have heard that?"

"Why, yes; are you not?"

"Look at me."

"You weep; is it with joy?"

"Do you think so?"

"Does my presence offend you?"

"Oh, no."

"Then you make me very anxious. Is it possible that I may be of some use to you, even if my presence has no attraction for you?"

"Monsieur le Comte, I have no right to ask anything at your hands."

"Perhaps not, but I have the right to offer you something."

"Nothing, nothing, I beg you. Turn your back on me, for I do not deserve that you should be my friend."

He drew nearer to her.

"Are you at liberty to go to Paris?" he asked.

"Why?"

"To make your début at the Comédie-Française; I have an order to that effect."

"Then you still take an interest in my fortunes?"

"Always. It is a friend's right."

"Even though you thought I was happy?"

"I knew very well that you were not. I know all; the man whom you chose — "

"Say no ill of him, he is so unfortunate!"

"I meant to say only that he was not worthy of you."

"It was a mistake on my part, — an act of madness born of your desertion."

"Therefore I deem myself the cause of your misfortunes; and that thought led me to come to your assistance, to rescue you, if there is still time and if you are willing."

"Speak, Monsieur le Comte."

"You must make up your mind, Olympe, to leave this man who makes you miserable and is ruining you."

"You know, then?"

"Everything, as I told you. You must leave Monsieur Bannière; be brave enough for that."

"Alas! it is already done."

"You have left him?"

"Poor boy! we are separated. Yes, he was arrested but a short time ago."

"What had he done, *mon Dieu!* He will disgrace you, the wretch!"

"He has done nothing, poor fellow! He was arrested in pursuance of a reclamation by the Jesuits. He is a rebellious recruit of that order; you know what that means, perhaps."

"Indeed I do. And the official caused his seizure?"

"In my house!" she cried, weeping.

"In your house! Here?"

"Not a quarter of an hour ago."

"Ah, *mon Dieu!* by six archers and a commissioner?"

"Yes."

"Was he not a tall, dark fellow, slender and well set up?"

"Yes, yes!"

"How pale he was!"

"Did you see him?"

"I met him in the custody of the archers on my way hither."

"*Mon Dieu! mon Dieu!* then he must have seen you!"

"He even heard me pronounce your name and ask your address."

"Oh, the poor boy! it will kill him!"

"It will kill him!" cried the colonel, in surprise; "why so?"

"Because he is jealous of you; because he knows well—"

Olympe was on the point of betraying herself, of divulging the secret of her heart. It seemed to her at that moment to be influenced by sincere feeling, — that heart which had been led astray for a year by no one knows what illusions and vagabond enjoyment.

"What does he know?" asked the colonel, softly.

"He knows," said Olympe, firmly, "that I have always had much respect for you, Monsieur le Comte."

"Respect?"

"That is the only sentiment which I could allow myself to retain for you," murmured the young woman, whose tears burst forth afresh.

The colonel took her hand and pressed it.

"Do you regret him?" he said; "do you pity him?"

"Yes, I do pity him, and I regret him too, — not the life which he has made me lead, alas! although I loved him and led him on. For I will not be a coward and deny my affection, even though it were unworthy. No, I do not regret him; but I cannot help saying that he is now much to be pitied, and that all his life the unlucky fellow will not only suffer, but will lay his suffering at my door."

"You gratify me, Olympe, by speaking thus," said the colonel. "Loyal I always found you, and loyal I find you still. If you knew how one's heart glows to find that its affection is worthily bestowed! You are a generous woman. I will rescue you. I did not know that the fellow was arrested, but I knew that he was making your life unendurable, and that you sometimes had thoughts of cutting loose from him. I should have been deeply disappointed to have you deny him, or to find that you still love him."

"May I hope then that I have your esteem at least, in default of your love ?" said Olympe.

"Rely upon all my sentiments; but let us attend to the most pressing business first. Make your preparations, and let us start."

"For Paris ?"

"Yes, Olympe. I have horses and carriage in waiting."

"I will say nothing about my engagement here, for I know that the king's command overrides everything; but I must speak about a certain ill-fated prisoner, who will die of grief if he learns of my departure in his dungeon. He will accuse me of cruelty or ingratitude, if of nothing worse; for after all it was for me that he left the Jesuits."

"However we can't share his imprisonment with him."

"You can use your influence to procure his release."

"I have no power in ecclesiastical matters."

"Try."

"By no means, my dear; you are wrong in looking upon yourself as under obligations to the man. He is in prison; let him stay there. Congratulate yourself rather upon being thus freed from your embarrassment."

"Never! it would be dastardly. I am incapable of it. I will not abandon him in his misfortune."

"That is chivalry thrown away."

"No; my heart tells me what to do."

"In any event you cannot compel the magistrate to release a culprit duly convicted."

"No Paris for me, if that poor fellow is not free. You fancy me a woman without heart, capable of forgetting in his dungeon, because she has ceased to love him, a man whose ruin she has wrought; a woman without pity, capable of enjoying life in Paris while the lover whom she once chose is dying of rage and grief in a convent cell. No, no; you would despise a woman who would yield to you upon this point, Monsieur le Comte; you could not love her."

"Olympe, Olympe, you are not yet cured! You have something more than compassion for that man."

"Do not insist," said she; "you will make me doubt your feeling for me, if you fail to understand me."

"Olympe, if I should rescue that man for you, you would succumb again to his allurements."

"Oh!"

"That sort of people have no spinal cord, they are like reptiles; supple and easily crushed when they are threatened, they raise their heads when the storm has passed. The serpent has tempted you, daughter of Eve, and will tempt you again."

"Monsieur le Comte, promise me that the poor wretch shall be free in two hours, and I will be upon the road to Paris in fifty minutes."

"Ah, that's something like!"

"Promise."

The count reflected a moment.

"You are quite sure of yourself?" he said.

"Give me your word as a gentleman in exchange for mine as a girl of noble birth."

"Done!" said the count; "now help me to find a pretext."

"Oh, I'm of no use in that direction; I am, as you see me, completely prostrated. Ideas, Monsieur le Comte!

I have n't had one a week on an average for a year; and
I shall not have another for a year to come."

"Wait till I think up something, then."

"How good you are!"

"I see no way to arrange it. To get a priest out of a
priest's hands is like enticing the devil into holy water.
One is sure to get splashed."

"How about the archbishop?"

"Bah! we are at swords' points, and the Jesuits would
play me some trick. Wait — I see a way."

"Ah!"

"Yes; but your protégé in order to escape one form of
slavery will have to step into another."

"Is it a milder form?"

"Yes, indeed, and has the great advantage of being
more in the open air."

"What is it?"

"Let him enlist in my dragoons. The Jesuits will
claim him, but we will tell them that their monk is a
dragoon, and that the dragoons are the king's; they will
have to let their prey go."

"That is, indeed, a happy thought," said Olympe,
joyfully.

"You understand, my dear, that instead of demanding
the liberty of a man, I charge the Jesuits with having
taken my dragoon away from me; that will change the
face of things, and put them in the wrong."

"You are a man of good heart and quick wit," said
Olympe, sweetly, "and I am as grateful to you as
Bannière will be."

"All right; but I rather prefer your gratitude to his.
So the idea commends itself to you?"

"Marvellously!"

"You have duly reflected?"

"I have."

"You will have no return of your affection for him?"

"Never!"

"The embryo Jesuit tempted you, and the embryo dragoon will be at least as seductive."

"You know, Monsieur de Mailly, that if I did yield to the mad caprice which was near being my ruin, it was after you left me."

"I know it, Olympe."

"You know, Monsieur, that I never deceived you while your love was alive."

"I believe it."

"My word is sacred, and my hand goes only with my heart."

"I do you that justice."

"Then trust me always. I have promised you to love Monsieur Bannière no more; that settles it, and I will love him no more."

"But I know why I said that."

"Why?"

"Because we have got to induce this youth to sign the enlistment papers; it is a delicate proceeding, and only you can undertake it, and at such a crisis the heart of the most courageous of word-givers may waver. Now you just told me, to reassure me, that you had never deceived me so long as you were mine; that is true. But now you are not mine, you are Monsieur Bannière's."

"Oh!" said she, gazing at him with eyes so eloquent that he felt a thrill of love reach the inmost recesses of his heart, — "whether I am Monsieur Bannière's or not, what matters it?"

"You must see," he replied, "from my seeking you out here, and bringing you an order for your début, that I love you still."

"Upon your honor?" said she.

"Upon my honor."

"Well, then," said Olympe, "I will prove to you that I have the strong heart of a man when resolution and confidence are essential. Twelve o'clock is striking; it is the hour at which I was awaiting you at Avignon a year ago, day for day."

"It is true, Olympe, and that day, or rather that night, the king recalled me; but I would have done well not to read his letter till the morning."

"Let us forget that year, Comte," said she. "You love me still, and it is for me to prove to you that I have always loved you. I will accept the king's command and will go with you to Paris. Now are you afraid of seeing me waver when I go to set that unhappy prisoner free?"

"I will go with you myself to the prison," replied the count.

Soon after the Mailly dragoons were heard in the street shouting boisterous refrains, which made the commissioners and the archers shudder as they returned from the prison where Bannière's name was entered.

That poor fellow hardly suspected, as he lay upon his straw pallet under the damp arches, that two generous hearts were working together for his deliverance.

It was true, however, — as true as his misery.

XXXV.

THE ENLISTMENT.

BANNIÈRE was still lying on the straw in the darkness the next morning, when a turnkey came to tell him that he had a visitor.

We cannot describe the state of frenzy to which solitude and neglect had driven him.

He was one of those nervous prisoners who lose their wits in a week, and die in six, more exhausted than others in six years.

He had already passed through all the successive stages of hope, discouragement, and despair, which others never reach before verdict, sentence, and torture.

His most bitter pangs were suspicion and jealousy.

He suspected Olympe of having caused his incarceration; he suspected her of having made an appointment with the colonel of dragoons.

Worse than all, he had heard, as the archers were carrying him away, that that colonel was Monsieur de Mailly.

Imagine his anger and his distrust.

In such a frame of mind was he when Olympe's visit was announced.

He bounded toward her as soon as he saw her, with an impulse of mad delight, which was moderated at once by the sense of what his dignity required as well as by the glacial air with which Olympe had armed herself.

"Ah!" exclaimed Bannière, "here you are at last!"

"Did you not expect me?"

"I did not believe, Mademoiselle, that you would have the face to come and mock at me, after casting me into the abyss."

"Don't waste words, Monsieur Bannière; you seem to play in hard luck in this world."

"Ah, but you helped me wonderfully to lose the game!"

"What do you mean?"

"Is it not to you that I owe my present imprisonment?"

"If you mean to reproach me because you loved me and abandoned your profession for me, you are right, and I am the cause of your imprisonment."

"That's not what I mean at all; I mean that I loved you, and you denounced me to the police."

"Oh, you know very well that I could never be guilty of such a dastardly piece of work."

"Can the same be said of that colonel of dragoons who was looking for you last night, and who doubtless found you?"

Olympe turned pale in spite of herself; although she expected the thrust, she was well aware that she had no valid defence.

"You saw Monsieur de Mailly, did you not?" said she, in a tone perceptibly tinged with pity.

Bannière took her evident grief as a sign of regret or of fear.

"Oh, well," said he, "I have convinced you, have n't I? It is perfectly clear now that you and your old lover conspired to ruin me."

"That is so far from being the case, Monsieur Bannière, that I have come from Monsieur de Mailly to bring you a chance of regaining your liberty."

"Liberty!" cried the young man, in amazement.

"You are arrested because of a reclamation by the Jesuits; you belong to them. Well, it occurred to Monsieur de Mailly to have you enlist in his dragoons. In that way you will belong to the king, who will also reclaim you, and will be at no loss to lay hands upon you."

"That is very generous!" said Bannière, satirically.

"You do wrong to speak of a kind action in that bitter tone. Monsieur de Mailly was under no obligation to do you this service."

"Ah, you take his part against me; you care more for his nobility than for my misfortune."

"Your misfortune, Monsieur Bannière, was richly deserved," said Olympe, gravely; "but this is no time for recrimination. Here is the enlistment in blank, the enlistment which will save you from the Jesuits,— from everlasting seclusion, that is to say, and from the ecclesiastical profession, for which you are little suited; do you choose to sign it?"

"In the first place, tell me what you are going to do with me; for there is an air of decision in your tones which surprises me. Explain — "

"Nothing until you have signed this paper."

"But it is impossible for me to accept a favor from a man whom perhaps you still love."

"That does not concern you, Monsieur Bannière; first of all, sign."

"What interest have you, pray, in being so anxious to bind me thus?"

"To rescue you, to prove to you that I had no hand in your incarceration by opening the doors of your cell. Sign!"

Bannière took the pen handed to him by Olympe, who had everything in readiness. He signed his name without reading the document which insured his freedom.

She folded the paper after she had dried the signature, and put it away in her pocket.

"Now," said Bannière, kissing her hand, "tell me that you still love me."

But without replying to him, she said, —

"Armed with this paper, Monsieur de Mailly will claim you this morning. You will be free this afternoon at four o'clock, when there will have been time to go through all the indispensable formalities."

"You did n't answer me, Olympe," said Bannière, gently; "I asked you if you still love me."

"Don't be anxious if there should be some little delay," continued Mademoiselle de Cléves in the same tone. "The magistrate will be reluctant to let go his prey, but Monsieur de Mailly has decided to act peremptorily."

"Olympe!" Bannière interrupted once more, and more forcibly.

"It also occurred to me," she continued, without appearing to notice the prisoner's burning eagerness to change the subject, "that you would lack means of subsistence here; so I have brought you some money, so that when you leave the prison you will be in condition to assume at once the swagger and jaunty air which a soldier should have."

"Look here, Olympe," said Bannière, in desperation, "don't you propose to answer me? I asked you if you still love me."

"I do not propose to reply, in fact, Monsieur Bannière."

"But I propose that you shall reply."

"Then I will speak frankly, as I think. No, Monsieur Bannière, I do not love you."

"You do not love me!" cried Bannière, terrified by Olympe's words, and more than all else by the tone in which they were spoken.

"No!" she said again.

"Why not?" stammered the poor wretch.

"Because you have worn away, strand by strand, the golden thread of my love; because, even before it broke, you had sullied and tarnished it, and dimmed its lustre; and because, with a woman, illusion is the great preservative of love. You deceived me, then mocked at me, then maltreated me; my illusion has vanished, consequently I have ceased to love."

"Olympe!" he shrieked, grovelling at her feet, "I swear that I have never deceived you!"

"I do not believe you!"

"Olympe, I swear by my own life and yours that I never gave your ring to La Catalane."

"I do not believe you."

"Listen, Olympe! Since I am to be free and able to act, it will be very easy. If La Catalane is or ever has been my mistress, it must have been to gratify some sentiment or other, must it not? Either caprice or jealousy or weakness. Either she provoked me or I besought her. In any case her self-conceit will make her boast of it. I ask you to come to her with me, and she will tell you all that has taken place between us. If she says that I have been her lover, if she says that I gave her your ring, do with me as you please. Kill me, — no, do even more than that, — leave me!"

The unfortunate man uttered these words so forcibly and naturally, he put so much heart and so much passion in them, he writhed at Olympe's feet in such an agony of despair, that she was moved, and she let him see it.

"How can you conceive," he continued, "that I could

have loved another woman, even for a moment, when you were my whole life and my whole heart? An infidelity of the imagination — *mon Dieu!* you will pardon it; I would pardon it in you. See now whether I love you. If you should tell me that Monsieur de Mailly has returned, that he went on his knees to you to return to him, that he persuaded you, for you were weak — Olympe, I am a miserable, cowardly devil, my love is paltry and good for nothing, but I would forgive everything if you told me that you still loved me! "

Olympe felt as if her heart stopped its beating; she feared that she should waver and weaken, and abandon her hand to the fervent kisses of this man to whose words the eloquence of true love gave such irresistible force.

Her only salvation lay in violence and brutality. She hardened her heart and resorted to that stern obduracy which women fall back upon when they have ceased to love, or believe that to be the case.

"Very well! " said she; "you have saved me the trouble of telling you what I desired to conceal. Monsieur de Mailly has returned; he did go on his knees to me, and did persuade me. I was weak, and I no longer control my own actions."

As the words fell from her mouth, she saw the blood leave Bannière's cheeks, his lips and his neck, as it flowed roaring back to his heart.

He seemed a pitiable object to the woman who was shaking his very soul.

"Ah, Olympe, Olympe! " he muttered.

He trembled in all his limbs, and his legs gave way under him. From his knees he fell back to a sitting posture, then rolled over on his side, and would have measured his whole length on the floor if he had not fallen against the wooden stool which was the only seat provided for prisoners.

She maintained a gloomy silence, while he struggled to recall the life which seemed to be leaving his body.

"You will not be inflexible," he said at last, with an effort, "on the ground of a crime which I did not commit, when I am not so in respect to a sin which you have admitted. I forgive you, Olympe; give me back your love."

"Bannière," said she, in a stifled voice, "if I had not believed you guilty, I never would have been false to the faith I plighted to you — Do not interrupt me. You repent now, I can see; you appreciate now what I am, but it is too late."

Bannière looked at her with the expression of one whose wits are wandering.

"Henceforth, Banniére," she continued, growing bolder, "we are separated; let me say to you that if you had chosen I would have been faithful to you forever — "

"Oh, *mon Dieu!*" he muttered, as he had done the night before when he saw Monsieur de Mailly.

"Don't interrupt me again, Monsieur Bannière; as I have told you, I no longer control my own actions. Live, work, and forget, — it will be very easy for you, — and believe that of our two destinies yours is the happier. To-day you regret; who can say that to-morrow I myself shall not be the one to regret?"

With these words, which attested her affectionate and generous nature, Olympe made a step toward the door. As he saw her on the point of leaving him, Bannière made a leap, or rather started to make one.

"No," said he; "it's of no use. She is no mere flirt. When she says that she has ceased to love me, it is because that is the fact."

He fell back again prostrate upon the floor.

Olympe approached him, and seeing him in that condition, bordering upon lunacy, she held out her hand to him; he did not notice it.

She slipped between his fingers the purse of gold she had brought; he gave no sign that he perceived it.

Then she moved again toward the door, and he did not lift a finger to prevent her.

Her heart was almost bursting with anguish; with her eye fixed upon the poor youth whom she was deserting, she felt drawn to him by every sentiment of duty and loyalty.

It may be that a word from Bannière, a tear, a sigh, or even the slightest movement would have called forth a last proof of tender emotion; but the man was dead to all intent, and required no further attention.

She caused the door of the cell to be opened, and went out, more terrified than ever, swiftly as a ray of light, fearing, even when she was in the open air once more, that a reaction would take place, that a shriek from the poor fellow, a heart-rending appeal to the old love, a beating upon the inflexible doors, would fall upon her ear, to reproach her for her decision and make her courage waver.

Nothing! She heard no sound except the rustling of the paper upon which Bannière had signed his enlistment as a dragoon, and the corners of which were in revolt against the heavy silk of her dress.

XXXVI.

HOW BANNIÈRE BECAME A DRAGOON IN THE MAILLY REGIMENT.

BANNIÈRE, deserted by Olympe, passed the second night after his arrest at Lyons upon the straw pallet of his dungeon, rolling and twisting about, and beating his head against the wall.

There are sufferings which the most practised pen will never attempt to describe, because such a pen knows that description has its limits, while grief has none.

The next morning, crushed and ground and bleeding, he had fallen into that sort of lethargy which resembles sleep much as death resembles repose.

Toward eight o'clock, through the cloud which weighed upon his mind and veiled his intellect, he thought that he heard the door of his cell open and saw several men approach him.

Soon a sensation altogether material helped to draw him from his torpid state.

He felt that he was being vigorously shaken; he opened his eyes, cast an expressionless glance around him, and with a mighty effort succeeded in making out what was going on.

Two dragoons, leaning over him, were shaking him with all their strength to arouse him; while a brigadier who stood in front of him, seeing that their efforts had no result, ordered them after every fruitless shake to shake harder, and that in the same tone and the same phlegmatic air with which he would have conducted the manual of arms.

Bannière was so annoyed by the shaking that he made an effort to recover his voice equal to that he had made to recover his sight, and succeeded in articulating a few words.

"What do you want with me?" he asked.

"Brigadier," said the dragoons, "he has spoken."

"Yes," replied the brigadier; "but I did not understand what he said."

"No more did we," said the dragoons. "Hallo, there, friend!" they shouted, beginning their shaking again; "repeat, if you please, what you just said. The officer did n't hear, nor did we."

"I asked what you want with me," Bannière repeated in a die-away voice.

"Brigadier," said the two soldiers, "he asks what we want."

"*Pardieu!* I heard him," said the brigadier; "I am not deaf."

Then he turned to Bannière.

"What do we want? We want in the first place, comrade," said he, "to set you on your feet if possible, then take you to the barracks, then put on your back a uniform like ours, then teach you to ride, then instruct you in the sabre and carbine drill, — in short, to make a pretty dragoon of you."

"Make a pretty dragoon of me," repeated Bannière, wondering vaguely what the words meant.

"That is to say, as far as it 's possible," added the brigadier, who, as he saw Bannière's bruised and bloody countenance, did not seem to form an extremely flattering opinion of his future companion's physique, and consequently did not wish, as they said in the regiment, to promise him more butter than he could spread on his bread.

"Ah, yes," muttered Bannière, "sure enough. I enlisted yesterday in the Mailly dragoons." He added with a sigh: "I had forgotten it."

"The devil!" exclaimed the brigadier, "you have a short memory apparently, comrade; look out, — that's a serious defect in the military profession. There is a little article in the code on that subject; I recommend you to study it."

Bannière made no reply; he had relapsed into the gloomy reverie from which the repeated and progressively more violent shakings of the soldiers had aroused him for an instant; it is more than probable that he did not hear a word of what the brigadier said.

That was a great misfortune.

However, they got Bannière upon his feet, and once on his feet he could walk; and once under way, he was soon outside the walls; once outside the walls, he breathed the fresh air, and then his faculties gradually returned.

He was a dragoon.

But he was no longer a Jesuit.

They were taking him to the barracks.

But they had no motive for confining him there.

He would leave the barracks, we will not say some day or other, but some hour or other.

He would leave them probably even before nightfall; he would go to La Catalane, and compel her, willy-nilly, to give him the ring; then he would go to Olympe, and however obstinate she might be, he would prove his innocence.

But if he could not satisfy her, he would blow out his brains at her feet, and all would be over.

This little plan, irrevocably determined on in Ban-

nière's mind, gave much strength to his legs and
elasticity to his arms.

He had a momentary idea of using this latter quality
to overturn the two soldiers who were walking beside
him, and then to bring his legs into play and lose himself
in one of those labyrinths of streets where it is impossible
to follow a man. But he reflected that the alarm would
be given at once, and that he could not fail to be retaken
before he had paid to La Catalane and Olympe the double
visit he was contemplating.

It was better to pay those two visits first, and trust to
chance for the rest.

So Bannière shook his head as if to drive away these
foolishly premature ideas, and with a more tranquil
countenance kept on toward the barracks.

He was almost smiling when he arrived there. The
clocks were striking nine as he entered.

The barracks were at one end of a great square
courtyard which was used for the regimental drills and
manœuvring.

At the moment of Bannière's arrival the regiment was
engaged in going through the drill on foot. We believe
we have already said that the dragoons had the privilege
of belonging to both the cavalry and infantry arms of the
service.

Before the enemy, and under fire, every horse-dragoon
was a cavalryman; but when his horse was slain, he
changed temporarily into the infantry, and wielded a
musket in place of his sabre.

The regiment then was going through the foot-drill.

The two dragoons and the brigadier conducted Bannière
to the armory. As a man must be at least five feet four
and at most five feet six to belong to the dragoons, the
uniforms made upon that basis were never too long or

too short. It sometimes happened, however, that they were too broad or too scant.

The regimental tailor surveyed Bannière, and said very knowingly, —

"I know what will fit this rascal, as if I had his measure. Make him wash his face, and have his hair cut, and then send him here. I'll look out for the rest."

Bannière went down into the courtyard, washed his face at the fountain, and submitted his head to the shears, wherewith his locks were clipped according to the rules in five minutes.

Then he went and put on his uniform; and when that was on his back, it was agreed that Bannière really made, as the brigadier had ventured to predict, a very pretty dragoon.

Bannière, absorbed as he was in more serious matters, did not fail to cast a sidelong glance upon the fragment of a mirror, nailed against the wall, which the dandies of the regiment used when they put the last touch to their toilet.

This piece of broken mirror was responsible for the vanished tranquillity of many Lyonnais beauties.

Bannière, then, cast a glance in its direction, and saw, to his great satisfaction, that the uniform was by no means unbecoming to him, whence he derived the hope that having won Olympe's heart in his Jesuit garb, he might have a fair prospect of winning it back again in the brilliant uniform of a dragoon.

There was always that haunting spectre of Monsieur de Mailly behind all Bannière's dreams.

Olympe had told him, as a proof that she was no longer his, that she had returned to her former lover; but might she not have said it in a moment of anger to repay him for the injury he had done her?

Besides, he had himself told her that he was a coward, like every man who truly loves, and who is ready to sacrifice everything. even his honor, to his love.

Oh, well! if Olympe had done as she said, it would be for him to forgive, when he had proved that he had never deceived her; for then he would be the innocent and she the guilty one; and then, oh! then how gladly he would forgive her!

He had reached that point in his forgiving impulse when his brigadier instructor put a gun in his hand, and stationed him among the new recruits who were learning to charge in twelve time.

Bannière passed an hour carrying arms and presenting arms, after which he was told that he was free to dispose of himself as he chose until noon, when he would receive his first lesson in horsemanship.

Bannière asked the brigadier if it would be safe for him to go boldly into the city and defy the Jesuits.

The brigadier replied that under the safeguard of his Majesty's uniform he might be absolutely without apprehension, — that he could safely go up to the very windows of their college, and make the most irritating and contemptuous gestures to the very faces of the black-robed gentry.

Bannière did not wait to be told twice; he saluted his superior, and with his sword under his arm, and his helmet slightly tilted over one ear, he walked across the courtyard to the outer gate, the topographical situation of which he examined with great care, and heedless of observation.

XXXVII.

HOW BANNIÈRE CALLED UPON LA CATALANE, AND
FOUND THE HAIRDRESSER THERE, AND WHAT
TOOK PLACE.

BUT, as we know, Bannière's purpose in going out was
not purely and simply to examine the architecture of the
barracks gate.

His purpose was, first of all, to go to La Catalane,
recover the ruby, and ascertain how that ruby came
into her possession.

He had stormed and raged inwardly ever since the
morning, as we have said; his first thought had been to
gain his freedom at all hazards, so that he might effect a
happy solution of this terrible episode which had wrought
such frightful disaster to him; but he had thought better
of it, and had chafed at the bit during the two hours consumed by his toilet and his lesson in the manual.

All this, as may well be imagined, had not failed to
exasperate him still more against the cause of all his
trouble.

And so, as soon as he had turned the corner of the
barracks, he bent his steps toward the theatre, in the
neighborhood of which La Catalane lived.

Notwithstanding his great haste, however, he stopped
at an armorer's to purchase a pistol, powder, and balls.
They cost him two louis, which he took from the hundred louis contained in the purse Olympe had handed
him, and which, upon reflection, he had concluded not
to cast aside, as they might be very serviceable to him.

The pistol bought and loaded, Bannière put it in his pocket and resumed his way toward La Catalane's dwelling.

It was not simply as a means of threatening, not as a mere weapon of intimidation, that he had provided himself with the pistol; by no means. As the moment of his meeting with that woman drew nearer, Bannière's cheeks grew paler, his lips were closed more tightly, and his decision became more fixed to force the proof of his innocence from her, and if she refused, to blow her brains out.

This decision did not impart a very loverlike expression to his features as he knocked at La Catalane's door.

It was the hairdresser who answered his knock.

As he was reasonably sure that this creature was familiar with all that had taken place, he was not sorry that chance had served him so well as to bring the two together at that time.

The hairdresser recoiled a few steps as she saw who it was, and thereby enabled Bannière to step quickly into the hall; and when he had done so, he closed and locked the door behind him.

"*Jésus Dieu!*" cried the hairdresser, "what does this dragoon want of us?"

Bannière understood that it was not politic to alarm his prey at the outset; so he contorted his features into a ghastly smile, as he said,—

"What! dear Madame, don't you recognize me?"

"*Mon Dieu!* it's Monsieur Bannière," ejaculated the hairdresser. "No, no, no, I did not recognize you."

"What! you don't know your friends?" said Bannière, imparting the mildest note that he could manage to his voice.

"Oh, but you have a fierce look!"

"It's the costume which gives me that appearance. But a word with you, my girl."

"What is it, Monsieur Bannière?"

"Is La Catalane at home?"

"Why, yes; oh, she will be very glad."

"Why so?"

"Why, to see you. She is very well disposed toward you, my indifferent gallant."

"Bah!" said Bannière, "you're making game of me."

"No, upon my word! Besides," she added, with a cynical smile, "you can assure yourself of the truth of what I say no later than this very minute."

"Oh, well, perhaps we will ascertain about that! Oh, hairdresser of my heart, just take me to her."

"Why, you know where she is, — in her boudoir."

Since her dealings with the Abbé d'Hoirac, La Catalane had a boudoir.

"No matter! do you show me the way nevertheless," replied Bannière.

The woman saw no objection to that course, and she preceded Bannière up the dark stairway.

Suddenly a bright light streamed into the hall; the hairdresser had opened the door of the boudoir, and Bannière could see La Catalane stretched out luxuriously upon that article of furniture whose indiscreet disclosures made the reputation of Crébillon *fils*.

"Look, Madame," said the hairdresser, "it's Monsieur Bannière."

Bannière entered in the wake of his guide, and closed and locked the door of the boudoir as he had done with the street door.

"Monsieur Bannière? Where is he?" asked La

Catalane, who did not recognize him in his new costume any more readily than her confederate had done.

"Here he is, in military rig. Just see how it becomes him; only it seems to me that it gives him a terribly fierce look."

At this moment Bannière, having finished what he was doing, and having put the key of the boudoir in his pocket for greater security, turned toward La Catalane.

He was pale no longer; he was livid.

La Catalane shuddered at the expression of his eyes.

"Oh, yes, very fierce indeed," said she, rising. "Pray, what's the matter, Monsieur Bannière?"

Bannière walked up to her with knitted brow, his breath hissing between his clenched teeth.

Without noticing her question, "Your hand," said he.

La Catalane slowly raised her right hand, murmuring in deadly terror, —

"*Mon Dieu!* what do you want?"

Bannière seized the hand she extended, and examined one by one the rings with which the fingers were laden.

Monsieur de Mailly's ruby was not on that hand.

"The other!" he said.

"*Jésus!* he is mad," muttered the hairdresser.

Bannière took the left hand as he had taken the right, by the wrist, and had scarcely glanced at it when his eyes shone.

He had recognized the ruby he had sold to Jacob the Jew.

"Oh," he cried, "it's true; there it is!"

"What?" asked La Catalane, trembling like a leaf.

But Bannière replied to her questions only by propounding questions of his own.

"Where did you steal that ruby?" he demanded.

"What! Steal!" cried La Catalane, attempting to assume an air of righteous indignation.

"Where did you steal that ruby, I say?" repeated Bannière, tapping the floor with his foot.

As he put the question, he squeezed her wrist so hard that the poor woman groaned with pain.

"Help!" cried the hairdresser, "help! murder!"

Bannière looked at her over his shoulder, and remarked without loosing his hold of La Catalane,—

"Come, a little less noise there!"

But as the tone in which the words were uttered was anything but reassuring, the hairdresser, instead of making less noise, redoubled her shrieks and gestures of despair.

Bannière released La Catalane's wrist, leaped upon the hairdresser, seized her by the neck with his left hand, and as he dragged her toward La Catalane, drew the pistol from his pocket, and held the barrel against her chest.

"Come," said he, with stern decision, "I have no time to lose in lamentations and jeremiads. About that ring, where did it come from, who gave it to you? Speak, or I'll kill you!"

La Catalane appreciated that her life hung by a thread.

"The Abbé d'Hoirac," said she.

"Then you are Abbé d'Hoirac's mistress?"

"But —"

"Then you are Abbé d'Hoirac's mistress?"

"Yes."

"Very well. You are going to give me that ring."

"But —"

"First of all, you are going to give me that ring."

"Here it is."

"And now you are going to state in writing that you are the Abbé d'Hoirac's mistress, and that he gave you the ring."

"But — "

"Thousand devils!"

"I will write whatever you wish," cried La Catalane, falling upon her knees, so terrified was she by the expression of Bannière's face.

The hairdresser meanwhile, to whom Bannière had paid no further attention than to tighten his grasp upon her neck as La Catalane's hesitations increased his rage to madness, — the hairdresser was writhing and twisting in his hands, like a serpent in the clutches of an eagle.

He saw at last that unless he let her go, he should strangle her. Moreover he had to hunt up writing-materials for La Catalane to make her statement.

He unscrewed the vice a little.

"Oh, let me go! oh, let me go!" muttered the hairdresser, indistinctly.

"If I let you go," said Bannière, "will you be wise and hold your tongue?"

"I will not make a sound," said the woman.

"Very well," said Bannière.

He relaxed his hold upon her, and she fell at full length upon the floor, begging for mercy.

Then he went to a little round table upon which his eye fell; and there he found pen, ink, and paper all ready for use, as if in anticipation of his visit.

He took the whole up bodily, and set it down before La Catalane.

"Now write," said he.

She had no inclination to resist, but her hand trembled so that it took her some moments to steady herself.

"Come," said Bannière, "calm yourself; I will wait."

He stood playing with the trigger of his pistol, cocking and uncocking it with a sinister, threatening sound, which was more efficacious in restoring La Catalane's faculties than all the salts and cold water in the world.

She took the pen and said, with a glance at Bannière:

"Dictate, and I will write."

"No," said Bannière, "you might claim, perhaps, that I had influenced you to say what I want. Write it yourself: only tell the truth, lucidly and as concisely as possible."

La Catalane wrote:—

"I declare, as being the solemn truth, that the ruby ring which I this day deliver to Monsieur Bannière was not given to me by Monsieur Bannière, but by the Abbé d'Hoirac, my lover."

"Good!" said Bannière, following with his eyes the words as they were written,—"good! Now sign it."

La Catalane signed with a long-drawn sigh.

"And now the ring," continued Bannière.

Another sigh, deeper still; but it was no time for haggling,—she gave him the ring.

Bannière examined it closely to see if it was really the same ruby, and having recognized it beyond question, put it on his little finger.

"Now," said he, "as I am no thief, and as it is no part of my purpose to do you any real injury, take this."

Taking a handful of louis from his pocket, he threw them in La Catalane's face, and darted from the boudoir.

At the door he stopped to listen; he feared that one or the other of the women might rush to the window to call the guard, and have him arrested when he went out.

But they were picking up the louis Bannière had thrown at them, to which the hairdresser, who was half strangled, claimed to have as undeniable a right as La Catalane, who was half dead with fear.

Bannière, seeing that he had naught to fear in that direction, leaped down the stairs and into the street, and ran off as fast as his legs would carry him, in the direction of Rue Montyon, where, as our readers will remember, Olympe resided.

XXXVIII.

HOW BANNIÈRE CEASED TO BE A DRAGOON IN THE MAILLY REGIMENT.

BANNIÈRE arrived, quite breathless, before the house so familiar to his eyes and his heart, and in which he had passed such blissful and such unhappy hours.

Everything was closed except a single window on the first floor, — the window of Olympe's boudoir.

Bannière's heart sank within him at the aspect of the house, which resembled a tomb, except that the solitary open window seemed to indicate that every spark of life was not yet extinct.

He seized the knocker, and pounded away furiously.

He thought at first that he was to receive no reply; his impatience lengthened seconds to minutes, and minutes to hours.

At length he heard a step approaching the door cautiously.

He knocked again, as there seemed to be some hesitation in the step.

"Who is there?" asked a woman's voice.

"It's I, Claire, — I."

"Who are you?"

"I am Bannière. Don't you know my voice, pray?"

"Oh, Monsieur Bannière, why have you come here?" asked Claire, without opening the door.

"Why have I come here!"

"Yes, I ask you that."

"Why, I have come home; I have come to see Olympe. I have come to prove to her that her suspicions were unfounded; I have come to tell her that I still love her."

"But Mademoiselle Olympe is no longer here, Monsieur Bannière."

"Olympe not here!"

"No, Monsieur Bannière; she has gone."

"Gone where?"

"To Paris."

"When?"

"At two o'clock this morning."

"With whom?" asked Bannière, as the color left his cheeks.

"With Monsieur de Mailly."

Bannière uttered a cry of anguish, as if a knife had pierced his heart. Feeling as if he were going to fall, he clung to the knocker.

Almost immediately a thought flashed through his mind.

"It's not true!" he said.

"What! not true!" cried Claire, offended that such a slur should be cast upon her veracity.

"Olympe is in there!"

"I swear that she is not."

"She doesn't want to see me, and has taught you your lesson."

"No, Monsieur Bannière, as truly as there is only one God in heaven!"

"I say that you lie!" cried Bannière.

"Oh, the idea!" said the maid; "I lie! Come in, Monsieur Bannière, and see for yourself."

Whereupon Claire, sure of her facts, majestically opened the door, and gave passage to the dragoon.

The liberty accorded him of entering the house, after

the long discussion through the door, proved to Bannière
that there was no hope for him.

But he went in, nevertheless, gloomy and crushed; his
purpose was, not to see Olympe again, for he was convinced that she was not there, but to see at least the
room in which she had lived.

Alas! it was easy to see that she had indeed departed.
At every step Bannière found some trace of her hasty
flight. The salon was crowded with boxes which Mademoiselle Claire had been occupied in packing.

He went from the salon into the bedroom.

He was suffocated with grief.

The bedroom was still redolent with subtle perfume,—
the same which La Catalane had successfully employed
to assist in deceiving the Abbé d'Hoirac.

Bannière knew it so well, alas! — he had been intoxicated with its fumes so many times, by her side from
whom he was separated forever!

He fell on his knees beside the untouched bed, took
in his arms the lace-trimmed pillow upon which Olympe
was wont to lay her head, and covered it with kisses.

Deep sobs burst from his overcharged heart, mingled
with sighs and tears and inarticulate sounds.

Claire observed his great sorrow compassionately.
Women are women all the world over; that is to say,
they have no mercy for the ills which they themselves
are responsible for, — with regard to such they are pitiless,
— but they are very compassionate for those ills which
other women bring upon us.

We must remember, too, that Claire had once thought
Bannière a fine fellow; and veritable grief, especially
when caused by unhappy love, always adds to a man's
attractions in a woman's eyes.

"Oh, Monsieur Bannière," said she, "you must not

give way thus! After all, Mademoiselle Olympe is not dead."

"Claire, dear Claire," cried the dragoon, recalled from hell by this consoling voice. "Oh, you are kind, indeed you are! You will tell me where she is, won't you, so that I may follow her and find her?"

"I would do so with much pleasure, Monsieur, but I do not know myself where Mademoiselle is."

"What! you don't know where she is?"

"No."

"But you are packing her trunks."

"True; but I am to await a letter from her to tell me where to send them."

"When ought the letter to arrive?"

"I don't know."

"But at least you know whether she started for Paris or for Marseilles?"

"Oh, for Paris, Monsieur, I am sure."

"Are you perfectly sure, my good Claire?"

"Yes."

"What makes you sure?"

"Because, as they were leaving, Monsieur de Mailly said to the postilion, 'The Paris road, by the Nivernais.'"

"Monsieur de Mailly!" exclaimed Bannière. "Oh, then he really was with her!"

"As for that, Monsieur Bannière, I should not think of concealing it from you."

"*Mon Dieu! mon Dieu!* Claire, what shall I do? what will become of me?"

"I don't think it is for me to give advice to a determined fellow so deep in love as you, Monsieur Bannière."

"Oh, if I only knew where I could hear of her!"

"Why, you can always hear of her at the Hôtel de Mailly."

"You are right, Claire; there I can surely learn where Olympe is, — at all events, by following Monsieur de Mailly. Oh, Claire, Claire, my child, you have saved my life!"

In his joy, he put his hand in his pocket, pulled out several louis, and put them in Claire's hand, kissed the pillow once more most fervently, and rushed out of the house smiling.

"Oh, *mon Dieu!* what an idiot I was! Of course I can learn everything at the Hôtel de Mailly."

But it was a hundred and twenty leagues from Rue Montyon to the Hôtel de Mailly. How was Bannière to manage that distance?

The question seemed not to cause the dragoon the least anxiety, for he hurried off toward the barracks with an almost placid expression on his face.

He arrived just as the cavalry drill was about to begin.

The brigadier-instructor was waiting, biting his mustache, and holding a long whip in his hand.

He was inclined to grumble, as his custom was; but as he glanced obliquely at the clock, he saw that Bannière was a minute ahead of time instead of a minute behind, so he had nothing to grumble about.

"Come here, comrade!" the brigadier said to him.

"Here I am, brigadier."

"Have you ever ridden?"

"Never."

"So much the better," said the brigadier, "for in that case you have no bad habits to unlearn."

Why did Bannière, who was as we have seen a passably good horseman, reply that he had never ridden?

Because he had his reasons for the falsehood, no doubt. Bannière was not troubled with such scruples as were eternally tormenting Champmeslé and laying snares for his feet.

The horses were on hand.

"Bring the trotting horse first," said the brigadier.

Turning to Bannière, he said: "You understand that you will be taught first to ride a trotting-horse, then a runner, and then a jumper."

"Why not begin at once with the runner?" asked Bannière, who seemed anxious to learn.

"Ah!" said the brigadier, "because you must learn to trot before learning to gallop."

"Very well," said the recruit; "then the runner, as you call him, will gallop if desired."

"He goes like the wind."

"And for a long while?"

"By riding judiciously, one can do twenty leagues in four hours upon his back."

"The devil!" exclaimed Bannière; "a fellow must be an expert to ride such a horse."

"Oh, that makes no difference; for when the rider falls off, he stops."

"That's very convenient," rejoined Bannière. "Well, brigadier, let's see the trotter."

"Aha! you are in a great hurry, comrade."

"Well, you see, brigadier, that I detest the Jesuit ceremonial as much as I adore the military drill."

"Good," said the brigadier; "I see that I was rightly informed about you, and that with time and good will, we can make something of you."

"*Dame!* I hope so," said Bannière.

The brigadier made a sign, and the trotter was led out; he showed Bannière how to gather up the reins, how to seize the mane with the left hand, and how with three springs he should be in the saddle.

We say "should be," because after his three springs Bannière was not in the saddle at all. He had lifted himself up; but after resting his stomach on the pommel for an instant, waving his right arm and left leg about wildly, much as a swimmer does, he fell back on the ground, amid peals of laughter from his comrades.

"Let's try again," said the brigadier, seriously.

Bannière did try again, and was more fortunate the second time. After some minutes of violent effort, he at last tumbled into the saddle.

"That's better," said the brigadier; "but we will begin again, so that we may get it perfectly."

"Begin again it is," said Bannière, bravely; "for I am like you, brigadier, upon my word! I take some pride in it."

The dragoons who were watching the lesson began to laugh.

"Silence!" said the brigadier. "The poor boy wants to learn at least," he added, "and I'm not sure that I could say as much of all of you."

Bannière made a third attempt, amid profound silence, and this time he came out of it without discredit.

"Ah!" he exclaimed triumphantly, when he was in the saddle, "here I am, brigadier."

"Very good, dragoon!" was the reply; "now turn the toe of your boot in, press the saddle with your knees, — the knees, dragoon, are the true horseman's support — Are you doing as I tell you, my boy?"

"I think so, brigadier."

"Well then, houp!"

He aimed a blow with the whip at the steed, who proceeded to justify his appellation by starting off at a fast trot.

Although Bannière was, as we have said, a fairly good

horseman, the gait of the horse upon which he was mounted had the advantage of being so hard that one could from behind see the sky between the rider's body and the saddle at every step.

For a moment it occurred to him to ride English fashion, — rising on the stirrups, that is, — but he reflected that he would betray himself if he did so, and he let himself be shaken up like a bag of walnuts, swaying from side to side.

Again he reflected that if he exaggerated the insecurity of his seat, the galloping lesson might be postponed till the next day; and as he was in a great hurry to pass from the trotter to the runner, he regained his equilibrium gradually, and ended by riding sufficiently well to draw forth words of encouragement from the brigadier, who at last uttered the words so eagerly awaited, —

"Very good; now, the runner."

Bannière was on the point of leaping from his horse at a single bound; but that, he thought, would be as culpable a piece of imprudence as the other he had so nearly committed, so he let himself down as awkwardly as possible to the ground.

"Oh, oh!" exclaimed the brigadier, losing a little of his enthusiasm for the recruit; "the next time, my friend, we must dismount in better form than that."

"Shall I try again, brigadier?" said Bannière, in his humblest tone.

"No, it's not worth while; we will attend to that to-morrow. The runner."

The runner was led out. He was a superb blooded horse, with legs as slender as spindles, and muscles of steel.

He stretched out his graceful and intelligent head toward Bannière, snuffed at him, and neighed.

"Good!" muttered Bannière, "good! before long, I'll make you neigh."

"Come, come," said the brigadier, "let's not lose any time; to the saddle, and see if you can mount this one better than you dismounted from the other."

"Oh, brigadier," said Bannière, "it's nothing at all to mount, as you will see."

Indeed, at the third spring, Bannière was firmly seated in the saddle.

"Not bad," said the brigadier.

"Tell me, brigadier," said Bannière, who seemed encouraged by the praise, "we don't go too fast at first, do we? I have never ridden at a gallop."

The brigadier began to laugh, and touched the horse so lightly with the whip that one could see that he had regard for Bannière's suggestion.

Yet the horse, notwithstanding his moderation, set off at a great pace, perhaps urged on by invisible pricks of the spur.

"Oh, brigadier, brigadier!" cried Bannière; "what's your horse doing? Stop him, I am falling. Brigadier, brigadier, your horse is bolting with me! Whoa! whoa!"

Bannière, without letting go the rein, crouched down on the mane of his steed, who, after making the circuit of the inner court amid the shrieks of laughter of the whole regiment, darted out at the gate and into the street, as if he needed more room to satisfy his ambition for speed.

The brigadier and the soldiers, still laughing, ran to the gate, and saw Bannière in the distance clinging to his horse, and crying in a most doleful voice, —

"Brigadier, help, help! I am going to fall! Whoa, whoa, whoa!"

This lasted until the horse had disappeared at the

corner of the street; then the horseman let go the mane, gathered up the reins, and leaning like Hyppolite over his horse's neck, he emitted a little whistling sound, which, seconded by vigorous spur-play, increased the speed of his mount twofold.

Meanwhile the brigadier and the soldiers were laughing as if they would burst. They were completely taken in by Bannière's stratagem.

The boy had not been a Jesuit ten years, and an actor twelve months, to no purpose.

XXXIX.

HOW BANNIÈRE'S HORSE RAN UNTIL HE STOPPED;
THE WORTHY PERSONS WHOSE ACQUAINTANCE OUR
HERO MADE IN A CERTAIN TOWN, THE NAME OF
WHICH HAS ESCAPED US.

THE horse was a fast runner, and Bannière realized the
need of speed. Consequently, when the horse gave signs
of weariness and slackened his pace, Bannière would
drive the spurs into his sides up to the rowels, whereupon
the spirited animal would make off again at a gallop.
The result was that man and horse covered a long distance in a short time without stopping for breath.

Two hours out of Lyons, however, Bannière was compelled to rest for a few moments, for his own sake as
well as his gallant steed's. These few moments he employed in discussing a bottle of generous Burgundy,
while his horse was regaled with a double ration of oats
in which he poured what there was left of his bottle.

In the two hours he had made almost eight leagues.
Man refreshed and horse fed, the man remounted the
horse and resumed his journey.

The wine and oats had a miraculous effect; the beast
had the devil in him, and his feet hardly touched the
earth. One would have said it was the steed of Faust
on his way to the witches' vigil.

To be sure, one would have looked in vain for
Mephistopheles on the crupper; but, visible or invisible,
every man has his Mephistopheles galloping beside him.

Bannière's Mephistopheles was at this moment a combination of every human passion, — in the first place, love
for Olympe, more violent than ever; secondly, a profound
hatred for Monsieur de Mailly, which grew more and
more bitter as the moments passed, for he imagined,
poor fellow! that Monsieur de Mailly during all this
time was at Olympe's side; then from time to time
another emotion crept into his heart, which though
something less exalted than the two noble passions, love
and hatred, which form the basis of so many thrilling
tragedies and exciting dramas, is no less importunate.

We refer to that baser emotion which is called *fear*.

Bannière was afraid of being followed and over-
taken. It was the second time that he had fled for
his liberty, — the first time from the Jesuits, the second
from the dragoons. But the first time Olympe was the
companion of his flight; and this time he was alone, save
for the invisible Mephistopheles which kept whispering
in his ear, —

"Haste! Bannière, haste! and you will overtake
Olympe and Monsieur de Mailly; and you will escape
from the dragoons as you escaped from the Jesuits.
Haste! Bannière, haste!"

Every word which fell from this spirit who was
urging Bannière on was translated into a vigorous dig
of the spur.

At last the horse, utterly exhausted, came to a stand-
still with trembling legs, covered with foam, and gasping
for breath.

Our embryo cavalryman had covered in five hours
fifteen honest leagues, equal to twenty-five leagues at
least by post.

Bannière was earnestly engaged in conversation with
his Mephistopheles when his horse stopped, and had not

noticed that he had reached quite a large village, and
that the dwellers therein, standing at their doors or sitting on benches against the house-fronts, were gazing
with an air of selfish well-fed comfort, which they were
at no pains to conceal, at the dust-begrimed horseman
and foam-covered steed, both of whom seemed in dire
distress, while they, worthy bumpkins, lazily turning
their heads without moving their bodies, were entirely
free from care, happy and motionless, enjoying to the
full that variety of well-being which the Latin poets, an
eminently slothful race, understood so well.

Witness Virgil's shepherd returning thanks to Augustus for the repose which he owes to him; and witness
Lucretius congratulating himself upon being able to sit
calmly on shore, while the angry sea is tossing ships
and sailors about upon its mountainous waves.

When the horse stopped, and Bannière succeeded in
opening his eyes, blinded with dust and suffused with
blood, he saw in the first place the large village of which
we have spoken, which consisted of a single street, at
the farther end of which the country was open again.
Then, when he directed his glance from the more distant objects to those nearer at hand, he saw a man with
a pleasant, rosy countenance holding his horse by the
rein, and another, less florid in appearance, holding the
stirrup on the dismounting side. At the same time a
voice which assumed to speak in gracious tones said at
his ear, —

"Good-day, Monsieur le Dragon!"

"Oho!" said Bannière, still somewhat confused, "are
they speaking to me, I wonder?"

But a moment's reflection was sufficient to assure him
that the voice could not be bidding good-day to any
other than himself, for the simple reason that he was

alone on the road, and there probably was not another dragoon within ten leagues.

He also observed that his horse had halted just at the door of one of those enormous inns which dotted the main roads of the France of former days, and which gave forth an odor of grain for quadrupeds and baked meats for bipeds that could be smelt a league away.

The spit was turning; chickens and partridges were browning before the fire, while the sweet-smelling hay was thrown down from the mow, and the teeth of the thirty horses in the stable were crunching the beautiful black oats.

" Good-day, Monsieur le Dragon," said somebody.

" Good-day, Messieurs," replied Bannière, trying to impart to his voice an accent of courteous gratitude, as he saw the two men offering their services.

" Oh, what a handsome dragoon! " said a third voice, which by its gentler modulations Bannière recognized as belonging to a person of the female persuasion.

" Devil take me! " thought Bannière, looking about for the proprietress of that charming organ, which, although its words terrified him, struck very softly on his ear. " Devil take me! I must change my rig; I am a little too military to appear in public in this neighborhood."

However he took courage, in that his male interlocutors wore civilian costumes, and that his panegyrist was a pretty girl of some twenty years.

The two civilians were, as we have said, one at his bridle, the other at his horse's side. The pretty girl was standing at the door of the inn. Bannière cast a hasty glance upon his surroundings, and seeing that there was nothing in or about the hostelry which savored of the provost, he alighted with an air of determination.

He was no sooner out of the saddle than his horse was led off to the stable by the hostler, and Bannière allowed himself to be gently impelled toward the dining-room.

There are, as we all know, invisible but irresistible currents which always draw a man in the direction in which he wishes to go. The beast wished to go to the stable and the man to the refectory, and both reached the goals of their respective desires at the same time.

The two civilians, whose demeanor was intended to inspire confidence, accompanied Bannière, as if to do the honors of the establishment; and Bannière, albeit rather surprised at their assiduous attentions, made no resistance.

She of the attractive countenance, in some mysterious way unfathomed by Bannière, perhaps upon fairy wings, vanished from the threshold of the outer door only to reappear upon the threshold of the dining-room.

Being thus guided by heart, eyes, and stomach, Bannière yielded with a good grace.

In the first place he had to undergo a series of inquiries very natural on the part of people who were so lavish of polite attentions; but they all substantially resolved themselves into this one,—

"Where are you going, dragoon?"

"Where am I going?" Bannière replied. "*Pardieu!* that's a simple question; I am going to Paris."

"Pardon! you would do better to go somewhere else."

"It seems that Paris is Monsieur's destination," said one of Bannière's questioners. "I, for my part see no harm in his going to Paris; I come from there, myself."

Bannière thought it was quite time for him to get some idea of the individuals who surrounded him; and while the table was being laid, he made a somewhat careful examination of them, as he was dusting his boots with his handkerchief.

The one who seemed to have some objection to Ban-nière's going to Paris was a little bourgeois of some fifty years, with a red face, plump and well-fed, with short, thick hands; he was dressed in a grayish-brown coat, breeches of the same color, and grayish-blue ribbed stockings.

The other, who was tall with a long, thin neck, wore a plume of feathers over his ear notwithstanding his bourgeois costume; he had long arms, a long nose, a small, dry hand, and a little, round black eye; and in his long nose, if we may be permitted to revert to that feature, there was a peculiar deviation from a straight line, which all people who are afflicted with it ought to have remedied at once by the operation of orthopedy, for there is no peculiarity of the physiognomy which so infallibly indicates moral obliquity.

Unfortunately Lavater, to whom we are indebted for this information, was not born at this time; at all events, he had not then written, so that Bannière could not have read Lavater.

He thought that the man with the long nose and the slant had got into the habit of wiping his nose from left to right, and that the infirmity we have mentioned was the result of that injudicious practice.

It may be, however, so absorbed was he in thoughts of Olympe's pretty little nose, that he neither saw nor thought anything at all concerning the great, ugly, crooked nose of the man with the plume.

That personage, moreover, bore himself very haughtily, and at the same time stroked his thigh, which was thrust forward in knightly fashion, and the hilt, once gilded, of a long rapier.

Sometimes he obligingly cast his little black eye down upon the pretty girl, his companion, who deserves, as well as the others, that ten or twelve lines should be devoted to drawing her portrait.

To be sure, we romancists never deal with pretty women, and the companion of the man with the plume was very pretty.

However, this is what she was like; take careful note of it.

Slight, fair, and rosy; large eyes of a deep blue shade; mouth well-shaped, smiling often, sometimes pouting, and at such times captivating; sweet little hands, delightful to look upon.

She saw that her turn had come to be examined, and she made a charming courtesy to Bannière.

The conversation became general, and dealt only with commonplace subjects, as is usually the case among people who are not acquainted.

The news of the road, the weather, and the traveller's horse were the principal topics.

Bannière was very reserved upon the first point; he had every conceivable reason for not divulging whence he came

Upon the second he talked freely; he confessed that it was hotter than the devil.

"Not so hot as it is in the Abruzzi, though," interjected the man with the plume.

Why he said "than in the Abruzzi," we shall see very soon.

On the third point, his horse, Bannière was as prolix as Ovid.

This can be easily explained; he had reasons for acting as he did.

We have already explained that he did not care to tell where he came from.

As to the second point, he could not prevent the

weather being what it was, — very hot. He might, to be sure, have discussed the degree of heat, and maintained that it was as hot as in the Abruzzi; but he did not do it, — perhaps because he was of the same opinion as his interlocutor, or because he did not care whether it was so or not.

As to the third, he wanted to sell his horse, which was, like all cavalry horses, branded with a *fleur-de-lis* upon the flank, and was recognizable — that is to say, compromising — wherever he might go.

The man with the blue hose and the man with the plume thereupon began to analyze the beast.

The man with the plume was lost in admiration of his beauty.

"Permit me, nevertheless," said the little man, "to contradict you, Monsieur le Marquis."

"Oho!" thought Bannière. "A marquis, eh? the devil you say!"

The more he looked at him, the more unpleasant did he, the lover of the beautiful, find that extraordinary nose.

"In what particular," said the marquis, "do you find fault with the horse? He is as you see him."

"He is foundered, Monsieur."

"Pretty good!" said Bannière; "if it would not be discourteous, I should tell you that you did n't know what you were talking about."

"Oh, as to that," rejoined the marquis, "I cannot agree with you. I stand up for the animal, which seems to be a very good one, and I am much pleased with him; but to say that Monsieur does n't understand horses! — oh, no! oh, no! I will never say that."

"Nevertheless — " Bannière began.

"Dear dragoon," said the man with the plume, in a

slightly patronizing tone, which went decidedly against
Bannière's grain, "Monsieur is a large dealer in silks,
who has killed more horses in his travels than your
regiment and mine have ever had slain in battle, even
though they fought against Prince Eugene and Monsieur
de Marlborough."

"Oho! you have a regiment?" said the dragoon.

"That is to say, Monsieur, I am captain in a regiment," replied the marquis, modestly.

"Monsieur le Marquis," said the little blue-stockinged
man in Bannière's ear, "is captain in the Abruzzi regiment."

"Ah!" said Bannière, "I see; that is why he said
just now, when I remarked that it was hot on the Paris
road, 'not so hot as in the Abruzzi'?"

"Exactly."

"I understand, then."

"He's a terrible fellow, of whom you certainly
must have heard."

Bannière executed that contortion of the eye and
mouth which is supposed to accompany an effort of the
memory; but he could not remember.

"What is his name?" he asked.

"The Marquis della Torra."

"No, — no," said Bannière. "The Marquis della
Torra? It's the first time I ever heard the name."

"At all events, you know now that he is a captain."

"And a marquis," said Bannière.

"And a marquis," repeated the little silk-merchant.

"So you say that the horse is foundered?" resumed
the marquis.

"I am afraid so."

The marquis rang, and a waiter appeared.

"Go to the stable," said the marquis, "and see what
Monsieur's horse is doing, and come back and tell me."

In a few minutes the boy returned.

"Well?" the marquis inquired.

"He is feeding," was the reply.

"There, you see!" said Bannière.

"What?" said the little man with the blue stockings.

"A foundered horse does n't eat."

"What's that?" said the marquis, who seemed to be going over to his companion's opinion; "we have known horses go two or three days, even when badly foundered, when they were of such stock as your horse is, Monsieur."

"Oh, as for the stock," said the little man, returning concession for concession, "he's of good stock; I saw that at once."

"As I say, they will go along for some days," continued the Marquis della Torra, "breathing hard, and then fall all of a sudden."

"Very well," said the little man; "just take the trouble to come to the stable door, Monsieur le Marquis, and you will see how Monsieur's horse is wheezing."

"What will your regiment say, dragoon," said the marquis, with the air of a superior officer, "when they see what a wreck you have made of your horse, for some little love affair, no doubt? For my own part," he added, becoming all captain, "I have my soldiers flogged when they ruin my horses."

The blood mounted to Bannière's temples, for it seemed to him an extremely impertinent speech, especially in the presence of the young lady aforesaid.

"In France, Monsieur," said he, proudly, "cavaliers are not flogged."

"No," retorted the silk merchant, "they are not flogged, but they are imprisoned."

"The horse is mine, and not the regiment's," said

Bannière, coolly; "it was a present from my father when I enlisted. Therefore I treat my horse as I choose."

"Pardon me," said the merchant, politely. "It is undeniable that if the horse was given you by Monsieur your father, he is yours, as you say, and, being yours, you can do what you please with him."

"Monsieur, excuse me," said the marquis; "seeing you in uniform, I took you for a common soldier, although when I heard your conversation, I at once said to myself, 'A strange soldier this;' and taking you, as I did, for a common soldier, in the kindness of my heart I was somewhat anxious, as I should be, for example, if you were travelling around the country without leave."

"I am quitting the service, Monsieur. I have my discharge."

"Oh, so much the better!" exclaimed the young woman, who had not spoken before, being wholly absorbed in devouring Bannière with inquisitive feminine eyes.

"Indeed, Madame!" said the Marquis della Torra, with a most dignified air.

"Indeed, what?" asked the young woman, with much less assumption.

"In what way does it concern you, pray, whether Monsieur does or does not leave the service?"

"Not at all, Monsieur."

"And yet you said, 'So much the better!'"

"Very possibly."

"You are wrong, Marion; the profession of arms is a noble profession."

In his warlike enthusiasm he waved his plume.

"Well," said Bannière, "noble as it is, I am leaving it, which is equivalent to saying that I should be glad to dispose of my horse."

"Really ? " said the captain.

"What use have I for him, I should like to know ? " said Bannière, in the tone of a retired bourgeois. "A war-horse is a very good thing for a soldier."

"True, true, upon my faith! " said the Marquis della Torra.

"Indeed, if Monsieur is leaving the service — " said the dealer in silks.

Marion said nothing; she looked at Bannière with an expression which was intended to convey the idea that if he was out of a place and would apply to her, she would find one for him.

"Will you dispose of your coat too ? " asked the captain.

"Oh, yes! coat and waistcoat, breeches and boots," said Bannière; "with the greatest pleasure. But what can you do with all those things, Monsieur le Marquis ? " he added with a laugh.

"What ? Oh, I should like the coat for a pattern for a new uniform. I mean to try to have that of our regiment changed; and I am sure that if the colonel saw your coat — "

"Oh, *pardieu !* it is quite at your service, Monsieur le Marquis," said Bannière.

"How much will you sell it for ? "

"I will not sell it."

"What do you mean ? I don't understand."

"I will exchange it for a civilian's coat. You are tall, so am I; you are thinner than I am, to be sure, but I like a tight fit. You see we can make a trade. Give me any coat whatsoever."

"Whatsoever! Indeed you are very easy to please. Any coat whatsoever! How sorry I am that my luggage has not arrived! I would have given you my gray velvet coat with red satin lapels, which is quite new."

"Oh, no, Monsieur, that would have been too much."

"Go to, young man," said the marquis, loftily; "in truth, it would be a fine sight to see a man like myself exchange on even terms with a dragoon. I love to oblige, my dear fellow, and it costs me a hundred thousand crowns a year. However, that is what God has put noblemen in the world for; it is for that that he has made them well-to-do, and captains of regiments."

"Monsieur," murmured Bannière, bowing low, overwhelmed by such elevation of sentiment.

"What a delightful man you are!" ejaculated the merchant, as if he could not restrain his rapturous admiration.

"Indeed, yes," said Bannière.

The young woman gazed abstractedly at a wretched picture hanging on the wall.

"But, unluckily," resumed the captain, "my trunks not having arrived — "

"Well?" said Bannière, inquiringly.

"Why, I have not those coats."

"But," said Bannière, "of course you have another. A man like you is not likely to be short of coats."

"Yes, upon my word! In order to travel more quickly, I left everything behind. I have nothing but a velvet dressing-jacket and a pair of cloth breeches."

"The devil! that's a night costume, I should say," said Bannière.

"Just that, my dear Monsieur, upon my word."

Bannière looked at the marquis with some astonishment. He was evidently wondering how a man of such importance in the world could start on a journey with no other coat than the one on his back. His eyes wandered from the captain to the merchant.

The latter gentleman thought that he could read in his eyes an inquiry as to the condition of his wardrobe.

"On my faith!" he hastened to say, "I am as badly off as Monsieur le Marquis, not by accident but on principle. I have no coat but this; I never change it. One does not easily forget poor beginnings. Economy, Monsieur, economy!"

"That same economy is the builder of fortunes," said the captain, emphatically. "Besides, if you had two extra coats, you could hardly make one for Monsieur with both of them; he is a third taller than you."

"Let's see," said Bannière, coming to a decision, "is this nocturnal costume so very absurd?"

"What! absurd!" said the plumed worthy, frowning, and looking askance at Bannière.

"Pardon, Monsieur, I meant to say laughable."

"Laughable, laughable!"

"Why, yes, of course, Monsieur; one is always a laughable object in such a costume," Bannière retorted with some impatience.

"Ah, very well, very well, I understand your meaning," said the marquis, more mildly.

"He's a very sensitive man," said the merchant in Bannière's ear.

It made but little difference to Bannière; however, he desired to be courteous.

"I hope Monsieur does not think that I wished to be offensive," said he.

"Oh, no! oh no!" said Madame Marion; "don't be alarmed."

"I will go and fetch the costume," said the Marquis della Torra; "I see that it will be a kind action."

"Don't disturb yourself, Monsieur le Marquis," said the merchant; "I will fetch it from your room myself."

And he went out.

XL.

HOW, WITHOUT BEING AS NOBLY BORN AS MONSIEUR DE GRAMMONT, BANNIÈRE PLAYED THE SAME GAME AS HE.

ALL these little courteous attentions gave Bannière a very exalted idea of the social position of Monsieur le Marquis.

To induce a rich merchant thus to play second fiddle to a captain, he thought, the captain must be at least a millionaire.

Then he began distractedly, for his heart and thought were still hastening after Olympe, to eye Madame Marion askance, without the least thought of evil, and only to seek some means of repaying her attentions.

The merchant was absent only a sufficient length of time to go upstairs and down; doubtless he was familiar with the marquis's apartment. He brought back the costume in question.

The jacket was of velvet, beyond controversy, — upon that point the Marquis della Torra had not lied; but the velvet was discolored and shiny, and its freshness had long ceased to be a memory even.

It must have been some old dressing-gown of the time of Monsieur de Roquelaure (the contemporary of Tallemant des Réaux, of course), the skirts of which being worn out (we are speaking of the dressing-gown) had undergone amputation, whereby the original garment was transformed into a jacket with sleeves.

The marquis saw that Bannière was examining in detail the object presented to him. and that the process was not advantageous to the object.

"Come, try it on, try it on!" said he, to divert the amateur's attention.

Bannière tried it on.

It must have been a trifle absurd, as Bannière had anticipated, for Madame Marion, well disposed as she had shown herself to be toward him, could not restrain a tremendous shout of merriment when she saw him arrayed in that ancient garment.

The fact is that a helmet, such as was then worn, red breeches, and cavalry boots made a most farcical appearance in connection with that jacket.

Bannière, while trying on the jacket, kept hold of his coat by the sleeve; but at last he was compelled to let it fall, and the spectators heard the sharp, silvery, yet deadened sound of a well-filled purse striking the flagstones, the metallic clinking being stifled, however, by the thickness of the cloth.

Thereupon, as if strung on wires, the Marquis della Torra and the merchant straightened up, and looked at each other with a brightening of the countenance which Bannière must have understood, if he had not been absorbed by the disgraceful spectacle of himself in that passé jacket with sleeves of unconscionable length.

Madame Marion blushed, and turned toward the famous picture on the wall, which she began to study anew.

The marquis, with all his pride of birth, developed at once a most earnest desire to make himself agreeable; the weight of the purse, no doubt, calculated mathematically by the noise it had made as it fell, convinced the marquis that he had no mere vulgar dragoon to deal with.

Indeed, it might very well be so. Many sons of families of rank enlisted in the dragoons, who were a privileged corps; and every son of a good family is an honorable friend in the eyes of a captain, when he has a purse as well filled as Bannière's seemed to be.

The purse, — that is the most satisfactory pedigree to a stranger.

They made Bannière try on, in like manner, the white dimity breeches; then they gave him a pair of slippers as badly worn as the rest, — more so, indeed.

But just as they were handing these articles to him, the captain said to the merchant, —

"One moment, one moment! What the devil are you doing! How fast you go, my dear fellow! My jacket, very good; my breeches, all right: they are things without any special value, and I am anxious to accommodate our young friend." As he spoke, the marquis glanced in fatherly fashion at Bannière. "But those slippers! No, no, no! I cannot do it; they were embroidered by my Marion, and I must keep them."

Marion, as the captain spoke, cast a glance of such singular meaning at Bannière, that the dragoon, forgetting Olympe for an instant, pushed his feet still farther into the slippers, and cried with a sly smile, —

"They have belonged to me for a second, so they can have no more value for you, Monsieur le Marquis; I appeal to Madame herself."

"Nothing could be better said," cried the dealer in silks. "No, Monsieur le Marquis, no, Madame la Marquise, you surely will not be so cruel as to offend this worthy gentleman by taking the slippers off his feet. Be firm, young man, be firm," he added in an undertone, "and the slippers are yours."

The marquis politely bent his head in token of acquiescence; Marion smiled sweetly, and the slippers remained in Bannière's possession.

To form an accurate idea of Bannière's opinion of himself, you should have seen him view himself in that remarkable costume in the little cracked mirror which graced the wall of the dining-room. In very truth, of all the more or less extraordinary outfits which the worthy ex-novice had had upon his back one after the other, not excluding the black robe of the order, there was not one, it must be said, so ill adapted to set off his natural charms.

So he sighed long and deeply.

The marquis, like a shrewd politician, grasped the condition of affairs.

"Yes, I understand, my gallant soldier-boy, you consider that that costume hardly does you justice; but believe me, young man, a military coat is sometimes very embarassing. We have many officers in the district, and some of them are inquisitive beyond measure. If one of these officers should take it into his head to want to look at your papers, and your papers should happen not to be all right, — why, you 'd be in a pretty pickle with your dragoon uniform! Upon my word, you will be much more comfortable in your mind in my shabby old velvet jacket."

This was Bannière's own honest opinion. The innocent manner in which he fell into the trap — that is to say, the silence with which he thought fit to receive the marquis's observation, — fully convinced the two strangers that they had rendered a great service to this wandering dragoon.

They looked upon him therefore from that time on as their own property; and, the soup being by this time upon the table, they all sat down together, Madame la

Marquise della Torra being placed at the left of her embroidered slippers.

Bannière was hungry, and the odor from the dinner was appetizing in the extreme; so the gastronomic quartette devoted the first few moments to discussing with due appreciation mine host's viands and wines.

After a while Bannière, recovering from the humiliating effect of his absurd costume, took the lead in conversation, and emitted a few clever remarks, interrupted by sighs.

The *bon-mots* were for Marion, the sighs for Olympe. He was too much in love, as we know, to be witty all the time.

When his eyes rested upon the marquise, he felt a strange sensation; memories of Olympe, mingled with memories of La Catalane, crowded upon his brain, — memories of joy and of hatred; rose-lined clouds, and clouds that lowered.

By a strange freak of chance, the Marquise Marion had La Catalane's lips and Olympe's hair. The result was that, simply from looking at her, poor Bannière was oppressed with visions of the past, — most unhealthy nourishment even for healthy minds, *a fortiori* for those which are diseased.

A curious effect was produced upon Bannière by this partial resemblance to Olympe; it caused him to forget everything except the image evoked by it, including the marquise and her two companions; he drank the wine and forgot it; he had sold his dragoon's coat, and he forgot not the coat alone, but the enlistment which had resulted in his assumption of that garment. Above the soiled cloth, among the lighted tapers, a graceful phantom was flitting, now losing itself in the dark corners of the room, and again reappearing unexpectedly and filling

the whole place with mysterious life. In the fire, in the
wine, and in the future Bannière saw nothing but Olympe.

He was aroused in the first place from his reverie by a
very pathetic sigh from the Marquise Marion.

But he relapsed immediately.

Then by an exclamation from the Marquis della Torra:
" *Sangdieu !* " he cried; " but our young friend has
no boots now! "

" Of course he has n't," replied the merchant, " since
he exchanged them for your slippers. "

" Then he will not be able to ride. "

" True again, " said the merchant.

" By Jove, that 's so, " said Bannière.

" No boots, " the marquise chimed in, " but something
to buy them with. "

With that she threw a glance at Bannière, which
stopped on the way, or if it reached its destination, was
not construed as it was intended to be.

" Oh, Monsieur, I am sure of it, " said the marquis,
with the same look which had already led Bannière to a
decision on one occasion; " Monsieur will be no more anxious to retain his horse than his uniform. "

Bannière started.

" And he will be quite right, " added the marquis, very
significantly.

" It is unfortunate that the horse is foundered, " said
the merchant; " I should like very well to own him
otherwise. He is really a fine-looking beast. "

" Well, buy him then, " said Bannière; " with a little
care you will bring him round all right, I 'll answer for it. "

" Impossible. "

" Why so? "

" Besides, is n't he branded with the regimental cipher,
or the king's *fleur-de-lis?* "

"He is branded with the *fleur-de-lis*, like every invalided horse."

"There, you see that you admit that he is invalided."

"Bah!" Bannière insisted; "what does the brand amount to? It can't be seen if the saddle is put on in a certain way."

"That's very well; put it on that way, if you choose, young man. But understand that, so far as I am concerned, the brand is a fault; but then, what's the use of talking about a foundered horse? No!"

"I should be very easy to deal with as to price, however," said Bannière, imprudently.

"No matter how cheap you would sell him, he would still be too dear," said the merchant.

"Anything which is good for nothing is too dear at any price," sententiously observed the marquis.

"But after all, Captain?"

"Arrange it to suit yourselves," replied the marquis, "and let me go to sleep; I am ready to drop, I'm so sleepy."

He stretched himself out on a couch near the chimney-piece, taking care to turn his back on Bannière and Marion.

Five minutes later the Marquis della Torra was snoring like a duke.

XLI.

HE WHO HAS GAMBLED WILL GAMBLE AGAIN.

THIS unlooked-for drowsiness annoyed Bannière considerably. He was very anxious to dispose of his horse, even though it should be no more advantageously than he had disposed of his uniform.

The merchant, too, seemed much put out.

"Ah!" he cried, "Monsieur le Marquis has gone off to sleep without giving me my revenge."

"Revenge for what?" asked Bannière.

"Oh, nothing of importance; revenge for a game of piquet, which we play almost every evening during our journey."

"Monsieur does not play," Marion hastened to say, trying to make herself more and more agreeable to Bannière, and taking advantage of the captain's siesta to use her eyes to that end.

The words, "Monsieur does not play," brought back to Bannière's ears the jingling of heaps of gold coins, the sound of dice rattling upon the cloth, and the ball rolling around upon the roulette table.

"Very seldom, Madame," he faltered.

"Very seldom is not never," said the dealer in silks; "then, too, there is playing and playing; to play for amusement is not playing."

"Very true," said Bannière.

"See," rejoined the merchant, lowering his voice as if to avoid waking the marquis, — "see, your unfortunate horse is not worth five pistoles."

"Oho!" exclaimed Bannière.

"No, he's not worth that. Very well! I will play you for him against — against what?"

The merchant looked about as if seeking something to stake against Bannière's horse.

The marquis ceased to snore, opened his eyes, and just as Banniére was about to reply, —

"Who is talking about playing?" he cried; "that damned merchant again! What a living dice-box! That devilish fellow is the very incarnation of gambling."

The merchant, who did appear to be an ardent gambler, tried to argue.

"But, Monsieur le Marquis — " he began to remonstrate.

"Let us have a little rest, for God's sake! Why, here's a poor boy who perhaps hasn't enough money for his wants, and you must needs make a hole in it! Oh, it's shameful! It's easy to see that you are of plebeian extraction, my friend. Let this dragoon go his way, and if he has any money, let him keep it. Gold does not grow in the streets, my good fellow."

"But, Monsieur le Capitaine — " the merchant insisted.

"Hold your tongue!" said the marquis, savagely; "it's a wicked thing that you're doing. Do you suppose that everybody has a fund of a hundred thousand pistoles to draw upon, as you have?"

"Oh, Monsieur le Marquis exaggerates!" cried he of the blue stockings, with a bow.

"No, indeed I don't exaggerate, for you have all of that; either in golden crowns or in silks, it's all one. But he would like to make me a gambler too, upon my soul! — me, who detest dice, and cannot bear the touch of cards."

Bannière, without regarding the significant glances of Madame Marion in his direction, undertook to plead with the indignant marquis in behalf of the worthy merchant, who had flushed up like a turkey-cock under , this reprimand.

"I assure you, Monsieur le Capitaine," he said, "that this honest citizen, whom you abuse so, has put no violence upon me."

"Indeed, indeed! He tried to compel you to play, he talked about your horse, or the devil take me! I am much mistaken if I did n't hear him."

The merchant seemed to make an effort to rebel against the marquis's assumption of authority.

"Suppose I did speak of the horse," he said with a degree of firmness which seemed heroic to Bannière, "does that prove that I am vicious? Don't you ever play yourself, pray, Monsieur le Marquis?"

"Zounds, yes! I do play, and like to play too, but for the purpose of losing. If I thought I should win, understand that I would never play, Monsieur. I presume that, rich as you are, you will hardly think of comparing your fortune to mine. Even if I were to play so as to lose ten thousand livres a day for a whole year, my Della Torra estates would not be impaired at the end of that time."

"What delicacy of sentiment seems to animate these people!" said Bannière to himself.

"*Mon Dieu!* I know it," said the merchant, "I know it; but the moment that I should decline to lend you anything on your estates — "

"What 's that?" interrupted the marquis; "if you propose to adopt that tone with me, why, *mordieu!* I will give you as good as you send. You want to play, blackguard, do you? You want to risk your crowns, you dog, do you? So be it, then! put these famous crowns of yours on the table, pull them out into the light; they are dying for lack of fresh air."

"But, Monsieur le Marquis," said the merchant, whose features began to exhibit considerable concern, "I am not such a madman as you seem to think. I play without excitement."

"And so do I, by my blood!" cried the marquis. "Just see if I lose my head! Am I calm or not? I was asleep, as this youth will bear witness, and you waked me, my friend. Very well! I propose to lose a hundred thousand crowns this evening, or to ruin you; that's business."

"Upon my word, you terrify me, Monsieur le Marquis."

"Come on, come on, Monsieur Gambler."

"But this is no game that you propose; it's a duel."

"How much have you?"

"Upon my person?"

"Yes, or in your chest."

"Why, Monsieur le Marquis ——"

"Pshaw!"

"What?"

"To the table! to the table, quickly!"

"But, Captain ——"

"Ah! he declines. Oh, yes, I understand; brave as a lion when he has to do with the empty purse of our little dragoon, my rascal backs down when the strong box of Della Torra is to be reckoned with. Come, come, have we the pluck? Yes? All right, then, out with the great crowns and the louis d'or, and the bank-notes, when the crowns and louis are exhausted; damned be he who cries quarter!"

"Come on then, if you will," said the merchant.

"If I will! I should think so!"

"You're absolutely sure?"

"Absolutely."

Then he turned to Bannière.

" This deuce of a fellow," he whispered, " has the heart of a king. Pity me, dragoon, for I am a ruined man."

With a sigh the merchant took his place at the table.

In an instant the stakes were laid.

The marquis displayed a pile of bank-notes, huge enough to make a lucky Mississippi shareholder stare; while the merchant, fumbling in his pockets, and drawing them out one by one, produced modestly fifteen louis or thereabouts, glistening among ten or twelve pale silver crowns.

At sight of the louis and the bank-notes, Bannière felt all the gambler's instinct spring into life at the bottom of his soul, while his clinched hand played with the fifty or sixty louis remaining in his pocket; then with his chin in his hands, burning eyes, and tightly closed lips he leaned his elbows on the table and watched.

The Marquise Marion, nibbling at sweetmeats, supported herself partly against a chair and partly upon Bannière's shoulder.

It was evident, however, that the dragoon's emotion did not communicate itself to her. She must have been accustomed to such sights.

The battle waged furiously; for it was, as the merchant had said, a veritable battle rather than a game.

The marquis had the advantage at first, and joked his opponent very pleasantly. All the merchant's louis save one solitary louis made acquaintance with the marquis's pile of notes.

But with the last remaining coin the luck turned, and the merchant had his turn at winning, in such fashion, however, and with such rapidity that the pile of notes melted away like butter from the marquis's side, and took their way one by one to the merchant's right hand.

Bannière was lost in admiration; it was impossible to lose with more grace and nonchalance than was displayed by the noble marquis.

Mere spectator though he was, the ex-novice felt the perspiration gather upon his brow. If one is a true gambler, one has no need to play to experience all the emotions; it is enough to watch others play.

The sums which had disappeared from the bundle of notes grew to be enormous. The poor merchant seemed more and more embarrassed. He was ashamed of his good luck. It was a veritable battle royal between grandeur on the one side and honesty on the other.

Bannière had tears in his eyes. He felt that it was not in his nature either to win or to lose thus.

"Ah, Monsieur," said the merchant,—"ah, Monsieur le Marquis, let us stop, I implore you. You have struck an unlucky vein."

"Pshaw!" replied the captain; "a good deal of fuss you're making over a paltry fifty thousand livres or so! Come, let us go on, let us go on!"

"Madame la Marquise," cried the merchant, with clasped hands, "beg Monsieur le Capitaine to stop."

"Bah! my wife will have a diamond or two less in the jewel-box which I expect to give her on her birthday," said the marquis; "and she will not make any wry faces at her husband on that account, will she, Marion?"

The marquise shrugged her shoulders.

"It is an extraordinary run of luck, is it not?" said the merchant to Bannière.

"Indeed it is," replied the dragoon; "I never saw anything like it. Monsieur le Marquis is in a fair way to lose all that he possesses this evening."

Bannière had hardly finished speaking when a combi-

nation of aces swept away two thousand livres more from
the marquis.

" Oh, this is too much at one time! " cried the merchant;
" I decline to play, I am winning too much. "

He threw down the cards as if disgusted with his
good fortune.

" Come, my friend, " said the marquis, " one last stake
of ten thousand livres! "

" Oh, Monsieur le Marquis, reflect! "

" About what? "

" Reflect that you are in bad luck, and that it will
be throwing away ten thousand livres. "

" No; I have an idea. "

" What is it? "

" That I shall recoup on this last stake. "

The merchant shook his head.

" Go on, go on, one last stake! " said Bannière,
intensely interested.

" So be it, " said the merchant, " since you insist
upon it. But how shall we play for the ten thousand
livres? "

" The one who has the best ' point ' on the deal wins. "

" Done! "

The cards were dealt.

The marquis had a point of six in diamonds, but the
merchant had one of seven in hearts.

He gathered up the ten thousand livres, and said,
rising from his chair, —

" Upon my word, Monsieur le Marquis, I am confused with my luck, and I hope you will remember
that you compelled me to play. "

" That's all right, " said the marquis, smiling; " when
two men play against each other, it's absolutely necessary that one or the other should lose. I only ask one

favor of you, and that is that you will give my wife that beautiful damask gown which you are keeping for the Princesse de Beaufremont."

"Yes, indeed, Madame, — that and two others with it, if you will accept them."

Bannière wiped his forehead with his handkerchief.

"Never did I see such a game or such gamblers," he said aloud.

"Yet how sad it is," cried the marquis, looking philosophically at the ceiling, "and how blind is fortune! Here I have been losing sixty thousand livres to a millionaire, while I have under my eyes a poor fellow whom the third part of that sum would perhaps make happy for life."

"Oh, twenty thousand livres! Yes, twenty thousand livres would make me very happy," murmured Bannière, thinking that of the twenty thousand he would spend fifteen to find Olympe again, and that it would be very hard if he could not do it with that sum.

"And yet," continued Della Torra, plunging deeper and deeper into the realms of philosophy, "what would have been necessary to effect that result? Simply that Monsieur," indicating Bannière, "should have been seated in the chair of that asinine merchant, and that the asinine merchant should have been seated in his."

"*Dame!* what would you have, Monsieur le Marquis? it's fate," said the winner.

"No, it's the lucky vein. In your place the dragoon might not have won, perhaps."

"Oh, yes, he would," the merchant interrupted, in a tone of absolute conviction.

"Bah! why so?" asked Bannière.

"Because, Monsieur, the vein belongs to the seat, and not to the man who sits in it," said he of the stockings, sententiously.

"Do you think so?" said Bannière.

"He's right," said the captain; "upon my word, I believe he's right!"

"So you agree with Monsieur, do you?" said Bannière.

"Oh, perfectly! There's no obstinacy in my character."

"Sit down there a minute, Monsieur," said the merchant, pushing Bannière toward the famous seat, "and try it; we'll see how it works."

"Oh, no, no!" said the marquis; "enough of that sort of thing. My hands are positively weary with shuffling the cards."

"Go on, go on!" the merchant insisted.

"No, the luck would not last; it follows the money on the cloth, not the idea in the gambler's brain."

"Oh, well!" said Bannière, "we might try it for a few crowns."

"Just one crown, out of curiosity," said the marquis.

"Impossible!" said Bannière, in his most high and mighty tone.

"Why so, pray?"

"Because I only play with gold."

"Very well," said the marquis, carelessly; "venture a louis then, if you really insist."

Resuming his seat nonchalantly, he shuffled the cards with the languid air of a man little accustomed to take so much trouble for so small a stake.

Bannière cut, and the marquis dealt the cards.

The former took up his hand, and found in it three aces, three kings, three queens, and a point of six. He discarded two queens and a king, and took up the fourth ace and the last two cards of his point.

He lay down his hand, and won the stake.

The marquis tossed him a louis, laughing uproariously.

"Oh, it's very strange," said the merchant; "do go on."

They began again; and Bannière still won, as he did the third time.

Then the merchant suggested that they double the stake, to see how much Bannière could win while the luck lasted.

The demon of play was upon the dragoon, muttering in the depths of his heart, —

"Gold! gold! gold!"

He accepted the suggestion, and in half an hour he had won two hundred louis in bank-notes.

Then the luck changed; the vein was worked out, no doubt.

Bannière began to lose and was delighted, for he had begun to be ashamed of his good luck, as the merchant was. But he continued to lose so persistently that the enchantment came to an end. However he had lost only what he had won; he might consider the games played as a mere experiment, stop there, and not encroach upon his store of louis.

But he was a true gambler, and had not the courage to stop. He began to stake his louis.

Once he had begun upon them the louis stole away, two by two, four by four, six by six. He had sixty louis, and they lasted about half an hour.

Sixty louis, — that is to say, more than he needed to take him to Paris to find Olympe.

The marquis thereupon, coolly and without any visible sign of satisfaction, bowed to Bannière, and pocketed his sixty louis. The dragoon attempted to borrow two louis to help him to entice back his luck. Two louis seemed a very trifle for a marquis rolling in wealth.

But to his unbounded amazement, the captain shook his head.

"My principle," said he, "from which I never depart, because it rests upon true morality, is not to encourage the young to ruin themselves. So, Monsieur, if you please, we will stop where we are."

Bannière was considerably confused; but in the words of the marquis he was forced to recognize that gentleman's superiority to himself, — a gentleman, too, who had lost sixty thousand livres without winking; so he lowered his nose like a school-boy.

Then the merchant leaned over to him in a friendly way.

"Come, young man," he said, "you still have your horse. What the deuce! Make Monsieur le Marquis disgorge. The horse against ten pistoles."

"What 's that?" said Della Torra.

"I say the horse against ten pistoles," the merchant repeated.

He added, in an undertone, to Banniére, —

"*Pardieu!* if you lose, you don't lose much."

It was the marquis's turn to shuffle.

He had in his hand on the last deal just what Bannière had in his on the first.

That was very curious.

Such tenacious winning amazed the dragoon, who began to look dark in spite of himself.

He had nothing left with which to pay his reckoning at the inn.

He made a remark to that effect, laughingly; the laugh, however, went no deeper then the end of his lips.

But the marquis, to Bannière's vast astonishment, instead of playing the grand seigneur and offering to accommodate him, turned on his heel, and made for the door.

The dealer in silks had already vanished.

Bannière was overwhelmed. The thought that he had lost all means of overtaking Olympe and inducing her to return to him, drew a sigh from his bosom, and two great tears from his eyes.

Marion was about to leave the room in the wake of the Marquis della Torra.

She turned as she heard the sigh, and her eye perceived the two great tears. She was evidently touched thereby, for she raised her pink finger-tip to her lips, and winked significantly at Bannière.

He understood her to mean "Wait," and consequently "Hope." He had no particular hope, but he waited.

Twenty minutes had not elapsed ere Marion appeared at the window, and rapped with the tips of her fingers upon the glass.

Bannière opened it hastily.

"Monsieur," said she, in a low voice, "you have been robbed."

With that she fled precipitately, or, rather, she flew away like a bird, without waiting even for Bannière to kiss the fair fingers which had drummed so gracefully upon the window.

XLII.

IN WHICH BANNIÈRE TAKES HIS REVENGE.

BANNIÈRE stood a moment speechless and motionless. He was simply struck dumb by what he had heard. His love and his self-esteem were alike deeply wounded.

After a moment, however, he recovered the power of speech.

"Robbed!" he muttered, while a shiver ran over his whole frame. "What! the Marquis della Torra, captain in the Abruzzi regiment, and the worthy millionaire merchant, leagued together to rob me! Impossible!"

These reflections passed through his brain very rapidly, — so rapidly that they had taken shape before Marion had reached the middle of the stable-yard, and yet the graceful creature's step was as light and swift as air.

But Bannière was light of foot, as well as she, especially when spurred by some violent passion. With one leap he reached the hall, with a second the courtyard, and at the third he reached her side and seized her in his arms.

Feeling the arms clasped about her, and the burning breath on her cheek, she began to turn pale and shiver, as if she were under the influence of a sorcerer.

Night came to her aid; if the dark-eyed goddess, daughter of Chaos, and sister of Erebus, does sometimes shelter robbers, as the fable tells us, it has also favors to grant to honest people now and then.

"What did you mean, dear Marion," whispered Bannière in the young woman's ear, " by saying that I had been robbed ? "

" I meant nothing less than just what I said."

" Robbed ? "

" Yes. Do you know what a Greek is ? "

" A Greek ? " said Bannière, wonderingly; " to be sure, I do, I learned it at college; it is a man born in Greece."

" Oh, no, my dear Monsieur! "

" Pray, what else is it ? "

"The Greeks are clever folk who use their skill to repair the neglect of fortune."

" Sharpers, eh ? "

" 'Sharpers' is a very hard name; 'Greeks' is more courteous."

" So the merchant is a Greek ? "

" Precisely so."

"And the marquis is a Greek too ? And your husband, the captain — "

"Oh, Monsieur, he is no captain; neither is he my husband."

" In any event, whether he is all that or not, you are an angel."

To prove to Marion that his words were the index of his thought, he took two hearty kisses, whereat the young woman's heart beat very fast.

"One word more, little Marion. How did the marquis — I call him marquis, because I must call him something."

" He robbed you by means of a system of signals with the merchant."

"But all the coin, and all the notes which they waved in my face. Surely it was coin, and the others were notes ? "

"The coin was genuine, and comprised the whole stock of our pretended millionaires; the notes were false, as you could easily have seen if you had looked closely at them."

They had reached that point in their conversation when a window on the first floor opened, and they heard the captain's voice, —

"Marquise Marion! Marquise Marion! Well, well, where are you, I should like to know?"

"He is calling me, do you hear?" said the young woman; "he is calling me. Oh, Monsieur, let me go! He will kill me."

She released herself, returned Bannière one of his kisses, and disappeared in the darkness.

Bannière remained alone in the middle of the gloomy courtyard.

Then all that he had heard of clever sleight-of-hand performers, who can make a cup dance under one's nose without its being seen, came into his mind. He remembered that in every game he had played with the pretended marquis, he had continually seen or felt or imagined, as you choose to put it, one card longer than the others in the pack, and that two or three times while he was shuffling, he had tried to push that card in so that its edge would be even with the rest.

He remembered also that the noble marquis invariably left that card underneath in cutting, so that it was one of the stock left for the dealer when he discarded.

"Marion was right," said he; "I see how they did it. Now, Bannière, my boy, you must be as clever as these gentlemen; a Greek and a half against a Greek."

He began to consider, and if it had been daylight his sombre features would have been seen to clear gradually under the inspiration of that internal fire which is called thought.

In five minutes his countenance was perfectly serene once more; he had made up his mind.

"I have them," said he.

He turned about without further delay, and, guided by the lighted window which served him as a beacon, found his way to the quarters of the false Marquis della Torra, who, with the false dealer in silks, was drinking coffee, strong coffee, flavored with a liqueur which was very grateful to sight and smell.

Marion had just come in, flushed and breathless, poor child, and was undergoing a little lecture, which Bannière interrupted by knocking at the door.

"Walk in," was the reply without too much delay.

Bannière walked in, rosy and gracious and smiling; his whole bearing spoke of perfect good-humor. The actor had made over the gambler's face.

"Monsieur le Marquis," he began, "I have a little secret to tell you."

The merchant rose. He was a very tactful gentleman, and wished to withdraw so as to leave Bannière and the marquis alone and free to speak.

But Bannière fathomed his purpose, and insisted upon his remaining.

"Don't go, Monsieur, I beg of you," said he. "Are not all secrets safe in the breast of such a gallant fellow as you?"

The marquis was not altogether at his ease, despite the appearance of extreme courtesy.

"What is it, my dear fellow," said he, assuming his noble manner; "what do you want of me?"

"Monsieur," rejoined Bannière, "it is a hard thing to tell, but I must come to it."

"Say on, dragoon."

"You see that I am here. Monsieur."

"I am listening."

"Monsieur, I am not honorably retiring from the service; I am running away."

"We suspected as much," replied the captain, harshly; "but beware, young man, these are not such secrets as the Marquis della Torra, captain in the Abruzzi regiment, can hear with approbation."

"Alas! that is true, Monsieur, yet I hope that you will be indulgent to a poor young fellow, and do me a great favor."

The Marquis della Torra thought he could smell a loan in the air, and he assumed the expression of a banker locking up his vaults.

He was just about to interrupt Bannière when that gentleman interrupted himself.

"Hush! listen!" said he, mysteriously.

Instinctively the two men approached; they began to get scent of something out of course.

"My purse," Bannière continued, "was not my only source of supply; I had besides — "

He looked inquiringly about.

"What? What had you?" asked the two men in one breath.

"I had a great bag of money."

"Ah!" exclaimed the captain and merchant in unison, their interest being renewed by this confidence. "A bag?"

"Yes."

"A large bag?"

"Containing ten thousand livres."

"Ten thousand livres!"

The two men licked their chops, and cast a sidelong glance at each other.

"Pray, what did you do with the precious bag,

dragoon?" the marquis asked with fatherly solicitude. "Tell us."

"I thought I was pursued when I was just entering this village, a quarter of a league back; and as my horse was dead tired, and the bag very heavy, I threw it into a ditch under the willows, taking careful note of the place where I left it, so that I might find it again when it should be dark."

"Oho!" exclaimed the confederates.

"So that, now that night has come — "

Bannière made a significant gesture to the two Greeks, who looked at one another in utter bewilderment. They had never encountered such an unparalleled ass as this dragoon, who was not content with being plundered once, but was in such haste to go through the same operation a second time.

"Well," said Bannière, "now do you understand?"

"No, not perfectly," the marquis replied.

"If Monsieur le Marquis does not understand perfectly," said the merchant, "please understand yourself that I do not understand at all."

"Why, I want you to go with me."

"Oh, with pleasure!"

"With a lantern?"

"Yes."

"But why go with you?"

"For several reasons: in the first place, because you know the country much better than I, and will help me not to lose myself; secondly, because I don't like to go abroad alone at night; and lastly, because the landlord might be suspicious and uneasy if he should see me leave his hotel alone at night, with a lantern. Indeed he has already exhibited considerable astonishment at my transformation from a dragoon to — whatever I am."

"True! true!" said the two worthies; "at your service."

"Then do you take a club," said Bannière to the pseudo-dealer in silks; "Monsieur le Marquis will take his sword, and I my sabre."

"But why take all those things?"

"To guard against robbers, of course; a bag containing ten thousand livres is worth the trouble of defending it."

"True enough," was the reply.

"How about me?" said Marion; "am I to carry nothing?"

"You, Madame," said Bannière, mingling a little gallantry with his affected simplicity, "may carry the lantern, if you please, and light our way."

Each one did as agreed. Marion took the lantern; the merchant armed himself with a club; the marquis girded on his sword, which he had laid across a chair in order to sip his coffee more conveniently; and Bannière, discarding belt and scabbard, took his bare sabre under his arm. The procession left the hostelry with careful step, ears pricked, and noses in the air.

Marion, anxious and perplexed, overflowing with admiration of Bannière's *sang-froid* and with curiosity as to the result, marched at the head, performing the duties of will-o -the-wisp with her lantern.

Bannière set the pace, and it was a rapid one, so that they were soon outside the village.

It was eleven o'clock in the evening; the fields were dark, deserted, and peaceful. On the horizon some belated light would twinkle for a moment, like a star, and now and then in the distance could be heard the barking of a dog.

On the right of the road they were travelling, ran the famous ditch, bordered with willows, separating the road from a level field whose velvety carpet shone green as emerald in the rays of the lantern.

They had travelled in this wise for a quarter of a league or thereabouts, when Bannière halted, and seemed to be trying to locate his position.

"This is the place," said he. "Madame la Marquise, give me your hand and jump the ditch."

Marion was tempted to reply that she had leaped wider ditches than that; but she liked to touch Bannière's hand, so she accepted it, and sprang across.

The Marquis della Torra stretched his long legs, and landed on the other side. The merchant made a little short leap,— too short, alas! for he came down upon the sloping side of the ditch, and as his legs failed him, he slid gracefully down into the water on his face.

Neither the marquis nor Bannière paid any attention to him, and he was compelled to extricate himself from the difficulty as best he could. He finally succeeded without other loss than that of his club, which he let drop as he fell, and which was carried down stream.

Meanwhile Bannière had stopped, and with Marion and the marquis formed a group, which the merchant soon joined, dripping wet from his waist down.

"Well?" said the marquis, inquiringly, when the group was complete.

"Well?" echoed Bannière.

"Where is what we are looking for?" the marquis continued.

"What we are looking for?"

"Yes, the stuff that you lost, I mean."

"The stuff that I lost is there," cried Bannière, "there in your pocket, and you are going to restore it to me on the instant."

"Upon my word!" cried the stupefied marquis.

"Oho!" muttered the merchant.

"No noise!" continued Bannière. "You are not a marquis, you are not a captain, your name is not Della Torra; you are a Greek, a sharper, a thief."

"I?"

"Yes, you; I knew all the evening that you were playing the long-card game on me."

"Villain!"

"Come, no words! You have a sword, and I a sabre; draw, and quickly, unless you want me to kill you on the spot with your sword in its sheath. It's all one to me so long as I kill you."

The merchant undertook to come to the assistance of his comrade, and in default of the club, which had gone swimming off by itself toward the village, he drew a knife from his pocket; but Bannière made a pass at him, and dealt him a blow which split his brown coat from waist to shoulder.

The merchant did not ask for the balance of his reckoning; he beat a hasty retreat, with a groan which proved that the lining of his doublet was punctured.

As for the marquis, he seemed to have taken root as he stood there pale and trembling, without even drawing his sword.

"Come, come," said Bannière, "let us do something. As we do not fight, let us empty the pockets."

Marion looked on at this triumph of the dragoon over the captain, half terrified and half delighted; she smiled and cried, and stamped her little feet.

It is incredible how a woman will always prefer a man whom she never knew till the day before, to the man whom she has known for years. Does this mean that woman is fickle, or that man does not improve on acquaintance?

At last the marquis, driven to desperation by Bannière's insults and Marion's equivocal behavior, drew his sword.

But his trembling hand was very weak; and Bannière had no sooner crossed blades with him than the marquis's weapon fell from his hand.

He thought that he was a dead man, and fell on his knees. But Bannière had a merciful heart; he contented himself with dealing the marquis a few vigorous blows with the flat of his sabre, and then set about the principal work, the investigation of his pockets.

But in vain did he turn the wretched pockets inside out and back again; of the sixty louis which the marquis had swindled him out of, he found, after much searching, only two or three.

"Ah," cried Marion, sorrowfully, "if I had only known that that was what you were looking for!"

"What then?" asked Bannière, still fumbling, but to no purpose, among the captain's clothes.

"Then I would have told you that the merchant is the cashier of the party."

"The devil!" cried Bannière, angrily.

But as he was a youth who made up his mind quickly, he said at once, —

"Let us run, let us run; perhaps we may overtake him before he reaches the inn."

"Yes, let us run," echoed Marion, who had made up her mind to make common cause with our hero; "let us run, we may overtake him."

Having given the marquis a postscript of two or three blows with the flat of the sabre for good measure, Bannière started to return to the inn, with Marion clinging to his arm and running beside him as light of foot as Atalanta.

The marquis remained a prey to grief and shame at seeing Marion so happy in his overthrow, Marion the accomplice of a stranger! He uttered a cry which much resembled a roar. He undertook to pursue the fugitive damsel; but Bannière turned upon him, and he stopped where he was. Thereupon the youth made a step in his direction, and the marquis turned on his heel and fled.

Bannière resumed his course. He relied upon the brevity of the merchant's legs to overtake him; but fear had elongated them, and not only did he not catch him, but when he reached the inn he found that the rascal had had time to get clear away.

Like Bilboquet, he had saved the chest.

Bannière rushed to the stable, hoping that he had at least forgotten the horse; but the merchant's memory was excellent, and notwithstanding all the bad points and infirmities he had detected in the beast, he had saddled and bridled him, and ridden away at a gallop.

Thus there remained to Bannière absolutely nothing but two louis and Marion.

The poor boy was in utter despair when he had assured himself of this last blow; but the disaster was irreparable, and it was well to put as good a face as possible upon it. He summoned the landlord and began to tell his story, the result being that mine host made him pay upon the spot for his own dinner and that of his three table companions,— a demand to which Bannière submitted without much demur, being by no means anxious to have any trouble with the authorities of the place.

Of the two louis there remained in his possession only eight crowns — and Marion, who was lovely and loving enough to have been sufficient consolation under any circumstances, if Olympe were out of mind.

But Bannière's heart had room for but the one love; and so as his eye fell upon the lovely child gazing tearfully and imploringly at him with clasped hands, —

"Alas! my dear," said he, "unfortunately you have before you a man bankrupt in heart and in purse! I shall never forget the service you have done me, but I will not insult you by offering you less than it is worth. Listen! You are fair enough to have known what love is. Well, I love to distraction a woman whom I am now hastening to join, and who has twice been the cause of my desertion, — once from the Jesuits, and again from the dragoons. I am well aware that you have left that blackguard of a marquis for me, but it may be that I have done you good service in that respect. Some day he would have compromised you, and you would have lost your life, or at least have been imprisoned. So we will part now, if you please, dear Marion."

Marion heaved a sigh, and gazed at Bannière.

"Alone in the middle of the night," said she.

She pronounced these words in a tone so full of pathos that Bannière's heart was deeply moved. He returned her gaze, sadly shaking his head.

"Without money or a place to lay my head," she added in a lower tone.

She hung her head, and Bannière instinctively felt that her eyes filled with tears.

"I have eight crowns," said he; "here are six of them for you."

A fascinating siren was this woman, and there were tones in her voice which would have softened the wise Ulysses, much more Bannière, who had never set himself up as the peer in sagacity of the King of Ithaca.

However history does not tell the particulars of his parting with this chance companion; but it is cer-

tain that Marion was all alone at the inn the next
morning.

She deserved a happier fate than was in store for her,
poor child! Her nature was such that her life might
surely have been turned to better things, had the good
angels but come to her before her evil genius had taken
full possession of the field.

XLIII.

BANNIÈRE AT PARIS.

BANNIÈRE in his jacket of chocolate-colored velvet, dimity breeches, and slippers, was destined, as may well be imagined, to produce a most striking effect upon the highways over which his route lay; every passer-by stopped to look at him, and only went on again when he was well out of sight.

He was the cause of delay to those who stopped to gaze at him, but nothing delayed *him*.

He had but three crowns with which to accomplish a journey of a hundred leagues, — three crowns because Marion had compelled him to retain that number, and had absolutely refused to accept more than five. Even then he had a struggle with her, for she said it was too much for her to take five crowns out of eight, especially as he had so much longer a journey before him than she; and then, too, a pretty woman is never so much incommoded without money as a man in the same plight, even though he possessed in his single person all the charms of Endymion and Adonis.

Oh, well! even with these three paltry crowns — incredible as it may seem, and yet I hope the gentle reader will believe it as soon as he has my word for it — Bannière contrived to save, and with his savings he bought a pair of shoes.

Poor Marion's slippers had done all that brave slippers could be expected to do; they held out for twenty leagues, after which the uppers dropped off on one side and the soles on the other.

The matter of food was of the least importance to Bannière. He lived at the expense of the vines and walnut and hazel-nut trees; and as every good meal ought to include a vegetable or two, he would take a carrot or an onion from the first field he passed, often amid the sharp expostulations of the peasants; but when he would tell them (or their wives) that he was hungry, and had committed that petty theft to satisfy his hunger, the peasant, male or female, who had begun by shrieking at him would often end by dividing his bread with him.

He subsisted in this way, asking shelter at stables or barns, and when it was refused, sleeping under the bright stars, in some haymow or beneath some thickly leaved tree.

This was the only expedient Bannière had been able to find for avoiding adventures and lovelorn females; for it should be said that wherever the unlucky fellow showed his face, he made an immediate conquest.

"Alas!" he would say as he sat over his humble repast, "why am I not possessed of a magnet which attracts metal, rather than one which attracts the female heart? With the former I should already have more wealth than I should need to buy Olympe back, though she were in the harem of the Grand Turk himself, and he should ask by way of ransom the sum which Amurat demanded of the Duc de Bourgogne for the Comte de Nevers."

Now and then Bannière insensibly displayed his learning, which was one of the results of his early education at the Jesuit convent.

After eight days of desperate travelling, Bannière looked at himself one morning, like Narcisse, in the mirror of a clear spring, and saw that his beard closely resembled that of Polyphemus. He had no choice but to get shaved.

He rose to his feet, after he had washed down his frugal breakfast with several deep draughts of limpid water, made for the nearest village, and found a barber, who performed the operation required.

While the razor was at work, Bannière, for the sake of saying something, asked the name of the village.

The barber gashed his chin as he replied, —

"The village of Vertus, Monsieur."

"How many leagues from Paris?" asked Bannière, trying to get a glimpse out of the corner of his eye, — a difficult feat! — of the drop of blood which was rolling down his chin.

"Two leagues, Monsieur, two short leagues."

The barber said "short leagues" because he thought he owed his customer something by way of compensation for cutting him.

Bannière leaped for very joy. He had not dreamed that he was so near Paris, which the morning mist had prevented him from seeing in the distance.

Paris is indeed a lovely city for men of wealth, — but we, though we should be charged with perpetrating a paradox, maintain that it is even lovelier for the poor; but above all has Paris attractions beyond compare for the adventurous fisherman who comes thither, like Bannière, to cast his net into that fathomless sea in search of a priceless pearl.

He had just one crown when he entered the capital; unfortunately he had also the velvet jacket and dimity breeches.

Perhaps it will be interesting for meditative minds to see how he will get clear of such an outfit; and they who

saw him dress ought to be really anxious to observe his
manner of undressing.

Let us lift a corner of the curtain. Oh, you may
look, Madame, though you were as great a prude as
Madame de Maintenon herself; there will be nothing
indecorous.

The dragoon, we ought to say, attracted little notice
in the faubourgs. Paris swarms with eccentric characters. In the first place, Bannière arrived, as we said,
in the morning; now the morning is the time chosen by
a large number of poor government clerks or merchants'
apprentices to do their daily marketing, and they show
themselves, without ceremony, to their fellow-citizens
in a costume which tragedy dignifies by the epithet
" simple."

Racine; see *Britannicus*.

But by the side of the simple garb in which Junia
presented herself to Nero, Bannière's costume was an
extremely complex one.

Everything went well in the Faubourg Saint-Marcel;
but the dragoon had no sooner passed through Rue de la
Harpe, crossed the Pont Saint-Michel, and entered Rue
Saint-Denis, than he realized how essential a respectable
attire would be in prosecuting the plans which he was
revolving in his brain.

To clothe himself decently would require six crowns
at least, — just the number he had tried to force upon
Marion, and twice as many as Marion had left with him.

As he had but one crown, it was of course out of the
question; but that fact did not prevent him from gazing
at a coat hanging outside the door of a dealer in old
clothes.

Every one knows that the unwritten law of the second-
hand clothes-trade is that the purchaser pays something

to boot, even though he exchanges a good article for a poor one, or a passable one for a worse.

Now this was not the case, for the Marquis della Torra's jacket ranked among the very worst. But this Bannière was born with a silver spoon in his mouth. He who had determined to kill a man to recover what he had lost, had the luck to fall in with a woman.

It was just the reverse of the experience of Captain Pamphile, whose negress was a man; Bannière's old-clothes man was a woman.

He presented himself before her most courteously; his theatrical experience had accustomed him to make striking *entrées*. The merchant was about thirty, — still young, that is; she was almost pretty. She saw this handsome youth embarrassed by his shabby, absurd garments, and she smiled upon him.

Bannière made his request, and half laughing, half imploring, offered his crown for the coat.

The woman looked him over again, smiled again, and without a word took the coat from its hook and passed it to him.

He asked leave to go to the rear of the shop, and it was accorded with another smile even more gracious than the first two.

But Bannière in his wisdom had decided to pay no more attention to smiles. He passed into the back shop, and gently closed the door behind him.

Two seconds later he emerged, with the satisfaction of seeing himself attired in a fine summer coat, although the season had advanced as he had, and autumn had arrived, when he arrived at Paris. He had selected the coat, however, a linen one, as a better match for his dimity trousers than broadcloth or velvet.

The dealer gave Bannière a fourth and last smile; but

he disregarded it, and left the shop.   It required some
courage on his part to go away and leave that smile behind him, for its language was at least more cheerful than
his self-communings.

This is what he was saying to himself, —

"I have nothing left with which to buy food, — not a
sou, not a denier, not an obolus, — but I will not be ridi-
culous.   If I continue to fast, which would be absurd in
this city which feeds eight hundred thousand souls, so
much the worse for my stomach, that's its affair; so
much the worse too for my wit, for that would prove it
not to be fertile in expedients."

This monologue did not prevent Bannière from thanking with all his heart the gracious old-clothes dealer, who
was following him with her kindly eye.   Several times
he turned about, partly to wave his hand to her, and
partly to see if the passers-by were turning to look at
him.

No one seemed to take any notice of him, to his ex-
ceeding delight.   It proved that he had ceased to be
grotesque.

With a tranquil mind he at last reached the Boulevard.
He sat down between two stones, leaning an arm upon
each as if he were in an arm-chair, and amused himself
by watching the dogs, who were more fortunate than
he, in that they were enjoying their first meal of the
day.

But it was something quite other than the dogs who
knew he seemed to be looking at them, or their repast
in which he seemed to be absorbed, which kept his eyes
staring into vacancy and his mind active; it was his very
serious anxiety to know how he could, in his present
destitute condition, begin to adopt the necessary means
of finding Olympe.

"She fled," he was saying, "with Monsieur de Mailly; he left Olympe before to be married, and since he has a wife he cannot have taken Olympe to his own house."

No; but he must have installed her in some secret establishment.

"Of course!" said Bannière to himself; "that's the way it is; now it remains for me to learn where the secret establishments of the wealthy are located."

Thereupon he hailed a rustic who had in his hand a little perfumed note.

"Friend," said he, "tell me, please, where one should go in Paris to find abandoned women?"

The Auvergnat, for such he was, began to laugh, and went his way without any other reply. Bannière judged from his silence that the question was either too deep or too stupid, and that he did not understand it.

His judgment was correct.

This bad beginning made Bannière distrustful of himself.

"If I involve myself so," he said, "I am quite capable of making a fool of myself all the time. I don't know how it is, but I always begin at the wrong end.

"Why am I a fool in Paris, when I had some wit in the provinces?

"Because I am hungry and have on a thin coat. Now the longer I go without eating, the hungrier I shall be; the colder the weather grows, the thinner my coat will be.

What to do without a sou?

That question, the everlasting problem of the destitute and the ambitious, Bannière propounded to himself as he plunged his hands deeper into the pockets of his linen coat.

"What to do without a sou?" said he.

Suddenly he exclaimed aloud, and his right hand moved excitedly in its pocket.

Oh, happiness! he felt something cold against the end of his fingers, and recognized the presence of a piece of money.

To seize it, pull it out, look at it, and dance for joy was the work of a single second.

The good-natured creature had realized Bannière's need of his crown, and had stowed it away in the pocket of the linen coat.

And so he still had a crown, and was twenty-five times as rich as the Wandering Jew.

His first impulse was to rush back to the shop, and kiss the merchant on both cheeks. But he soon thought better of it, and determined instead to honor her thoughtful kindness by restoring himself to his normal condition through the agency of an abundant and satisfying repast.

Acting upon this determination, he entered a cook-shop in Rue du Ponceau.

XLIV.

HOW BANNIÈRE BREAKFASTED IN THE RUE DU PONCEAU COOK-SHOP, AND WHAT TOOK PLACE THEREAFTER.

SINCE the somewhat distant period in which the action of this tale is supposed to take place, the people of our country (of the only country, that is, where men really *eat*) seem to eat more than in old days, whereas they really eat much less.   A hundred eating-house keepers like those who poison us to-day, are not worth, from the stomach's point of view, a single *rotisseur* of Rue de la Huchette.

The shop of the *rotisseur* of former times was a world in itself, something of which only Monsieur de Humboldt's *cosmos* can convey an adequate idea.   The *rotisseur* himself was a multiple being, — fruiterer, provision-dealer, grocer, eating-housekeeper, and pastry-cook. He was everything, in short, except the wine-merchant, who maintained his specialty against all the *rotisseurs* in the world.   With his chicken-gravy (we are speaking of the *rotisseur*, of course) he made delicious soups; with the chickens themselves, certain mysterious fricassees, of which none but the *rotisseurs* knew the secret.   He served salads, eggs and game in all shapes, and even condescended to use the frying-pan for certain of his dishes.

Then, too, the *rotisseur*, as we have said, pressed the pastry-cook hard, and cooked all sorts of fancy dishes in his oven, while the enormous spit, turning incessantly with a grating sound in front of the vast fireplace, furnished grease enough to supply all the kitchens of the quarter.

A famished man, if he entered one of these cook-shops could not possibly leave it in the same condition; however lean his purse, he was sure to find in that wonderful larder the means of eating to satiety.

From the lark at three sous to the fat pullet at three francs, from the humble pigeon to the golden pheasant, everything was to be found there, two-legged and four-legged, even to a whole ox, if it had been called for; and besides all that, the *rotisseur* plied his trade in private houses, and at very moderate cost, thanks to him, one could enjoy in his own dining-room a delicious repast, cooked as it should be.

Genuine cooking disappeared with the downfall of the *rotisseurs ;* they will rise again some day, we have no doubt, as a necessity of the society of the future.

For our own part, no Homeric festival with its bubbling fat, nor the *pinguis forma* of Virgil, has ever tickled our palate and sense of smell in our halcyon days of enormous appetite, like those delicious sizzling roasts, smoking hot, which in imagination we have seen turning round and round over the dripping-pan of a *rotisseur* of the eighteenth century.

Bannière then entered the cook-shop. He selected a chicken at forty sous and a salad, which were carried for him to the nearest wine-shop, — a place (to find its like we must go back a hundred and thirty years) where wine was sold, real wine, the honest, unadulterated juice of the grape.

Bannière ordered two dozen oysters and two bottles of Burgundy.

Then by an effort of the will which underlies every
well-organized mind, he forgot all his troubles, and settled
himself comfortably in a corner, determined like a man
of spirit to make a brave fight against the vampire called
ennui and the demon melancholy, the two abandoned
sons of love and separation.

He ate.

Right here we desire to give utterance to our respect
for the public, and our liking for physical and moral
refinement. No one likes better than we do to exhibit a
hero of romance in glowing colors under all circumstances.

But we must confess that Bannière's stomach had
rebelled; and in so doing had changed the man's
whole nature, whereby his moral excellence was much
diminished.

The stomach, if it is in bad humor, reacts upon the
heart and the brain. It is needless to add that it also
tends to render arms and legs of no account.

So it happened that the ex-dragoon had no sooner
washed down the succulent oyster into his discontented
stomach with a draught of generous wine, and the gentle
warmth of the gastric juices had no sooner begun to
mount to the eyes and play around the temples of the
half-starved youth, than he seemed on the instant to view
his situation through such rainbow-hued hopes as he had
not known for a fortnight.

One would have said that the good Burgundy was no
other than that magic beverage which Thessalian Canidia
used to pour upon the tombs at midnight, to evoke the
spirits of the dead. Under its influence Bannière was
born again, his eyes were reopened, and he saw again, in
his imagination of course, at the same moment the object
which, of all the world contained, he most longed to see,
— Olympe!

Olympe, to see Olympe again! — a thing that had seemed impossible the night before! But to-day it was the simplest thing in the world. For was not Olympe in Paris? And was not he, Bannière, in Paris also? The hardest part of the task was done, then, since he had already left behind him ninety-nine hundredths of the distance which had separated him from her.

Paris alone remained between them, — Paris, a more trackless labyrinth than that of Dædalus.

But, after all, what was this Paris? A city only seven leagues in circumference; consequently three leagues and a half in diameter in its widest part.

A trifling matter that for legs which had already made one hundred and thirty leagues, and had forgotten all about them, thanks to the oysters and the Burgundy, the chicken and salad.

He would find Olympe, then, by dint of searching everywhere on those famous legs of his.

Where was *everywhere?*

Everywhere, indeed! The *everywhere* of pretty girls is limited in extent. Although the Savoyard did not answer his question, Bannière well knew that a pretty girl's *everywhere* is the secret establishment of a nobleman; and among all the noblemen whom Paris held at that moment, there was no room for hesitation. Olympe had denounced herself in his cell at Lyons. It was Monsieur de Mailly who had come in quest of her, and it was Monsieur de Mailly who had spirited her away. Olympe then was installed in Monsieur de Mailly's secret establishment.

But where was it located? That was what remained for him to find out.

Oh, well! he would find out. But from whom?

Why, from Monsieur de Mailly himself, of course.

He would go at once and ask Monsieur de Mailly where his little place was, and by persuasion or force would prevail upon Olympe to leave it.

It was a very simple idea, but one which had not come to him until he had discussed the oysters and the chicken and the salad, and especially the good Burgundy, and which in our opinion would not have come to him at all without them.

How sad it is to be forced to admit that the moral being is so submissive to the tyranny of the physical! And yet it must be admitted; so we will admit it and resume our narrative.

Bannière, having finished his second bottle and laid out his plan of campaign, footed up his reckoning, and found that he had used up his crown all but three sous. But as he no longer felt the need of anything except Olympe, the three sous were of no use to him; so he very majestically bestowed them upon the barmaid of the wine-shop where he had spent an hour to such good advantage.

Now the linen coat was too warm, and the dimity breeches too thick: he was too well dressed; after his soul-satisfying breakfast he needed no other clothing than his youthful ardor and his heartfelt love.

With nose in air, and hand on hip, Bannière jauntily took his way toward the Faubourg Saint-Germain, where was situated the Hôtel de Nesle, in which Monsieur de Mailly dwelt, in all probability.

There existed at this period a certain species of the *genus homo* which has since been lost to sight, as all other curious things have been since the Deluge, and as all the monstrosities of Nature were before it.

Never fear, dear reader. We have no purpose to deliver a disquisition upon mastodons, or a thesis on fossil bones; these remarks are preliminary to nothing more than a slight digression upon Swiss indoor men.

These personages, whom we were privileged to gaze upon with awe in our infancy, whose dignity was shattered in the Revolution of 1830, and who ceased to exist as a class in the Revolution of 1848, — these personages held despotic sway over that portion of the house which separates the exterior from the interior, and they were armed sometimes with halberds and sometimes with simple disdain, as the weapon with which to carry out the orders transmitted by the first valet-de-chambre, or the favorite lady's-maid.

It was one of these Helvetian bull-dogs whom Bannière at first encountered; but the Swiss, summing up with perfect accuracy at a glance the total cost of a linen coat and dimity breeches, and estimating the whole outfit at three crowns, refused admission to Bannière in most lordly fashion.

"But, Monsieur le Suisse," said Bannière, "I asked you for Monsieur le Comte de Mailly."

"Monsieur is not within," replied the Swiss.

Bannière understood upon reflection that his linen coat and dimity breeches were the great obstacle to his entrance.

"Oh, have no fear!" said he, with as much dignity as he had ever imparted to the rôle of Hérode; "I have not come to beg."

"It makes no difference; clear out!" said the Swiss, little moved by Bannière's clear exposition of his social standing.

"I come from Monsieur de Mailly's regiment," he insisted, "and I have matters of importance to tell him. Beware of refusing to admit me, for the consequences will fall upon your head, not on mine."

The Swiss again took stock, somewhat more carefully than before, of the four or five ells of cloth which went to the making of our hero's costume.

"From the regiment?" said he, uneasily.   "You say that you come from the regiment?"

"Yes."

"Oho!"

"You are wondering at my costume, are n't you?"

"Yes."

"Well, never mind that."

"Oho!"

"I am one of Monsieur de Mailly's dragoons; and as I have come on affairs of state, I disguised myself in order not to be arrested *en route.*"

"Aha!" exclaimed the Swiss, almost convinced.

"Let me pass, then," said Bannière; and he made an attempt to slip between the halberd and the giant's body.

The Swiss brought the halberd to his side, and thereby blocked Bannière's passage.

"Well?" said Bannière.

"But Monsieur le Comte de Mailly really is not within."

"Upon honor?" asked Bannière.

"Upon honor!   Madame alone is at home."

It was true.   Bannière, who had acquired experience upon the stage in reading the eyes of his interlocutor, at once saw that the worthy Swiss was telling the truth, by the tranquillity of his expression.

"Madame," thought Bannière, "Madame! the devil! that's not what I want."

"But, after all," he said to himself reflectively, "Madame can answer questions about Monsieur."

Thereupon he turned again to the porter.

"Very well!" said he; "that's all right."

"What's all right?"

"It is Madame with whom I wish to talk."

His bearing was so business-like that the Swiss no longer hesitated.

Summoning Madame's maid, for whom he had a special bell in his office, he informed her as soon as she appeared that a messenger, who had arrived in great haste from Lyons, where Monsieur de Mailly's regiment was stationed, desired to speak with the countess.

In this way did Bannière, at ten o'clock in the morning, procure admission to the impenetrable sanctuary of a woman.

XLV.

MONSIEUR BANNIÈRE DISCOVERS INEXHAUSTIBLE RESOURCES IN HIS LINEN COAT.

MADAME DE MAILLY, a lovely person, with bright black eyes, curly hair, a soft, dark complexion, and in whom the severest critic of the time could find no other blemish than a lack of fulness in her cheeks, had married, as we said in an earlier chapter, Monsieur le Comte de Mailly, the lover of Olympe.

She was one of the five Mesdemoiselles de Nesle, who were destined, as every one knows, to cut a great figure in their day.

The four others were Madame de la Tournelle, Madame de Flavacourt, Madame de Vintimille, and Madame de Lauraguais.

All were beautiful; some were more beautiful than Madame la Comtesse de Mailly, but not one of them had the charm which Nature and training had bestowed so lavishly upon the countess's whole being. A woman is not always beloved because she is the fairest; there are charms which take precedence of personal comeliness.

Madame de Mailly was worthy to be adored.

Bannière's first thought, as he was admitted to her presence, was of the powerful influence such a woman might exert over men who were the most difficult to move.

The countess, on her side, as her glance fell upon the youth, experienced a strange sensation as she observed the contrast between his bearing and his costume.

"How absurdly he is dressed!" she said aside to her maid; "and why this disguise?"

The maid looked Bannière over knowingly, and shook her head.

"Monsieur de Mailly's men are carefully selected," she said, "if the whole regiment is built upon the pattern of this specimen."

The fact is that the countess's first thought had been, strangely enough, that if Bannière were suitably clothed, he would be a very agreeable object to look upon.

At sight of a good-looking man the most modest woman almost always finds some thoughts come creeping into her mind which she does not confide to her husband, and often not to her confessor.

"Well, my friend," said the countess, very pleasantly, "you asked to speak with me?"

"Yes, Madame la Comtesse," replied Bannière.

"What do you want to say to me?"

"A secret which compels me to beg Madame la Comtesse to grant me a private interview."

People of the world are naturally suspicious. The extraordinary costume, the perfect courtesy, the perfumed honey which the lips of a dragoon are not wont to exhale, but which came from Bannière's lips, arrested the countess's good-nature just when it was about to expand as it might in a woman without rank.

"This fellow," she thought, "is no dragoon; he bows too well."

She winked at her maid in a fashion which meant, "Remain in the room, Mademoiselle;" and the maid therefore remained.

Bannière, who had cast several sidelong glances at her as if to give her leave to withdraw, without regard to her mistress. determined not to utter a word or move a finger in her presence, and stood in one spot, motionless as a milestone, dumb as a fish.

We must not forget, in order to the understanding of certain mysteries, which become no mysteries at all if we go back to the past, that this tale is almost contemporaneous with the Regency, and that the lovely young women of that epoch, queens of love and pleasure, knew, when they chose to remember, how many times and in what fashion the Lauzuns in the last century and the Richelieus in this had disguised themselves as a means of gaining admission to their presence.

Madame de Mailly, then, guided amiss by ordinary female instinct, fancied that she saw in this mute individual an aspirant for her favor more audacious than others, and more clever too, — in other words, more dangerous; and she began to knit her brows. Lovely as she was, she became almost ugly, so inimical is virtue to beauty, — such annoyance does Minerva cause Venus, as the Abbé de Bernis, whose madrigals were just beginning to be fashionable, might have said.

"If you have come here for no other purpose than to stand there in front of me as you are doing, and without a word to say for yourself," said the countess, coldly, "be good enough to return whence you came, Monsieur, and don't disturb me again."

The word "Monsieur," was pronounced with an inflection which betokened the most abrupt dismissal that ever disguised gallant received.

But Bannière was not moved by it in the slightest degree.

"Madame," he replied, bowing, "I am, upon my honor, a dragoon of Monsieur le Comte's regiment. My name is Bannière, and God forbid that I should have the slightest purpose of insulting you!"

"Speak, then. You have some favor to ask at the hands of Monsieur de Mailly, have you not? and you hope to obtain it through my intercession? Speak, then; when I ask you to speak, you must do so, quickly and clearly."

"In that case, Madame, all that I have to ask is the simple question where I may find Monsieur de Mailly."

"For what purpose do you wish to find Monsieur de Mailly?" asked the countess.

Bannière had not anticipated that question, although he should have done so. Thus his imagination, instead of suggesting some pretext, failed him completely.

"Allow me to remain silent, Madame," said he.

"If you need to see Monsieur le Comte de Mailly for some purpose which you cannot divulge to his wife, you should not have come to his wife to ask his address. Adieu, Monsieur."

At this point Bannière began to lack tact as well as imagination. He adopted a violent course with Madame de Mailly, just as he had done with the Greeks.

"Madame," he cried, "I am seeking Monsieur de Mailly because he has robbed me of my dearest possession."

"What can Monsieur de Mailly have robbed you of?"

"A woman!"

The countess started.

Bannière imagined, in his innocent, ignorant heart, that by making such a revelation to her he should arouse her to irritation against her husband, and thus loosen her tongue.

He had based his calculations upon a grisette, and not upon a great lady.

"What woman?" the countess asked.

"Mademoiselle Olympe! that is to say, my life and my soul!"

The countess shuddered at the flames which shot from Bannière's eyes, while the soubrette avowed ingenuously to her own heart that if her name were Mademoiselle Olympe, Bannière would not have had to run after her, — very far, at all events.

"Who is this Mademoiselle Olympe?" continued the countess, determined to probe the matter to the bottom, and to use such parts of the revelation as suited her purpose and let the rest go.

"An actress, Madame."

Madame de Mailly shrugged her shoulders, with an expression of lofty scorn impossible to describe; then in a tone which the most skilful student of womankind would have been unable to interpret according to its true signification, she said, —

"You are either a madman or a liar."

Bannière was overwhelmed.

"Madman! liar!" he cried.

"Just so, Monsieur, for none but a madman would make such statements to a woman about her husband if they are true; and if they are false, why then, as I just said, you are a liar."

"Oh, you are right, Madame!" said Bannière; "yes, I am mad with love."

The countess glanced at Bannière out of the corner of her eye, shrugged her shoulders again, and entered her bedroom.

Bannière rushed after her.

She stopped upon the threshold, and turned her head so as to look at him over her shoulder.

"Ah!" she exclaimed dryly, with a freezing glance quite capable of breaking off all the magnetic currents which run from the zenith to the nadir.

Bannière, in despair at the impending utter failure of

his mission, felt a growing impulse which urged him on; the soubrette did all that she could with her two little hands to drag him away from the spot where he had been guilty of such a monumental piece of doltishness.

He yielded to the exertions of the soubrette, who was desirous to be as sympathetic as her mistress had been cruel. At the door she comforted poor Bannière with a pressure of the hand and these words, —

"You had better go. Madame does not believe you because she has a heart of stone; but I with my soft heart, — alas! I believe and pity you."

Bannière made no reply; he left the house in a state of mental depression, seeing nothing before him on earth save the abyss into which his happiness had fallen.

The stomach no longer performed its cheering functions; the ungrateful organ had gone through the process of digesting, and in the course of that process had forgotten.

It would be difficult, even for a much more eloquent pen than ours to describe the frame of mind in which the unhappy Bannière found himself after this scene.

His hope had vanished, — not of finding Monsieur de Mailly; oh, no, nothing was easier than that, for he had but to wait at the door of his hotel, *pardieu !* he was sure to return there some day or other: but to find Monsieur de Mailly was not to find Olympe; and to fail to find her was, in Bannière's estimation, a fate far worse than death.

The worst feature of the situation was that the more deeply he pondered, the more profound was his despondency, — no money, consequently no resource.

He fell into a state of prostration more complete in proportion as his joy had been more expansive.

Suddenly something like a ray of light passed over his face, but it was more sad than joyous.

"I have my ruby," he said; "it is worth, at least, three hundred pistoles; I can borrow a hundred upon it. I will have a document proving my possession of it drawn up in proper form by a notary, — something unimpeachable and not to be doubted. With the money I will find Olympe, and will take her with me to the notary, and show her the ruby, if meanwhile I have not been able to redeem it."

In another moment he thought better of that scheme.

"Oh," he cried, "to risk the loss of my ruby, the only proof which I possess of my love and my absolute devotion to the service of my mistress! To intrust the precious ring to other hands than my own! No, I was mad to think of such a thing. Is it not quite possible for a pawnbroker to become bankrupt and fly the country? May not a Jew be arrested and imprisoned, and his property confiscated? May not a notary's house be burned down, or his chest robbed? *Dame!* such things have been seen, and there are even well-known notaries in his Majesty's galleys at Toulon and Brest. And then, before a notary I should be obliged to give my whole name and my history, — Jacques Bannière, runaway from the Jesuit convent at Avignon, deserter from the dragoon barracks at Lyons. Impossible! However, it's decided, whether or no; I have got my ruby again, and it shall never go out of my hands."

He pressed it in amorous folly to his lips, and sought upon its cold surface the warmth of the kisses which Olympe had imprinted upon it in days gone by.

The mere thought of parting with the bawble, for a month, for a day, or even for one short hour only, so horrified him that he beat his breast, — a reminiscence of his old monkish habit.

The linen coat received the blow. It was very thin,

the poor coat, and like swaddling-clothes adapted itself
to all the contortions of the body.   But under the blow
which Bannière dealt it with his fist, it assumed an attitude of resistance, and the flimsy stuff did duty as a
shield for the heart.

Bannière felt an unusual thickness in the lining.   We
beg the reader's pardon for leading him astray when we
said in the lining, for the coat had none.   We should
have said that Bannière felt something like a lining in
one spot.

He investigated with a sensation of surprise not un-
mixed with awe; he investigated, and discovered, sewn
on the inside of the linen, just at the location of the
heart, a square piece of white cloth, bearing some resemblance to the patches which serve to repair the ravages
of time in garments hoary with age.

"There's a bad place," said he; "I wonder if the old-
clothes woman cheated me ?   No; there's thickness
there, real thickness; let's see what it means."

Ripping out the stitches with eager fingers, he found
inside the square of cloth a sort of sachet-bag, made of a
band of gray and a band of red satin, the whole in
wretched condition, all worn out and discolored, but
with a coarse figure of Saint Julien worked upon the red
satin with these words, —

Ora pro nobis.

"A scapulary!" cried Bannière; "why, the coat must
be enchanted!   Can it be that this scapulary led to my
finding a crown in the pocket, I wonder ?   That's hardly
probable, though, unless Saint Julien, the patron saint
of travellers, is also a patron of the coat to the extent of
supplying it with a crown every morning.   Let's look
in the scapulary."

He proceeded to examine it with most scrupulous care.

" Empty, quite empty ! A religious emblem, pure and simple, without craft or ornament ! "

Two little silk ribbons were attached to the scapulary, making it evident that it was intended to hang from the neck upon the chest.

Bannière therefore devoutly suspended it around his neck, and invoking the kindly offices of good Saint Julien, under whose protection he considered himself thenceforth, he took the first street he came to without the least idea whither it would lead him. Henceforth that was none of his affair; it was for Saint Julien to direct his steps aright.

He had gone scarce a hundred feet when he noticed a number of people collected at a street-corner.

As he was in no sort of haste, he approached them to see what they were doing, and found that they were reading a theatrical poster.

Bannière heaved a woful sigh; he recalled the time when, given over entirely to his art and his love, he used to play Hérode with Olympe, and go home to supper with his Mariamne, restored to life.

What were they playing at Paris, at that famous Comédie-Française of which he had heard so much ?

He stood on tiptoe to read over the heads of the people in front.

Suddenly he cried aloud.

The poster bore Olympe's name in huge letters, and announced her first appearance at the Comédie-Française for that very evening.

XLVI.

MAN PROPOSES AND GOD DISPOSES.

THE film which came over Bannière's eyes made him so dizzy that he must have fallen face forward against the poster itself, except for the resistance offered by the back of the party over whose head he had seen the fateful words.

It was, indeed, unheard of, that Saint Julien should perform miracles after this manner; the scapulary was vastly more than a treasure, since it thus fulfilled on the instant the wishes of him who possessed it, — a feat which money can only accomplish after some time has passed, and then not always.

Bannière, recovered from his vertigo, read and read again, and being convinced that he was not mistaken, that it was indeed Olympe who was to appear, and to appear that very evening, he was near dying with joy upon the spot.

The result of the discovery he had made was truly incalculably important.

In the first place Olympe was found again; in the second place Olympe was free, — for a woman, when she takes to the stage, does not wish to be kept in seclusion, nor can she be. The duty of rehearsing requires her to go abroad continually; and the only man who does not see an actress is the one who does not care to see her, or who does not know enough to watch in the neighborhood of the theatre.

Bannière ran directly to the Comédie-Française. In that way he avoided the necessity of thinking about dinner, and in his destitute plight that was the wisest thing he could do.

But it may have been because there were a great many people in Paris as curious or as penniless as he, he found a crowd already assembled at the door.

Bannière, being quite at home in the customs of the theatre, walked along the line without taking his place therein, presented himself to the doorkeeper, and asked Mademoiselle Olympe's address.

Thereupon he discovered something which he did not suspect,— that the Swiss servants of great noblemen are much to be preferred to the same species in the employ of the theatres. The experience was dearly bought; but one seldom learns anything new without paying for the increase of knowledge with the death of a hope or an illusion.

Bannière was shown out much more roughly than he had ever been in his life, for a door was slammed in his face with such violence that he was fain to renounce all hope of information from that quarter.

Had Monsieur de Mailly commended Olympe to the vigilance of the Swiss, or had she commended herself? She was quite capable of it.

Bannière studied the poster once more on the walls of the theatre. It bore in bold characters these words:

BY ORDER

BRITANNICUS. Tragedy by M. Racine.

Mademoiselle Olympe will make her début in the rôle of JUNIE.

"By order!" Bannière read it over again; then he repeated it to himself. "By order! what does it mean?"

he asked. "Can it be that the king is responsible for my love's début? It is possible, but hardly probable. Is it Monsieur de Mailly who has caused her to return to the stage? It is not the act of an amorous man; or if of an amorous man, surely not of a jealous one."

He realized that his condition of uncertainty would last forever if he confined himself to his own imaginings; so he made inquiries of one of the idlers, whose appearance was less forbidding than that of his friend the doorkeeper.

"Monsieur," he asked, "can you explain to me the occasion of this function which is in preparation?"

"To be sure."

"If you can, you will do me a great favor."

"Monsieur," replied the lounger, "you must know that our dear little king has been ill?"

"Yes, indeed, Monsieur; and very dangerously. I did know it, as you say; and the proof is that, like all good Frenchmen, I had a taper burned for his convalescence."

"Ah! very good, Monsieur!"

"I did only my duty, Monsieur; but to return, if you please, to this performance — "

"Oh, yes! the king is better, Monsieur, and this evening he is to appear at the play. It is his first visit to the theatre since his illness. You can imagine what a throng will attend to see him and applaud him, especially as his presence is coincident with an important début."

"Yes, that of Mademoiselle Olympe; I see that on the bill. Do you know this Olympe, Monsieur?"

"Not personally. I am a draper in Rue Tiquetonne, Monsieur, and do not affect the society of women of that class."

"But have you heard nothing about her?"

"I have heard that she came from Lyons, where she has had great success, and that she was expected to make an even greater hit here in Paris; and as I have considerable curiosity to see this Columbine, I will take my place in the line, with your permission, Monsieur."

"I share your interest so thoroughly," said Bannière, "that I think I will fall into the line too."

He suited the action to the word, without duly considering the fact that he had not a sou in his pocket, and hurriedly joined one of the groups, thus helping to form one of the vertebræ of that creature with a movable backbone which is called the public, and whose tail, like that of the monster evoked by Theseus, is sometimes twisted into tortuous folds, sometimes stretches out like an endless serpent, and sometimes — too often, alas! — presents to the view of the spectator naught but three or four rings, — very slender ones too.

On this occasion it was a veritable Python, with incredible elaborations.

Bannière, when he was fairly encased in the vertebra of the monster, thought more seriously than he had done hitherto of his poverty, which was no better than absolute destitution.

But he reasoned after the following fashion: —

"Everybody can't get in; there will be a row, and a jolly one too. In the scrimmage there will be plenty of opportunities to thump the Gardes-Françaises, and that same insolent doorkeeper, whose halberd I vow to break over his back the first chance I have, and I hope that that chance is near at hand. The result will be that a lot of idiots will be unable to get into the theatre, although they are ready to pay, but that many clever fellows who care little about keeping their linen coats intact, like myself for instance, will succeed in fighting their way in for nothing, and will find scores of good seats in the pit."

This line of reasoning, our readers must agree, was not so very illogical for a man who was hungry and in love. If Bannière under such circumstances had adopted any different course, he would have belied all his practical and theoretical knowledge of things theatrical; especially would he have run counter to the all-powerful mediation of great Saint Julien, whose scapulary he wore upon his breast.

Meanwhile, behind Bannière and the lounger with whom he had the conversation we have reported, the crowd, like a ram with many horns, began to butt against the doors of the Comédie-Française, which asked no better fate than to be carried by storm; and so they were, as soon as the box-office was opened.

For five minutes all went well; but at the end of that time the impetuosity of the crowd, abetted by a number of arguments similar to that which Bannière had used upon himself, began to have their effect upon the general good order which had been maintained up to that time. Bannière, with unspeakable delight, saw that about ten paces ahead of him fisticuffs had begun to be exchanged with such regularity that they might be expected to continue.

At this crisis, as at most other times, Bannière had reason to congratulate himself upon his height, thanks to which he could see hats flying about, and the levelled gun-barrels of the archers, who were hustled about in the hurly-burly, and swayed this way and that, like the poor willows during the fierce squalls of spring and autumn.

Only ten minutes more of fighting on the part of the advance guard, and a like period of patient waiting on the part of the centre where Bannière was, and his triumph was certain.

The ten minutes passed, and matters turned out much better even than he expected. The tempest became a cyclone, and the guards were forced back, and disappeared like wisps of straw in the clutches of a whirlwind.

There was nothing more to do but to push his way in; there was no need even of breaking anything over the doorkeeper's shoulders.

But our readers must have noticed one thing, and that is that bright ideas fly about in the air like flocks of birds, so that when a man has a bright idea, and naturally thinks that he has it all to himself, he is sure to see it acted upon by somebody else, just as he was about to avail himself of it.

Thanks to the battle which was raging at the door, and in which the armed force had been worsted, more than forty men, who had the advantage over Bannière and his friend of having taken their places in the line ahead of them, had already reached the porch without having occasion to put their hands into their purses.

Bannière's turn came at last; he calculated that in another minute, in a second, he too would have passed under the blessed porch; he was already preparing for a spring to overthrow the last two lines which separated him from the entrance, when these same lines, which were wavering and almost in a panic, like the famous column of Fontenoy before the charge of Monsieur de Richelieu, suddenly turned upon Bannière and forced him back to the gutter.

It was not till then that he saw that the doorkeeper whom he had thumped so soundly in his fancy, had been to seek reinforcements and had found them; that the defeated archers had multiplied, as the soldiers grew from the dragon's teeth of Cadmus; that the Gardes-

Françaises did not consider themselves beaten by a simple repulse; and that sundry, very determined-looking bayonets, very straight and very numerous, had driven out those would-be spectators who had gone beyond their rights, and were advancing in good order to discipline the others. This check, however, was not calculated to discourage a combatant so interested in the fight, and consequently so implacable, as Bannière. A resolution like his does not surrender to a few pieces more or less of flesh and blood or of cold steel.

Therefore he was obstinate, and instead of falling back, as most of his neighbors did, his energy increased twofold, and, like a true soldier, he constituted himself commander-in-chief of a mob of mutineers, who yelled *Vive le Roi!* with all their might, and undertook to carry the doors and barriers of the theatre by storm.

The good example set by Bannière emboldened all the fugitives, who turned about when they saw that the day was not hopelessly lost, and who rallied around their new leader, and made a path through the ranks of the archers and police, crying, *Vive le Roi!* more frequently than ever, — an ingenious bit of tactics, always employed by insurgents, whereby the disturbers of the peace sought to make it appear that they were breaking down barriers, bursting open doors, and assassinating guards for no other purpose than to demonstrate their zeal and their affection for his Majesty Louis XV., who was still called at this period " Louis the Well-Beloved."

But, unhappily, as we have learned in our own days of revolution, nothing imparts so much force and obstinacy to the bayonets of the troops as the resistance of plain, every-day citizens.

There has been of all time most intense emulation between the citizen's coat and the uniform. in the direction of inflicting annoyance upon each other, and tearing each other to pieces.

The uniforms, then, did horrible execution among the coats, and we can easily understand that Bannière's unsubstantial garment, which was at the centre of peril, was not spared.

After all, however, it was stubborn to the point of ferocity; in itself alone it was as good as a whole army. The valor and wrath and devotion which it displayed on that field would have sufficed to win for the Romans the three battles of Trébie, Trasimène, and Cannæ.

Nevertheless God was on the side of the battalions. Numbers carried the day. Ten or twelve archers gave their undivided earnest attention to the gallant youth, who deserved to have been better supported, or attacked with a smaller force.

Thereupon — and it was a grievous sight to see — the hapless coat which had hitherto avoided such rough scenes was torn to tatters by their vindictive hands.

Bannière, who in spite of everything, and like those whose good luck he had envied, had succeeded in forcing his way into the vestibule of the theatre, saw that he would be quartered alive if he continued to shower blows with feet and hands, to right and left, in front and in rear, as he had been doing; so he clung with feet and hands to a pillar, as if he would have uprooted it; and then there was enacted under that porch a scene which was certainly more curious than that which the lovers of sound literature had come thither to witness.

He yelled *Vive le Roi!* did poor Bannière, with such vehemence that his cry became a roar. He embraced the stone column with such power that the archers abandoned the attempt to break his hold upon it.

One would have said he was one of those pieces of

sculpture of the Middle Ages with which the architects of the cathedrals of Strasburg and Cologne adorned the huge pillars of those structures.

Alas! why cannot such instances of courage and devotion, like that of Cynegirus at Salamis, be allowed to triumph, that posterity may gaze upon the gratifying spectacle of virtue rewarded?

But it was not to be. A commissioner appeared, made inquiries, looked about, and instead of subscribing to the general sentiment of admiration which enveloped Bannière's glorious defence like a halo, issued, in that shrill voice which is characteristic of officials of his class, certain clear and concise orders in these words, —

"Archers, take that man, alive or dead, and bring him before me."

Bannière, understanding the significance of "alive or dead," and knowing as he did that resistance to the orders of a commissioner had more than once been followed by strangulation, or torture quite capable of causing death, — Bannière, who was willing to fight against superior force, but did not care to offend the majesty of the law, untwined his feet, straightened out the joints of his fingers which were clinched around the pillar, and put himself in the hands of his persecutors, as an oak which has already been uprooted by a tempest bends and sways and falls before the first breath of air.

The commissioner had withdrawn to his den, and the archers escorted Bannière thither, — some holding him by the wrists, while others pushed him with a will from behind. He was well acquainted with that process which seemed to be part of the tactics of all the archers in France. It was the same which had already been put in force upon him when he was taken to prison from Olympe's house at Lyons.

Having learned prudence by experience, and remembering his former arrest, Bannière, upon the pretext of rearranging in consonance with the demands of decency certain portions of his attire which had suffered tremendously, drew his precious ring from his finger and quietly slipped it into his mouth.

It will be noticed that in all the troublous periods of his life Bannière's first thought was for the ruby.   The feat was performed to his entire satisfaction, and no one remarked it.

Thus Bannière, hustled and frowned upon by fate, was haled before the commissioner, who was preparing all his eloquence and the thunderbolts of his wrath for the process of questioning him.

When the *mise-en-scène* was all arranged, the inquiry began.

Bannière listened calmly to the questions which were put to him in the peevish tone and with the absurd pedantry which distinguish Messieurs the Commissioners of Police of the fair kingdom of France.   But, as we have said, Bannière had his ring in his mouth; he was afraid that if he should put it between his teeth and his cheek and try to talk, it might fall out and betray itself; so he kept it in the centre of his mouth on his tongue,— which means, of course, that he did not speak.   For it is quite impossible to speak with a jewel upon the tongue; and thus, as will be seen, we prove the falsity of the fabulous verses in which the poets speak of pearls and gold issuing forth with every word.   Homer, apropos of the aged Nestor, mentions only honey as flowing from the lips of the King of Pylos, and leaves to Hesiod, less severely accurate than he in matters philosophical, the chains of gold which drop from the lips of Eloquence.

Nothing, then, came from Bannière's mouth, and we

know why; but the commissioner, who was far from sus-
pecting the reason, thinking that his obstinate silence
was caused by sullenness, got tired of putting questions
which evoked no response whatever, and, in accordance
with his undoubted right, committed Bannière to prison.

The same archers took him away to the For l'Evêque,
— the poor boy, but recently so full of fire and energy,
now walking along with dull eye and bent head, like the
coursers of Hippolytus.

XLVII.

LOVE-MADNESS.

NOTHING of moment occurred on the way. Bannière continued to maintain absolute silence, much to the astonishment of the archers, who had heard him shouting, *Vive le Roi!* so vigorously.

They took him to the For l'Evêque, as has been said, and entered his name upon the books with the customary formalities.

During the process of registration he said no more than he had said before the commissioner and on the way to the prison.

Once regularly registered and locked up, he breathed more freely, took the ring from his mouth, and hid it in a little hole in his wall (the king's wall, we should say); then he drew his cot in front of the hole and lay down upon it, so as not to lose sight of the ring even in his sleep, as Monsieur de la Palisse, who said so many good things, might have said.

It was not without reason that he acted as he did, for they searched him with the utmost care — no very difficult task, by the way, as he was more than half naked.

They were especially diligent in scrutinizing the scapulary, which was seen to be empty and harmless, and was looked upon with some awe, as such articles commonly were in those days, when the archers still believed in the religion for which it was their duty to enforce respect, although perhaps the priests had ceased to believe in it.

This time it was no mere commissioner who undertook to interrogate Bannière, but a magistrate of the Châtelet; it was an imposing ceremony.

Up to that time Bannière had said very little; but from that time on he talked too much.

" Your name ? "

" Bannière. "

" Your age ? "

" Twenty-five years. "

" Your occupation ? "

" I have none. "

" Your dwelling-place ? "

" I have none yet, for I only reached Paris this morning. "

" Your means of existence ? "

Bannière held out his arms, — a famous means of existence! The archers knew a thing or two about them, and could certify to it if need were.

" Why did you fight with the guard ? "

" Because they prevented my going into the theatre. "

" What were you going to do there ? "

" *Pardieu!* to see the play. "

" But they searched you, and you had no money. "

At this point Bannière was embarrassed, even more so than he had been with Madame de Mailly, for this time, instead of making a foolish reply, he could think of no reply at all; and yet with a little presence of mind, the reply would almost have suggested itself, — he had only to point to the numerous gaping wounds in his coat, and say, —

" Do you suppose my purse would remain long in a coat torn like that ? "

That manner of reply would also have indicated a purpose to claim damages and interest.

But Bannière never thought of the lie, simple as it would have been.

He stood overwhelmed with confusion by the statement of the magistrate. We ought, however, to tell the whole truth to the end that the reader may not make Bannière out to be a worse idiot than he really was.

While the magistrate was at work upon him, Bannière's mind was occupied exclusively with the possible means of escaping from the prison.

This desire manifested itself very suddenly, and just when the magistrate least expected it.

"What time is it?" he demanded of that functionary, who looked at him in utter amazement.

"What to do?" he retorted banteringly.

"What to do? *Parbleu!* to go back to the Comédie, of course!" cried Bannière.

The judge looked at the archers.

"Come, quick, quick!" almost shouted Bannière; "I may still be there in time to hear Junie say, 'Oh, my prince;' and that is the moment of all others when I should like to see her. Olympe was so lovely, so pathetic, so touching!"

"What's that!" exclaimed the judge.

"Hurry, for God's sake!" Bannière went on; "for if you delay any longer, I shall never get there in time to hear her say, — to Agrippine, you know: 'Pardon this transport, Madame!'"

"The deuce take me!" stammered the magistrate, "but what in God's name is the matter with this fellow?"

"Come, have you finished?" continued Bannière, in a tone which indicated a renewed outbreak of the rage which he had held a moment in restraint.

"Look here!" cried the judge, gazing at Bannière

with a sort of terror, " are you mad ? Why, I had made
up my mind that you were almost innocent, and was just
about to show some indulgence — "

" *Parbleu !* " said Bannière, " it would be much better
than to treat me rigorously. Have I done anything
wrong ? They beat me, tore my new coat to tatters, and
my dimity breeches which I was wearing for the second
time only, and all because I wanted to see the performance, and was crying, *Vive le Roi !* "

" Yes, and he was shouting it out in great shape too, "
said an archer; " we must do him that justice. "

" He seems not to be a bad man, and he expresses
himself very well, " said the judge.

" Quick, then, quick, open the doors, " cried Bannière,
" since I am entirely innocent ! "

" But, " the judge added, " he is mad ! "

" Mad ! I ! Nonsense ! "

" Be calm and we will see. "

" You tell me to be calm ! "

" Yes. "

" But I tell you that she will be leaving the stage. "

" Who ? "

" Junie. "

" Who 's Junie ? "

" Junie ! ten thousand devils ! Do you mean to prevent me from seeing her when she leaves the stage ? "

" Oho ! the attack is coming on again, " said the magistrate, glancing at the archers, as if to make sure in
advance of their courage in case that he should have to
call upon them.

" Look, my little judge ! " said Bannière; " now she
will be undressing. "

" Who, pray ? "

" Why, Junie ! "

"Junie undressing!" exclaimed the scandalized official.

"Of course, yes! Do you suppose that she will go home in her tunic and her peplum?"

"Well! what is that to me, I should like to know?"

"But it is much to me; I have no more than time by running to meet her when she leaves the theatre. Let me go."

"Certainly he is a madman!" said the judge.

"He's a madman!" echoed the archers, delighted to agree with the judge.

"A madman of the erotic variety!" the magistrate added.

"And yet," one of the archers ventured to say, "I saw him arrange his dishevelled clothes with great care."

"Oh, he has lucid moments," said the judge.

Bannière started toward the door; the archers, at a sign from the magistrate, held him back, and the struggle began again.

The archers forced him down upon the flags, and while they held him there with three sturdy pairs of arms, the magistrate walked around him, gazing at him with interest mingled with curiosity.

"Messieurs," said he, "this man is afflicted with one of those mental maladies which physicians call love-madness. It is sometimes very dangerous, and a careful watch must be kept upon him."

Having delivered this judgment, the magistrate muttered a few words, wrote a few others on a piece of paper which he handed to the chief of the archers, and made his escape, not without enjoining upon the four to keep Bannière in the same recumbent position until he was outside the door.

Bannière, who had not taken his eyes from him, had grown more excited rather than calmer, had threatened him, and even struck at him. His madness, alas! was a sort of love-madness, although not of that variety which the judge had in mind.

When that functionary had taken his departure, they released Bannière's legs, but continued to hold fast to his arms.

"Come, my boy," said their leader, "get up now with good grace."

"Get up? We are going—"

"We are going to see Julie," said the archer, who had understood him to use that French name instead of the Latin name used by Monsieur Racine.

Bannière leaped to his feet, thinking that he was really to be set at liberty. He was careful to resume possession of Olympe's ring; and he slipped it into the scapulary, — a perfectly safe hiding-place thenceforth, so thoroughly had it been searched.

He was quite right to hide the ring so cleverly, poor Bannière; for after taking many steps in the streets of Paris, in a direction which was not that of the Comédie-Française, so far as he could judge, the archers put him into a fiacre, and said to the driver, —

"To Charenton."

An hour later Banniere and his escort alighted in front of a large house. As he was led through a wicket, his name was entered (upon information furnished by the archers, for Bannière refused to answer questions, understanding nothing of what was going on) as an "Erotomaniac."

The archers took their leave, and left him to himself. Upon the strength of the report of the magistrate who had questioned him, he had been committed to an asylum for the insane.

As he was still in a state of rebellion against the

frightful persecution to which he was subjected by fate, there came strong men who bound him hand and foot, and cast him into a cold cell, where they left him alone with his despair, which was sweetened by only one circumstance, — that in all his misfortunes he still had Olympe's ring.

XLVIII.

MEANWHILE the theatrical performance which had such deplorable results for Bannière, had turned out more satisfactorily for the peaceable spectators who had paid for their seats.

The king had arrived at the appointed time. He had taken his place in his box amid the joyful shouts which can be explained only by the insensate affection which at that time reigned in the hearts of all the subjects of his Most Christian Majesty.

Louis XV. had just passed his eighteenth year. He was in the very bloom of youth, in the very flower of his beauty. He had been the loveliest child in France; he was the most beautiful youth in the world.

In addition, no man possessed in such perfection grace united with nobility of demeanor.

The potent charm which he wielded over the whole nation, which saw in the peaceful beginning of his reign the glorious dawn of a long period of repose and of unbounded prosperity, may be explained by the incessant dread by which the people had long been oppressed, on account of his feeble health, always threatened, so said the friends of Madame de Maintenon, by Monsieur d'Orléans and his confederates.

But Monsieur d'Orléans had died, loyally performing the trust which God had given him, of preserving for

France this slender lily swaying upon its stalk; he had died bequeathing to the French people the trust which he had received from God.

At last this royal youth, the object of such anxious solicitude, had arrived at man's estate.   He was sufficiently vigorous in health to reassure his anxious subjects, yet frail enough to be interesting still.

His pallor, the result of a sickness from which he had risen as from the tomb, was an additional reason for loving and admiring and applauding him more than they had ever done in ordinary times.   Never, in very truth, had his eyes shone with a gentler flame, never had his beautiful white hands appeared more caressing and delicate, to the enchanted gaze of the ladies.

When the enthusiastic reception accorded by the Parisians to their idol was at an end, they began to pay some little attention to what was taking place upon the stage.

It was indeed Olympe who took the part of Junie. The poster which Bannière had perused, and which had led him straight away to Charenton, had told naught but the truth.

Perhaps the time has arrived to give our readers some account of what had taken place previously.   Of the events which we have narrated covering Monsieur de Mailly's return to Olympe, and her departure from Lyons, we have seen only the surface; let us look a little deeper than that.

A marriage, as we have already said, had been arranged, under the auspices of the king, between Louis Alexandre de Mailly, and Mademoiselle Louise Julie de Nesle, his cousin.   It was one of those alliances which unite great fortunes, which bind closer the ties of blood relationship, which are arranged between the heads of families, and which the young people concerned almost never rebel against, because they combine all the advantages of good-fellowship at least, if not of true happiness.

It should also be said that a marriage at that epoch was a much less serious affair than in our day. People married then to have heirs to inherit their fortunes and to perpetuate their race.

To reach these two results it was sufficient, from the husband's standpoint, to have one son; now this son, the first born, the husband could almost always be sure was really his, unless the wife was extraordinarily wanton. With that assurance it mattered little to him who begot her other children, for they did not bear his name or share in his fortune. One was put into the army, and another into the Church; it was " Monsieur le Chevalier " or " Monsieur l'Abbé." See Molière, for instance; Molière, who died of jealousy, — Molière, clever delineator of the morals of his days, — never once makes use of the word *adultère*. It is a French word, it is true, but a poetical word, like *coursier* (courser) instead of *cheval* (horse), or *flamme* (flame) instead of *amour* (love), or like *trépas* (demise) instead of *mort* (death). The ordinary word in common use is *cocuage* (cuckoldry), — that is to say, the word which conveys only the idea of absurdity. Of this double masque, which wears, like Janus, the double face of marriage, one sees only that which laughs; the face which expresses grief, which is furrowed with tears and contorted with despair, remains in the shadow, and no one ever sees it, except perhaps the husband, when in the privacy of his own apartment, alone with his thoughts, he lays aside the other, and looks at himself in the reproachful mirror of memory.

To-day it is quite different: cuckoldry has become adultery; the fault has become a crime. Has society

improved in morality?   Yes, at first sight; we maintain
that it is so, and it would not be hard to prove it.   Then
the law came in, and took a hand in enforcing morality;
the law abolished *majorats*, rights of primogeniture
and trusts; the law decreed the equal division of the
father's property among all his children.   No more clois-
ters for the daughters,   no more boarding-schools for
younger sons;   all have the same origin, hence all ought
to have equal rights.

From the moment that the husband came to see that
his children had, under the law, equal rights to his inher-
itance, he chose that they should have equal natural
rights; and from that moment *adultère* (adultery) became the real word,—that is to say, synonymous with crime
for the parents and with deprivation of rights for the
child.   That is how the nineteenth century came to take
seriously the word which the eighteenth had taken only
in joke; that is why Molière wrote " Georges Dandin,"
and I, " Antony."

The Nesle and Mailly families had arranged one of
these marriages in the persons of the two cousins whose
names and prefixes we have duly set forth.   Monsieur de
Mailly had left Avignon for that purpose, had come to
Paris, and married his fair cousin in about the same length
of time that Cæsar used in whipping the King of Pontus.
He came, he saw, and he conquered.

Madame de Mailly was a lovely young woman of some
seventeen or eighteen years.   I know that there has been
much discussion about her age; but we maintain that she
was born in 1710, that is to say, the same year as the
king.

We drew her portrait when Bannière was ushered into
her presence, and consequently have no need to draw it
now.

Monsieur de Mailly had known his cousin from child-
hood, so that it would have been difficult for any new
sentiment to be born of their closer union; they were
both young and both beautiful, and we are glad to believe that there was nothing positively distasteful to either
in their new estate.

But Monsieur de Mailly, accustomed as he was to
Olympe's gracious and delicate attentions, soon began to
draw comparisons between the wife he had taken and the
mistress he had deserted, entirely to the advantage of the
latter. In addition, Monsieur de Mailly had discovered
in his new wife a tendency to melancholy and to self-
absorption; one would have said that some strange
sentiment, which she was concealing from all others, and
from herself too, perhaps, was working at the bottom of
the young woman's heart, concealed in some dark invisible corner, and revealed its existence only by that sharp
sting which every partially stilled passion makes every
time that it awakes.

Now, as there was no criticism to be made upon Madame de Mailly's conduct, and as Monsieur de Mailly,
after carefully studying the tone of voice and the expression with which his wife talked, not only with those
friends whom he had introduced to her, but with all the
noblemen she met at court, had become convinced of
his wife's cold demeanor to all alike, he had decided that
she was naturally cold, and had not demanded of her,
despite his jealous disposition, any further assurances than
she had volunteered to give him.

But he found, nevertheless, that as Madame de Mailly's
husband, something was lacking of the happiness he had
known with Olympe.

Whenever his heart felt a breath of sadness, it turned
instinctively toward Olympe, and a sigh would wing its

way from Paris to seek that lovely being wherever she
might be.

At last he arrived at the stage of regretting her so
bitterly, and of missing her so seriously, despite all his
efforts to forget her, that he determined to make the
journey which all his sighs had made one after another,
and to do what his sighs had been unable to do, — bring
Olympe back to Paris.

But would he find Olympe free? Would she consent
to go with him? Would she consent to take up with
him again after he had deserted her? That was the
question, as Hamlet says.

But such questions propounded to a man's self-esteem
are soon answered. Where in the provinces could Olympe
find a cavalier sufficiently accomplished to make her
forget Monsieur de Mailly? In Paris itself, in whose
favor the regent had decentralized Versailles, — in Paris,
the very centre of beauty and fashion, Monsieur de
Mailly was esteemed a handsome and fashionable cavalier.
So of course Olympe could have found nothing equal to
what she had lost, and equally of course she must still be
sighing regretfully for those two happy years as Monsieur
de Mailly was himself sighing for them.

Now Olympe, being in such a frame of mind, and she
could be in no other, would regard his return as a piece
of great good-fortune, which she might long for but
would not dare to expect.

However, every contingency must be provided for, and
it might be that Olympe, in despair at his desertion, and
renouncing all hope of a dramatic career at Paris which
he and she had so often discussed, had made an engagement with some provincial manager; in that event the
engagement must be cancelled, — a very simple thing to do,
for an order to appear at the Comédie-Française over-
rode all other engagements.

Monsieur de Mailly procured such an order from the first gentleman of the chamber, and started for Lyons with it in his pocket.

Although he really counted upon Olympe's love and her fidelity to the souvenirs of the past, he was not sorry, by way of rekindling her love and confirming her in her fidelity, to present himself as her patron, and to arouse a feeling of gratitude in addition to the other sentiments which Olympe had doubtless preserved for him.

We have seen under what circumstances Monsieur de Mailly arrived at Lyons; how he had found Olympe in despair, and how in her despair she had given herself back to him.

Bannière's liberty was the result at least, if not the condition, of her return to her former allegiance, which had almost driven the poor boy mad when she bluntly announced it to him in his cell.

Monsieur de Mailly, then, had found Olympe, if not happy to go with him, happy to leave Lyons, and to seek in her work upon the stage, and the studying she would have to do, some distraction for that love for Bannière which she had believed to be destroyed by contempt, but which was in reality overshadowed for the moment by jealousy.

And what had happened? This: Olympe, after leaving Bannière, had discovered that she still loved him, and, after taking up with Monsieur de Mailly, had discovered that she cared nothing for him.

Thereupon, like a desperate woman who no longer believes in anything since she has lost her happiness, like an exile who cares for nothing since she has lost her country, Olympe had clung to the only passion which women still have when they no longer have aught to love.

She resumed her independence; and that to her meant the stage.

Thereupon Monsieur de Mailly, who had seen what was going on in her poor heart, had tried to keep Olympe entirely to himself by inducing her to abandon all thought of a dramatic career, and not to use the order to appear with which he had armed himself with contrary intent; but Olympe, wounded in the depths of her heart, and unable to hold any one responsible for the wound, had said, —

"Not to Bannière, nor to Monsieur de Mailly, but to everybody, — that is to say, to nobody."

Reminding the count of the order to appear of which he had spoken when he came to Lyons, she imperiously demanded that it should be put to some use.

The count could not refuse, and the result was Olympe's début in "Britannicus."

XLIX.

MONSIEUR DE MAILLY TAKES THE WRONG ROAD.

INSTEAD of taking note of Olympe's melancholy, and seeking for its real cause among the ideas, old or new, which ordinarily harass the other sex, Monsieur de Mailly, like all jealous men, allowed his own prejudices to run away with him.

He assumed a most gracious expression, and approaching Olympe with a jaunty air and a smile on his lips, he said, —

"Dear Olympe, you had a colossal success this evening."

"Do you think so?" said she, wiping the rouge from her cheeks.

"Moreover, my dear love, you acted the part to perfection."

"Ah!" said she, nonchalantly, "so much the better."

"Do you know," continued Mailly, "that people are talking of your talent?"

"Indeed?" rejoined Olympe, in the same tone; "and does that gratify you?"

"No, quite the contrary."

"What! quite the contrary! Why so?"

"Because there is nothing pleasant about it for me."

"What! there is nothing pleasant for you in my having talent, and people saying that I have?"

"No, indeed there is not."

"Ah! that requires explanation, do you know."

"It's very easy to explain."

"Go on and explain, then."

"Suppose one were jealous, for instance?"

"Oh, well, in that case one would be altogether in the wrong."

"That may be," retorted Mailly, archly, "but one would suffer none the less."

"Suffer?"

"Cruelly."

"Why, *you* are not jealous, are you?"

"I hardly know."

"Bah! Of what should you be jealous?"

"What! *Mon Dieu!* I know that you love me," said the count, with that extraordinary assumption of self-possession which always denotes an absolute lack of equilibrium.

Olympe turned her head, and made a face at her mirror, which in a woman less well-bred might have passed for a grimace.

The count had something else to think of, and saw neither Olympe nor the mirror nor the grimace.

"However that may be," he continued, "I am not entirely reassured."

"What must I do, Count, to bring you to that state of mind?"

"Ah, my good Olympe, certain things which, unhappily, you will not do."

"Oh, I can do many things," said she.

"But not things which you have already refused to do."

"Women are capricious," said she.

"So that I ought not to lay aside all hope?"

"You must agree, my dear Count, that I cannot know how to reply to that until I know what you are talking about. Is it one or several things which you desire?"

"When one desires a thing from you, Olympe, it is not worth while to be modest in one's desires."

"Well, begin."

"Where shall I begin?"

"With the most important or the most difficult to grant of all the things you wish. Take the bull by the horns, as they say."

"Well, dear Olympe, would you like to make me the happiest of men?"

"I ask nothing better."

"Leave the stage."

Olympe raised her head; in her look there was a restrained fire which made the count shudder.

"What!" said she, "you come to seek me at Lyons with an order for my début, you bring me back to Paris to make my début; now I have made it, and have scored a success, and you call upon me to leave the stage the self-same evening. If I were to do that, I should be mad; if you were to make me do it, you would be mad. Off the stage, I should bore myself and you to death; trust me, and do not insist upon this, for we should both lose too much."

Monsieur de Mailly chose to insist, nevertheless.

"But, dear Olympe," said he, "you know that this is not the first time."

"Very true; I know it is not the first time you have asked this of me, and I know also that it follows that it's not the first time I have refused you. Well, I beg that it may be the last, my dear Count."

"But —"

"Oh, enough of this!" said she; "if you insist upon this, Monsieur, it is evident that you have too little esteem for me."

"Alas! dear Olympe, on the stage opportunities are so frequent!"

" Opportunities for what ? "

" Why," stammered Monsieur de Mailly, startled by the cool manner in which she propounded this strange question, — " why, for being loved and falling in love."

" It is not for *my* ears, I think, that you intend what you have just said, Monsieur le Comte."

She fastened upon Monsieur de Mailly that piercing, terrible gaze which transfixes the heart, like a blade of steel.

He was somewhat overbearing by nature, and in addition he had some bad leaven in his heart that evening, the dear count.   His unlucky star urged him on too.

" My dear," said he, " allow me to protest against your grand airs."

" Why so ? "

" Because, unfortunately for me, it would not be the first time that you had seized one of these opportunities."

" I think you must be losing your mind, Monsieur le Comte," said Olympe.   " In this connection you do not refer to Monsieur Bannière, do you ? "

" Why, yes."

" Very well! it was you who made that opportunity, and I did accept it."

" You see, my good friend, it is a calamity to which I do not want you to be exposed henceforth."

" You are mistaken again, Monsieur le Comte. My friendship with Monsieur Bannière was in no sense a calamity for me; but it was most assuredly, on the other hand, a dire calamity for him."

The count saw that the conversation was becoming a duel.

He checked himself, but he was too late.

The wound, like a wasp's sting, was gradually spreading its poison through Olympe's veins.

"You are not willing to make this sacrifice for me?"
said the count.

"No, Monsieur."

"Once more I ask you."

"No."

"If I were to beg, to implore you?"

"It would be useless."

He sighed.

"Oh, *mon Dieu!*" he exclaimed; "I swear to you
that I have n't the least uneasiness. I know that you are
the noblest of women; but though your soul is noble, your
heart is capable of receiving impressions."

"Assuredly."

That word made Monsieur de Mailly shudder.

"You see," he said; "that is just what I dread."

"Oh!" said she, "when that time comes, be assured
that I will tell you of it."

Another blow for the poor fellow.

"Do you know that what you promise me, while very
loyal, is far from pleasant to think of, dear Olympe,"
said he, frowning; "for you admit the possiblity of
changing."

"One must admit the possibility of everything," said
Olympe, calmly.

"What! admit everything! Even that your affection
may change?"

"Do you know anything immutable in this world?"

"Well, admit it then; but I say that it is a great pity
that you will not give me the means of combating my
unhappy thoughts."

"I will grant everything except what you just asked
me."

"You will give up to me in everything except the
matter of the stage?" cried De Mailly, eagerly.

" In everything."

" Thanks.   I begin then."

" What are you going to do ? "

" I am going to pack up your jewels and give them to your maid."

" What for, pray ? "

" To be given to my servant, who will take them — "

" Where ? "

" To my little place in Rue Grange-Batelière."

" To your house ? "

" Where I beg you to come and take up your abode this evening."

Olympe opened her great eyes to their fullest extent, in wonder.

" But the suite I have hired ? " said she.

" It would very soon be invaded by the crowd of admirers whom you have created for yourself, while they will think a long while before coming to my house."

" So you condemn me to imprisonment ? "

" Almost."

She was silent for a moment.

" You hesitate ! " he cried.   " Oh, Olympe ! "

" *Dame !* a prison ! " she muttered.

" You said, *in everything.*"

" But a prison ! "

" We will gild the cage, my lovely hermit ; we will try to make you regret your liberty less than anything else."

" Liberty ! " murmured Olympe, with a sigh.

" One would say that you cling to it."

" Cling to it ! " she ejaculated.

" Ah, Madame," said the count, " there are bad days, and I have fallen upon one of them."

" What do you mean ? "

"I mean that I am unfortunate this evening, for I have discovered in you a tendency to frigidity of demeanor, when perhaps I had the right to expect something different."

Olympe, who had fallen into a profound revery, aroused herself suddenly, and said, shaking her head,—

"Come, let us not argue any more; it tires me. You ask me to leave the stage?"

"Oh, no, no, I don't dare."

"You ask me to leave the world, then, do you not?"

"I ask you to consent at least to go with me to my little house, which you know of, and to install yourself there with your women."

"Very well, it's agreed," said she, rising; "I am off for the little house."

"But reflect," the count began.

"Reflect! you tell me to reflect! Don't speak to me of that, Count. It's agreed, I said; but it is only on condition that I shall not reflect."

"I don't want to take you there under false pretences, Olympe. If I ask you to go there to live, it is because I wish to hide you."

"Agreed."

"It is because I wish to select the people who shall visit you."

"Agreed, agreed. Count, is it your pleasure that I should not go out at all? Count, is it your pleasure that I should not see a soul? Speak, command,— or no, do not speak, I will divine your wishes."

"Olympe, you enchant me and terrify me at the same time."

"Good! good! your arm, Count, and let's be off."

The count, transported with delight, put Olympe in his carriage, which was waiting at the actors' entrance, and told the coachman to drive to his little establishment on Rue Grange-Batelière.

Olympe said not another word; she looked, without seeing them, at the priceless objects which surrounded her, and which, Monsieur de Mailly told her, were all her own; then she sat down to supper, but ate nothing, smiled when the count spoke to her, but could not muster up a laugh. In short, she did her feverish utmost to retain an appearance of amiability until he had taken his leave.

When she was finally left alone, she dropped into a chair by the fire.

"Oh, how bored I am!" she said. A terrible word that, of which men never appreciate the full significance until it has done its work and produced its results.

Monsieur de Mailly, for his part, returned home very happy over his success in inducing Olympe to divorce herself from the excitement and noise of society. He had no suspicion, poor wretch! of the deadly enemy with whom he had left her face to face in his house on Rue Grange-Batelière.

"The battle was a hard one," he said to himself, "but the victory is mine, and I have her under my hand. The king shall not see her except at the theatre, and if he sees too much of her there, why, I will absolutely forbid her acting; my friends of the chamber will assist me."

Unhappy Monsieur de Mailly! he had sunk up to his knees in the quicksand of love, in which poor Bannière had been three quarters drowned.

L.

MONSIEUR DE RICHELIEU.

ON the evening of this noteworthy performance, throughout which the king followed so attentively the character
of Junie, as represented by Olympe, a momentous event
took place, which came very near destroying the striking
effect of the young monarch's appearance at the Comédie-
Française.

The news of this event fell like a bombshell among
the audience.

" Monsieur de Richelieu has returned from Vienna! "

In fact, about six in the evening, a heavily laden carriage drawn by four sturdy horses who seemed to have
adopted the gallop as their ordinary gait, passed the bar-
rier of La Villette, drove down Rue Saint-Denis to the
Boulevards, turned into Rue de Richelieu, and so into
the courtyard of a noble mansion on Rue Croix des
Petits-Champs.

The mansion stood between the courtyard and a
garden.

Hearing the noise made by the carriage, several servants with torches came running out. Some stood on
the porch, others rushed to the stepping-stone and opened
the door of the carriage, through which there hastily
stepped out a youngish man wrapped in a cloak of sable.
He acknowledged with a wave of the hand the salute of
his whole household, who ran to meet him, and cried to
the servant who had come with him, and had alighted

from the box: "Rafté, I am absolutely not at home to anybody except the person you know. I trust you to see that I am undisturbed."

Whereupon he entered the house and disappeared in the suite of apartments which had been made ready and heated beforehand, proving that the traveller's return was expected.

We have said enough to indicate that this traveller was Monsieur le Duc de Richelieu, who returned from his Viennese embassy in the early days of November.

It is with no purpose of offending the well-informed reader, who has followed out the court intrigues of the eighteenth century in the contemporaneous chronicles: nor is it to deserve the name of a prolix writer, that we pause here to sketch in few words the portrait of the then Duc de Richelieu, as well as several others, which were associated so closely with his, in 1728, that they seemed to be nothing more than its frame.

The Duc de Richelieu was then thirty-four; he was the handsomest man in France, as Louis XV., at eighteen was the handsomest youth. He had won notoriety by his adventures with the regent's daughter, with Mademoiselle de Charolais, Madame de Gacé, Madame de Villars, etc., etc., as well as by his threefold experiance of the Bastille as a place of abode, and by his mad antics generally; he had become a famous diplomatist, too, and had been accredited to the Emperor Charles VI., at Vienna, the object of his mission being to persuade that monarch to break off his alliance with the Queen of Spain, who advanced the claim that the crown of France should go to her family in case of the death of Louis XV.

This purpose was not easily accomplished. The Emperor Charles was a man endowed with a vast amount of cautious energy, which was little short of barbarism.

Moreover, the Austrian court was a terrible place for a man accustomed to the luxurious life of Paris, and its politics made a rough apprenticeship for one who had been trained to the frivolities of the Œil-du-Bœuf.

Vienna had, in European eyes, two claims to superiority which no one denied, — generals who had almost always whipped our generals, and diplomatists who had seldom failed to throw dust in the eyes of our diplomatists.

The Duc de Richelieu, who was capable of anything, even of a good action, as was said of him by the regent (that other man of shrewd intellect whose real worth was not appreciated until he was succeeded by the Duc de Bourbon), fulfilled his mission with honor, and returned from Vienna, as we have said, toward the beginning of the year.

To be sure, Prince Eugene's mistress had materially assisted him in all his diplomatic intrigues; like Ariadne, she had given him the ball of thread to help him out of the labyrinth of Schoenbrunn.

However little versed one may be in the *chronique galante* of the day, one can understand that as soon as his return became known, all Paris hastened to call upon him; whence the duke perceived that, even though he had been forgotten for two years, the poorest memories need only to be refreshed.

He alighted at his hotel, as we said at the beginning of this chapter, enjoining his people to allow no one to intrude upon him; and the order was observed with military strictness. It is well known that Monsieur le Duc de Richelieu was as well served as any nobleman in the realm.

Disappointment was visibly painted upon the faces of the inquisitive or affectionate friends who had hastened to come and knock at the great doors or the secret doors, on the street or on the passage-way in the rear.

For that evening the trusty servant of Monsieur de Richelieu stood on guard behind one of these secret doors, his ear on the alert, and his eye applied to a hole in the wall, near the hinge, taking careful note of all the sounds in the passage-way.

At last, after almost an hour of waiting, a hired carriage stopped not far from the garden-wall. A woman, whose shape and face were carefully concealed, alighted from it; whom by her quick gait, and her curious manner of dismissing the coachman, the servant recognized as the person whom he was told to look out for.

The snow was falling, and it was quite dark. No one was abroad in the neighborhood.

The servant opened the door he was guarding, before any knock was heard; and the young woman glided through the opening, and directed her steps across the garden, like one accustomed to the place.

When she reached the house, she fairly fell into the arms of the duke, who was standing at a door on the ground floor, and who embraced her affectionately, crying, —

"Ah, my lovely princess, you have come at last! I have been waiting so impatiently for you, and had abandoned all hope of seeing you again."

Princess in very truth; for this young woman who laughingly returned the duke's embrace, and placed her little hands in his with the utmost friendliness, was called Mademoiselle de Charolais, and was not only a princess, but a princess of the blood.

She made no other reply to the duke's apostrophe than a lover-like kiss. He led her then into a large room, luxuriously furnished, heated to the temperature of a beautiful spring day, the walls of which were hung with tapestry, whereon amorous shepherds and shepherdesses disported themselves amid flowers and verdure.

A table laid near the fireplace, two comfortable easy-chairs, a sideboard laden with porcelain, which was an extravagance seldom indulged in at this time, when the Pompadour cult had not risen above the norizon, and the soft radiance of the candles, inspired a feeling of general well-being, which made the manifest pleasure of the princess even more expansive.

"Now, Duke," said she, "before we sit down to supper, let me have a look at you."

She took her stand squarely in front of him.

"Look at me, Princess! what for, pray?"

"Why, so that I can be sure it's really you."

"Ah, Princess, your memory is not so good as mine, it seems."

"How so?"

"Because I recognized you at once."

"You don't think I have grown too plain?"

"You are still the loveliest of all princesses, born or to be born."

"But why don't you ask me how I think you are looking?"

"Oh! it's useless."

"Pshaw! why?"

"I don't count now; I am an Austrian, a savage, I have become accustomed to being looked at by the Germans. So give me time, Princess, to lay aside the air I have acquired; it will be a matter of a week or so, and when I have become a Frenchman, yes, a Parisian, again, I will come and stand between you and your mirror."

"So you think you have changed, do you?"

"Tremendously."

"You have become ambitious."

"'T is true, Princess."

"I was told so, but I would not believe it."

"Nevertheless it is the exact truth."

"Well, let us sup, shall we? You have already told me how love attacks young girls; and while we are at supper, you shall tell me how ambition attacks men."

"Believe me, I shall always be happy to teach you anything; but meanwhile, dear Princess, as you suggest, let us sup."

The princess took her place at the table.

"Do you know," said she, "that I have acquired an enormous appetite in two years?"

"For what, Princess?"

"Alas!"

"Oh, what a pitiful sigh!"

"To what do you attribute it?"

"To what does one usually attribute the female sigh?"

"To love, you mean?"

"Dame!"

"Well, you are in error, my dear Duke. I am not the least bit in love with anybody."

"You say that like one who would like to be still in love, or soon to become so."

"No, upon my honor!"

"Indeed?"

"You may believe me or not, as you choose; but in your absence — "

"Well?"

"I said 'adieu' to love."

The duke laughed aloud.

"You flatter me," she continued; "but you can't make that which has ceased to exist exist, or bring the dead to life."

"Ah, Princess, then you don't believe in ghosts?"

"What's the use of believing in them when they are only unsubstantial shadows?"

"Princess, there are ghosts which come from a greater distance than the other world, — from Austria, for example, — and which, I swear to you, are honest flesh and blood; and if you doubt it, Princess — "

"No, Duke, I never doubt a thing when you say it's so."

"Well, then — "

"Well, then, it doesn't change my decision. I shall never love again, Armand."

"And who is the wretch, the man abandoned by heaven and earth, who has inspired such a feeling as that in you?"

"The man? Why, have there been any men in France, Duke, since you went away?"

"Thanks, Princess."

"No, upon my word! I speak as I think."

"At least you will tell me the source of this aversion for the pain or the pleasure; for, as you know, true lovers are like true gamblers, and rank the pain of losing next to the pleasure of winning."

"Duke, there is neither pain nor pleasure at the bottom of my determination."

"But think of me. I return because I am bored to death there in Vienna; I perform prodigies of diplomacy in order to earn the right to return to France, and you come and tell me such things as that you are bored at Versailles!"

"Look! I have grown fat."

She held out a lovely arm to the duke, who pressed his lips upon it in a long kiss.

It was so long that Monsieur de Richelieu did not

just know how to end it, and Mademoiselle was interested to see how he would end it.

"How about the king?" he said at last, restoring
her captive arm to the princess.

She looked at him, and almost blushed.

"What! the king? What do you mean?"

"Oh, nothing; I simply meant to ask you about his
health."

"It's very good," said Mademoiselle de Charolais,
pronouncing the words in a curious tone.

"That 'very good' does not satisfy me."

"How must I say it, Duke?"

"I would like you to say it either more gayly or in
more sober fashion; in the former case it would sig-
nify a happy woman, in the latter a jealous one."

"Jealous! I? Jealous of whom?"

"Why, jealous of the king, of course."

"Jealous of the king! What induces you to say such
absurd things, Duke?"

"Oh, well! when the time does come, — and I sincerely hope that he will give you reason to be one or
the other —"

"I made happy or jealous by the king? I?"

"Princess, upon my word, one would say that I was
speaking Dutch."

"The fact is that I no longer comprehend you, my
dear Duke; have you heard nothing from France for two
years, pray? I imagined that ambassadors carried on a
regular correspondence, two indeed, — a public and a
secret correspondence, one dealing with politics and
one with the affections."

"Princess, I have not carried on two systems of
correspondence."

"No, you have had a hundred, I suppose."

"It's a fact that everybody, except you, has written to me."

"Then they have told you that the king — "

"That the king is handsome, yes."

"And that he is virtuous also ? "

"They have told me that; but as I know that Monsieur de Fréjus had all my letters opened, I did not believe a word of it."

"You were wrong."

"Why so ? "

"It is as true as the truth, Duke."

"What! that the king is virtuous ? "

"Yes."

"The king has no mistress ? "

"No."

"It's incomprehensible. Aha, Princess, I see, I understand."

The duke roared with laughter.

"What is it that you understand ? " said Mademoiselle de Charolais.

"*Pardieu!* You don't want to denounce yourself, and you wait for me to arrive with the proofs."

"Nonsense!"

"Take care!"

"My dear Duke, the king has not so much as looked at me for two years."

"Suppose you make oath to that."

"By our former affection, Duke!"

"Oh, I believe you, — for you loved me almost as much as I loved you, Princess."

"Those were happy days!"

"Alas! as you were just saying, we were young then."

"Come, come! we are relapsing into the dismals, Duke, and you seem to have an especially depressing effect upon me."

" How so ? "

" You make me out an old woman. "

" My mind was running on one subject, Princess. "

" What is that ? "

" If the king has no favorite, the court must be in terrible confusion. "

" My friend, it is simply chaotic. "

" It must be; for in that case Fleury governs France, and France is a seminary. "

" There are seminaries, Duke, which are places of wild dissipation compared to the France of to-day. "

" Naturally, when the king is virtuous, everybody else wants to be the same. "

" Duke, it is positively sickening. "

" The result must be a sort of overflow of virtue from the court into the streets, so that the people will be submerged. "

" Everybody has the disease now. "

" And the queen ? "

" In the queen virtue is carried to such a height that it has become absolute ferocity. "

" *Mon Dieu !* I will wager in that case that she dabbles in politics, poor woman ! "

" You have said it. "

" With whom, in Heaven's name ? "

" With whom do you suppose ? Certainly not with the king. "

" Why ? "

" My dear man, she is so virtuous that she is afraid of her husband turning lover. "

" Bah ! is some one advising her ? "

" Yes. "

" She has taken a tutor in politics, then ? "

" Yes; that is to say, she has kept the one she had. "

"And it is still — "

"It is the one who made her Queen of France; and there is nothing like the gratitude of these Poles, especially of the women."

"They are not like the French women, are they, Princess?"

"Oh, no!"

"So she is conspiring with Monsieur le Duc de Bourbon?"

"Precisely."

"Who is still one-eyed?"

"*Mon Dieu!* yes."

"And who is humpbacked too?"

"The fact is that his backbone is doubling up. I don't know whether it is caused by the weight of affairs of state."

"Ah! that cunning De Prie never wrote me a word of all this."

"Oho! so the De Prie wrote you at Vienna, did she?"

"To be sure."

"Then I don't know why you care to question me, Duke."

"Why, to learn something."

"When the De Prie has dealt with a subject, is there anything more to be learned about it?"

"Well, now, my dear Princess, you may not believe me — "

"I warn you that I shall not believe you."

"I swear to you — "

"An oath! that makes it all the worse."

"I swear to you that there is nothing more between the marquise and me than between yourself and the king."

Mademoiselle de Charolais shrugged her shoulders with an incredulous smile.

"Because you are just from Vienna, do you fancy I am just from Lapland?" said she.

"Go on, my dear friend," said the duke, seeing that it was quite useless to argue with the incredulity of the princess.

"What shall I go on with?"

"What you began to tell me. You were saying that the queen is conspiring with Monsieur le Duc de Bourbon?"

"Yes."

"To overthrow Fleury?"

"To overthrow Fleury."

"And why does she desire to overthrow Fleury?"

"Because Fleury is an old curmudgeon, and has kept her short of money. Speaking of money, do you, who are the friend of the De Prie, tell her, pray, that she has shown execrable taste in her protegée."

"What protégée?"

"Why, the Polish woman!"

"Oh, Princess, that poor queen, pity her; she is more to be pitied than blamed."

"But I do pity her more than you do yourself; I pity her particularly for having been made Queen of France by that scheming marquise."

"Upon my word, Princess, you amaze me when you say that you have been bored these last two years. When one hates as you do, there is always more or less amusement. Come, keep on the right side of the marquise, if it were only for Monsieur le Duc's sake."

"No, no, no, I loathe the very sight of the wretch; she made the queen queen."

"It was her right, since she was intrusted with the mission."

"Very good! but was it also her right to carry a trousseau to the poor princess, — to count her stockings, skirts, and petticoats, as if she were the laundress of a provincial bride ? "

" Listen, Princess, the marquise was Leblanc's daughter-in-law."

" Well, I am reconciled to you again, and I return to Monsieur de Fréjus."

" To our curmudgeon, that is."

" Knowing that the queen had no money, he sent Orry, the Comptroller-General, to her, endowed with full powers to negotiate a loan in the name of poor Marie Leczinska; and he represented to Monsieur de Fréjus that the poor princess was not in a condition befitting her lofty rank. Fleury admitted the justice of his remark, mingled his pity with that of the Comptroller-General, and took from his cash-box — for he has a cash-box, like Harpagon — "

" Took what ? "

" Guess."

" *Dame !* you say like Harpagon."

" Duke, cover your face; he took out a hundred louis! We are governed by a man who gives a hundred louis to a queen! You were that creature's ambassador at Vienna! "

" If I had known this feature of his character, I swear to you, Princess, that I would not have remained there twenty-four hours. What must he have said when he heard that at my formal entry I had the horses of my suite shod with silver, and my own with gold ? "

" Yes, and that you had so managed it that they were all without shoes when you arrived at your hotel."

" Let us return to Monsieur de Fréjus. You have no conception of my interest in what you tell me."

" Well, he took a hundred louis from his cash-box for the queen. Orry turned as red as a peony, and argued with the minister that her Majesty was in need of money.

"Fleury sighed.

"'If she really needs money,' said he, 'why, we must bleed ourselves;' and he added fifty louis to the hundred."

"Oh, that is n't possible!" cried Richelieu; "you 're romancing, Princess."

"Say that it seems incredible, and I am with you. But wait till I am done, I beg."

"There is more to come, then?"

"Orry's color changed from bright red to white; seeing which Monsieur de Fréjus suspected that he was going to complain again.

"'Oh, well,' said he, 'I will add another twenty-five louis, but she must not ask for any more for a month.'

"With that Harpagon closed his cash-box."

"One hundred and seventy-five louis!"

"Twenty-five less than I used to give your servant, Duke, when he brought me a note from you on New Year's Day."

Richelieu bent his head politely.

"Princess," said he, "I must confess that while I have been away most unearthly things have happened. So the queen is in a rage with Monsieur de Fréjus?"

"A furious rage."

"Well, well! won't she turn the king against him?"

"Just fancy, Duke; on the other hand it is Monsieur de Fréjus who is trying to turn the king against her!"

"What, the virtuous bishop!"

"I tell you that it is an abomination!"

"And the desolation will follow, Princess; don't dream of doubting it. So there is criticism below and aloft?"

"Everywhere."

"Are there Fréjusians and Bourbonians?"

"In battle array! The guns are loaded and the matches alight."

"Then this is the contention,—to get the king in subjection by some means or other?"

"Exactly."

"And Monsieur de Bourbon and Monsieur de Fréjus are both seeking this means?"

"You have hit the mark."

"Monsieur le Duc by trying to maintain the queen's influence?"

"He will not succeed."

"You think so?"

The princess put her mouth close to Richelieu's ear.

"The king has been complaining for a week," said she, "that the queen has kept herself secluded."

"Oh, the poor king!" said the duke, bursting into laughter; "does Monsieur de Fréjus know it?"

"Of course he does."

"And he, more clever than Monsieur de Bourbon, is thinking, no doubt, of placing some new star in the sky?"

"What did you mean, pray, by saying that you knew nothing of what was going on? *Tudieu!* what a diplomatist you are!"

"Surely, dear Princess, I shall never go astray about Monsieur de Bourbon, so long as I have the same opinion of him that I have always had."

"What has been your opinion?"

"That he was an idiot."

"Why?"

"Because the queen is alive."

"Oh! but the king is very virtuous, Duke."

"There you go again, Princess. Oh, don't make me so suspicious."

"Of whom and of what?"

"Of you and of beauty."

"Where do I come in, Duke?"

"Princess, Monsieur de Bourbon is on the watch, Monsieur de Fréjus is on the watch; while I, just returned from Vienna, have found without watching at all."

"Found what?"

"The means."

"It is——"

"It is you! The king must fall in love with you, my dear Royal Highness, and he must be guided by your superior wisdom."

"Oh, Duke!"

"Well, then, what have you to say? Something prudish?"

"Pshaw!"

"Come, doesn't the bait of governing the kingdom offer some allurement? Do you object to making the fortune of your old friends?"

"It isn't that; but——"

"Isn't it true that among all the women by whom his Majesty is surrounded, you are the one most capable of inspiring in him the desire to be ruled with a loving hand? In short, Princess, make the attempt. What makes you hesitate?"

"Frankly now, aren't you joking?"

"I? Oh, the idea!"

"Did no one write you anything at Vienna?"

"About what?"

"Have you heard nothing since your return?"

"About whom?"

"About me."

"No," said the duke, with the most innocent expression.

"Well, Duke, the same idea occurred to me as to you."

"Really? And why did you renounce it?"

"I did not; quite the contrary."

"What! Did you put it in execution?"

"So far as it depended upon me, yes, Duke."

"And—"

"And I was repulsed."

"You, repulsed! Impossible!"

"It is, as I have the honor to inform you, however, my dear Duke; and I tell you this, because I prefer you should hear it from me rather than from somebody else. After all, perhaps my failure was due to one thing in particular."

"Don't ask me to divine what it was, Princess; I give it up at once."

"I am going to tell you."

"Say on."

"I was in love with the king."

"You, Princess!" cried Richelieu. "Oh, what a mistake!"

"*Mon Dieu!* yes, I was, Duke, and that took away all my power."

"I understand; you seated yourself in a corner, and sighed, waiting for him to look at you, and—he did n't look at you."

"No, I did n't do just that, Duke. I scribbled off a verse or two, passable enough. I wrote them out in my best hand, which the king knows almost as well as you do, and I slipped them into the king's pocket."

"A declaration?"

"Something like it, upon my word! It ought to be worth something to be a princess of the blood."

"True, she may select her own partner for the dance.

Oh, what a pity that your memory is not good, Princess!"

"Why?"

"You could recite your verses to me; and we would decide whether they were as good as mine, or Rafté's rather."

"Impertinent!"

"Who wrote yours, Princess?"

"Myself."

"Then you ought to remember them."

"I rather think that I do remember them; if they had done any good, I would have forgotten them."

"I am listening, Princess."

"Here goes: —

> Vous avez l'humeur sauvage,
> Et le regard séduisant."[1]

"Ha, ha!" laughed the duke. "Arouet himself does no better."

"Let me go on, then."

"I should be very sorry to stop you on such a fine road."

The princess continued: —

> "Se pourrait-il qu'à votre âge
> Vous fussiez indifférent?"[2]

"And he was indifferent to such poesy?"

"Just wait till the end, Duke! the point is at the end, as they say."

"Let's see the point."

> "Si l'amour veut vous instruire —"

"Oho! that's very tempting!"

[1] You have a savage disposition and a fascinating expression.
[2] Is it possible that one so young as you can be indifferent?

" But he did n't allow himself to be tempted.

> Cédez, ne disputez rien,
> On a fondé votre empire
> Bien longtemps après le sien."[1]

" Oh, my Princess, that was altogether admirable, superb. And did not the king, when he found such verses in his pocket and recognized your handwriting, fall at your feet? "

" He was too young."

" Let it go at that, then, Princess. And now? "

" Oh, now it's another matter altogether. I would not write such verses now."

"Why not? "

" Because I am no longer in love, and because I would not for anything in the world make a downright declaration to a man whom I care nothing for. That is why I have no chance of success with the king, who absolutely requires to feel real affection himself, and to be able to inspire a similar sentiment."

" Come, come, come, that's a woman all over, dear Princess, to talk like that."

" No, it's perfectly true."

" Well, that's what I mean."

" It strikes you as it does me, then? "

"I am convinced."

" You renounce your project, Duke? "

" No, but I will seek a more efficacious instrument."

" What do you propose to do with your humble servant? "

" You? Oh, I beg you to consider yourself still my friend."

---

[1] If love desires to give you lessons, yield to him, do not resist. Your empire was not founded till long after his.

"A truce to pleasantry, Duke; I really mean that I am done with love."

"What! nothing but friendship at your age?"

"Duc, you still have a week of Austrian manners to get rid of; you said so yourself. Go about it, pray! I am a Parisienne, I tell you."

"Good!"

"We are friends?"

"Good, good!"

The princess rose, and toasted her little feet before the fire; the duke then ordered a carriage to be ready at the end of the street, and himself escorted Mademoiselle de Charolais to the carriage, — both, like Paul and Virginia, wrapped in the same cloak.

"Duke," said the princess, "a week from now you will know all the news, and I shall be little better than a savage compared with you. If you hear anything which will interest me, come and tell me; you know the way."

"Is it open?"

"Too open, alas!"

With these words they parted. The princess entered the carriage. Richelieu waited until it was out of sight, and returned to the house, much embarrassed by what he had learned this first night at Paris.

His servant handed him a list of twenty-seven women whom he had turned away on account of that useless princess.

"Bah!" said he, as he buried himself luxuriously in his well-warmed bed, "this is the politician's night; to-morrow I shall have the ideas of a cardinal."

As the clocks struck twelve, he went to sleep.

LI.

MADAME DE PRIE.

RICHELIEU had fallen asleep thinking of all the fair dames who had been denied admittance, and wondering which of them would do most, as the king's favorite, to help him to acquire the political influence which was a necessity to him now that he had become ambitious.

If reflections of this sort are not enough to deprive a diplomat of thirty-four of his sleep, they may at least give him agreeable dreams.

Thus, toward one in the morning, — about an hour, that is, after he had gone to bed, — and just as the multitude of pleasant thoughts he had been revolving in his brain were beginning to lose their distinctive colors and become mingled together in the mezzotints of sleep, he fancied that he was really asleep and dreaming.

In his dream he heard something that seemed like a persistent voice in front of the garden window of the room on the first floor where he was lying.

A man's voice denying, and a woman's voice insisting; in short, the voices of a man and woman quarrelling.

It also seemed to the Duc de Richelieu as if the tones of the female organ were not strange to hear, and its every vibration evoked delightful memories.

So he yielded to the charm of this alluring dream, and desired to follow it to the end. Has it never happened to you, dear Madame, to form the desire, even during your sleep, to make those delightful dreams which you sometimes dream last as long as possible ?

The will is such a beautiful and powerful faculty. It comes to us so directly from God, the all-beautiful and all-powerful, that, even when we are asleep, it sometimes produces similar effects.

So the duke left only one ear awake, and with that ear he listened.

"No, Madame," said the male voice, "you can go no farther; it is quite enough for you to have forced, how I'm sure I don't know, the door of the old courtyard. In truth, Madame, things are not done in that way now."

"Villain!" thought the duke, still convinced that he was asleep.

"Whether I did or did not force the door of the old court," retorted the penetrating female voice, "I am in the house, am I not?"

"You undoubtedly are, but by a trick."

"I am here at all events, no matter how I got here; half of the task is done. Now let me see the duke."

"Impossible, Madame. Monsieur le Duc retired an hour ago, very tired from his journey, and he is asleep."

"Look! here's something to make a noise with; wake him."

The duke heard the musical sound of an indefinite number of gold pieces shaken together in a purse.

"Oho!" muttered the duke, still dreaming, "she is giving money to my servant. A pretty piece of business! the rogue's place is a good one."

"But, Madame," replied the obstinate lackey, who was determined to sustain his master's reputation as a favorite with the weaker sex, "Monsieur is not alone."

The duke sighed, stretched out his legs and arms as if to assure himself of his solitude, and murmured the word. "Scoundrel!"

"Well, what difference does that make?" continued the female voice. "I am not here to interfere with his love affairs; I have business to discuss with him. Come, boy, open, open!"

"But Monsieur le Duc forbade me—"

"Because he did not know that I was coming."

"Madame, I swear to you that he will wake up and overhear us, and that he will order me to show you the door,—which would be very discourteous on his part, while my entreaty to you not to insist is only in pursuance of my orders."

"That infernal lackey talks very well," said the duke from beneath his eider-down coverlet. "Now let's see what reply the lady will make. Ah!"

"On the other hand," she replied, "I am willing to wager that Monsieur le Duc will not dismiss me, especially if I give my name."

"Madame, take the thing on yourself, and knock on the window."

"No, no," replied the voice; "I don't want to take my hand out of my muff; it's freezing cold."

"*Diantre!*" thought Richelieu; "she must be a great lady, to be so afraid of the cold. Why doesn't she give her name at once? And upon my word, if she is pretty, I will agree with her about the weather."

"Come, boy, knock," continued the unknown female; "knock, and I will say that I did it."

"Madame, I will do it, since you force me to; but I would like to know your name."

"So would I," said Richelieu.

"Why so? If I tell it to your master, isn't that enough?"

"No, Madame; for if my master discharges me for this, you will owe me some compensation."

"That is no more than right, and you are a sharp boy. Compensation! See, here is something on account of what I shall owe you."

"More bribery!" muttered the duke; "this creature is determined to see me. Such things only happen in dreams."

"Now," said the servant, "I only need one thing more."

"What is that?"

"To know your name."

"Ah, Monsieur Rafté, you will end by irritating me."

"You see, Madame! since you know my name, I am entitled to know yours."

"Well, then, the Marquise de Prie —"

And at the same moment a vigorous blow was struck upon the duke's shutters.

"Madame de Prie!" cried Richelieu, pulling his head out from under the bed-clothes. "What! Did I dream that? Did I dream that Madame de Prie, Monsieur de Bourbon's mistress, was in my garden, wrangling with Rafté about five degrees of frost? A charming dream!"

At that moment another blow, followed by several more, quick and impatient, shook the long window.

"Why no, I was not dreaming after all; they are really knocking!" cried the duke.

"Duke! Duke! open!" cried the female voice, hoarse with the cold, aided by some little irritation.

"Open!" cried the duke, jumping out of bed and into his stockings and a dressing-gown which was at hand.

The servant entered the room.

"Where's the marquise?" said the duke, eagerly.

"Here I am, Duke," said Madame de Prie, appearing on the threshold. "Are you out of bed?"

"Yes, Madame, at your service. Lights, Rafté, lights!"

"What! dressed already!" said Madame de Prie.

"Ay, ay!" said the duke.

"You heard me, then?"

"Yes, and recognized your voice."

"After all, Duke, you're not such a fop as they say."

"Why?"

"Because a fop would not have got up."

"You forget, Marquise, that I have been away two years. But be seated, pray! Fire, Rafté, fire; don't you see that the marquise is shivering, my friend?"

"It would appear that after midnight the house is so full that you are obliged to use the garden for a ladies' reception-room," said the marquise, jokingly.

"On the contrary, Marquise, I was expecting you."

"Yes, sound asleep."

"Is it not thus that one awaits good fortune?"

"Oh, delightful, Duke!"

The marquise took the easy-chair which Richelieu offered her. Richelieu assumed one of his most graceful attitudes, and both began to laugh. The fire blazed up, and Rafté went out.

"Ah, Marquise," said the duke, "do you know that one o'clock has struck?"

"Yes, and it's cold enough to split the rocks."

"Was Monsieur de Bourbon's fire out, that you come here?"

"Upon my word, Duke, it was absolutely necessary that I should speak to you first."

"Pardon me, but how did you succeed in getting in? Just now, when I was half-awake and half-dreaming, I thought I heard either you or Rafté speak of a door that you had forced."

"Forced, no; opened, yes."

"How was that, Marquise?"

"Why, with a key of course!"

"What! you have a key to my house, and I go tranquilly to sleep exposed to such danger?"

"Why, Duke, you gave me one in the old days, if I remember aright."

"Yes, so I did; but I thought that you had returned it."

"What a cruel memory he has!"

"I should think so, — a statesman! However, whence got you that key? You understand, Marquise, that I ask you the question for my own satisfaction."

"Yes, there might be a factory devoted to making them. Indeed, that would not be a bad speculation."

"Marquise, you terrify me."

"Don't be alarmed; this key —"

"Well?"

"Came to me from a less honest source. It is not a false key, but a real one."

"But where did you get it?"

"Two years ago, before you left for Vienna, you gave several of them around in Paris."

"Yes; but how do you think that I could conceive of a woman of our days keeping an absentee's key two whole years, — unless indeed she had put it in her Massbook and forgotten it?"

"Ah! there's where you are in error, Duke; we have become very devout, you see. Piety is fashionable. Oh, there have been vast changes in Paris since you went away; you left Monsieur le Regent at the Palais-Royal, and you return to find Monsieur de Fréjus at Versailles."

"All this does n't answer my question as to where you fished up that key; and unless you stole it from some one —"

"Stole it! For shame! You treat me like a princess of the blood, my dear Duke; you take me for Mademoiselle de Valois or Mademoiselle de Charolais. Stole it! For shame! I bought it."

"Bought it! Oho! Who sold it to you?"

"A lady's-maid who didn't know what she was selling. You understand: one sees a key on the floor, takes possession of it, and no one knows anything about it; by and by along comes some one who gives twenty-five louis for it. If the mistress asks for it, one looks astonished and says, 'What key, Madame?' It's tempting for a soubrette."

"And then, too, as you say, Marquise, the key of a man who is at Vienna. Aha! people must have thought seriously that I should never return from Vienna."

"Yes; everybody except me, who, in my capacity of Minister of Foreign Affairs, knew that you were on the way home."

"Of course."

"Therefore I acquired possession of the famous key, thinking that you would not have your locks changed until the day after your return. That was a clever calculation, was it not?"

"Very accurate, as you see."

"So that the key will be worth to me, I hope, a little more than it cost me. But it is strange, Duke—"

The marquise drew in three or four long breaths through her nose.

"What is it?" asked Richelieu.

The marquise continued the process noted above.

"I can smell a woman here," she exclaimed.

"Nonsense! I am alone."

"I tell you that there is a woman here whose perfumery I am acquainted with."

" Marquise — I swear — "

" It 's a princess's perfumery."

" Ah! you flatter me, Marquise."

" Coxcomb! he is the same as ever."

" So are you, Marquise; only you improve every day."

" Yes; at least, that is what my flatterers will tell me so long as I am in favor."

" And you are now at the very top notch of favor, Marquise."

" I think so, and I have come to prove it to you."

" Ah, let us have the proof! "

" But first of all, Duke, be frank with me. Have you any one here ? "

" No one."

" Upon your honor ? "

" Faith of Richelieu! You hesitate ? "

" Duke, if it were of love affairs that I have to speak to you, I would take your word in a moment; but as we are going to talk politics, and in politics the least indiscretion may be fatal, permit me to do as Saint Thomas did."

" *Vide pedes, vide manus* (Behold my feet and my hands !) "

" You say that to make me think that you are a Latin scholar."

" God forbid that I should make any such claim! "

" Well, then, prove what you say."

" Marquise, I will take the candlestick, and we will explore every nook and corner of my apartments; will that satisfy you ? "

" If you please, Duke."

" Shall we begin with the fireplace ? But there 's a fire there; you hardly suspect that anything is hidden there, I fancy ? "

"Unless it should happen to be a princess of the blood; those ladies are as incombustible as salamanders."

"Why might one not say as much of the princes of the blood, Marquise?" said Richelieu.

The marquise smiled at the hit.

"Let us examine first the space between the bed and the wall," said she.

"It's empty," said Richelieu; "go and look."

"The trunk-closets."

"Empty, empty, empty. Do you wish to look under the coats?"

"Useless; if any one were there, we should see the legs."

"There's the secret stairway."

"Useless. The bolts are thrown, and the hall is not heated; while we have been talking a lady of quality would have frozen to death, and consequently would have ceased to be dangerous to me."

"Well reasoned!"

"As we are alone, let us talk."

"Let us talk," echoed the duke, leading the marquise back to her chair.

LII.

THE POLITICS OF MADAME LA MARQUISE DE PRIE.

The marquise resumed her seat, and the duke leaned upon the back of her chair.

"Marquise, my dear Marquise," said he, taking her hand, "if you knew how much I regret that your bad temper compelled me formerly to ask you for the key."

"Why?"

"Because if you had cared for me, to-day, after two years of separation, we should be mad with love for one another."

"Duke, I came to talk business. Come, let my hand go; time flies."

"As you please, Marquise."

And the duke retained her hand.

"I was telling you — "

"That you are more in favor than ever."

"Does that surprise you?"

"Well, yes, it does."

"How so?"

"On account of the bitter warfare which old Fleury seems to be waging against Monsieur le Duc."

"We are giving him as good as he sends, thank God!"

"He has the king on his side, Marquise, and you know that when they deprive the king of his old preceptor, he weeps and shrieks."

"Yes; but we have on our side the queen, and when they deprive the king of the queen — "

"Look out, Marquise. They say that the queen is turning very virtuous,— too virtuous, in fact,— and that the king is beginning to fear her more and to love her less."

"Ah, they have told you that?"

"They have told me more than that."

"What then?"

"They have told me that Louis XV. has begun to live apart from her, — an entirely new thing."

"It is true."

"Very well! So it seems to me, Marquise, that you are leaning upon a broken reed in the person of the queen, — a queen who, as the king says, keeps herself secluded."

They both laughed at this; but in the midst of her hilarity the marquise, looking at the duke with the expression of one who proposes to deal a decisive blow, said to him, —

"My dear Duke, do you know why the king is living apart from her?"

"*Dame!* because he prefers to."

"Do you know why the queen keeps herself secluded?"

"Because it suits her to do so, I suppose."

"Well, no, not exactly; it's because she is *enceinte*, Duke."

Richelieu started at this intelligence, and uttered an exclamation which showed the marquise how deeply interested he was in it.

"Ah, very good!" said he, after a pause.

"You can understand, Duke," continued Madame de Prie, "that with a dauphin in the world, our fortune is secure; let the queen once be a mother, and she will assume the demeanor befitting her rank. Already her character is very serious; she has admirable ideas, and she is ambitious, — I should say, rather, thoroughly saturated with ambition."

"By whom, Marquise."

"Oh, play the know-nothing, do! Look here! is Vienna so far from the Duchies of Bar and Lorraine that you do not know how eager Stanislas is to have a hand in managing our affairs?"

"I understand you, Marquise, and I think it may well be that you are right."

"You do think so, don't you? And I at once thought of you as one whom we must have among our friends."

"I trust I am already in that category, Marquise."

"Oh, of course! but I am speaking of friends of another variety, — political friends."

"May I be one of them?"

"Oh, it depends entirely upon yourself."

"Tell me something of your plan."

"It is this: evidently Monsieur de Fréjus means to monopolize everything."

"Even to the cardinal's hat; yes, it's very plain."

"And to disgrace Monsieur le Duc?"

"And to disgrace Monsieur le Duc."

"To effect that he must have two sources of influence: first, the king himself, — he has him; secondly, some one who governs the king. Would it not seem to you the proper thing, morally speaking, that this domination over the king should be wielded by the queen, — by the wife over the husband?"

"It would indeed be a most exemplary moral spectacle, Marquise."

"We must hold fast to morality in every possible way."

"I suggest that you make use of immoral means, Marquise."

"Why, my dear Duke, the king is as virtuous as a girl."

"Agreed, Marquise. But girls have been known to cease to be virtuous. Indeed we see instances of it every day; nothing is more common."

"The queen will keep him in the straight path; we must combine to support her."

"Nothing easier. All we have to do is — "

"To surround the king with good examples, instead of parading all sorts of sin before him. You would never imagine the inventions of that abominable old priest to fill the poor little prince's mind with such ideas as best suited his schemes. I declare that it is sickening to me."

"*Dame!* in his place would I have done the same? No, no! I would have sent the king another preceptor, and I would have selected you to make his lessons delightful to him."

"Now, you 're joking again instead of talking seriously. And yet, my dear Duke, it 's worth while under the circumstances."

"Yes, Marquise, yes; I see your plan. You wish to make the court of the present king while he is in the bloom of youth what the old king's court became when he was in his dotage: thus Louis XV. will be Louis XIV., the queen, Madame de Maintenon; Monsieur le Duc will play the rôle of Le Tellier, and you will be Père La Chaise, — is n't that it?"

"Almost, omitting the ennui and the old age."

"Well, well, Marquise, you must be relying upon a twofold conversion on my part, to make such propositions as this to me."

"I rely upon you because you have really changed. I rely upon you because you have been too frivolous not

to become serious, because you have compromised your
reputation too often not to be discreet at last."

"Marquise, dictate to me what I must do."

"I will do so, and will also give you a glimpse of your
prospective emoluments."

"I am listening and looking."

"You must appear at the queen's card-party to-morrow.
What do I say? To-morrow means to-day, as it is half-
past two in the morning."

"Very well; it was my purpose, Marquise."

"You will make a sensation."

"To tell you the truth, I rather expect I shall."

"I don't know whether the queen cares much for
you?"

"I can relieve your uncertainty on that point. I know
that she doesn't care for me at all."

"You must try to bring her to a better opinion of you;
everything is easy for you, if you only choose."

"I will try. She is a Pole, and I will be a German,
which is about the same thing."

"Good! Once on good terms with the queen, you
will praise her perfection to the king; by so doing you
will soon make friends with the king, Duke."

"Yes, if I amuse him."

"Oh, you'll amuse him."

"To do so morally, you see, is difficult."

"He is passionately fond of hunting, in the first
place."

"Very good; but he doesn't hunt all the time, especially at night."

"He is fond of gardening."

"Yes, I know that Monsieur de Fleury taught him to
dote on plants and lettuce, and that he likes to watch
them grow and wither. As for myself, I could never

bring myself to the point of digging in the ground and
killing the caterpillars on lettuce. It would need a fourth
sojourn in the Bastille to induce me to raise violets, notwithstanding the example of the great Condé."

"You can tell him stories."

"I don't know any now."

"Invent some, then."

"You see, Marquise, there are only three things on
earth which never fail to divert crowned heads."

"What are they ? "

"Look at Louis XIV.; there was a king who in his
youth was never bored, but was so well entertained all
the time that when he grew old, nothing under heaven
would amuse him. Well, Louis XIV. loved these three
things, — women, war, and extravagance."

"Oh, Duke! Duke! "

"You will tell me that the queen is too jealous to
allow him to speak to a woman, too tender-hearted to
allow him to go to war, and too economical to allow him
to spend money as he chooses."

"Do you think so ? "

"To be sure I do. Doesn't this worthy princess
ordinarily ask before buying anything, 'How much does
this cost ? ' "

"She asks, 'How much *does* it cost ? ' because Fleury
invariably asks, 'How much *did* it cost ? ' "

"Never mind; I have spoken none the less like an
oracle."

"Your deduction from all this ? "

"Is that it will be very difficult for me to guide the
king, Marquise."

"Ah, *dame !* doubtless it will if you create difficulties
as you go along; if you don't choose to deal with each
one according to his or her character; if you refuse to

see that Louis XV. is naturally inclined to virtue, and that everything about him savors of the worthy bourgeois, who thinks of nothing but having a family to be a good father to; if, in short, you measure the king with your own yardstick. Ah, Duke! Duke! everybody does n't deserve a taste of the Bastille at seventeen."

"Good! now you 're insulting me."

"What! on the contrary, I am only too flattering; come, no more resistance, and above all no more paradoxes."

"I bend, Marquise."

"Then you consent to be on the queen's side ?"

"I will tell the king that she is the most entertaining of women."

"And you agree to amuse the king ? "

"Yes, if you do not limit me in the class of amusements."

"I limit you to conjugal love, that 's all."

"Oh, no, Marquise, that 's barred; that 's your business, not mine. A man can always play at virtue with women, — that 's good form; but with men it 's rank hypocrisy. Strike that off the list, Marquise, strike it off."

"Then you don't care to become minister of state, or to be sent to Flanders some fine morning to assume the baton of a marshal of France ? "

"Bah! if it ever rains that sort of merchandise, Marquise, I promise you that I shall be one of the first to stand under the gutter."

"Well, what must be must, and I turn the king over to you; don't corrupt his morals, that 's all that I ask of you.

"I promise that, and now for something to bind the bargain, Marquise."

"Duke, you will undervalue the importance of the negotiation if it is paid for in advance."

"You are a perfect demon of wit and grace, Marquise."

"Oh, don't pretend to sigh, Duke! You know very well that you care nothing for me any more. I am a woman in politics, and you would find no charm in my affection now, for I am all for the main chance. I am of no use to any one except pages who want to become ensigns and make their fortunes with my consent. Let us return to our conclusions."

"Very well. First."

"First, you will come to the queen's card-party this evening."

"Yes, Marquise."

"Second, you will reinstate yourself in her good graces."

"It's as good as done."

"Third, you will join forces with us against Monseigneur the Bishop."

"That is in accordance with my inclination."

"Fourth, you will worm your way into the king's favor."

"I have no need to promise to do what I can in that direction; it is my most earnest desire."

"Fifth, you will leave the king virtuous as he is, you will do nothing to corrupt him, you will put aside all suggestions of giving him a mistress."

"I promise neutrality, if the king exhibits no inclination that way."

"Never fear, I will answer for that."

"Very well, Marquise! and now?"

"What?"

"On your side, what undertakings do you enter into? There is no contract, you know, unless there are two contracting parties and mutual consideration."

"On our side, we bind ourselves —"

" First — "

" Oho! you want an undertaking in several articles, do you? "

" Why not? "

" So be it; first, to give you within the year whatever embassy you select, or a minister's portfolio. "

" The latter also to be selected by myself? "

" Yes, provided you don't select Monsieur le Duc's. "

" Of course, — honor to whom honor is due. "

" Oh, it would not be the first time that you have laid your hand upon what belongs to him. "

" You confess it yourself, Marquise. "

" Second, " said she, quickly.

" I am listening. "

" Second; to appoint you lieutenant-general at the first opportunity, and marshal at the second. "

" How much time do you ask to fulfil these engagements? "

" Let us say two years, if you please. "

" It 's very short, take care! "

" Oh, no! Fleury will die with rage in less time than that, — with rage or age, as you choose. "

" I prefer rage; it 's surer. "

" With rage, then, so be it. Your hand, Duke! "

" Why, Madame, for an hour I have been holding them both out to you. "

" Come, kiss me, — I have no rouge, — and adieu! "

She rang quickly.

Rafté appeared.

" Marquise, Marquise, " said the duke, in an undertone; " this has an air of hostility. "

" Now do you want me to tell you something? " said she, standing at the door.

" Say on. "

"Well then, Duke, if you are as well-disposed toward us as I have been ill-disposed toward you for the last hour, Monsieur de Fleury will be under our feet within a month."

She pressed his hand with the tips of her saucy pink fingers, gave him a last glance overflowing with mischievous coquetry, and darted into the garden, dragging behind her Rafté, who could hardly keep up with her rapid step.

"The devil!" mused Richelieu, alone once more, "I am very curious now to know what proposals Monsieur de Fréjus has to make to me."

LIII.

A NOCTURNAL ADVENTURE.

MADAME DE PRIE had scarcely taken ten steps toward the carriage which was waiting in the distance, and which drove toward her as she left the garden, and Rafté, who was watching her to guard against accidents, was about to close the door, when three men came running along the passage at full speed, and threw themselves violently against the door, like three rabbits trying to get into the same burrow.

Rafté tried to hold the door against them, but their three strengths united were too much for his. He saw that he was going to be beaten, and beat a parley.

The tallest of the three men replied that there was no time to talk, the negotiation might be prolonged; and therefore he summoned the garrison to allow him and his companions to enter peaceably, or they would force their way in.

"But, Messieurs! but, Messieurs!" cried the servant.

"'But' as much as you choose! The patrol are after us, and we have no desire to go to the guard-house."

"So much the more reason to keep you out, Messieurs; if the patrol are after you, you must be law-breakers, Messieurs. I will call for help!"

"Devil take you, triple idiot!" said the same man who had already spoken; "for whom do you take us, in God's name?"

"Oh, thieves dress very well sometimes."

The patrol were on the way; they could be heard rapidly approaching.

"Come," cried the smallest and probably the youngest of the fugitives, for his voice seemed almost boyish, — "come, force your way in, Messieurs!"

This voice imparted so much courage to the other two that they speedily entered the garden over the body of Richelieu's man-servant.

The tallest of the three men at once attended to the secure fastening of the door; while Rafté, in a state of bewilderment, rose from the ground and ran off as fast as his feet would carry him toward the house, muttering as he ran, —

"Is it possible, *mon Dieu!* is it possible?"

He entered the duke's chamber just as that gentleman had got into bed again, and was trying to go to sleep.

Rafté entered the room, we said; we made a mistake, he hurled himself through the door.

"Well, well! what's the matter now?" the duke demanded.

"Oh, Monsieur, Monsieur!"

"What has happened?"

"Such an adventure as never falls to the lot of any one but you, Monsieur."

"Has the queen come to call on me, by chance?"

'Better than that, Monsieur, better than that; at least I think so. Dress yourself quickly, Monsieur; dress yourself."

"Oh, pshaw! must I?"

"Yes, hurry up, Monsieur le Duc, hurry up!"

The duke leaped out of bed as he would have done in case of a night attack in a campaign.

"In full dress, Monsieur!" said Rafté; "in full dress, Monsieur."

"Explain yourself, will you, villain ? "

"Monsieur, there are three of them."

"Suppose there are! Do you think you know them ? "

"Masked, Monsieur, masked! "

"Oho! the balls at the Opera have begun, I believe; but where are these three ? "

"In the courtyard, Monsieur, in the courtyard."

"They forced the door, then ? "

"Yes, Monsieur."

"And you allowed them to do it ? "

"I resisted then, Monsieur; but they passed over my body."

"Did they, indeed! Give me a gun, then! "

"Oh, Monsieur, don't dream of such a thing! "

"Why not ? Three men force my door and ill-treat my servant at two o'clock in the morning, and — "

"Monsieur, among these three men there is a certain voice — "

"A woman's voice ? " asked Richelieu, eagerly.

"Monsieur, I can say no more, lest I seem an idiot in Monsieur's eyes, if I am mistaken."

"Very well, then, go and leave me in peace! "

"No, Monsieur, no; take the trouble to come where they are, and you shall see — "

"What ? "

"What you shall see."

The duke slipped on his stockings and his dressing-gown again, took his sword in his left hand, and followed in Rafté's wake.

The three men were crouching behind the little door, and listening with much hilarity to the remarks which the watch were addressing to them from without the wall.

"Aha ! " said the sergeant, "well, well, well ! They are in the hotel of Monsieur le Duc de Richelieu ! "

"Well! in the hotel of Monsieur le Duc de Richelieu, yes. What then?" asked one of the runaways.

"Very good! very good!" replied the sergeant; "Monsieur le Duc has just returned home, and is beginning his pranks already."

"Hallo!" said Richelieu, drawing near, "it seems that somebody here is masquerading under my name."

The trio roared with laughter.

"Oh, yes," said the sergeant; "insult respectable females in the street, and laugh in the face of the king's officers! A duke and an ambassador! I shall make an official report of this business."

"The devil! the devil!" exclaimed the duke; "I have no part in this. What, Messieurs, have you been engaged in insulting respectable women on the street?"

"They screamed much too loud to be respectable," said one of the masks.

"You treat this matter very lightly, Monsieur Mask," said Richelieu approaching, that one of the three who had spoken; "it's easy to see that your name is not Richelieu, as mine is, and that you have no need of making a reputation for morality."

"The duke! it's the duke!" exclaimed the three men in a low voice.

"Messieurs," Richelieu continued, "I desire to think you gentlemen; such am I, and with gentlemen I know where I stand. However, I wish to know, and you will understand me, — I wish to know whether you are or are not gentlemen, so that I may know what to do with the bad impression you have made on me. Unmask, therefore, I beg."

At these words there was a very pronounced exhibition of uncertainty among the masked men.

"Messieurs," said the duke, "I hope that you will not

force me to open my gate to the archers of the watch with my own hand."

Thereupon the tallest of the three left the group, and walked directly to the duke.

"Do you recognize me?" he asked, raising his mask.

"Pecquigny!" cried Richelieu.

"Himself."

"What the deuce are you in a row with the watch for?"

"It's like this. We went to the ball at the Opera after the play; after the ball we had supper; after supper, being a little heated, we started to take a walk around the city."

"Yes, I see, and you insulted some decent women."

"Oh, no; that's the merest nonsense, my dear fellow."

"Allow me to ask you a question, my dear Pecquigny."

"What is it?"

"You have unmasked."

"*Dame!* yes, as you see."

"Wait a moment! — you have unmasked — and I don't know a better gentleman in France than you. But why, when you have unmasked, do your companions still wear their masks?"

"They have good reasons."

"But what are the reasons? It seems to me that I might be allowed to know them."

"Do not insist, Duke."

"Are they women? But no, it's impossible; they are too tall."

"Duke — "

"Perhaps they are princes of the blood?"

"I swear — "

"My dear fellow, if they are not women or princes of the blood, I can imagine no reason which can prevent their unmasking as you have done."

Pecquigny was still hesitating. Meanwhile the archers, in a furious rage at receiving no other reply than shouts of laughter to their summons to surrender, began to hammer at the little door with the stocks of their muskets.

The duke, beginning to lose his temper, took Pecquigny by the sleeve.

"Look you, Pecquigny," said he, "I have come back from Vienna very virtuous, very peaceable, and very philosophical, but for all that as irascible as a turkey-cock when I am cheated out of my sleep. Now you pull me out of bed, you mystify me, and compromise me with the police authorities; I declare to you that as surely as my name is Richelieu, if you don't tell me the names of these two insolent masks who insist on remaining covered on my premises, I will attack you, with Rafté, who acts as my provost when occasion demands. Ho there, Rafté! go and get a sword, and have at them, have at them!"

"Hold, hold!" cried Pecquigny, who knew the duke's intractable character, and saw the gleam of his naked weapon; "hold, O thou peaceable philosopher! thou virtuous ambassador! do you not guess who the smallest of the three is, come?"

"What! how the devil do you suppose I can guess? I'm no Œdipus."

"The smallest of us — "

"Well?"

"Is the greatest."

"The king!" Richelieu could not restrain the words.

"Hush!"

"What! that virtuous and uncorrupted monarch goes about the streets at night insulting women!"

"Silence!"

"How did such things happen? Really, my dear

fellow, the more you tell me, the more inquisitive you make me."

"*Pardieu!* it's very simple; while we were seeking an adventure we fell in with a lady and her maid."

"Wait, wait! In the first place, my dear — "

"What is it?"

"Let me get rid of these villanous archers, who will end by arousing the whole quarter."

Pecquigny realized the advisability of that step, and withdrew a few paces.

The duke opened the door in his dressing-gown, lantern in hand.

"What's all this, Messieurs?" said he, in the tone of one accustomed to command, "and what are you doing at my door at this hour?"

"Oh, pardon, Monsieur le Duc," said the sergeant, suddenly descending from his tower of wrath, which grew very fast before a closed door, but melted away before an open one.

"Well, well! what grudge have you against him, this Monsieur le Duc, to spoil his night's rest in this way?"

"Monseigneur! Monseigneur! it is — "

"What is it?" demanded the duke, majestically.

"It is that three of your people made a disturbance in the street, and we are looking for them."

"How do you know that they were my people?"

"Because we saw them take shelter on your premises."

"That's no reason at all."

"It makes no difference, Monsieur le Duc; whether they were your people or not, those who made the disturbance are on your premises all the same, and your residence is not considered a church, and therefore a safe shelter."

"Upon my word! pleasantry, Monsieur blackguard!
We have sown wit so plentifully that everybody is
gleaning a little of it, upon my honor! What sort of a
disturbance did these gentlemen create, pray?"

"Monseigneur knows all the beautiful women in Paris,
does he not?"

"Yes, almost."

"Whether princesses of the blood, noble ladies, or
common citizenesses?"

"What then, sergeant?"

"Monseigneur should know *la belle* Paulmier, then?"

"The hostess of the *Lion parlant?* I know only that
of her."

"She is a virtuous woman."

"Indeed!" said the duke; "go on."

"Well, she was passing through Rue Saint-Honoré
with her maid. Your people — "

"I have already told you, sergeant, that those gentlemen were not my people."

"Those gentlemen, then," continued the sergeant,
"approached her more than familiarly, and the smallest
of the three began to kiss her; yes, to kiss her, — a
most humiliating thing."

"Upon my word!" said Richelieu.

"Meanwhile," the sergeant continued, "the tallest
was chucking the maid under the chin. So these
two honest persons began to scream, fit to break your
heart."

"But what were they doing in the streets at such a
time of night, these two estimable creatures?"

"They were going to call the guard, Monsieur le
Duc."

"What! going to call the guard! Did they foresee
that they were going to be insulted?"

"Oh, no, Monsieur le Duc, they wanted the guard to separate some people of quality who were having a fight in Mademoiselle Paulmier's house."

"Why did n't they tell the little fellow so? That would have had a restraining effect upon him perhaps."

"Oh, indeed! the little fellow! a perfect demon incarnate, Monsieur le Duc. 'The guard!' he cried. 'Ah, you want the guard! good; wait!' And taking Mademoiselle Paulmier by the waist, he dragged her off, in spite of her heroic struggles, kissing her all the while, mark you, as far as the post of the Swiss guards of the Louvre."

"Well, when he got there, what did he do?"

"There, Monsieur le Duc, there the real offence began; because, you understand, to kiss a young woman, even though she be pretty, prettier than Mademoiselle Paulmier, — which could hardly be, however, — is not a crime; but the little rascal, mimicking an august voice, began to call — "

"To call whom?"

" 'Forestier,' he cried, 'Forestier!' "

"Who is Forestier?" asked Richelieu.

"He is the commandant of the Swiss at that point, Monsieur le Duc, the real commandant."

"Very good."

"No, very bad, on the contrary; for out comes Monsieur Forestier, thinking that he recognized the king's voice; out comes his sword in the midst of his men, and he shouts, 'It's the king who calls; *mordieu!* it 's the king.' And thereupon all the Swiss jump for their swords and their carbines. They rush about and tumble over one another, and search the street — "

"And find?"

"Mademoiselle Paulmier in a terrible state, and not

another thing; the little villain, the little impostor, had made his escape with his companions."

"And the Swiss ? " asked Richelieu, laughing heartily in spite of himself.

"Ah, Monsieur le Duc, the rage of the Swiss was beyond all bounds; but as Mademoiselle Paulmier told her story, as the virtue of our well-beloved king is well known, and as the guard-house had been left unguarded, and Monsieur Forestier suspected a surprise, he ordered a retreat."

"It was prudent."

"So the Swiss went back to their post; but luckily they met us, just as we were consoling the heart-broken Mademoiselle Paulmier. She informed us as to the direction her assailants had taken, and we darted in pursuit of them. After five minutes we discovered them walking tranquilly along the street, just as if they had not been turning the whole quarter upside down. We charged them, and they escaped us only by entering your grounds."

"A bad business this! " said the duke affably to the sergeant of the squad, — "bad for everybody except you, my friend, and your worthy soldiers; for although I do not desire that my people should be arrested as they deserve, I do desire that they should pay the cost of their frolic. Come, gentlemen, come, pay up! " said the duke, turning to the culprits.

He held out his hand.

Three well-lined purses fell into it.

"My children," said the duke to the archers, "take this, and be cautious, even after you have drunk up all that these purses contain in honor of my safe return."

The sergeant received the gold with palpable satisfaction, shared it loyally with his acolytes,— that is to say, he gave them one purse, and kept two for himself alone; then he and they disappeared.

"Now," said the duke with perfect courtesy, "excuse me, gentlemen, for not having received you as I should have been glad to do; beneath a mask every man is free, and authorizes freedom of treatment from others."

With these words the duke made a reverence with a manner quite free from embarrassment. The three men saluted him in return; and when Pecquigny had seen that the coast was clear, they left the garden.

The smallest of the three, as he went out, made a motion to Richelieu, which was meant to be expressive of his gratitude.

The duke remained alone with Rafté in his garden.

They gazed at one another.

"Well, Monsieur le Duc," asked Rafté, "what do you make of this?"

"*Cordieu!* Rafté, you were right," said the duke, absorbed in thought.

"Have I a keen scent, Monsieur le Duc?"

"Oh! I never doubted it, Rafté!"

"Now, Monsieur, you can safely go to bed again."

"Do you think so, Rafté?"

"I am sure of it, Monsieur. In adventures, as in gambling secrets, there is a regular progression, of which the culminating point marks the end. After what has just happened, expect nothing more, or rather expect everything."

"Rafté," said the duke, "you are a delightful fellow. Do you know how to read and write?"

"What, Monsieur le Duc?"

"I ask you, Monsieur Rafté, if you can read and write?"

"Oh, I can scribble and stutter."

"Rafté, from this moment you are my secretary; and if I am ever elected to the Academy — "

He paused a moment.

"You shall write my discourse."

"Oh, Monsieur le Duc!"

"You shall, or the devil take me!"

"Will Monseigneur retire once more?" asked the valet-secretary.

"No, I cannot; I have too much to think about; no, leave me, Rafté."

"The fire is burning, Monsieur le Duc; so I will leave you."

Richelieu was left alone.

"And that's the temperament which Madame de Prie expects me to play the censor of morals to! What! give myself so much trouble to annoy this charming youth, instead of catering to his pleasures at so little pains!"

He mused a few moments more.

"Let others scorch themselves in the flames of virtue," said he. "I certainly was not born to be a kill-joy. I have vigorous lungs, the spark is all prepared, and the matter is combustible; let us blow on it. *Morbleu!* let us blow on it! Moreover, I could not extinguish it if I tried."

LIV.

THE QUEEN'S CARD-PARTY.

MONSIEUR DE RICHELIEU did not fail, however, notwithstanding his reflections, to go to the queen's assembly that same evening; he had made a promise which he could not break without embroiling himself with the marquise.

He was expected. All the restrained impatience of the court burst forth when he appeared. The queen alone did not seem to notice him.

This excellent princess had made Richelieu her bugbear. The duke's prowess had reached her ears when she was still nothing more than a lowly young girl; and all this parade of vice, which seemed such a fine thing at Versailles, was, in the eyes of the chaste daughter of King Stanislas, varnish awkwardly laid on to cover up shocking crimes.

So she had sworn active hatred against this corrupter of morals. On his side the duke found it impossible to care for her; and the result of this mutual enmity could not fail to be disastrous for the schemes of Madame de Prie, which depended for a successful issue upon the cordial co-operation of Monsieur de Richelieu and the queen.

The queen was constrained, so to speak, to look at Richelieu, whom she would have preferred not to see. The duke approached and made his reverence with that perfection of courtesy in which he was without a peer. With marvellous tact he had realized the queen's hostility to him as soon as he crossed the threshold, simply by the almost imperceptible movement of her shoulders when his name was announced.

"Bonjour, Monsieur," said she, coldly, and turned her attention at once to her game of cavagnole.

The duke was not the man to sue for favor, he knew too well that that brings one into contempt; nor was he the man to humble himself too far before a woman, though that woman were the queen: he knew too well that women prefer the arrogant to the humble.

But his reputation as a courtier and a man of spirit demanded that he should not be content with so cold and so evidently unfriendly a reception.

What would be said in diplomatic circles? A diplomatist meeting with such a rebuff on his first appearance would have lost his prestige at once.

The duke had come home with his memory burdened with a crowd of German princesses, Polish portraits, and souvenirs dear to the heart of Marie Leczinska; he was sure that at the first hint of this family gossip the disdainful princess would at once give him her ear. Monsieur de Richelieu speculated upon everything, even upon good qualities.

"Madame," said he, "I cannot take leave of your Majesty, engrossed as you seem to be in your game, without repeating all the messages, affectionate for the woman, and respectful for the queen, which the Princesses of Brunswick, Wolfenbuttel, and Nassau charged me to deliver."

The queen turned quickly around.

"Ah!" said she; "so they still think of me in those parts?"

It was Richelieu's golden opportunity to perpetrate one of those compliments which he so often found effectual;

he contented himself however with bowing modestly, and, having effected his purpose, withdrew from the queen's side.

She watched him as he walked away, and became thoughtful; she would have been glad that the interview should continue. For a long time she struggled against the desire, but at last, being weaker than her heart, she yielded to it.

She was something more than a kind-hearted princess, was our poor late queen; she was a woman of many excellent parts.

"Monsieur le Duc," said she, "did you not see my dear friend the Comtesse de Koenigsmarck at Vienna?"

"Indeed I did, Madame," replied the duke, returning to her side with respectful eagerness; "and Madame la Comtesse never spoke of your Majesty without tears in her eyes, — it was very affecting."

"What!" cried the queen, with some constraint; "affecting! I thought that the emotions of the heart were considered absurd by men."

"Madame," rejoined Richelieu, gravely, "deign to believe that whatever demonstrates sincere feeling affects men of good heart very deeply; and when the admiration which his queen inspires is in question, a good Frenchman, a gentleman, prides himself upon never being indifferent."

This reply produced considerable effect upon the queen, who glanced stealthily at the duke, and said nothing.

Richelieu had won his case.

Certain it is that at that moment the duke might, if he had been bent upon it, have begun negotiations in accordance with the plans of Monsieur le Duc de Bourbon.

Virtue was enthroned.

But at this point the king came in. His Majesty was resplendent with youth and beauty. Nothing in France at that time, as was universally admitted, equalled the adorable and gracious majesty of her youthful monarch.

The king seemed to be very much absorbed in the demeanor of his wife.

When the duke saw how handsome he was, he was interested to observe what effect his appearance would produce upon the queen.

Marie Leczinska rose, made the customary reverences, and took her seat again, having given to etiquette what etiquette demanded, nothing more.

The king, on the other hand, had blushed as he caught sight of the queen, who, if not beautiful, was at least interesting, with her air of suffering and languor.

But when, instead of the fire which burned in his own glance, he detected in the queen no signs of sympathetic ardor as he would have liked to do, a cloud, almost like the shadow of anger, passed across his face; he sighed very low, and began to look with more attention at the beautiful blushing creatures who were courtesying on all sides, and exhibiting to his gaze, by virtue of their court costumes, a most entrancing vision of white shoulders and dazzling arms.

"Marie Leczinska," thought Richelieu, "is her own executioner; she 's not even jealous."

Indeed the queen went on calmly arranging her markers and counters.

Louis XV. with heaving chest eagerly inhaled the perfumes and the incense of the ladies.

He caught sight of the duke standing respectfully apart, ready to pay his respects when the king should pass near him.

As he approached, the king's face wore a slight smile, instinct with sly good-humor.

The conversation, which had been so restrained and cold on the queen's part, was carried on very earnestly and warmly by the king.

Richelieu, when questioned concerning his travels, framed his replies in a manner to inflame the king's imagination and arouse his interest. But after a while, having noticed how impenetrably silent the duke was upon the subject of the events of the night before, the king, who was very bashful, and, like all bashful people, very fond of everybody who did not annoy him, laid a hand upon Richelieu's arm, and said, —

"Duke, you have seen the queen, and you have seen me; now you must seek out Monsieur le Cardinal."

"Such was my purpose and my wish, Sire, and I await only your Majesty's permission."

"Very well! Monsieur le Cardinal will be much pleased with you, I am sure."

"My respect for him will endow me with the power to please him, Sire."

"The cardinal is a very learned man, and an excellent adviser. You have had much experience yourself, Monsieur le Duc."

This word "experience," in the young king's mind, denoted all the longing admiration of youth for the science of good and evil in which they of maturer years were so well informed, particularly Monsieur de Richelieu, who had nibbled so early in life at the tree which bears it.

"Enough, Sire," replied the duke, "to enable me to render my services more useful to your Majesty."

"Duke, I shall never forget it. Go, pray, and see Monsieur le Cardinal, and say to him that — "

He looked cautiously about. Richelieu listened attentively.

"Say to him," continued Louis, with a gloomy expression, and a frown which would have made the Olympe of Versailles tremble, had it appeared upon the brow of Louis XIV.,—"say to him that I am weary and bored."

"Your Majesty bored!" cried Richelieu, simulating utter amazement.

"Yes, Duke."

"With your youth, your beauty, your manly vigor, and with the kingdom of France?"

"It is just on account of all those things that I am wearied and bored to death, Duke. My youth and my vigor prevent me from ruling as I would like; the kingdom of France prevents me from amusing myself as I might do."

"Sire, ennui is a fatal disease; I would not allow your Majesty to be without a physician."

"Good! the cardinal would laugh if he heard you; he has always insisted upon it that a man cannot be bored on this earth."

"Sire," said the duke, "it is very clear that Monsieur le Cardinal has not confided to you all his expedients for diverting his mind."

It was the first time that ever courtier had ventured a pleasantry before the king upon the subject of his venerated preceptor. Monsieur de Richelieu realized that he was running a great risk, but he chose to play a bold game in the hope of winning more.

The king was not angry; on the contrary, after a moment's silence, he replied very graciously,—

"Duke, Monsieur de Fleury has done very well not to teach me all the ways of diverting myself at once; if I have any time to live, I shall at least have some new things to learn."

"I will answer for it." said Richelieu.

" You will help me, Duke ? "

" At your Majesty's commands. "

" Go to see Monsieur le Cardinal, then, I beg you. "

" To-morrow, Sire. "

" And say to him — "

" That your Majesty is weary; yes, Sire. "

" And that I would like to go to war for amusement, " added the king, with a hypocritical smile, which aroused the duke's deep admiration, after their free conversation in which he had thought that he caught a glimpse of the king's heart, and had construed his inclinations as being much more amorous than warlike.

" Sire, " said he, finally adopting the part which was assigned to him, " I shall make it my glory to serve your Majesty in whatever direction you desire my services; I hope that my interview with Monsieur le Cardinal will result in some plan which will make your Majesty more contented. "

The king turned upon his heel, and Richelieu bowed to the ground.

" Unless Madame de Prie ranges herself with me, I shall not be on her side; that's decided, " said the duke to himself.

His carriage awaited him; he exchanged a few words with Pecquigny, who overtook him at the door.

" Well, Pecquigny ? " said he.

" Well, Duke, you have made a conquest of the king. "

" Nonsense! Tell me who the third of last night's masks was ? "

" Bachelier, the king's first valet-de-chambre. "

" Thanks. "

Richelieu returned home quite alone.

END OF VOL. I.